Additional Acclaim for Stephen Amidon's *Human Capital*

"[A] powerful, well-crafted novel about failure and anxiety. Long on character and texture . . . it's also expert social commentary."
—*Chicago Sun-Times*

"Beautiful and terrifying . . . This roaring read cuts to the heart of how we live now in America."
—Colin Harrison, author of *The Havana Room*

"Just as you think this novel is degenerating into soap opera, it strikes home again . . . the better to strike deeper chords. Even the epilogue startles."
—*The Hartford Courant*

"From its very beginning, *Human Capital* seizes us and plunges us into the grand delirium of reading about characters whose fates we eagerly, agonizingly follow to the last lovely page."
—Scott Spencer, author of *A Ship Made of Paper*

"*Human Capital* is truly marvelous."
—*The Toronto Star*

"Amidon moves it all along swiftly and skillfully. . . . [His] knowledge embeds the novel . . . with an authenticity that few contemporary novels achieve."
—*The Washington Post Book World*

"Amidon stirs this social soup, moving easily between classes and generations; building his characters as people we actually care about."
—*The Miami Herald*

"*Human Capital* deftly slices open the rich, corrupt heart of suburban America today and lets its dark secrets bleed out. . . . [A] smart, realistic portrait of how one man's near-fatal high-stakes wager is played out with all-too-human assets."

—*Elle*

"An engrossing, well-paced novel operating, like the work of Scott Turow, near the boundaries of commercial and literary fiction."

—*Newsday*

"*Human Capital* turns over the rock of NASDAQ affluence and lets us see the squirmy things underneath. . . . An entertaining, scathing, very American fable."

—Stewart O'Nan, author of *The Good Wife*

The New City
The Primitive
Thirst
Splitting the Atom
Subdivision: Stories

HUMAN CAPITAL

STEPHEN AMIDON

PICADOR

FARRAR, STRAUS AND GIROUX

NEW YORK

For Clementine, Alexander, Aurora and Celeste

www.picadorusa.com

Picador® is a U.S. registered trademark and is used by Farrar, Straus and Giroux under license from Pan Books Limited.

For information on Picador Reading Group Guides, as well as ordering, please contact Picador.
Phone: 646-307-5626
Fax: 212-253-9627
E-mail: readinggroupguides@picadorusa.com

Designed by Debbie Glasserman

Library of Congress Cataloging-in-Publication Data
Amidon, Stephen.
    Human capital / Stephen Amidon.
        p. cm.
    ISBN 0-312-42424-8
    EAN 978-0-312-42424-4
    1. Fathers and daughters—Fiction. 2. Divorced fathers—Fiction. 3. Male friendship—Fiction. 4. Suburban life—Fiction. 5. Teenage girls—Fiction. 6. Connecticut—Fiction. 7. Hedge funds—Fiction.   I. Title.
PS3551.M52H86   2004
813'.54—dc22   2004043985

First published in the United States by Farrar, Straus and Giroux

First Picador Edition: October 2005

10 9 8 7 6 5 4 3 2 1

PART ONE

1 Drew Hagel was going to be late for the banquet. He knew it the moment he pulled out of the parking lot and saw the stationary line of traffic on Federal. He'd wanted to leave the office no later than five-thirty, allowing himself plenty of time to make the six-mile drive up to the historic village. The roads could be tricky at this hour, and finding a parking place near Country Day during a school function would be next to impossible. Thirty minutes would guarantee he wasn't late. In fact, he'd probably get there early. That was all right, giving him some time alone with the Mannings. The invitation to join their table had been a piece of rare good fortune; he had every intention of savoring it.

But just after he'd finished packing, there was a perfunctory knock on his office door and in walked Andy Starke. He seemed friendly enough as he performed his usual sly, loose-limbed greeting, though his eyes were ominously grave. They had been exchanging phone messages for the past week—or more accurately, Drew had been avoiding the other man's calls—and now Starke had taken it upon himself to force the issue with a surprise visit. There was no escape. Starke had the look of a man owed serious money as he lowered himself into the chair opposite the big oak desk. Moments like these made Drew wish he hadn't let Janice go. She'd have sent Starke packing with little more than a ferocious look. She was smart and loyal, and she'd learned the business under Drew's father. Unfortunately, her loyalty hadn't extended to working without a salary.

"I was just in the neighborhood," Starke said.

A low-voltage joke: His bank was two blocks away. It was only by careful maneuvering that Drew had avoided bumping into him on the street.

"Been trying to get hold of you," he continued.

"Sorry about that," Drew said. "Things have been hopping."

Starke's expression briefly registered the office's sepulchral stillness.

"Glad to hear *that*. Anyway, thought I'd stop by and save you a call."

Drew nodded, ceding control of the conversation.

"How's Ronnie?" Starke asked.

"Good. Well, you know. It's getting to be something of a load."

"She still working?"

"She's going to try to give it another month."

"And Shannon?"

"Great. It's her senior banquet tonight. In fact—"

"Senior," Starke said, refusing to be rushed. "That must freak you out."

"I don't know if I feel too young to have one her age or too old to have babies on the way."

Starke nodded at this, his chin jutting in rumination, as if this were some nugget of profound wisdom. And then he got down to the matter at hand.

"So. Drew. I was sort of under the impression we were going to get us some of that long green last week."

"Andy, what can I tell you. This lawyer in New York is dicking me around on an escrow."

"So what's the deal?"

"Next week," Drew said before he'd really thought about his answer.

Starke began to nod, that long jaw still jutting.

"Next week's good. It's not last week, but then again it's not the week after next." He sighed. "You know my problem here, right?"

Drew nodded. Starke told him, anyway.

"This is the third month you've missed. Bells and whistles time. *Sixty*-day delinquencies are supposed to go to Collections. I've held them off this far but . . ."

"I've got about five sales in the works. Honestly. Tell them that."

"I *have* been telling them that."

"Andy, come on. This is me you're talking to."

Starke didn't appear to take much comfort from this information.

"So I can tell them next week for sure?"

"Yes," Drew said. "Absolutely."

It was a minor lie; he'd be able to give the bank its money in a little less than a month. Starke stared at him blankly, then gave a capitulating smile. They talked for a while about sports and the economy and Shannon's decision to attend Oberlin. Although the tone was friendly, Drew couldn't help but feel there was something punitive in the way Starke lingered. Finally, he slapped the chair's weathered arms and stood, scowling for a moment, as if he'd just eaten something disagreeable.

"Hey, and Drew, for future reference?" A note of offense had crept into his voice. "A little respect. Return your calls."

Drew gave him a minute to clear the building before rushing from the office, his leisurely procession across town now set to be a mad scramble. As he rode the building's groaning elevator, he fought off the temptation to be angry with Starke. The man was only doing his job. He'd been a good friend to Drew, arranging the loan and then its extension. And he'd clearly been responsible for the bank's leniency so far. They'd known each other for the better part of a decade, working together on the financing for dozens of sales, meeting for regular drinks at Bill's Tavern. Drew wished he could tell him how good everything was about to become, though Starke would be furious if he knew what he'd done with the money. He would just have to keep stalling him for the next few weeks. After that Starke would be happy. The credit card people and the bursar at Oberlin; the contractors and the obstetrician. Everybody would be getting his due.

Drew's pleasure at this thought evaporated when he saw the wall of cars at the parking lot's exit. Traffic in Totten Crossing was getting worse with each season. Twenty years ago the only obstacle to traveling from one end of Federal to the other was a solitary flashing yellow, fooling no one as it winked with jaundiced indifference at the occasional drivers. Now there were a half dozen lights on the town's main street, programmed by a suite of remorseless Scandinavian software to slow everything to a sluggish crawl. As Drew waited for a space to open, he briefly contemplated a shortcut through one of the neighborhoods surrounding downtown, a route he remembered from boyhood bicycle journeys. But these streets had changed as well, reconfigured to be terminal, twisted into cul-de-sacs or blocked by steel security gates. Passing through was no longer an option.

Someone let him in. Traffic started to move. Drew popped open his briefcase and removed a few shortbread cookies. He was hungry, and there was no telling what they'd be serving at the banquet. As he rolled forward, he allowed himself to believe that the delay wouldn't be so bad. Fifteen minutes, tops. These functions never started on time. People would be slow getting to their tables; the kids, giddy with spring, would horse around. Shannon and Ronnie would certainly be there by now; his daughter would stay at school, while his wife finished work with her four o'clock bulimic. Their presence would cover his lateness. In fact, a late-but-not-too-late arrival might be good. Drew pictured himself making his way across the crowded dining hall, nodding to people who wondered where he thought *he* was going, answering their questions by taking his seat at the thirty-thousand-dollar table just a few strides from the dais.

But then traffic came to another stop, blocked this time by the bad intersection of Federal and Totten Pike, the old post road crossing that had given the town its name three hundred years ago. It would take ages to get through, especially if you wanted to make a left. There were at least two dozen cars ahead of him. By the time the intersection cleared there was only time for three of the turning cars to get through. He looked around for an escape route, quickly determining that if he cut behind the dry cleaners, then through the Cumberland Farms parking lot, he could bolt across the pike and take one of the unbarricaded lanes to Old Totten Village. It was risky—people wouldn't exactly be falling over one another to make room for him once they saw what he was up to—but if he didn't take a chance, then he would certainly show up unacceptably late. Come on, he thought as he slid a last chunk of shortbread into his mouth. Make a decision. Be bold. You're supposed to have changed—prove it. Be the new Drew Hagel.

He made a quick left, cutting off an oncoming Audi. The driver flashed his high beams, a wagging finger of light that suggested he was one of the transplanted European bankers seen frowning over the sausage selection at Earth's Bounty. The alley behind the shops looked more like the Totten Crossing of Drew's youth: flattened beer cans, teeming Dumpsters, and smudges of crushed mammal. He took another deep breath and plunged through the stalled traffic on Totten Pike. After that his plan worked perfectly. The back streets were clear. He made it to Old Totten within two minutes.

Although the settlement's brick buildings had closed to tourists for the night, the road was lined with cars that had spilled over from the Country Day lot. The senior banquet was a big pull. Only a handful of misfits failed to attend, a group that might well have included the Hagels if not for Quint's invitation. Like everything else at Country Day—the silent auctions and benefit performances and class trips— the banquet could rapidly empty Drew's already thin wallet. The idea was that groups of parents would band together, creating "table totals" that would determine their proximity to the platform from which student awards would be dispensed. Ten years ago this naked elitism had been nothing more than a rumor; now it was explicit policy. As things stood, Drew could barely make the minimum of two hundred dollars per seat, a donation that would place him in a far-flung Siberian exile with the financial aid crew. With Shannon about to graduate, there was no reason to spend an evening on the fringes of conspicuous consumption. The Spring Fling auction had been bad enough, with Drew's sole bid on a weekend at somebody's place on Martha's Vineyard beaten by an offer that was five times greater. It would be better not to go at all.

Then Quint had called. Or rather, it had been his assistant, asking the Hagels to join the Mannings at the banquet. Drew had haltingly replied that he wasn't sure how much he could contribute, remembering that last year's top tables had gone for something like thirty grand. For ten seats. There was a chilly spell of silence.

"You would be Mr. Manning's guest, of course," she said, her voice stiffening.

He'd tried to sound cool as he accepted, though he was secretly elated to receive such a gesture from Quint. It had been almost three months since they'd last spoken, and Drew was getting worried. He'd directed a few guarded remarks at Shannon to see if she could find out anything from Jamie, though he had to be careful, since his daughter didn't know about his involvement with Quint's fund. She hadn't been able to tell him much. Quint was busy. What else was new? Drew had called the Mannings' house a few times on the pretext of getting a tennis game together, but the messages he left on the machine had gone unanswered. All sorts of dark scenarios had begun to play through his mind, especially once he stopped being able to meet the hefty payments on his equity credit line. And then Andy Starke started calling and Drew felt the first faint stirrings of panic. He was getting ready to make an unannounced visit to Quint's office when the banquet invitation had come through. There was nothing wrong at the fund. Quint was a private man. He was busy. In a few weeks it would all come good. Forty-four percent. A hundred and ten thousand dollars of clean and absolute profit.

Drew's elation had been tempered by the prospect of convincing his wife and daughter to attend. To his surprise, both had been pushovers. Although Ronnie would hate the thinly veiled parental warfare that was sure to take place at a senior awards ceremony, she was eager for the chance to improve her relationship with Shannon. The fact that Quint was paying didn't hurt, either. She was scheduled to be on call but promised to switch with a colleague.

Shannon also agreed without hesitation. Until recently it was doubtful she had any intention of celebrating her time at Country Day. After trying on just about every kind of relationship with her classmates—petulant rebellion during her freshman year, pathetic stabs at conformity as a sophomore, her startling ascendance to the class's vanguard while dating Jamie Manning as a junior—she had finally settled on utter alienation. She'd missed the cotillion and the senior trip to Nova Scotia, and Drew never heard her speak about her classmates at all, never heard her talk about a single subject she was studying.

But everything had changed in the past few weeks. His daughter had become an enthusiastic member of the senior class. Drew had been shocked by the transformation, especially after having heard so many bitter diatribes about the school's stupidity and superficiality. Shannon began attending parties, staying late after school, taking day trips to the shore. Much of this time seemed to be spent with Jamie, leading Drew to wonder if they were seeing each other again. Whatever the reason, she'd finally found her place at Country Day. When he told her that they were going to the banquet after all, she accepted without hesitation. And so it was set. They'd all be going, guests of the Mannings, whose table by the stage was reachable only by a long walk across the crowded floor.

As he feared, the closest open parking space was several hundred yards from the school. He strode quickly along the swept dirt path fronting the restored houses, each bearing an embossed brass plaque chronicling the slaughter and deprivation that had been visited upon the settlers. Country Day had started as a slightly cranky alternative school shoehorned into the village's drafty old meetinghouse, but over the past few decades it had spread into a complex of new buildings. There was currently a new science center in the works, beneficiary of tonight's largesse. They'd need the room; the school's waiting list now numbered well over one hundred, even though the tuition had nearly doubled in the four years since Shannon had enrolled.

Drew moved through the school parking lot, packed tightly with North European steel. He was finally able to relax when the main building came into view. People were still arriving. He paused between two cars to catch his breath, his eyes coming to rest on a familiar black Lexus in the next row. It was Carrie Manning's. There was someone in the driver's seat. Drew moved a few lateral feet to confirm that he was looking at the unmistakable sweeping blond hair of Quint's wife. He waited for her to get out so he could accompany her into the dining hall. But she appeared to be staying in the car. He wondered if she was on the phone. That was all right; he could wait out a call. If you arrived with Carrie, you were by definition on time.

But she wasn't on the phone. She was weeping. Not crying—that was too mild a term. There was an abandon that went far beyond tears. Drew could see her shoulders heave, a sight made all the more strange by the fact that he couldn't hear anything through the car's sound-proofing. He stood perfectly still, uncertain whether to approach her or walk away. Something must have happened. One of her sons had been hurt. Quint had died in a car wreck. But if her family was in trouble, she wouldn't be sitting alone in a school parking lot. She'd be at the hospital; she'd be working the phones or huddling with lawyers. Whatever was provoking her tears was none of Drew's business. He slowly backed away from her car, his eyes locked on her the whole time to be sure she hadn't seen him. Once clear, he beat a retreat back to the swept dirt path, only daring to sneak a look at the Lexus as he neared the school's front entrance. Carrie was still in the car.

Drew stepped into the lobby, checking to see if his own wife was waiting for him. He was desperate to tell her about what he'd just seen. Carrie Manning had been the topic of much conversation between them, especially after the overwrought dinner parties they'd attended up on Orchard last fall. The resulting verdict was that she was a handful. She was lively and beautiful and had been genuinely pleased when Shannon and Jamie dated, but there was something vaguely out of control about her that didn't quite fit with the rest of Quint's world. The bare feet at the school picnic. The community theater dramatics and Amnesty International fund-raiser. Spending all that money to turn the decrepit Garden Theater into some kind of vintage movie house. And the wine, the extra few glasses she had whenever the occasion presented itself. Ronnie had an explanation for her behavior, saying that control freaks like Quint often attached themselves to volatile personalities, especially those who, even after three kids, still looked great following the maître d' to a corner table at Le Cirque.

Drew could see that his wife was not in the lobby. She was probably already in her seat; her feet had been swelling recently. He joined the slow migration into the cafeteria. A low-frequency hum of parental expectation filled the big room. There were about thirty large round tables, draped in white linen, each bearing candles, their eerily unwavering flames reflected in the neatly arranged cutlery and glass. People had begun to sit, the scrape of chairs on the parquet floor like the lowing of some hungry herd. At the far end of the room was the raised platform with its dais and table covered with neatly arranged trophies and plaques and citations. Drew couldn't see which of the tables beneath it was the Mannings'; there were still too many people milling around for him to get a clear view. On the wall behind the platform was the Country Day mural, painted over each year by the graduating class. This year's was a lopsided multiethnic throng, big on vibrant colors and sly fashion references. The faces were strong and smiling, though what was most notable were the eyes, which all bore the same jaded, slightly vacant expression. It was impossible to say whether this was by design or simply marked the limits of the young hands that had drawn them. Either way, the effect was jarring, as if the people at the banquet were being watched over by a race of giant, disapproving children.

He passed by the outermost table, two hundred bucks a seat, fifteen people instead of the usual ten, a life raft of parents and their resentful offspring. Drew's rightful place if not for Quint. It was so near the exit that the stream of hip-checking guests made it seem to sink into the parquet floor. Drew moved past them, still too preoccupied with the sight of Carrie in tears to savor the moment. Quint's table came into view as he reached the hall's center. Jamie was the first person he saw, seated next to his friend Jazz Mahabal. Both of them were up for several awards, most notably Jamie, who was one of the favorites for the Carswell. Their conversation was being watched by Jazz's parents. Godeep was Quint's jolly, terrifying general counsel; Drew had never exchanged more than simple greetings with Sonia. He wasn't even sure she spoke English, a suspicion enhanced by the matching lavender sari and bindi she wore tonight. Ronnie sat next to her, locked in earnest conversation with Quint, who listened with a slightly canted head as he ran his finger idly around the rim of his water goblet. Drew felt a momentary pulse of panic; he didn't like the sight of his wife talking to Quint. But he soon put his worry aside. Quint wouldn't be telling her anything about their business. Shannon was nowhere in sight. Drew figured she was table-hopping before things got going.

Quint was the first to notice him, raising his chin slightly in greeting, though he kept his attention focused on Ronnie.

". . . and then the losers wind up with me," she was saying.

Drew slid into the closest empty seat, misjudging the distance slightly, his bulk rattling the glasses and knocking a dusting of pollen from the floral centerpiece. The table's occupants all looked at him.

"Talking about me again?" he asked his wife in tones loud enough for everyone to hear.

The joke fell flat.

"Ronnie was just explaining how she thought all this competition was a bad idea for kids," Quint explained.

Drew shot her a look. He couldn't believe she was saying this. She had to know Jamie was up for the Carswell.

"I don't know," Drew said tightly. "They seem to handle it."

Ronnie didn't register his cautionary tone.

"I just think it's crazy to single out certain young people for praise," she continued. "I see the fallout from that sort of pressure every day."

Her words brought a brief silence to the table, conjuring images of damaged youth, the stupefied and sullen who wound up in her office. Drew looked at Quint. If he was offended, he wasn't showing it. Jamie, too, was unfazed, his handsome face maintaining its customary slack affability. Still, Drew wished there were a subtle nullifying gesture he could direct toward his wife, some private code he could deploy to stop her from pursuing the subject. But the code was something he'd developed with Anne. You didn't get codes the second time out. Everything had to be stated.

"But isn't this competition just preparation for life?" Godeep Mahabal asked in the rolling British accent that seemed perpetually on the verge of laughter. "Part of the education we are all paying for so dearly?"

"For the winners, maybe," Ronnie persisted. "But not the losers."

"I'd have thought it would have been especially instructive for *them*," Drew said.

He'd intended the remark as a conversation-ending quip, but once again no one was laughing. This was all wrong. He had to stop this before it got out of hand. Nothing came to mind.

"Sounds like that camp Mom sent us to," Jamie said.

He looked at his father, and Quint smiled wryly, causing Drew to wonder how much gentle mockery they would be directing toward Carrie's pretensions if they knew she'd just been weeping in the school parking lot. Drew was also struck by the likeness between father and son, the pale blue eyes and black hair and strong jaw. According to Ronnie, this was where the similarity ended. Jamie, she said, lacked his father's strength and intelligence and adamant determination. She continued to say so even as he placed fifth in his class and was accepted early at Duke and captained the squash team to a winning season. When Shannon broke up with him last fall, she seemed almost relieved.

"It was this sort of New Age place," Jamie was saying. "Lots of singing and lentils. And all the sports were noncompetitive. I remember this one game: They gave us this big, mushy ball and said, okay, get going. Play."

"There weren't any rules?" Jazz asked.

"Only that there couldn't be teams and nobody could keep score. Anyway, everybody argued for about ten minutes; then a bunch of guys started playing smear the queer."

"What on earth is that?" Ronnie was aghast.

"One person runs with the ball and everybody else tries to tackle him. I guess technically they were following the instructions. It was every man for himself, and there was nobody keeping score."

"Didn't you play?" Godeep asked.

"Not at first," Jamie said, his voice growing a little quieter. "But then somebody threw me the ball and that was that. I got pounded. I started to cry and so they stuck me with it again and I got tackled even harder. I remember, there were all these kids on me; I couldn't move my arms or legs. I kept on crying and they wanted to give me the ball again and so I went and hid beneath my cabin for the rest of the afternoon. That night I called my folks to come get me, but I guess I was there for the duration."

His eyes were focused on the table in front of him, lost in unhappy memory. The story had cast the table into a sudden, uneasy silence. Drew could see Quint's smile waver.

"So did you have to play again the next day?" Ronnie asked softly.

Jamie looked up. He noticed his father's gaze. His troubled expression disappeared, replaced by that self-confident smile Drew could never bring himself to like.

"No, this kid from Putney got his arm broke." He shrugged with a late-night comic's timing. "After that we did a lot of hiking."

Drew joined the laughter, but Ronnie only smiled politely, aware that she could no more convince this table of the evils of competition than she could persuade a congregation of fundamentalist Christians of the emptiness of hell. In the brief silence that followed Drew realized that his daughter was still nowhere in sight.

"Shannon here?" he asked Ronnie.

"I haven't seen her."

"Did she call or anything?"

Ronnie shook her head. This baffled him. She'd have called if there was a problem.

"Has anyone seen her?" he asked generally.

No one spoke. He turned back to Ronnie, who shrugged, having long ago given up on playing an active part in her stepdaughter's life. Drew looked around the dining hall. Nothing. He turned his chair slightly away from the main table and speed-dialed her on his cell phone. He got her voice mail.

"Strange," he muttered as he hung up.

Conversation ensued, though Drew found it hard to track. He was worried now. How could she possibly make herself late? The kitchen doors flew open; underclassmen emerged with big trays. Drew was frozen with indecision. He wanted to search for his daughter but didn't have the slightest idea where to start.

And then Ronnie's beeper sounded. Shannon, reporting in, though it was strange that she hadn't called him on his cell phone. He watched as his wife read the message, her ginger eyebrows elevating slightly.

"Is it her?" he asked, a bit too loudly.

"Work."

Drew felt a fresh pulse of angry confusion. Ronnie was supposed to have traded off her call duties. She beckoned for Drew's cell phone, and he watched in growing desperation as she called her service. Though no one else was paying attention, Drew felt as if this were the only thing happening at the table. She hung up and nodded once to him. Meaning she had to go. Drew couldn't believe this. First his daughter was a no-show, and now his wife was leaving. Several thousand dollars' worth of chair space, Quint's gift to his family, was about to empty before his eyes.

"I'm sorry," Ronnie said to Quint. "I have to deal with this."

"You don't have to apologize, Ronnie," Quint said. "It's what you do."

It was such a gracious comment that even Ronnie, not the world's greatest Manning fan, was momentarily struck by it. She stood laboriously, her thin frame weighed by the bulk of her pregnancy. Drew went to help her, then trailed her until they were just out of earshot of the table.

"I thought you were going to get someone else to cover for you tonight."

"I tried," she said. "But I couldn't find anyone."

"Well, yeah, but this looks bad, just walking off like this."

"I'm not just walking off, Drew," she said patiently. "I'm going to see someone who is having serious difficulties."

"It's just . . . I mean, Shannon being late and now you going."

"Drew, relax. Everyone knows why I'm going. And Shannon will show up." She put her hand on the side of his head. "Don't get yourself all worked up. It's just a silly little dinner."

Drew watched her walk off with the splay-footed gait she'd developed in the past few weeks. She was right, although that didn't change the fact that the night was turning into a disaster.

"I'm sorry about this," he said to Quint as he returned to the table.

"It really isn't a problem at all. An emergency's an emergency." He looked around. "I'm starting to think my own wife has abandoned us, too."

Drew suddenly wondered if he should have told him about seeing Carrie in the parking lot. But the moment had passed. It would look strange if he said something now.

"So, it's been a while," he said feebly.

"Crazy times," Quint said. "We've been incredibly busy."

"I've missed our games."

"Yeah, we've got to try to get those going again."

"That would be great," Drew said, patting his gut. "I've got to do something to take care of this."

"Well, the babies will keep you running. When are they due, anyway?"

"Eight weeks."

The conversation was interrupted by the arrival of the food, breaded chicken and wild rice and broccoli, all of it covered with a coagulating beige sauce. There was no appetizer. People wanted to get to the prizes. Drew dug into his food with joyless efficiency, swallowing with only minimal chewing as he brooded on the humiliation of his family's abandoning him. When he was done, he looked around and saw that everyone else was still in the early stages of consumption. Sweat lined his scalp and his stomach churned. He checked the table to see if anyone else had noticed his gluttony. Quint had begun speaking to Mahabal in a quiet fiscal undertone; Jamie and Jazz were laughing together. Only Sonia was looking at him, her face fixed with a gentle, opaque smile. She'd seen him wolf down his food, but he couldn't tell what she thought about it, this stranger with a dot in the middle of her forehead, born in a land of starvation and now mistress of a three-million-dollar Colonial. Turning away from her gaze, Drew was struck by a terrible thought: He had no business at this table. His presence was a mistake. His eyes wandered to the mural, those giant children staring down at him with their eerie scorn. Telling him that he didn't belong here. At least his wife and daughter had the good sense to stay away.

"Ah, here she is," Quint said.

Drew turned, desperate for it to be Shannon. But it was Carrie. She smiled merrily as she arrived at the table, though Drew detected the signs of her weeping around the edges of her eyes. Stranger still was the presence of a pronounced welt on her forehead. Her husband and son looked at her, then exchanged a glance.

"So," she said as she slipped into her chair. "Are we having fun yet?"

2 Birds were foraging on the just-seeded lawn, feeding with the skittish movements of creatures whose luck was too good to be true. The gardeners had been generous; there was plenty for everyone. Occasional squabbles ended almost as soon as they started. For those who missed out there was always the multistoried feeder on the patio, with its squirrel-baffling escarpments. Carrie let her gaze drift past the birds to the orchard. Shadow was just beginning to fill its empty spaces. The sky's afternoon blue had turned into a smoky gray, creased by the bright orange plume of an eastbound jet. She tightened her focus on her body's blurry reflection in the bedroom's big window. She was naked, but that didn't matter. No one could see her through the glass. And even if anyone could, too much land separated her from the rest of the world. Eight acres, although it could have been eight thousand. She was as good as invisible.

The birds were suddenly in flight, scattered by a commotion at the edge of the lawn. Dillon and Nick emerged from the trees, laughing and shoving, wielding branches like swords. They carried their running battle right over the tennis court, leaving behind a flurry of footprints in the swept clay. The sticks began to flail wildly, one of them passing just inches in front of Nick's eyes. Carrie was about to go down, but just then the kitchen's sliding door rumbled and Sabine was calling in her loud, undeniable voice. The boys obeyed instantly, dropping the sticks and racing inside.

Go, she told herself. Do what you have to do to get out the door.

This is Jamie's night, and you don't want to spoil it. Quint had offered to come by after work to pick her up, but she told him not to bother. She could hear in his voice that he wanted to stay at the controls until the last possible moment, managing this latest crisis. Fluctuation. Plummet. Whatever language of loss they were using these days. Besides, he'd sense her anger about the Garden and want to talk about it. But talking would only make it worse. The decision had been made. It wasn't going to happen.

The boys started yelling in the kitchen, but their uprising was quickly quelled by Sabine. They got like this during a crisis. They'd sense their father's distraction and go wild. Jamie, too, though his rowdiness took place farther from home, filtering back to Carrie in vague reports she was then expected to keep from his father. Dented fenders, a lost wallet, a morning spent puking in his bathroom. Quint had told him that if he was caught drinking again, he would lose the Wrangler for the summer. Because she was soft, Carrie still refused to rat on him. And now Quint was vanishing into the realm of bad numbers and Carrie feared there would be no controlling her son.

She chose a simple black dress from the closet and went back into the bathroom to do the things she did to her face. The tiles were still humid from her bath; she had to wipe away the mirror's fog. When she was done, she reached for the cell phone she'd left by the sink. It rang just as she touched it, like an animal startled awake by a stroking hand.

"I'm out the door." Quint's voice sounded as if he were calling from outer space, as in some ways he was. "You sure you don't want me to pick you up?"

"The boys still need to be fed," she said, her voice flat as it echoed off the tiles.

"Did Sabine go already?"

"Don't worry, Quint. I've got it under control."

Control, control, control. The Manning family motto.

"That isn't what I meant. I just thought I could come home and help out."

"We'll manage."

"*Mom!*"

Nick was at the bottom of the stairs, his voice shrill. She cupped her hand over the phone.

"I'll be down in a minute!"

"Carrie, I wish you wouldn't be so angry. This really is beyond our control."

That word again.

"Mom, Dillon is being a total dickwad! He took all the chocolate milk!"

Dillon was shouting now, defending himself. Where was Sabine?

"Quint, look, I'm all right. All right?"

They entered a silence. He was waiting for her to hang up first, the way he always did. She obliged him.

The kitchen smelled of meaty smoke. Cheeseburgers. There were home fries as well, cobs of corn streaked with melting butter. Sabine's idea of American food. Carrie had tried to wean her off all that fat and sugar, rocket fuel to the boys, but gave up after the veggie burger fiasco that had left a blackened mass clogging the waste disposal. The argument seemed to be on temporary hold as Sabine probed the Sub-Zero's mist. Dillon clutched a muddy glass, a crescent of chocolate above his upper lip. Nick was looking murderously at him. He turned to his mother in mute indignant appeal when she entered the room.

"What?" Carrie asked, the depth of her voice's weariness surprising even herself.

Sabine stood and shook her head. Carrie understood. There was no more chocolate milk. She felt something sink inside her. She didn't need this.

"I'm sorry, Nick," Carrie said. "How about a Snapple?"

"Uh, forget that noise," he said with an ominous chuckle.

She briefly contemplated running down to the convenience store, but that would make her seriously late. She wondered who in town would deliver the vile brown sludge she now let her sons drink, and then she wondered what sort of person would send out for chocolate milk. Of course, there was a solution to the whole problem—locking them in their respective rooms without dinner—but she didn't have the heart for it. Dillon belched loudly.

"Dillon, does that help?"

He shrugged and began to eat. Helping wasn't his concern. Nick continued to stare at her, slack-jawed, awaiting justice. Sabine shut the refrigerator door, deferring to Carrie. Why did they expect her to make these decisions?

"How about a shake?" she asked.

Nick looked skeptically at her, not happy, but not dismissing the idea, either.

"Define shake," he said.

"Nick, honestly. You put milk in the blender and drop in a scoop of ice cream."

Nick gave a probationary shrug, deferring acceptance until he saw the result. Sabine had moved to a neutral corner of the kitchen to watch. Even though she could be as ferocious as a drill instructor, she recused herself the moment Carrie or Quint was present. The fundamentals still applied. They were, after all, not her children.

The Cuisinart was coated with the calcified remnants of one of Jamie's protein concoctions. She'd have to use the Osterizer, last seen in one of the big storage compartments above the stove. She got the retractable footstool from the broom closet and set it up. The boys were temporarily subdued by the unprecedented sight of their mother climbing a ladder. The blender was wedged between other appliances. As she pulled it out, the free-swinging plug smacked her forehead with surprising force.

"Damn it!"

Her sons found this hilarious, laughing hysterically and then pretending to laugh hysterically. She threatened from on high to call the whole thing off, but this only caused an interval of barking. Sabine had taken a step forward, reconsidering her neutrality. But it was too late. Carrie was *doing it*. After slamming the blender on the counter, she opened the freezer, wondering now if they had an acceptable flavor of ice cream. There were two cartons visible, one an ancient banana sorbet she'd used for a forgotten dinner party, the other some Heavenly Hash, purchased no doubt for its vaguely druggy undertones. She held them up for her youngest son to choose.

"Uh, no way," he said, groaning emetically.

"Just pick one, Nick. There is a limit, you know."

He shook his head, frankly and without animosity. The existence of a limit was clearly news to him. Everyone was staring at her. They were waiting. For a decision. An explosion. Anything. Her forehead was aching where that damned plug had hit her. How could a simple plug be so heavy?

She chucked the cartons into the sink and looked back through the freezer. Billowing horror movie clouds obscured her view. Organic peas. Bricks of meat wrapped in Earth's Bounty butcher paper, including the months-old slab of venison she was going to have to make a decision about. Whole wheat waffles. A bottle of viscid Stoli. And then she saw it. Tucked behind the ice maker. A big, collapsed cardboard box of ice-cream sandwiches. Frost crackled as she pulled it out.

"Gentlemen, we have liftoff."

Nick flashed her a thumbs-up when he saw what she was holding. Dillon's mouth fell open, ready to stake his claim.

"Don't worry," she said before he could protest. "We'll make enough for you both."

"You want I . . ." Sabine asked.

"I've got it, Sabine," she said, lady-of-the-house cool, her voice charged with retribution that would never come, since there was no way Carrie was going to look for someone new. She dropped three of the sandwiches into the blender and then splashed in enough milk to cover them. There were a dozen buttons. Any of them would do the trick. She chose one near the middle. Noise filled the kitchen as she turned it all into a sweet, smooth mush.

Carrie didn't fully start to dread tonight's dinner until she drove down the sharp, scary bends on Orchard. She'd been to dozens of these things; countless more loomed in her future. The Mahabals would be at the table: Sonia, who never said anything; Godeep, whom Carrie was mad at about the Garden. At Jamie's insistence Quint had also invited Shannon and her folks. Carrie had never been too comfortable around Ronnie, though she admired her calm sanity, her refusal to get involved in the school's status wars. Drew she liked well enough, though he became hopelessly tongue-tied around Quint, putting on ice the ironic spirit she'd liked when she first met him. Carrie wondered if their mandated presence meant that Jamie was once again dating Shannon. She'd be sure to sit next to her in order to find out, even if she had to chuck someone out of a three-thousand-dollar seat. Jamie back with the only decent girl in the whole school: That would provide at least some salvation to a terrible week.

Traffic slowed on Federal just as she came alongside the Garden. She tried not to look, but its shabby brick mass proved too compelling. The COMING SOON message on the marquee had become a bitter joke. They'd put it up in March after Jon found the box of letters in the office. And now it wasn't going to happen. Dead because some cybernumbers hiccuped. A year of work wiped out because a fraction didn't square up with a guess about that fraction.

She'd coveted the old cinema since they'd moved to town eight years ago and she first saw the building in its lovely desuetude. She'd immediately taken her idea to Quint, but he had just bought the old tap and die complex and there was no money around for another renovation project, much less one that showed no reasonable expectation of profit. So she'd bided her time, living in constant low-level fear that some speculator would turn it into a shopping arcade. But it remained resolutely dark, even as the economy went crazy and money started sprouting everywhere. Carrie didn't understand at first—it was a perfect location for another monstrous commercial superfluity—but she'd eventually discovered that the owner, Rex Gilman, was something of a crank who owned several such theaters throughout New England, part of an old family empire that had fallen on hard times with the advent of multiscreens. For some reason he refused to sell, even as the old buildings turned into crumbling bulldozer bait. It turned out that several offers *had* been made on the Garden, including one by the horrible women from PMG. Each had been met with comprehensive silence.

Then, last summer, Carrie learned that Gilman was facing a potentially ruinous tax bill and would be willing to sell if the new buyer planned to maintain the property as a theater. He wasn't a crank after all, just someone who loved the old cinemas he'd inherited. He'd planned one day to restore them himself, but he now understood this was beyond his means. Carrie went immediately to Quint and told him that the Garden was something she *really wanted*. This time there was plenty of money around. A plan soon emerged, as it always did with Quint. Although she'd hoped that they could buy the building outright, Mahabal advised them to set up a nonprofit and restore the cinema as a landmark. They would thereby qualify for low-interest government loans, though WMV would provide the lion's share of the money in the form of charitable donations to Carrie's foundation. She would get her theater and Gilman his peace of mind; the people of Totten Crossing would be treated to big-screen classic movies, and Quint's fund would have a tax break. Everybody would win.

The Garden Film Society was born, incorporated with endless documents and endowed with a daunting amount of cash that Carrie soon understood she controlled. Because Mahabal didn't want to be forced to countersign every last check, he gave her the ability to transfer money by wire when he was away on business or locked in epic negotiation. Coming up with a password to allow her into the account was the only fun she had during these long meetings. After considerable thought she settled on Octave, after her all-time favorite screen character.

The work became even more onerous when Carrie learned that the foundation would need a board of directors. Her plan had always been to make all the decisions herself, but this was impossible if it was going to be a charity. At least four other people, disinterested parties with legitimate qualifications, were needed. Carrie press-ganged Myra Carter-Scheine, the head of the town's arts council, then called the provost at the university and the editor of the local paper for their recommendations. The university put forward someone called E. Cottrell from its film studies department. The *Recorder* didn't have a film critic—it bought in from the wire services—but the features editor recommended Jon Watts, a local writer who worked for an online film review site. The final board member would be Mahabal, who would furnish the legal expertise.

Putting the property deal together proved difficult. Applying for government funding was a nightmare. The inspector's report was a grim litany of hidden water damage, colonizing mold, and rodent-

chewed wiring. And then there was the potential deal breaker, Mahabal's refusal to agree to any contractual clause specifying that the
building must be used as a cinema. Gilman would just have to take
Carrie's word for it. By year's end the entire project had seemed likely
to fall through, and when a small section of roof gave way under
the first accumulation of snow, Carrie had trouble not taking it as
an omen. But she wouldn't give up. She took the plump, awkward
Gilman to lunch, to explain her plans to restore the cinema to its former glory and screen the sort of films the local chain operators didn't
have the guts to show, works you could now only see on the cramped
screens of libraries or colleges. She invoked the holy names of Kuro-
sawa and Welles and Renoir. Thus seduced, Gilman finally agreed.
The contract would not specify any particular end use. Carrie Manning's word would suffice. They closed the deal on February 1. She
immediately arranged for Ruud de Vries, the architect who had designed their house and Quint's office, to give the place the once-over.
After walking from one end of the moist carpet to the other in his er-
gonomic shoes, he simply shrugged.

"Well?" Carrie asked impatiently.

"We'll need a structural engineer."

"But it's doable?"

He shrugged again.

"Hey, you have the money, anything's doable."

He'd have a plan by the end of March; work could begin soon after.
With a January launch now in mind, Carrie called the first meeting of
the board of the Garden Film Society in early February. She held it at
her house to keep things informal. Myra Carter-Scheine, longtime
beneficiary of Manning largesse, made it clear the moment she walked
in the door, head scarf flowing, that she planned to defer to Carrie in
all matters. She really didn't know much about film; she was a potter.
Jon Watts turned out to be about Carrie's age, a lean, sort of shy man
with a self-deprecating manner and a warm, private smile. Mahabal
arrived, looking uncomfortable; he would be making a brief presenta-
tion to start the meeting and then cede his proxy to Carrie for all votes
on artistic content. In the future he would appear only if major bud-
getary matters were being decided.

It was E. Cottrell who caused trouble. The university's representa-
tive arrived fifteen minutes late, rolling through the Mannings' security gate on a sputtering unmuffled Yamaha. She was pierced and
patronizing, clad in ripped jeans and an ill-advised leather jacket. She
performed a little dumb show of contempt when she stepped into the
house, wouldn't meet eyes during introductions, then sat staring at
her amply chewed nails while Mahabal spelled out the board's legal
and fiscal obligations. She looked bored during Carrie's opening remarks, though she came to a nasty sort of life once the conversation
turned to content. E. Cottrell immediately hijacked the meeting with
her outrageous suggestions. Baltic heist movies and Japanese manga;
an Iranian vampire flick and a pseudodocumentary about a Canadian
all-girl porn rock band. Carrie thought: *Porn rock?* On Federal Street?
Each of her proposals was met by silence. Carrie started wondering
what the E. stood for. Eleanor. Elizabeth. Finally, she felt that she
had to say something. Choosing her words carefully, she explained
that the series was not really about exploring the fringes, but rather
about showing films that might benefit from the Garden's restored
splendor.

"Such as?" E. Cottrell demanded.

"I don't know," Carrie said, winging it. "Something like *Salaam
Bombay*."

"Indian cinema? Aren't you sort of missing the boat?" She turned to
Mahabal. "No offense."

"None taken," he said, snapping shut his briefcase. "I was born in
Clerkenwell."

He gave his eyes a private roll for Carrie's benefit before leaving the
room, making a beeline for the basement, where Quint and the boys
were watching Duke.

"Or what about *Topsy-Turvy*?" Carrie said. "That was in and out of
Cinema Six in a week."

E. Cottrell actually scoffed. Carrie looked at her in blank disbelief.
No one had scoffed at Carrie. Ever. Cool it, Edwina, she thought.

"Why not just go ahead and book in a season of David Lean?"

Lawrence of Arabia, of course, was high on Carrie's list, something
she decided to keep quiet for the time being.

"But I think Mike Leigh is just the sort of filmmaker our audience would go for."

"Oh." E. Cottrell smiled mirthlessly. "*Our* audience. I see."

"Well, yes, our audience. It's a subscription series."

"I'm just wondering where your taste and mine might intersect, is all."

Carrie felt like giving that nose ring a firm tug. Esther. Ernestine.

"I suppose you had someone better in mind?"

E. Cottrell shrugged, insulating herself with boredom.

"Well, if you want British cinema, you could at least have Jarman or Greenaway."

"Watching Peter Greenaway films is like being embalmed before death."

They were Jon's first words of the meeting. Carrie shot him a grateful look and saw that he was actually somewhat better-looking than she'd first thought. Although there was no reason to suspect he was defending her—E. Cottrell was sufficiently obnoxious to invite attack in her own right—Carrie allowed herself to feel gratitude. The professor looked at him with an expression that cataloged the deficiencies in his gender, politics, taste, and education, then smiled privately, making it clear she was rising above whatever devastating remark featured in her acidic little mind. They finished without making any decisions, but at least they had established a procedure. Everyone would nominate a dozen films, which they'd gradually whittle down to twenty overall. Carrie would screen any films people wanted to see in the viewing room downstairs, the first being A *Touch of Evil*. Even E. Cottrell conceded the film had value, if only because people could laugh at Charlton Heston's makeup.

That night Carrie was tempted to tell Quint that she couldn't do it. The idea of dealing with E. Cottrell, on top of the designers and suppliers and contractors, was too much for her. But she'd resolved to see this thing through, even if they wound up showing *Road Warrior* and *Rocky Horror* to stoned teenagers. She did, however, solicit her husband's advice on how to rid herself of E. Cottrell.

"That's a tricky one."

"Can't we just vote her off?" Carrie asked.

"You need cause."

"We have it. She's a condescending jerk."

"Boards are supposed to be fractious. Remember, this thing has to withstand public scrutiny."

"Public scrutiny. As if anyone cares."

This was what drove her crazy about her husband, this insistence on rectitude, even when people weren't looking. She wished she'd checked out E. Cottrell before recruiting her. Quint could sense her disappointment.

"You could always buy her off."

"How do I do that?"

"Easy. Make her an offer to resign."

"What if she refuses?"

"Raise it slightly. If she turns that down, make her an offer that's slightly *less* than the previous one. And then offer less than that. She'll accept the moment she understands what you're doing."

Carrie shot him a dubious look. She'd never been very good at negotiating.

"You want me to handle it?" he asked.

The idea of Quint giving E. Cottrell her walking papers was not without a certain appeal, though Carrie remembered her resolve to take charge of this project. She called the university the following morning. She started at five hundred dollars. E. Cottrell made that scoffing noise. Carrie offered her five-fifty and this time was greeted only by silence.

"How about five twenty-five?"

The silence now had a different quality.

"Five-ten?" Carrie asked.

"Do you have my address?"

To replace her, Carrie dug up Don White, a retired media studies instructor from the community college with a deep passion for the films of Billy Wilder. The four members of the newly constituted board worked easily together. They would meet at Carrie's house once a week to watch a film in the basement viewing room, then discuss its merits over a few glasses of wine. There was usually agreement about films they would schedule—*Raise the Red Lantern, Spirit of the Beehive, The*

Magnificent Ambersons, Fanny and Alexander, Danton—and ones that weren't quite right: *Delicatessen* and *Wild at Heart* and that screeching Almodóvar thing. A list soon began to take shape. More films: *Rules of the Game* and a Preston Sturges double bill and Carrie's all-time favorite, *Shoot the Moon*. They would easily meet the August deadline. A subscription brochure would be ready for an autumn mailing.

After that rocky start Carrie found she loved this even more than she'd hoped. Although Myra Carter-Scheine and Don White were just two more people in her crowded life, she found a kindred spirit in Jon, his initial putdown of E. Cottrell an overture to what soon became a real friendship. The more they talked, the more they discovered they had in common. Both loved Catherine Keener and Patrice Leconte and Sluizer's original *Vanishing*, though absolutely not his Hollywood version. Zombie movies and David Thomson. He told her about work she'd never heard of, like *Come and See*, with that amazing scene where those poor peasants built Hitler out of mud. She tracked down a copy for the board to watch, leading to its only real deadlock. Don White and an unusually animated Myra Carter-Scheine found it to be too heavy going, while Jon and Carrie thought it would perfectly define an outer edge. Carrie reluctantly employed her Mahabal proxy. Don and Myra didn't mind. It was only a movie.

The restoration plans were completed as all of this was taking place. As Ruud de Vries had predicted, the project was going to be a lot more expensive than anyone anticipated. Quint frowned when he heard the news but still authorized the transfer into the Society's account. Carrie was vaguely aware that things weren't going so well at WMV, even though they were supposed to prosper in a sinking economy. Her first clue came when Quint mentioned that he regretted pledging so much to the senior banquet, an almost unprecedented spell of second-guessing on his part. When Carrie asked if the fund was having problems, he told her not to worry. She was able to bring a model to her board's first April meeting. The builder was given the word. Preliminary construction was due to begin in June.

She soldiered on, though she could see the storm clouds gathering all through April. The way Quint's hours would stretch past dark; the empty bed she'd wake to in the morning. He began to ride Jamie even harder than usual. And then, last week, he'd arrived home late to tell her that they might have to put the Garden's restoration on hold. Still, Carrie held out hope, figuring this would mean at most a six-month delay. She was used to cycles; she was used to good patches and bad. But matters grew worse. Quint started taking late-night calls from Europe in his home office. His attention wandered; his blue eyes grew increasingly worried.

Finally, two days ago, he'd sat her down to give her the news. The fund was having its first major crisis since he'd started it eight years earlier. They were taking big hits on their capital reserves. He was laying off nearly a third of his staff. Some investors were being told their money was going to have to be locked up for another year, and even then there was no guarantee they wouldn't lose everything. Obviously, extraneous projects like the Garden would have to go. Extraneous. That was the word he'd used, not thinking how hurtful it would be, forgetting that this had been the focus of her own passion, her own long days. Carrie didn't appeal to him to make an exception; she didn't beg him to think of another way. They were clearly beyond that now. She asked if she would have to transfer back the nearly half million dollars still in the account.

"Leave it there for the time being," Quint said. "Godeep's figuring out a way to recoup it without us getting killed on taxes."

"In that case, could we use some of it to mothball the building until we can get back on track?" she asked, still not getting it. "I mean, the roof still needs to be fixed, and if we don't do something about the mold . . ."

"Carrie, you're going to have to sell the building."

"Sell?"

"I can't continue paying the mortgage given what's going on."

"Quint, we can't sell. I mean, to who?"

"Whoever makes the highest bid," he answered, as if she'd asked him the color of the sky.

"You mean some developer?"

Quint nodded. This was why he'd let Mahabal refuse an end-use clause in the contract. To him, the Garden was only so much square footage, a trinket that would now have to go back to the jewelers.

"But I told the owner we wouldn't do that."

"There's no provision for that in the contract."

There it was. The magic word.

"Carrie, listen to me. Next week I'm going to start telling investors there will be no dividends this year. None. And that's the best-case scenario. How do you think it would look if we started renovating an old theater while I was doing that?"

Old theater. Carrie was tempted to ask him how he thought it was going to look for her, going back on the promise she'd given to an eccentric little potbellied man. But she didn't bother. There was no point. A contract had been signed. The markets had spoken. It had been decided.

She lucked into a recently vacated place in the Country Day lot. She turned off the motor and reached for the door handle but found herself unable to get out of the car. It was as if some great gravitational crush were now at work in the cramped space. After two numb days, the sadness and anger finally hit. Jamie would soon be off at Duke; her younger boys were growing more distant from her every day. Quint was becoming a stranger, buried by the weight of looking after other people's fortunes. And now the Garden was gone as well. Hadn't anyone seen how much she wanted this? Hadn't they noticed how hard she'd been working, dealing with bureaucrats, opening her house to strangers, deploying all her charm on characters like E. Cottrell and Rex Gilman? Carrie suddenly felt powerless, a silly, gratuitous woman who couldn't even shoulder open a car door. She wondered if this was where she'd been heading all along, to be sitting alone in a sixty-thousand-dollar vehicle, with nothing to do but watch the things she loved vanish.

The intensity of her tears shocked her. It had been a long time since she had really cried; she'd forgotten how scary it could be. The muscles in her stomach began to cramp; a raw, constricting pain gripped her throat. Her mind told her body to stop—this was ridiculous; someone would see her—but she could not stop. Seconds, minutes, she had no idea how long the crying lasted. It ended only when it was ready to end, leaving her exhausted and angry at herself. She adjusted the mirror so she could see her face. It looked puffy and red. The small knot on her forehead, which had started to shrink on the ride over, was now engorged. Feeling ridiculous, she took a tissue from the armrest compartment and touched her smeared makeup. But the moist puffiness still had to be dealt with or Quint would know she'd been crying. The air conditioner would be good for that. She turned on the car and then angled the vent so the clean, phony cold washed her face. It felt as good as water. Ronnie emerged from the building, forcing Carrie to slump in her seat. The last thing she wanted was for Shannon's stepmother to see her in distress. She'd ask what was wrong and Carrie just might tell her.

Before long she was as presentable as she was going to be. The car door opened easily this time. Dinner had already been served when she arrived at the table. She took a quick inventory of her guests. The Mahabals, friendly and bland; Drew, a big dog waiting on her husband's favor. There was no sign of Shannon. Carrie took the first available seat, directly across from Quint. He looked even more shattered than he had last night, although no one at the table except her would have noticed.

"What happened to your head?" Jamie asked.

Carrie touched the welt.

"You should see the other guy."

Steve Buscemi in *Fargo*, though no one caught the reference. Quint looked at her strangely, and she figured that she should probably shut up. This was Jamie's night, and she'd already messed things up by arriving late. He'd begun chewing the cuticle next to his thumb. Although people—well, his father—fully expected him to win the Carswell, it was by no means a sure thing. The award was named for Clinton Carswell, a student who had dropped dead on the lacrosse field fifteen years earlier after an errant ball struck his chest and sent his heart into a fatally irregular rhythm. It was given each year to the senior who "best personified the values of Country Day." Whatever those were. Until recently it had been presented by the dead boy's parents, but they'd moved to West Palm Beach. Students, teachers, and staff all had equal votes to keep it from being a simple popularity contest among the kids. Jamie was considered a front-runner, though MIT-bound Jacob Hsu, with his second-place tie at National Robot Championships, and Madison McNabb, whose video diary *Soul 2 Seoul* had recently been shown on MTV, were also prime candidates. A few weeks ago at dinner Carrie had joked that parents should be allowed to bid for the award the way they did everything else at school, a crack that was met with identical frowns from her husband and son. There was a prize to be had. The Manning boys were ready.

Keeping quiet, being good, she let her eyes drift between her husband and son, Jamie the picture of his father when he was seventeen. The smile like a shield of teeth, the unblinking eyes, the way his brow would furl into an expression that somehow mixed insecurity with utter confidence. He was almost as smart as Quint if you didn't count math; easily more popular and arguably better-looking. What he lacked was his father's will. There was just no comparison. People would say this resulted from a pampered life, but Carrie knew better. It was deeper than that. It was his inheritance from her. Softness. Fragility. Indecision. Whatever was left in the artistic soul when the talent was taken away. The part she'd foolishly tried to nourish with the alternative camps and photography lessons and her advocacy of Shannon Hagel. She should have known she had nothing to tempt him from the fruits of Quint's legacy, the customized Wrangler and the Springsteen concerts and the adoring male posses. The irony, of course, was that Jamie's choice had done nothing to dispel his father's feeling that his eldest son didn't quite measure up to the model of a boy Quint had devised before he was born. You should have chosen me, she thought as she watched Jamie. All is forgiveness here. You win just by showing up.

Carrie shook off these unhappy thoughts, looking around the table for a friendly face. Shannon still hadn't arrived. Carrie worried that there was a problem, that Ronnie's departure had something to do with her absence.

"Is Shannon coming?" she asked generally.

Nobody knew. Drew looked pained, although no one who knew the Hagel family could possibly hold him accountable for his daughter's behavior. Further conversation was prevented by the dimming of the lights. Tricia Windham, the school's black-haired, brown-nosed head, took the platform as if she were stepping onto the set of an infomercial for a revolutionary diet supplement. The very first thing Carrie had ever heard her say was that "kids are our most precious commodities." She'd been hired for her fund-raising prowess; people joked that her capital campaigns could be listed on the NASDAQ.

"It's *super* that everyone could make it tonight," Windham said. "A really *terrific* end to a, well, *terrific* year."

She droned on about how sad it was that not *everyone* could get an award; how they were all winners. Finally, the ceremony started. Kensington Smith won for drama; Jacob Hsu bagged math; Chun Kyu Kim won for French. Cheyenne Newsome was awarded best personal Web site. Bright, avid faces collected their due. There was a controversial moment when Jazz Mahabal won for male athlete of the year; though he had led his team in scoring, that team happened to be *girls'* field hockey. Godeep had played the sport back in England, and after discovering that there was no boys' team for his son to carry on the family tradition, he'd threatened suit unless Jazz was allowed to play with the girls. The school had caved. You did not go to court against Godeep Mahabal. Jazz, utterly unashamed, went on to lead the team to its first championship season. The whole controversy had turned out to be a monumental waste of time; Jazz, 130 pounds soaking wet, was a finesse player who was easily shrugged off the ball by the ample-thighed daughters of Connecticut.

More prizes. Jamie won a community service award for his all-night squash marathon. He stood, shooting his famously shy smile at the crowd, the same one Carrie had recently caught him practicing in the bathroom mirror. Just before he reached the dais, a solitary male voice sounded from the back of the hall.

"This Bud's for you!"

There was knowing laughter that Jamie pretended not to hear. Carrie shot a look at Quint, who stared darkly at his son as he returned to the table. He then turned his gaze upon her, a stern question in his eyes.

More awards. Precocity and more precocity. Jesse Schoenbrum for creative writing; he'd had something published in a review. Maura

Hughes-Shapiro, already interning for Chris Dodd, won for government. There was a sixteen-way tie for perfect attendance. As the parade continued, Shannon arrived, simply materializing in the seat next to Carrie. She waved an apology to Quint and resolutely ignored her father's probing glance. Carrie took the chance to examine Jamie's former girlfriend. The clothes were still a disaster: baggy cargo pants, a cheap sweatshirt, and ragged sandals. Antifashion, clothes at their most rudimentary. And her plain brown hair looked as if it hadn't been brushed in days. But there was no hiding those big beautiful eyes and that sexy mouth, and she seemed to have shed a few pounds since the last time Carrie saw her.

"What have I missed?" she whispered to Carrie.

"We won for community service. But there was heckling."

"Oh, yeah?"

"Beer was mentioned."

Shannon balled up a napkin and threw it at Jamie. Carrie once again found herself hoping they were getting back together. And then there was a ruffle of renewed concentration in the dining hall. The name of poor Clinton Carswell had been invoked. Carrie looked at her son, who was staring down at the table with a nervous smile, then turned to her husband, who was watching Tricia with his usual expression of benign entitlement. The winner's name was read out. There was a flutter of excitement at another table, and Jamie looked at his father, who turned his eyes toward his son, and they were not happy eyes. Jamie looked back down at his empty plate as an ecstatic Madison McNabb tore herself away from her ecstatic table to collect her award.

3 "I have to get going."

"Half hour more."

He was coiling around her, not letting her go anywhere. If she didn't break free from him now, then she would never make it back to school.

"Come on, Ian. I can*not* miss this thing."

He pulled back to look at her in the room's fading light, understanding now that she meant it.

"Yeah, I should get myself together, too. My uncle and I are supposed to have this big talk."

"What about?" Shannon asked.

"The future. Or his idea thereof."

She didn't like the sound of this.

"Man, he's really getting serious about North Carolina."

"That's because my birthday's coming up."

The old bed's rickety frame shuddered as Shannon stood. She endured a moment's dizziness; it had been hours since she'd last been on her feet. Her plan when she arrived had been to kiss and talk for a short while. But her resolve meant little once she was in his room.

"So you up for anything tonight?" Ian asked as she collected her clothes.

"Least popular student." She shrugged to let him know it didn't matter. "But Jamie's up for stuff. He got his father to invite us to sit at his table. I have to be there."

"I'd like to meet this Jamie."

There was no jealousy in his voice. He was genuinely curious. He'd seen the house; he'd heard the stories. Shannon smiled agreeably, though it was something she had no intention of arranging.

"Come on. Let's go."

He grasped her hand but then smiled mischievously, pulling her back down on top of him. They kissed for a while, but then she pushed herself decisively away. She really did have to go. Jamie was scared to death about losing the Carswell, especially in front of his father. And her own father would be suicidal if she didn't show up.

Ian got up as well. Unlike the overgrown babies at Country Day, he knew when it was time to be serious; he'd learned that there was more to life than getting exactly what he wanted as soon as he wanted it. They kissed once more out by her car, though she pulled back quickly, picturing his uncle's sudden arrival. She had yet to meet him and didn't want it to happen by accident. This was what they'd decided. Until Ian's birthday no one would know anything about them.

"Call me when you get home," he said.

"It might be late."

"I'll be up. I never close."

She followed the long rutted driveway off the property. Once on Totten Pike she tuned the radio to the punk retro show on the university station. She loved the band names, which, like Shannon, seemed to defy the notion that they would ever be popular. Prefab Sprout. Mission of Burma. Half Man, Half Biscuit. It was ten miles from his house to town, a straight shot on Totten Pike. For the first half of the journey there were only sporadic glimpses of set-back houses. Once she passed Shaker, however, development took over: expensive subdivisions and low-lying office parks. The sprawl Ian hated. Prefab sprout.

Traffic got bad as she approached Federal. She checked the time. Almost seven. She was going to be very late. As long as she showed up before the Carswell, she would be all right, even though her father would be in agony. In the last few days he'd become so excited at the prospect of being at the Mannings' table that Shannon wished she'd told him Jamie had been behind the invitation.

The banquet. One more thing to get through. After this, only the graduation ceremony remained, and then she'd be finished with it all. She hadn't wanted to attend either event, but she knew her father would start to wonder about her long absences from home if she didn't tell him she was hanging out with kids from her class. Once school was done it would be easier. Ronnie would have her babies, and no one would be paying attention to anything Shannon did. And then Ian would turn eighteen and they would be free. But summers were short, and she still had to decide about the fall. It had been agreed that she would be attending Oberlin—agreed by everyone but Shannon. Because she'd been wait-listed there before they finally let her in, she'd also had to accept admission at the nearby state university. She was supposed to send in a postcard withdrawing her acceptance, but she was holding off on that, secretly leaving open the possibility that she could still attend if she wanted. And then she could still be near Ian for more than just a summer.

They'd known each other for only eight weeks. That was what amazed her. How the most real thing in her life could have happened so suddenly. Everything else that was real—her mother's disappearance and the awfulness of school and her father's bringing a stranger into their house—had accumulated like sediment at the bottom of some dead lake. But Ian turned on a few minutes that weren't even supposed to have happened. She'd lost her keys. It was that simple. Her father was out, which meant she'd had to go by Ronnie's office after school to borrow hers. When she saw that there was a boy in the waiting room, she'd wanted to knock on the inner door, but interrupting one of her stepmother's sessions was strictly forbidden. She shot a quick look at him. He looked harmless enough. He had a thin, tapered nose like John Lennon and intense blue-gray eyes and a small, gentle mouth. Long, unruly hair, full of waves; broad, sharp shoulders; and thin wrists. Everything she liked in a boy, in fact. He was tapping gently on the aquarium glass, his face catching the neon light. Not bothering the fish, really, just trying to get their attention. He didn't have that ravaged look of some of the kids Ronnie treated. Shannon wondered if he'd come to pick someone up, a wayward brother or a friend. She turned away when he looked at her, though the way she reacted to his eyes startled her. She picked up a copy of *Newsweek* and took a seat as far away from him as possible. The words proved a meaningless jumble. When she looked back up, he was staring at her, and she could see now what she'd sensed when she first laid eyes on him. He was beautiful.

"This your first time?" he asked.

"For what?" she asked, her voice sounding bitchier than she'd intended.

He gestured toward the inner office door with his chin.

"I've been with her four years," she said, keeping the joke to herself.

"Four years? You must be more messed up than me."

Shannon could see that the boy was a patient. Maybe her joke wasn't that great.

"You don't want to know," she said, eager now to cut off the conversation.

She knew what he was thinking. That she was some rich kid who'd come to moan about her parents' divorce. One of those girls who swapped one syndrome for another to get a little leverage on the world. Shannon was tempted to tell him he had it wrong, though it didn't matter what he thought. He was just a good-looking boy she'd never see again.

The office door opened a few minutes later. Two parents emerged with their daughter, a tall teenager who looked as if she weighed all of eighty pounds. There was a rumor of vanished beauty about her, though her face was now nothing but cheekbones and eyes. Her skin had a greenish undertone; her hair was stiff and brittle. Her baggy clothes did not intersect with her body at any point. The teat of the water bottle she clutched had been chewed into a cabbagy paste. Her father's gaze was steadfastly averted, as if he wanted nothing more than to get back to the office and give somebody a very hard time. Mom was an older, puffier replica of her daughter. Her eyes were red and the rims of her nostrils inflamed. They were followed by Ronnie, dressed with her usual sobriety, the folds of her suit like curtains drawn to hide her pregnancy.

"So I'll see you next week," Ronnie said in a sad but hopeful voice.

The mother muttered something and followed her husband

through the door. The daughter trailed behind them, drifting weightlessly in her parents' mass.

Ronnie noticed Shannon.

"Is everything all right?"

Shannon could sense the renewed intensity of the boy's gaze.

"I locked myself out," she mumbled.

Shannon followed her stepmother into the office, surprised to find herself wondering if there was any way to get more information about the boy. But Ronnie never talked about her patients, even that time when one of them blew his brains out while his mother was calling everybody down to Thanksgiving dinner, his CD player turned up so loud it drowned out the blast. The mom had sent up her youngest son to get him, and now *he* was a patient.

"So how's school?"

"Same as always," Shannon answered.

Ronnie nodded, accepting the nonanswer. This was how it was between them these days. Everything cool; everything proper. Shannon made sure to say thanks after taking the key and headed back through the reception area. The boy, bathed in the faint aquatic glow, watched her pass. She hazarded a quick look at him, but his attention was already focused on Ronnie, his doctor, her stepmother.

She saw him again three days later. She'd gone down to the Starbucks on Federal after school with Jamie and Jazz and some other kids, including a junior named Layla who was supposedly hooking up with Jamie, though Shannon knew it wasn't going to happen once she spent a few nights in the presence of the Bad Jamie. It was the usual performance, everybody talking at once over sweet, frothy drinks that were more like ice cream than coffee. Shannon said precisely nothing, drinking latte until she had to use the bathroom. When she came out, she navigated toward the door, bored enough to head home.

"I know you," a voice said.

She turned and it was him. He sat alone, a big drawing pad in front of him, cooling black coffee next to it. There was a book on the table as well, something titled *One-Dimensional Man*. After hesitating a fatal second, she nodded and walked on.

"I'm sorry," he said.

This stopped her. No one ever apologized to Shannon except her
father, who did it so often that it no longer meant anything. She
looked back down at him, startled by the bold expression in his eyes.
Kids at Country Day didn't look at each other this way.

"About what?"

"Thinking you were with Dr. Traynor. I didn't know she was your
mom."

"She's not my mom," Shannon said. "She's just married to my dad."

"Well, I'm still sorry."

"Yeah, well, I better . . ."

"Take a seat," he said, his eyes remaining locked on hers.

She tried to think of a way to say no. But nothing came to mind, so
she slid into the booth, sneaking a look at that pad as she did. The
page had been divided into panels, most of them filled with pencil
drawings that looked like kids floating in space. They were good,
though before she could get a real sense of them he'd gently closed
the book.

"So do you know all about me?" he asked with a smile that let her
know he wasn't angry with her for trying to see what he'd drawn.

"No way. Ronnie never talks about her work."

"Ronnie? Is that what you call her?"

"Among other things."

He laughed quietly. He had a nice laugh. It wasn't a boy's laugh.

"It must be weird," he continued. "Living with someone who's so
together."

"It's kind of a pain," she said after a moment. "I mean, being in the
same house with this person who believes people should be happy
and well adjusted."

"What, do you prefer the alternative?"

He was smiling, though he was being serious as well. She liked
that.

"I guess we had a bad start and haven't really got over it."

"Sounds like my life."

His life. She had the feeling she was on the edge of something very
steep.

"Look," she said, pulling back, "I don't think this is such a good idea, talking about her. I mean, she'd kill me if she knew."

"Then don't tell her," he responded matter-of-factly.

"Look, I'd better go."

She began to slide out of the booth.

"So don't you want to know why I'm seeing her?"

Once again, she found herself frozen with surprise at his words.

"I got busted for possession of a controlled substance last year, and they said I had to see somebody or become a guest of the state."

"Controlled substance?"

"Marijuana. It wasn't mine, but I didn't feel like narcing out the owner. They said that if I attended counseling until I'm eighteen, I wouldn't have to go to jail." He smiled and shook his head. "It's a joke, really. I spend an hour a week talking about a problem I don't even have. I mean, the night in jail was all the convincing I needed."

Shannon shook her head in sympathetic disgust. It was typical of Ronnie to wind up on the side of the cops and the courts. She tried to be liberal and compassionate but was just as much a part of the system as the rest of them.

"Do they make you do anything else?"

"I gotta have a job. And work toward my high school equivalency, which takes about ten minutes a week. It's okay. In a few months it's my birthday and I'm free."

Shannon was unable to fathom what it would be like to spend a night in jail or be on parole. Those words brought to mind the slouching, stringy-haired men on her father's beloved police shows. But this boy was nothing like that.

"I just thought, it was sort of hanging over us," he said.

Hanging over us.

"So what do you talk about?"

"With your mom? Sorry—stepmom." He shrugged. "Just, stuff. My mom. My uncle."

"What's up with them?"

"Nothing with my mom. She died four years ago. My uncle, well, he's my guardian. So to speak."

"I'm sorry. About your mom."

"Yeah. Thanks. But what are you gonna do?"

Shannon didn't know, but she certainly liked the way he'd corrected himself about Ronnie's being her stepmother. There was movement in the corner of her eye. Her friends were heading toward the door. Jamie had raised his chin at her to ask if she was coming. But she waved him away. She was staying where she was.

They talked. His name was Ian Warfield, and he lived up on Totten Pike. Although he was Shannon's age, he hadn't gone to school very much in the past few years. Instead, he was educating himself. Ashamed of her own pampered life, Shannon said little in response.

"Well, I better get home," she said eventually, knowing she should get out of here before it became impossible.

"Can I get a lift?" He smiled. "They repossessed my license. I guess I'm one of those teen drivers people are always complaining about."

Their eyes held for a moment. Shannon could feel her heart beginning to pound.

"Sure," she said.

She didn't take him right home. Instead, they spent the next two hours driving through Totten Crossing, past the office complexes and the big fake Colonials situated on roads everybody now called lanes. They drove up Orchard, passing the Mannings' house, which looked a whole lot bigger than it had before. She told him about restless Carrie and inscrutable Quint and stressed-out Jamie, though she didn't say anything about going out with him last year. Ian said he hated the rich, though she could see that he was fascinated, like everyone else. And then they moved out into the country, through the apple orchards and state parks. She wanted to hear more about his wild days but somehow wound up talking about herself, hoping that she didn't sound pathetic when she complained about the horrors of Country Day, the girls who were always doing their nails and whining about their mothers and sending venomous instant messages; the arrogant boys who walked the halls like Romans with their sandals and flowing shirttails. Finally, she got around to the thing she never talked about: her mother's leaving.

"Wait—your mother left *you*?"

"When I was ten," Shannon said, not quite believing she was telling him this. "She fell in love with this guy named Timothy Purdy. I guess she'd been seeing him before she married my dad, and then he just came back. Only, he said he didn't want kids. And so . . . they're in Oregon now."

"Do you see her?"

"We talk on the phone every now and then. It's like talking to your grandmother."

"So basically we're in the same boat."

"Basically."

"No, wait. That's wrong. My mother didn't want to leave me. She went out kicking and screaming. So really, it's worse for you."

Shannon couldn't believe what a sweet and understanding thing he'd just said.

"Well," she said, "let's call it even."

Emboldened, she kept on talking, telling him how she was supposed to be getting excited about college, though she didn't even know if she wanted to go all the way to Ohio for more of the same social bullshit and academic pressure.

"Where are you going?"

"Oberlin?"

"Is that good?"

She shrugged, about to dismiss it, but then caught herself.

"Yeah," she admitted. "It's good."

Finally, it really was time for her to get home. He showed her his house, a small brick ranch fronted by a sloping yard full of broken-looking boulders. Seeing that his uncle's hot rod was in the driveway, he made her drop him on the street.

"So what's wrong with your uncle, other than his taste in cars?"

"He tends to dominate situations. It's always a good idea to go slow with him." He turned to her, not yet ready to get out of the car. "So how are we going to do this?"

This.

"Give me your number," she said.

He wrote his number on her American Visions notebook. It took him a long time, and Shannon started to think that maybe his not going to school wasn't so impressive, after all. But when he handed it to her, she saw that he'd drawn a picture of them standing together, their own perfectly rendered faces attached to pudgy little cartoon creatures. They both looked kind of freaked out, as if they couldn't understand what they were doing with these sexless little bodies. She laughed out loud, and for a moment she thought he was going to kiss her, but then he was shouldering open the passenger door.

"Call me," he said in parting. "Really."

She did. They got together nearly every night after that. At first, they would stay in her car, driving through the darkened orchards and surrounding towns. They soon found a pizza place run by hippies up by the university where they could spend hours. Sometimes she could hardly get in a word, Ian's mind running a mile a minute as he told her about a book he'd stayed up all night reading, something by Norman O. Brown or E. M. Cioran, books that were helping him figure out how to live outside a system that had so badly cheated him. His eyes sparkled with energy as he spoke; she'd never seen anyone whose brain could work so fast, not even Jacob Hsu. She began to find out more about him. He didn't have any tattoos. Nothing was pierced. He didn't smoke dope or drink beer; he had to piss in a cup whenever asked by his parole officer, a nice woman who thought Ian was doing just *great*. But even if he could get away with it, he wouldn't. His job was at the deli at Earth's Bounty, scooping out tubs of penne and slicing Parma ham for women who would linger over their choices as if they were buying precious gems. When he was eighteen years and one minute old, he'd quit without notice. After that he was off the grid, living on the fairly sizable chunk of money his mother had left for him to collect when he turned eighteen.

He talked about her, too. Virginia. Ginny. She'd been a dental hygienist for most of his life. Before that she was a biker slut. Evidently she'd had a rocky time with men, especially Ian's father, who was prone to violent mood swings, one of which swung him all the way out to California, where he crashed a motorcycle while driving 120 miles per hour, with predictable results. After Ian was born, she developed a pretty severe weight problem. When she found out she had cancer, she got religious and tried to make a deal with God to give her a few more years. But God clearly wasn't interested in her terms; she died in agony three months later. There wasn't much talk about Him those last few weeks she spent hooked up to the morphine drip. After she died, he went a little bit crazy, a situation that wasn't helped by the fact that he was put in the care of his uncle David, who was basically a good guy, though somewhat wild himself. Although Ian never said as much, Shannon was fairly certain that his uncle was the "friend" whose marijuana he'd been carrying when he was arrested. Recently David had begun talking about the two of them buying a bar in North Carolina with Ginny's insurance money. The idea had absolutely no appeal to Ian; he wanted to stay in the house his mother had given him and work as a graphic novelist, something Shannon had only vaguely heard about. It was like a cross between being a regular novelist and a comic book artist, although Ian joked that you never, ever were to use the phrase *comic book*. He was working on two different stories, depending on the mood he was in. One was called *Swimming Pool World*; Shannon guessed that was what she saw that first day at Starbucks. The other was about Michael Sojourner, a character he'd invented soon after his arrest.

"So when can I see these?" she asked.

"Eventually."

They finally went to his house after his uncle started working nights at his limo-driving job. It was there that they kissed for the first time, on an old sofa in front of a big curved picture window that overlooked Totten Pike. Shannon had been kissed by her share of boys, but she never felt anything like this. It was as if someone had drained all the blood out of her head and pumped it back into her heart. She could feel him getting excited and was starting to think she would let this happen but decided in the end that it was still too soon. Although the boys at Country Day weren't exactly fighting duels to win her love, she'd been with enough of them to know that going slow was a good idea. Stephen Dulea after a party, with his hammer-headed erection pressing against the zipper of his Dockers. Jesse Schoenbrum, the poet, who was just a frightened little boy hiding behind a sarcastic smile. And of course, Jamie, who had seemed so strong at first but had turned out to be just as young and frail as the others.

More kissing, more denial. It finally happened two weeks later, when her father and Ronnie had gone to Atlanta to attend a "Youth in Crisis" convention. It was perfect, infinitely better than those afternoons in Jamie's room. Shannon could remember everything about it. The jut of Ian's chin as he buried his head on her lap in the car when they turned onto Crescent Street; the soft tangle of hair in the center of his chest as she rested her cheek on him in her bed. Late that second night he read her the first few pages of a poem called *Howl*, stalking her bedroom like a big beautiful cat, that little black-and-white paperback in his hands as he invoked those brilliant people dragging themselves hysterical and naked through the streets at dawn, something Ian was, not hysterical, but brilliant and naked, his eyes like lightning as he read the words of what had immediately become her favorite poem.

But mostly what she remembered about that weekend was the sex. When he was inside her, she forgot she had a body; all she knew was how good her body felt. It had never been like this with Jamie. By the time her father and Ronnie returned from the airport she felt as if she'd been asleep for a week. It was everything she could do to keep from driving over to his house that Sunday night, risking discovery so they could be together for a just a few more minutes.

And so they were lovers. They would spend time at whichever house was empty, usually his, since his uncle worked so much. She'd almost gone mad with frustration during the four-day period last month when he had that strange bug that left him lying in bed without the energy even to tell her what was wrong. But he got better; his passion for her returned with a vengeance. She loved the sex so much that sometimes she would get angry when they were making love, knowing that they would soon have to stop. And—though she knew that this wasn't the reason they were together; she knew that this didn't really matter—she couldn't help but savor the fact that he was probably the one boy in a fifty-mile radius that nobody—not her father or Jamie or her stepmother or the kids at Country Day—would guess she was with.

She arrived in the cafeteria just after Jamie won the community service prize for the twenty-four-hour squash marathon he'd organized last fall to raise money for AIDS. The idea was to keep the ball moving from dawn Saturday until dawn Sunday, with each member of the school's twelve-strong team rotating through solitary half hour shifts. Shannon had stayed for most of it, leaving only for a few hours of sleep in the middle of the night. When she returned, Jamie was standing alone and determined in that echoing white emptiness, stubbornly hitting the ball against the streaked wall. The only other spectator was his father, who sat at the top of the stands his money had helped build. He was talking softly into his cell phone while he watched, his eyes never leaving his son. Jamie could have easily taken a break—the other boys were all asleep. But Quint would never tolerate this. People had pledged good money to keep the ball going. To stop would be to fail, and to lie about that failure would be to cheat. So Jamie kept on hitting the ball against the wall and his father kept watching. Two months later Shannon understood she had to get away from it all.

Quint was looking at his son with those same demanding eyes as Shannon slipped into her seat; her own father gave her a dirty look that she ignored. Ronnie wasn't around; the Mahabals beamed harmlessly at her. The only person Shannon was really glad to see was Carrie. In an ideal world, she sometimes thought, Carrie would be her own mother, or, probably more realistically, her older sister, the one who'd gone off to New York and wasn't quite making it on Broadway. Shannon had felt really bad for her when she broke up with Jamie. Carrie had invested a lot of time trying to make it work between them, treating them to trips into Manhattan, making sure to include Drew and Ronnie in her parties. Sometimes Shannon was tempted to go up to Orchard just to sit around and talk with her. But it would be too strange. She was no longer one of the Mannings.

She finally let her attention settle on Jamie, chewing the flesh around his thumb in anticipation of the big moment. Shannon knew that his anxiety this time out was justified. She'd heard the talk around the halls the past week. People were tired of his winning all the time; their classmates were sick of his acting so wild and nasty when he drank. The consensus was that maybe it was time to stop giving Jamie everything for free.

She pelted him with a balled napkin and rolled her eyes at the absurdity of it all. He rolled his back at her, though she knew he didn't mean it, not for a second. And then a hush descended, and Tricia Windham announced that Jamie had lost to Madison McNabb. As Madison pranced onstage, Shannon watched her friend endure his father's dark, disappointed look and his mother's awkward attempt at humor and Drew's feeble, unwelcome consolation that the kids who voted against him were just jealous. Shannon didn't try to speak to him until the evening had broken up and they were alone in the lobby.

"So," she joked, "community service. I know how much that must mean to you."

He smiled, but there was nothing in it.

"You want to go somewhere? Smoke some crack? Hold up a liquor store?"

"I don't know," Jamie said. "Shit."

"Come on," she said, hooking his arm with hers. "Let's go for a ride. I'll explain to you why none of this matters."

But he was resisting and she saw why. Wrestlers beckoned from across the lobby: loutish dimwits who had mysterious access to unlimited supplies of beer.

"Jamie, come on. Forget that. Let's go."

But his arm was already coming free from hers.

"Look, I'll catch you later, all right?"

He walked away and Shannon let him go. If that's what he wanted, then there was nothing she could do about it. She still had to remind herself of this on occasion. Jamie Manning was no longer her problem.

4 The passengers moved quickly, the way they always did when a plane arrived late. Most were solitary men with computer cases, their clothes twisted and flecked with peanut skins. Mingling among them was the usual random sample of humanity. There was a uniformed soldier whose too-small beret rode up on his shaved head like the loosened cap of a soda bottle; an old couple in matching sweaters who probably hadn't spoken since takeoff; a kid holding a deflating rubber dinosaur with a flaccid tail. A fat young woman lugged a sleeping baby, its slick red face and the resentful glances of nearby passengers indicating that a very long tantrum had just concluded.

David held his clipboard at chest level, angling it at likely-looking men. Eyes washed over it, but nobody stopped. Two other livery drivers worked the opposite side of the gangway, a sleepy Oriental guy and a blonde in a man's suit. Neither had been inclined to gossip, which suited David fine. The crowd began to thin down to stragglers and limpers. The other drivers made their connections, leading David to suspect that his trip had been a waste of his time. People who booked executive limos tended not to dawdle, especially after a long flight. They hit the concourse running.

A disheveled, muttering man strode through the gate, looking like the end of the line. He wove close enough to allow David to smell the sharp tang of multiple scotches. He feared that this might be his guy, which was all he needed tonight, a sloppy drunk who would probably want to stop for another bottle. But after a long, muttering look at the clipboard he staggered on, the tail of his shirt hanging loose from his wrinkled suit jacket. He made it as far as the bank of chairs that de-lineated the boarding area, collapsing into one already occupied by a ruffled newspaper.

"Fuck it," he said. "Fuck *it*."

Stewardesses began to emerge. David stepped up to the first of them, a curvy, short-haired woman with an off-the-clock scowl on her frosted lips.

"That it for this flight?"

"That it is." She nodded at the clipboard. "You miss your guy?"

"Doubtful. I think he's still in San Francisco."

"Can you blame him?"

Their eyes held for a moment, two grown-ups who understood the deeper implications of Californian revelry. And then she walked on, her hips swiveling testily, her wheeled case bumping along behind her. David was tempted to hurry after her and offer a chauffeur-driven ride home in a gleaming black Lebaron with leather seats and climate control and everything else that made people think of luxury these days. But he shook away the thought, pleasant as it was. He had to talk to Ian.

He hurried back to the parking deck, regretting his decision not to have called it quits that afternoon, when he found himself back at Camelot with nothing to do. It had already been a long enough day. He'd started at dawn, making two mind-numbing trips along the Mer-ritt and another to the New Haven train station. That was plenty of driving for one shift. Hamed and Jack would have no problem with his heading home. But just as he was turning in his keys, another driver crapped out on a four o'clock pickup at the airport. David grabbed it, figuring he would still be home in plenty of time to get dinner ready, only to arrive at the terminal and find the plane delayed by twenty minutes, which of course stretched into eighty. Meaning he would now hit Hartford during rush hour without a passenger. Mean-ing he could not use the diamond lane. If he was late, Ian could very likely take it as permission to skip out on their meal.

David tossed his clipboard on the seat and sped toward the exit, and of course, there was a big jam there, only a handful of those new booths currently in operation, your tax dollars at work. He called Camelot to say it had been a washout, then tried home on the off chance his nephew would answer. But it was just his own voice on the machine, leaving David to wonder if Ian had even remembered they were having dinner. After two weeks of amiable pestering he'd finally managed to get his nephew to agree to discuss the Cove. Although he had recently been resisting the plan, David knew that a friendly man-to-man would make him understand that this was a unique opportunity. A seventeen-year-old might think these chances rolled around as regularly as early-morning hard-ons, but David knew better. And they had to decide soon. David was off to Carolina to meet Gary Jeff Hill next weekend. Although he planned to pay the deposit out of his own savings, Ian had to be on board if they were to come up with the full price. Otherwise Hill would find another buyer. The man had put off his dying long enough.

He finally made it out of the airport, speeding freely along the feeder road, only to find himself slowed to thirty miserable miles per hour when he hit the interstate, those multiple-occupancy vehicles pounding by on the left. David allowed himself to think about how good it would be to quit this job. He was truly sick of it. Working all these hours; negotiating all this traffic. Everybody having important business, urging him to go that much faster. It had been a lot less stressful when he'd been on the stretches. All he had to do back then was take a bunch of sober people somewhere, hang around while they got drunk, and then get them back home. Proms, weddings, casinos, strip clubs: It was all the same big American fun. It was profitable, too. Drunks tended to tip better than sober people. He'd made some good money during the five months he'd driven the long limos. Once a group of studs celebrating a big dot-com killing had left him two hundred dollars for turning a blind eye as they gang-banged a Gold Club lap dancer while he drove aimlessly through sleepy suburban streets. On another night he'd been rewarded with five fifties for hauling that television chef to a trailer park meth lab. Money had been in the air back then, blowing around like roof tiles during Hurricane Andrew. All you had to do was reach out and grab it.

But last fall he realized that driving a stretch limo was a dead end.

Running executive cars might put less hard cash in his pocket, but it did provide him with the steadier lifestyle the lawyer had told him he'd need if the court was going to let him keep looking after Ian. Hamed and Jack had gladly accommodated the switch; reliable executive fleet drivers were hard to find. The passengers proved a completely different breed from the temporary high rollers who rented stretches. There was no bickering or making change. Everything was on account, a standard 20 percent gratuity factored in. He didn't have to grovel; didn't have to play emcee to all that low-rent entertainment going on in the back, the Vladivar vodka siphoned into the Absolut bottles, the Buttman videos on the nine-inch screen. These were people he could learn from. He could watch how they moved and listen as they spoke into their cell phones or dictation machines. Even their sleep seemed moneyed, their velvety breath popping at the back of their throats like small waves hitting the pier of a lakeside house.

The switch paid its biggest dividend two months ago. He'd just dropped off a passenger on Madison when he saw a familiar figure— tall, stringy-haired, emblazoned with tattoos—piloting a wheelchair through the roiling human midtown mass. David couldn't believe what he was seeing. Tib in New York made little sense; Tib pushing a withered old man made none whatsoever. His friend was equally astonished to see David in a black suit and tie. He introduced the chair's occupant as Gary Jeff Hill, who up close looked more sick than old, a pale formless man with intense, calculating eyes. There wasn't any time to talk, so they got together later that night at an Upper West Side diner. Hill was asleep back at the hotel, worn out from a day of being pushed around. The first thing David could see about Tib was that he no longer drank, which turned out to be sort of ironic when he explained that he'd spent the last four years working in a bar just outside Beaufort on the North Carolina coast. Gary Jeff Hill was the proprietor. They were in New York because Hill wanted to see it before succumbing to the disease that was eating away his brain.

"He's dying?" David asked, not particularly surprised.

"Well, he'll tell you we all are, he's just had an advance peek at the schedule."

"How long's he got?"

"About a year or two until he becomes locked in. After that, nobody knows."

"Locked in to what?"

"Hisself."

The thought drove them into an uncomfortable silence.

"So what's he think of the city?" David asked to break it.

"Not impressed."

It turned out that Hill planned to retire to a house he owned on Cape Hatteras, where he would spend his last days staring out at the ocean; he'd have to stare at something, and he'd rather it wasn't some nursing home's ceiling. The problem was, his insurance would run out before his brain cells did, and he needed money to fund a comfortable death. If it weren't for that, he would have just given Tib the bar. As it was, he would sell it to him for the barest minimum. But Tib's credit was shot from all the mistakes he'd made in Florida.

"The bank won't even trust me with a pen," he said. "I go in there, the first thing they do is chain them up."

"Buddy, I think they do that for everyone."

"I'm illustrating."

He talked about the bar for a while, how it was nothing like the Windjammer, that warehouse of sin and degradation where the two men had worked down in Daytona, getting college kids drunk on fizzy beer and Everclear, David encouraging coeds to lift their tank tops and then Tib bitch-smacking second-division linebackers if they got too excited by the sight. True to its name, the Cove was situated in a quiet inlet, directly on a pier where affluent people docked their leisure craft so the hurricanes wouldn't splinter them. Although it could be a lively place, customers behaved themselves. The beer wasn't the carbonated battery acid they'd served in Daytona but Sam Adams and Guinness and microbrews. On weekends people brought in instruments to play traditional music, Irish jigs and sea shanties.

"Pull in good money?" David asked.

"Enough to keep the wolves from the door, but not so much that some yuppie asshole wants to come in and fuck everything up."

David was certainly liking the sound of this.

"So you say you've become like a son to Gary Jeff."

Tib's eyes went distant as he nodded. If David didn't know him as a pipe-hitting Pensacola swamp rat, he'd have sworn they misted over.

"And there's definitely no chance of him just leaving it to you?" David asked.

"Your dad leave you anything?"

"Nervous and poor. So how much is he asking?"

Tib told him. Not that much more than Ian's inheritance.

"That all?"

Tib gave him a critical look.

"Why? You got that kind of money?"

"I just might."

For a moment the old Tib returned, storm clouds gathering across that vast forehead.

"Do not fuck with me on this particular subject, David Warfield."

David told him about Ginny's insurance money, how he'd been wondering what he was going to do to keep his nephew from frittering it away on childish things.

"Perhaps then you should come down for a visit."

David did just that two weeks later, driving straight through the night in his Chevelle so he didn't have to take time off work. He arrived early on a cold March morning, and he knew the moment he laid eyes on the place that this was where he had been heading the last two decades. Although the inlet wasn't the sort of spot anyone would put on a postcard, it was peaceful and largely free of man-made ugliness. The Cove Inn was a two-story wood-shingled building surrounded by a system of docks. Because of the time of year, there weren't many boats, and the ones that were currently berthed were covered with tarps. Even so, David could easily imagine how the predominant late-winter gray would give way to all manner of nautical color come spring. There was a boathouse on the southern side of the complex that was locked down; to the north was a ruined warehouse, home to a big colony of raucous seabirds. There were some bait shops and small structures of indeterminate use ringing the mostly empty parking lot that served the entire complex. To the east, through the inlet's narrow entrance, he could see the low line of dunes that constituted the Outer Banks.

The Cove fit Tib's description. It was nothing much; it was every-thing. There were booths and tables and a long polished bar. A wood floor and sturdy furniture. Gary Jeff Hill worked in the upstairs office, which had big interior windows that allowed him to keep an eye on it all. The things on the walls, the nautical instruments and jetsam, looked as if they had some business being there, unlike the job lot Taiwanese crap at the Windjammer. There was a good-size kitchen, though they had food service only for lunch, and a small stage with a few tables on it. There were no performances as such. When people made music, they simply pulled up chairs around one of the larger tables.

"You get much trouble?" David asked.

John Paul Thibault had been named Volusia County Bouncer of the Year in a contest run by 99 Kick Ass Rock—you had to throw a CPR dummy through a door from twenty feet—and had also served three months for hospitalizing a couple of Kappa Alphas in a disagree-ment over what constituted valid identification.

"Not really," Tib said, cracking his knuckles nostalgically. "As a gen-eral rule people take that shit down to Myrtle."

David stayed for the night. Since it was off-season, the place hadn't been very crowded, but the customers who came were loyal enough to keep the bills paid until the summer folk arrived. David sat at a cor-ner of the bar, nursing a bitter Irish stout and imagining what it would be like to cast a proprietary eye on it all through those upstairs win-dows. And then there was the music. People just unpacked their gear and started to play. There were fiddles and guitars and one big woman who played an accordion, the first time David had ever seen this done for something other than laughs. He'd never paid much attention to folk music, but tonight all those reels and jigs were just about the best thing he'd ever heard. There weren't any rules or structure to the play-ing. People just followed the logic of the sound. It was nothing like the Windjammer, where it had been Skynyrd tribute bands or 2 Live Crew on the juke. This was music with a history. Music that brought people together to do something other than fight and fuck.

The evening's only awkward moment came just after closing time, when Gary Jeff Hill descended from his office in a mechanical seat

that ran along the staircase's railing. At the bottom, Tib helped him
into his wheelchair and then rolled him to the small employees-only
bathroom behind the bar, where he picked up the sick man and carried him inside, the way you'd take a sleepy child to bed. David
thought back to the other people he'd seen Tib lugging around, cold-
cocked frat boys and blind-drunk coeds on the verge of getting date-
raped. This was so different. There was a tenderness to it that said all
you needed to know about how much Tib had changed since Florida.
David sat uncomfortably at the bar as the two spent what seemed to
be a long time behind the closed door. There was much urgent whispering and then a clamorous flush. Nobody met anyone else's eye
when they emerged. David stayed on Tib's sofa that night, and though
the men talked until nearly dawn, not a word was said about Gary Jeff
Hill.

David set to work on his nephew as soon as he got home. At first,
Ian seemed to agree that a change would do them both good. But
then, as luck would have it, he met his mystery girl. She was the first
real girlfriend of his life, clearly a more impressive proposition than
those kohl-eyed blow-job artists he'd been hanging around with at
Gryphon Games. David had hoped that it was a short-lived teen romance, but now, two months later, they were going stronger than ever.
He was hurt at first that Ian was being so cagey, though he remembered what he'd been like when he was young. In David's case, however, there had been a practical reason for stealth: his father's
tendency to rape anything female that passed before his eyes. David
had to admit, whoever the girl was, she was certainly a good influence
on Ian. They didn't drink or do dope together, and Ian was always in
one of his mellow moods after he'd been with her, the frantic babbling
and paralyzing five-day bouts of mystery flu things of the past.

All of which would have been perfectly fine if it hadn't been for the
Cove. David wished there were some way he could make his nephew
see that forging a long-term relationship when you were seventeen
was invariably a big mistake. Ginny was the perfect example of this,
falling so hard for Ian's father, only to wind up fat and broke. But of
course, there was no telling Ian that the first tanned and smiling face
he saw on the beach down in Carolina would look just as good. So he

decided to let matters run their course, hoping the affair would burn out before it was time to commit on the Cove. But now Tib was getting anxious, telling David that if Hill didn't have a decision soon, he would be putting the place on the open market. There could be no more procrastinating. The man's brain was crumbling like stale cake. David was going down next weekend to firm up the deal. Before then he would have to get his nephew to agree to the plan.

He got lucky in the end, making it home by seven forty-five; bad, but not a disaster. Ian was in his room, messing around with his drawing, listening to some of that yowling punk rock he favored. David told his nephew fifteen minutes, set some water boiling, then took a quick shower to wash off the day. In the kitchen he made a salad and opened a jar of Paul Newman. He then set to work cleaning the strainer, which Ian had neglected to do after last using it. Dried bits of broken pasta stuck out of some of the holes. That was another thing that was going to happen down in Carolina. People were going to start cleaning up after themselves.

When everything was cooking, he flipped through the mail. Amid the junk was a postcard reminding him that Monday was their joint session with Dr. Veronica Traynor. His heart sank as he contemplated another hour in that tidy little office. More distraction; more wasted time. Not that Traynor was a bad person. She was well-meaning in the way of people with too much education and not enough street sense. She certainly seemed to be fond of Ian, though there'd been a little bit too much talk of late about his nephew's independence. At least Ian had agreed not to tell her about the Cove. David was having enough trouble explaining it to the boy without her chiming in.

Finally, dinner was ready. Ian wandered into the kitchen, taking his own sweet time. But he looked happy enough.

"Good day?" he asked.

"Yeah," Ian said, dropping into a chair, squinting his eyes. "It was good."

"You want a Coke?"

"Sure. Whatever's in there."

"I'm gonna have me one of those Millers in a size twelve. You mind?"

Ian shook his head. He was good about that, though David would have gladly forsaken alcohol around him.

"You see this?"

Ian was flapping the postcard.

"We should talk about it before next Monday," David joked. "Get our stories straight."

"Okay. Whatever."

David's least favorite word in the English language. He imagined what old Chuck Warfield would have done to him had he used it. Ten with the buckle or twenty with the strap. Still, it was a lot preferable to what his poor sister got. David shook off the thought as he ladled the sauce onto the two large plates of spaghetti, big flat bowls with little flowers around the edges. Leftover Ginny gear. Like everything else in this house. The framed samplers and china figurines. The jars of potpourri that neither of them could bring themselves to throw away, even though they'd long since turned to dust.

"So," he said after a moment. "Tib's been on me about the Cove. He'll be needing our answer soon."

Ian nodded neutrally. David forged ahead.

"I wish you could come this weekend, but—"

Ian's probation kept him from leaving the state without a good reason. David figured visiting a bar probably wouldn't count as one.

"And I was thinking, I should probably have some sort of final decision by then."

Ian ate for a while.

"I don't know," he said eventually, his voice taking on the vague quality David enjoyed so very much.

"Don't know what, Ian?"

"It's just, I'm not sure I want to run a business."

David was glad for the opportunity to argue against something specific.

"But that's the beauty of it. *You* wouldn't be running a business. You'd be a silent partner. I'd do all the heavy lifting. You could simply kick back. Work on your books. Get a college degree, if you want."

"I don't need a college degree. I'm conducting my own education."

Another of the boy's strange notions, one David would have to confront at a later date.

"Well, then, there you go. You wouldn't have to get one. That's what being free is all about. You wouldn't have to hold down a job, neither. No more scooping salads or pissing in a cup."

"But I won't have to hold down a job, anyway, once Mom's money comes in."

"Now, you don't want to do that, bud. Spend your capital."

"But why do I have to invest the money in a *business*? Couldn't I just keep it in a bank?"

"Come on, Ian. You think you can live like that for long? A *bank*? They'd surcharge you, and nickel-and-dime you, and then there's the—what's it called?—the cost of living index; by the time you're twenty-five you'd be stony broke."

Ian was nodding, though David could see the doubt lingering in his eyes.

"This is a good deal, bud. You know I wouldn't steer you wrong. Not after what we've been through. This is what Ginny wanted you to do with what she left behind. This is why she put the money in a trust, so it wouldn't be frittered away. I mean, let's not lose track of what this project is all about, okay? It's about our *future*. Yours and mine. But mostly yours."

Invoking the memory of his dead sister could be seen as a cheap shot, but they didn't have a lot of time to play with here. Besides, setting himself up in a respectable business *would* have been the sort of thing she'd wanted him to do with his inheritance. All right, maybe not a bar, but that was just Ginny's prejudice after suffering their father's boozing for so many years. With this, Ian would never have to worry about his daily bread. He could concentrate on his mind and his spirit. All David had to do was make him see it.

"Ian?"

He was nodding again. Not agreeing, just nodding.

"I don't know. Can I think about it some more?"

"Think about it?"

"Just to get it straight in my head."

"Well, how much longer do you think you'll need?"

"When did you say you were going to go down there?"

"Next Friday."

"I'll let you know by then. Definitely."

Unsatisfactory as it was, his nephew's answer would have to be enough for now. A week was a long time. He'd be able to bring him around by then. All he had to do was stay positive and help the boy focus.

"All right, then," David said. "Now, eat up before it gets cold."

Listen to yourself, he thought. Starting to sound like he's your own kid or something.

PART TWO

5 Drew leaned over the footbridge's buffed railing, staring into the little river that twisted through Capital Park. He had fifteen minutes to kill before his meeting and didn't want to cool his heels in reception. He had a tendency to talk too much in these situations, being friendly with the wrong people, getting in the way of the right ones. It had been worst during the period of his divorce, the terrible hours he'd sat outside the mediator's door at the Relation Shop while Anne told her side of the story, her aggrieved monotone an instrument of torture designed for his ears alone. And there was also twenty years of chatter to bored home buyers, filling up the void with words that he regretted the moment they came out of his mouth. He'd done it again just the other night with his unwise attempt at consolation after Jamie's loss at the banquet. *They're just jealous.* He could see the irritation on Quint's face the moment he spoke. He had to be more careful. He still had to learn the language if he was going to be with these people.

The immaculate water, trapped in a series of effervescent eddies, slapped and gargled ten feet below. Sparkling fish darted among the smooth stones. Back when Quint bought the place the river was so polluted that the bleached bones of small mammals littered its corroded banks. These days Drew could baptize his impending newborns in the water if he were so inclined. A squadron of dragonflies patrolled its surface, their movements tightly choreographed as they hunted mosquitoes. The afternoon sun revealed startling colors in them, gossamer blues in the wings, electric greens on their bodies.

They'd been imported from California to combat the West Nile virus; rumor had it they'd been genetically altered to be superpredators. Drew wondered what they would feed on once they'd rid the area of their prey.

He looked up, letting his gaze take in the entire park. Quint really had worked wonders on the place. The undulating grass was cut to a uniform height, coated with the fine dew that emerged periodically from programmed sprinklers. The dirt pathways were carefully raked; the firs and magnolias lining them were trimmed into neat geometric shapes. Newcomers would never suspect that the park covered the pestilential rubble of a tap and die factory that had gone so spectacularly to ruin that Drew and his friends had been banned from playing here as boys. It was one of the few prohibitions they actually obeyed, scared away by stories of flagrant rashes and rabid bites. Now a team of groundskeepers eradicated any outcropping of wilderness, and the brazen jays and fat squirrels that moved over the grass were perfectly harmless. Drew had learned during last summer's tennis games that the pollution had been the complex's prime selling point, allowing Quint to buy it for a song, then get the EPA to foot the cleanup bill. Nowhere was this transformation more apparent than in the former factory buildings. The largest, occupied by WMV Capital Management, was buffed perfection, old stone salvaged, gaps packed and sealed. The two outbuildings were occupied by a roster of lesser companies, a sports paraphernalia retailer and a reverse auction outfit that brokered energy contracts. The rest had impenetrable names that relied heavily on the latter consonants. Drew had considered relocating here, but rents were on a par with midtown Manhattan. Until things improved, he was stuck in his father's place, with its cracked plaster and thirty-year lease.

He stifled a yawn and shook his head, trying to jump-start his mind. It had been a long, exhausting weekend, starting with Saturday's arduous shopping expedition to the mall for baby gear, a task they'd left this late because of Ronnie's omnipresent fear of another miscarriage. They'd visited a dozen stores, loading his old Saab to bursting. Luckily, none of his weary credit cards was rejected. Ronnie had gone to bed soon after their return, the pregnancy finally starting to slow her down. Drew had recently suggested she stop working, but she wouldn't hear of it. Leaving her clients before they'd been properly referred to new therapists was unthinkable.

After she was soundly asleep, Drew established himself in front of the television for his regular fix of videotaped catastrophe: flashlit cops and overhead angles on car chases; sports riots and animals gone bad. The two beers he'd allocated himself in reward for the mall trip stretched into four, and he only vaguely remembered going to bed. But then there was a voice in the darkness. Ronnie was sitting up, clutching a pillow to her stomach, telling him that something was wrong, the terror in her voice stoked by two previous miscarriages. They had the ER to themselves; Saturday nights were downtime at Mercy. The real action started just after dawn on weekdays, when weary hearts seized and brittle arteries burst, unable to handle another day, another ride into the city, another anthill of woe.

The news was good. As soon as the nurses and doctors got at his wife, Drew knew that it was a false alarm. There was none of the tight-lipped, whispering urgency that he had dreaded during their silent ride to the hospital. They wanted to keep her in for the night, anyway; twins occasionally baffled their gadgetry. Drew sat with up with her through the dawn, chasing those beers with bad coffee as he watched over her relieved slumber.

They were home by nine. He helped Ronnie into bed, then climbed in as well, spooning up behind her round hot body. They slept until noon, when the distant ringing of a phone woke him. He could hear it downstairs but not on the master bedroom's phone, which confused him until he remembered that he'd turned off its ringer after they got home. Ronnie slept on, her flush face serene in a plane of bright midday light, her ginger hair lit like some hothouse flower. Shannon was awake in the kitchen, the Sunday paper spread on the kitchen table, a spoonful of yogurt hovering near her mouth.

"Since when do you outsleep *me*?"

"We were at the hospital all night."

Her expression turned serious.

"Don't worry," he said. "False alarm."

"She really should stop working, you know."

"She feels responsible to her patients."

Shannon returned to flipping indifferently through the paper.

"So what did you do last night?" he asked.

"Party. End-of-the-year festivities have begun."

He still found it hard to imagine Shannon attending the series of rowdy house parties that accompanied graduation. It was a shame that she'd left it so late.

"Hey, who just called?" he asked. "I thought I heard the phone."

"Oh, sorry. It was Quint."

"Quint? Really? What did he want?"

"To talk to you. He left his mobile number. Wait, it's . . ."

She handed him a drugstore circular with a number penned in the margin.

"So what's up, Dad?" she asked. "What are you doing with Quint?"

Drew hated to lie to Shannon, after all those years when the truth between them was just about the only thing he had. But there was no other choice.

"Probably just wants to get the tennis thing going again."

He phoned from his study, wondering whether Quint wanted to give him the chance to up his investment now that the lockup was ending. It would be tricky; he'd probably have to bring Andy Starke in on what he was doing if he tried to borrow any more against the house. On the other hand, it would be embarrassing to turn down such an offer.

Quint sounded very far away, his voice layered with static.

"Drew, yes, I was wondering if we could get together tomorrow."

"Sure. Absolutely."

Quint broke away for a moment to speak to someone in the room with him.

"Hello?"

He came back on.

"Can you make it after lunch? About two?"

Drew had precisely nothing planned for the following day.

"That shouldn't be a problem."

There was an impatient chorus of voices in the background.

"All right. I'll see you then."

"Is there anything I should know or—"

But the connection was already dead.

Time to go. Drew plucked his briefcase from the bridge and strode through WMV's heavy, iron-framed doors. The receptionist invited him to take a seat. He would have to wait a few minutes after all; Quint was running a bit late. From where he sat he had a view of the entire open-plan office. The once-decrepit building was now perfectly clean and perfectly still, a place more appropriate for contemplation than high finance. There was nothing in the design to suggest the nail-chewing tension and split-second frenzy associated with Quint's business. The intervening floor had been knocked out to turn the small factory's two cramped stories into a single unbroken space; the stone walls had been uncovered and sanded. The light was natural, pouring through skylights and long vertical windows but mostly, at the far end of the building, through the sheer wall of glass that overlooked the park's gently rolling acreage. The main-floor area was populated by secretarial staff and younger associates. Hammered iron walkways ran above them on either side, lined by the offices. Just beneath that wall of glass was a common area with sofas and lounge chairs and tables. Above everything, Quint's office hung like the car of some great elevator, a floating glass cube. Drew could see him in there now, leaning back against his desk, talking to three men gathered in a tight crescent of chairs. His arms were folded across his chest; occasionally, his right hand would free itself to make a frugal gesture.

It was the same scene that had confronted Drew during his first visit to WMV last May, a meeting he'd been angling for ever since he and Quint became tennis partners. Drew had almost wrecked his car racing across town once the call finally came. In his office Quint was very different from the reserved, slightly shy man Drew had come to know on the court and at school functions. The polite wariness had been replaced by a clipped, almost conspiratorial tone. He talked nonstop for nearly ten minutes, telling Drew about WMV, explaining why it was different from other hedge funds. Drew lost his way occasionally in the jargon, especially a short interlude about "stochastics."

But he'd grasped the basics: Quint traded in the world's volatility, betting that incorrectly priced markets would eventually stabilize. His fund was "global macro"; he'd invest anywhere, anytime. Bonds, stocks, currency, futures. Emerging markets, established ones, markets that weren't even made yet. What stuck in Drew's mind was Quint's insistence that all markets were ultimately rational and that the key to making big money was to move into the temporarily irrational ones before they stabilized. How exactly he did this was a mystery to Drew; Quint had offered him a glimpse of a computer screen that was stacked with a series of crowded, mutating line graphs that could have been describing the workings of a bumblebee's nervous system. Quint also explained that a client's money would not be actually invested in the markets, but rather used as collateral for the very large amounts he borrowed.

"We're leveraged. Big time. And we can afford to be because we're right."

As for the rest, it was pure Greek. But the details weren't important. Drew had been to Quint's house; he'd seen the cars and tennis rackets and wristwatches of his clients; he'd listened to their talk about Gulfstreams and houses in Aspen and fifty-thousand-dollar March Madness wagers. Not that Drew was interested in any of that. He knew they were out of his league. All he wanted was the stability that would come with just a fragment of such wealth, the sense that he was no longer being buffeted by life. All he wanted was enough. To live as his father had lived, effortless and calm. Although Quint refused to quote numbers, Drew knew from his Web searches and what he'd heard at their Saturday-morning tennis sessions that last year investors in WMV had seen a return of 44 percent.

Forty-four percent.

"But we have to move on this," Quint said. "Minimum participation is two-fifty. And there's a one-year lockup."

It took Drew several long seconds to understand that the sum of $250,000 had just been mooted. He'd arrived thinking he could just about manage thirty.

"Obviously that's just the ante," Quint added. "You can participate at a more robust level. Most come in at about a million. Rookies I cap at two. Unlike Steinbrenner. After your lockup we'll talk about accepting further capital."

"Okay," Drew said. "Let me . . . can I let you know?"

"Let me know what?" Quint asked after a moment.

"My, you know, how much I want to put in."

Quint relaxed.

"Sure. But I need to know something by the close of play tomorrow. I want to get you set up for a June dividend next year. Plus I have a ninety-nine-partner limit, and there's a pretty hefty waiting list for this spot."

Drew had left in a gloomy trance. For some reason he'd thought Quint would understand he didn't have that kind of money to invest, that he was just after enough cash to pay for his daughter's college and knock down his credit cards. A strange notion, since as part of his effort to impress the men at the tennis games, he'd been hinting that he'd just closed on some fairly large property deals and was swimming in cash. As he drove back to town, he went though the motions of trying to determine where he could get his hands on a quarter million dollars. A futile exercise. Five years earlier he could have siphoned it out of Hagel & Son, but that money was gone. He had eighteen thousand in various bank accounts, half of which he figured he could dedicate to an investment. For the rest of the thirty he'd been planning to borrow against the big Northwestern life insurance account his father had set up for him when he was a boy. But that was it. Two hundred and fifty was an impossible number. By the time he got to his office he knew he had no choice but to beg off. He was clearly out of his league. His bluff had been called. Badgering Quint had been a foolish mistake, taking unfair advantage of their growing friendship. But he couldn't make the call. He sat at his desk for nearly an hour, staring at the phone, unable to bring himself to admit that he would never be able to join Quint's fund.

What amazed him was how easily the answer came to him. He'd borrow it from the equity credit line they'd opened a year earlier, when Ronnie was in her second pregnancy. Their plan was to use it to renovate the house once the baby was born. Although 33 Crescent had been heavily mortgaged to pay off Anne, the recent property boom had inflated its notional value far enough that they would be able to sap a couple of hundred thousand more dollars from its old wood. But then they'd lost the baby and the loan had remained dormant. Without ever saying so, Drew and Ronnie agreed that it would be spent only once a child was pinkly oxygenated and nestling on her chest.

Although he understood that there was no way he could use this money to invest in a private fund, the thought wouldn't go away. Within a few hours it became inevitable. It would be simple. Ronnie would never know. He'd do everything through his office. Even if she got pregnant in the next few months—an event that of course came to pass—he'd have received his first dividend by the time they were ready to start renovating. He would have to hustle to make the repayments for that first locked-up year, but come the following June the weight of his debts would be lifted. And it wouldn't be the ten or twenty thousand per year he'd anticipated when he first approached Quint, but a hundred thousand. More. He'd be able to pay down the credit line; Oberlin would be a snap; he could pay the builders. Five years down the road the credit line would be gone. Every penny he made from WMV from then on would be profit. Pure, weightless, frictionless money. He could help get Shannon going in life; Ronnie would be able to build her practice. And he'd never have to drag his tired bones out to show some lousy, crumbling, odoriferous pile that no one wanted to buy, never have to lose another listing to the harridans at Property Management. He'd be clear.

There would, he admitted to himself, be trouble if Ronnie found out. She was averse to all forms of risk. It led to stress, which was in her eyes a poison more deadly than leaked PCBs. Gambling with their house was something even she might never forgive. But she didn't understand. She hadn't spent those Saturday mornings with Quint and his partners. Nor did she know how desperate things were at Hagel & Son, what it was like to wake up at four in the morning and wonder how he was ever going to afford Shannon's college, much less the new family they so badly wanted to start. What it was like to pay two hundred thousand dollars to a selfish damaged woman in exchange for one scared and confused daughter to raise without an instruction manual and then, as an added bonus, to watch his father's business waste away to nothing in the distraction that followed.

And so he had met with Andy Starke at Bill's Tavern that evening, saying he wanted to increase the credit line by a hundred thousand to start the major overhaul of the house. Starke said it shouldn't be a problem. He knew Drew. He knew the house. Only a fool would refuse to lend against 33 Crescent. The following morning Drew had called Quint and told him that yes, he wanted in.

"Fantastic," he said. "I'll have someone drop off an accredited investor form and we're all set."

"Accredited investor form?"

"It's an SEC requirement. It basically says you make two hundred grand a year or have clear assets over a mil. Get that back to me, and we're good to go."

Filling out the form proved easy. It felt good, actually, fabricating big numbers for the income and asset columns, erasing all that debt. He'd been worried when Quint had him give the form to Mahabal, but the sharp-eyed lawyer didn't check closely. Why would he? Drew had spent the last few months as a regular guest on Orchard. His daughter was dating Quint's son. He was one of them.

"Mr. Hagel?"

Quint's assistant was standing above him. She was rail-thin and sharp-nosed, with the hard good looks of a television reporter. She led Drew silently through the young traders and clerical staff on the ground floor, up a spiral of metal steps and then past some recessed offices. Drew was momentarily struck by the notion that something was wrong in the building. A slight variation in the noise patterns, a ruffle in the atmosphere, too many empty desks. And he thought the three men emerging from Quint's office looked grim, like members of a basketball team down by thirty at halftime.

But this was mere anxious speculation. He didn't understand this place, what was essential and what was only appearance. He remembered hearing from one of the tennis players that it was all window dressing, anyway, that the big decisions were made by Quint. The assistant held the door for him, and Drew stepped into the hovering glass cube, feeling a brief pulse of vertigo. Quint was staring down at a computer screen, tapping his desk with a stiff finger. He looked up.

"Drew, come on in," he said softly, gesturing to a chair. He turned to his assistant. "Please ask Godeep to join us."

He moved around to the front of the desk and adopted his familiar posture, perched on the edge, his legs stretched out, his arms folded in front of his chest.

"Thanks for coming the other night," he said.

"Well, I'm just sorry Jamie couldn't, you know, win."

"Jamie's been burning some bridges with his behavior recently," Quint said wearily. "I hope this will be a wake-up call for him."

Drew nodded, a fellow dad who knew all about wake-up calls. There was a soft noise behind him. Drew turned. Mahabal was sidling into the office. He greeted Drew with a self-deprecating flap of his hand and took a seat in the corner. Quint took a deep breath and looked at the carpet for a moment, then met Drew's eyes.

"Drew, we've got a bit of a situation on our hands. We've taken a substantial hit in the past few weeks. Certain markets are proving more volatile than we'd anticipated, and our hedges against this eventuality aren't panning out. Fact is, none of our models anticipated the sort of spreads we're now seeing. Everywhere we're active is staying way overvalued. For no rational reason, in most cases."

"But up, that's good, right?"

"Well, not for us. We've shorted the volatility in these particular sectors."

"I don't—"

"We've bet that these markets would fall. But they haven't. They will, but for the time being they're remaining overinflated. Which means we're caught in an equity trap. We've borrowed money to make these investments, and now these debts are coming due. And so we're going to have dip into our fund's reserves to make those calls."

"Okay," Drew said, because he had to say something and that was all his mind could offer.

"Drew, what I'm saying is that your placement with us is down.

Substantially. Bottom line is that we're not going to be able to pay out any dividends this cycle."

"All right," Drew said, his voice sounding as if it were coming from elsewhere.

"Obviously, we're taking strategic measures to recover these losses, and I'm confident that they will pan out in the long run. But for now . . ."

He made a helpless gesture.

"How far in the long run?"

"Well, I doubt you'll be seeing anything in December, but by this time next year you should be looking at something."

"And how much is my placement down?"

There was a factual, merciless set to Quint's face that Drew had never seen before.

"As of this time you've lost about ninety percent of your position."

"How much does that leave?"

"About . . . well, just under twenty-six thousand."

Twenty-six. Not even enough to pay for Shannon's first year at Oberlin.

"But obviously that's not a meaningful number unless you want to talk about redemption, which for obvious reasons I would seriously advise against."

"No. Okay."

"I know this is a blow. But everybody's in the same boat here. And your real estate holdings must be doing well?" He gave a wry smile. "Speaking of irrational exuberance."

Drew nodded numbly. His real estate holdings. His castles in the sky.

"Well, at least *you're* hedged," Quint said. "Do you have any questions?"

"Um, you said a year?"

"Well, that's a presumption I'm making. Obviously, nothing is written in stone."

There was noise behind him. He turned to see Mahabal slipping out the door, which was then occupied by Quint's assistant. It was time for him to go. He shook Quint's hand and then followed the assistant through the office's hushed chaos. They'd gone only a short way when he remembered something.

"Oh, I forgot my briefcase," he said.

"I'll go," she said in a tone that left no room for debate.

She returned almost immediately, carrying his father's battered old leather case, holding it slightly away from her, as if it contained some of the toxic material that had once been beneath the building.

It occurred to Drew as he drove home that there were things he should be thinking about now. He would have to tell Andy Starke. And Ronnie, since it would be impossible to keep what he'd done secret from her. But she couldn't know. None of them could. The bank would call in the loan and his wife would never forgive him. He just had to focus. There must be a solution. There had to be a Plan B. It was just money. You could always get your hands on more money.

But nothing came. There was no Plan B. There were no fallbacks. The worst he'd ever allowed himself to contemplate was a diminished gain, 20 or 25 percent. But not a loss. Never a loss. This wasn't some roll of the dice. If Drew had wanted to do that, he could have taken a stretch limo out to Foxwoods. There wasn't supposed to be a downside with Quint. That was why he was so hard to get near. That was why he didn't advertise, why the men on the tennis court spoke in the clandestine tones and obscure syntax of insiders. WMV was a closed fund. These guys had it figured out. They were inside.

Drew reached the intersection with Federal, making a clean right; the evening rush was still a couple of hours away. He drove by the awninged bistros, designer clothes stores, and gourmet food shops that had replaced the five-and-dimes and nail salons of his youth; he passed the brick office buildings that had once been home to penny-ante insurance brokers and claw-fingered dentists but now housed cognitive behavioral psychotherapists, personal estate planners, and color consultants. The new travel agency offering helicopter ski packages and scuba diving expeditions appeared to be doing brisk business; artificially tanned agents spoke into headsets beneath Gauguin prints and posters of near-nude French girls bronzing at Juan-les-Pins.

He passed venerable Bill's Tavern, one of the few establishments on Federal that hadn't been transformed by the recent boom. It was still the same dingy repository of vacant stools and cloudy glass where his father had held court and Drew himself had spent the bad solitary days after his divorce. But at some point in the past decade the tavern had made the subtle shift from real to authentic. People came for the boozy end-of-the-line atmosphere they couldn't get at TGI Fridays. It was all there. The bench seats that deflated like popped blisters when sat upon. The ancient beer signs pulsing with anemic light. The zinc fixtures smeared with a thousand fingerprints; the noxious urinals surrounded by generations of graffiti. Even the tunes on the jukebox remained the same, the bond brokers and software engineers who now bellied up to the bar happy to waste a nostalgic quarter on Rare Earth or Eddie Rabbit. Drew felt a sudden temptation to take one of the back booths. But he drove on, knowing that Bill's wasn't the answer, any more than it had been in the bad days after Anne left him. He had to get back to the office. He had to keep working. A solution would come. All he had to do was keep working.

A delivery truck briefly blocked his way, and when it finally cleared, he saw a familiar face. Carrie Manning, standing beneath the Garden's marquee, looking impossibly elegant outside her theater. Her project. Paid for by Quint's money. And Drew's money. She'd been crying a few days earlier, but now she looked happy, because with a life like hers no unhappiness could survive for long. COMING SOON, the sign above her read. She was talking to Phil Ferris and Ruud de Vries, with their manes of silver hair and clothes of elegantly crushed fabric. The architect was speaking and Carrie said something and then they were all laughing.

Quint's wife was laughing.

6 Carrie didn't want to do this. She would have gladly never set foot in the Garden again. But she was the owner, or at least some legalistic permutation of herself, responsible for the minor repairs and cosmetic alterations needed to make it attractive to prospective buyers. So Ruud and Phil Ferris had agreed to meet her. It proved a bittersweet echo of their earlier walk-throughs, when everything had been splendid promise. They would be doing only the bare minimum. A more secure patch for the hole in the roof; a brace for a load-bearing beam that had been softened by dampness. The carpet would have to come up before it spawned the dreaded black mold that seemed to be everywhere now. And then the building would be ready to sell. There would be plenty of interest, developers eager to gut the place for shops and restaurants.

The two men were courtly and businesslike as they stepped gingerly over the swollen carpet. Carrie reckoned this sort of thing happened all the time. Somebody else would buy the place and hire them. How did that Dead song go? One man's ceiling is another man's floor.

They wound up standing beneath the marquee on Federal.

"Hey, what about that?" Ruud asked, pointing to the sign.

"Maybe I'll change it to GOING, GOING, GONE," she said.

They laughed quietly, and then the men went on their way, checking messages and digging keys out of their deep corduroy pockets. Carrie headed back inside to activate the alarm and close the emergency exit behind her. The realtor could handle the rest. She was thinking about hiring Drew Hagel instead of Property Management to help him out. Though Godeep would probably fight her on that one. PMG was all the rage now. If she didn't get the best, she would have to explain why.

As she walked down the aisle toward the ruined screen, Carrie was struck by how easy it was proving to erase a year's work. A few calls, a meeting or two. Once Godeep asked for the remaining money she'd call the bank and speak the magic word, and that would be it. She'd waited until Sunday night to inform the rest of the board, holding it off in the thin hope that Quint would tell her that everything was back on track. But she was just kidding herself. The situation at WMV was getting worse by the hour. Today he had begun telling clients that for the first time in the history of the fund, there would be no dividend payments. She'd barely seen him during the past few days. After the banquet on Thursday they'd fought briefly about that heckling. Quint had asked about Jamie's drinking; Carrie, the coward, had claimed she'd seen nothing. Luckily, Jamie had spent the night with Stephen and Matt, so they were able to avoid the usual scene, Quint speaking with that murderously slow voice, Jamie's soul withering a little more under the heat of his father's expectations. Quint had traveled to New York early Saturday to meet with institutional investors, that creepy gaggle of lipless functionaries, and then on Sunday he'd been up before dawn for a full day at Capital Park. It was well after dark by the time he finally made it home. They'd had dinner alone, Quint distracted and sullen, wolfing down his food, then sloshing his half glass of wine around in the fingerprinted goblet. Carrie briefly experienced the creepy Hopperesque ability to look in on her own life through the big windows. It was a scary scene, this gleaming silent kitchen late on a Sunday night, one person joylessly pulling the meat off a chicken's splintery rib cage and the other watching, chin in hand, both of them caught in their own grim calculations of loss. Carrie knew that this was the point where she should offer to rub his shoulders or drag him up to bed for some between-the-sheets therapy. But she couldn't bring herself to comfort him. She no longer cared about his investors and his status as boy wonder of the gilded world.

The relentless rhythms that had trapped her husband had nothing to do with her. She remembered a line from when she'd played Portia in *Julius Caesar* at drama school.

Dwell I but in the suburbs of your good pleasure?

"Hey, I've got a question," she said after five long minutes of silence. "Are we going broke?"

He looked up sharply at her.

"Of course not. That will never, ever happen. You know that."

"Then why are you tearing yourself up, Quint? What's the point?"

"People are taking hits."

"So? Isn't that the way the game is played? Winners, losers, everything adding up to that big fat zero sum in the sky."

Carrie knew she should probably shut up. But an unexpected anger was moving through her, fueled by a sense that a commodity a lot more precious than money was being squandered: the time of their life.

"Well," she continued, "I'm sorry if some big shot won't be able to trade up on his Gulfstream this year. I just don't understand why it has to turn our life to shit."

"They're my clients, Carrie. I'm responsible for them."

"Insert wife and children for clients, and you're closer to the truth."

He would not be provoked.

"Is it anyone we know? I want to prepare myself for the smoldering looks."

He reluctantly began to rattle off a list of names.

". . . Drew Hagel."

"Wait, hold on. *Drew?*"

She had no idea that he had graduated from tennis to business partner. Even though he gave off an aura of casual inherited wealth, Shannon had often commented on his money woes. WMV seemed far out of his league.

"His position has taken a serious loss."

"Exactly how serious?"

The sarcasm was gone from her voice now. The conversation had taken on the worrying texture of reality. This was Shannon's father. An actual human being. Quint gave his head a terse shake. He never talked sums. Not even with her.

"Quint, look, I don't think he has much money to play around with."

"He told me he'd made some killings in the property market."

"Killings? Not unless they were rats. Don't you know the dumps he sells? And Jamie says Shannon's started hinting about going to UConn to save money."

"Look, he's accredited. He filled out the forms. I saw them myself."

"Yeah, but did you *check* them out?"

"Carrie, come on. His daughter was dating our son. What did you want me to do? Audit him?"

She gave him a skeptical look. For someone who spent all day thinking about money, Quint was prone to a profound naiveté when it came to people who didn't have much. Like possessors of true love and good health, he found it hard to imagine that anybody could be living without the bounty he enjoyed. She decided to let it go. Maybe Drew really had made some money in property. It wasn't exactly rocket science, the way prices were rising. And Ronnie was far too sensible to let him do something rash. Anyway, it was no use talking to Quint about his work. He'd long ago made it clear that he wouldn't let her inside his magic circle of big numbers and steep graphs and split-second decisions. She watched him clear the table and load the dishwasher in that precise manner he had. She didn't offer to help; he'd only find fault with the way she did it. Restacking the plates in more efficient formations, moving things to the back.

The phone began to ring in his office. He hesitated.

"Go," she said wearily.

She could soon hear the air traffic controller strain in his voice, steady but anxious, interrupted by the squawk of the speakerphone. She knocked off the bottle of wine, then started phoning the board of the soon-to-be-defunct Garden Film Society. Don and Myra professed disappointment, though she could also detect relief in their voices. She called Jon last and was secretly glad when he was out. His disappointment would be real. She'd miss working with him, especially going to movies together. There was no one else. For a long time Quint had bravely accompanied her, sitting through films that held no interest for him, deploying the same polite attention he used when they were stuck at a restaurant with some moneyed bore. She finally relieved him of his duties halfway through the Fassbinder series at Lincoln Plaza. That was four years ago. Since then she'd developed a habit of going on her own, though she was never able to shake the feeling that this was a sad thing to do. No matter how mesmerizing the film, there was always the moment when she'd have to step into the light and patch together a day she'd just broken in half.

With Jon she finally had someone who could share her passion. They'd traveled into New York half a dozen times to see revivals at the Walter Reade; they'd gone to the university for the Buñuel season and seen all of Kieslowski's *Decalogue* at Bam Rose. Carrie could see he found a similar oblivion in films. And he noticed the little things. Stockard Channing's galumphing walk. The way Kenneth Branagh was a dead ringer for Jean Gabin. How Sterling Hayden had the exact same look on his face when slapped by Henry Gibson as he did when shot by Al Pacino. He'd made her a sweet sound track compilation for her birthday: *Cape Fear* and *Once upon a Time in America* and *The Taking of Pelham One Two Three*. She may have had little else in common with him, but they shared a sensibility, and at this point in Carrie's life that was an awful lot.

He'd become a creature of considerable fascination to her. He was very reserved at first, though she was gradually able to pry details out of him. He'd grown up in New Jersey's suburban wastelands and escaped to NYU, where he'd never quite made it through film school. He moved to London after meeting a Scottish girl and lived there for almost ten years, freelancing where he could, finally landing a job as the second-string critic for a national paper, five or six films a week in Wardour Street basements, plus features and interviews for the Saturday supplements. But then something had gone bad with the girl; there were visa problems and money problems. Still, he'd tried to find a way to hang on, but a new arts editor was hired at the paper and she had a mate just down from Cambridge and that was that. He'd come back to the States three years ago, deciding to give New York a second try, this time armed with a little wisdom and humility. He was renting a house east of town, close enough to get in for films and meetings but far enough out so he wouldn't have to squander his meager savings. The idea was to get himself established, then find a place in Manhattan. For now he was writing for critique.com, an online database that provided capsule reviews for newspaper calendar sections, library brochures, and cable guides. He was also working on a book, *Are You Talking to Me?*, a study of American cinema, 1967–1975, for which he sort of had a deal with Verso, though it wanted to see a few more chapters before an actual contract was offered. And there'd been mention of a script. It was a lonely, romantic life, vaguely sad but also noble in a way. If she had met him twenty years ago, she might have pushed him to finish his book and that script. But it was too late for that. For now she was simply glad for the company when the lights went down.

Of course, there was no reason to stop seeing him just because the Garden was dead. Films would still be shown, and she was bound to have even more time on her hands. But in the last few weeks she'd become aware of an erotic tension developing between them, little things, like the way their arms would brush as they took their seats or how she'd catch him looking at her when his attention should have been focused straight ahead. What worried her was that she'd started entertaining the notion of letting something happen. Not that anything would ever happen. She was forty; she was engulfed by sons. She was married to Quint.

Which left the question of what she was going to do with her days. She'd begun to suspect that she'd exhausted the possible means of distraction available to her. Volunteer work and little theater; Winsor Pilates and tae bo. Whatever new new thing they came up with, certain to be just like the old. The boys didn't need her anymore. In fact, it was strange to think that their need ever had been enough. More than enough. Jamie in particular. He was the perfect baby, his impossibly soft skin a pure extension of her own body. She remembered thinking this intimacy was all she would ever need, and now it was gone. Was this it then? Was this where she'd been heading all along? Quint had recently read a book by some genius down at Yale who was talking about the end of history; was this the end of *her* history? Was this how she was going to feel from now on, this absolute zero, this perfect stillness, interrupted by good restaurants and dream vacations and glittering prizes? She recalled something he'd said last year when asked to address some horrible orgy of new money self-congratulation in Jackson Hole. Oblivious, Carrie had daydreamed through his speech, though at one point her husband's words penetrated the smog. "Basing decisions on past performance is folly. History is the worst model we have. People who remember the past are doomed to repeat it." The statement was greeted by a susurrus of smug cackles. Fuck the past. Fuck where we've come from because *this* is where we're at. We are the new radicals, with our Ferraris and highlighted copies of George Gilder, our bootleg Partagas and cases of Château Petrus. History is for stiffs. Which was all well and good for Quint, though it still left the question Carrie had been asking herself more and more of late: What about her?

Twenty-five years with him. Eighteen of them married, though the first seven had belonged to Quint just as surely, even that four-year separation when they hadn't spoken a word, that time during which she'd always thought they'd both changed utterly, his personality hardening, hers scattering in any wind that happened to be blowing her way. Though maybe they hadn't really changed at all. Maybe this was just a personal myth she'd indulged for the past two decades. Surely he had always been the stronger one, even when she was beautiful and popular and he was a strange boy nobody yet rated. Surely he'd understood what it took her years to figure out: that she belonged to him.

She hadn't known what to expect when she traveled up to Deacon Williams Academy, but it certainly wasn't Wendell Manning V. She didn't even want to go. It was her father's alma mater, site of the oft described happiest days of his life, a fact Carrie had always found inseparable from the moldering desperation of his later years. Although he preregistered Carrie when the academy went coed, she'd always assumed that she would be able to talk her way out of going. She wanted to stay home so she could attend Brearley or Dalton. Her father could be convinced. She was already learning how to use her moods to get what she wanted from this distracted man whose resolve would evaporate at the first sign of her tears.

But then, when she was thirteen, he'd precluded debate by dying of a heart attack while perched on a toilet in the partners' bathroom. It was the purest sort of shock at the time, though in retrospect she could see that he'd been cultivating that deadly infarction for years. All that single malt; all that swallowed rage. Not that his death meant he was done with his family. People had always said Bert Delaney was a genius at estate planning, but Carrie didn't really know what this meant until she was confronted with the document that was to rule the next eight years of her life, his last will and testament. Among its numerous provisions was the stipulation that she was going to DWA. Period. The money was heading north. She could either follow it or attend the local public high school. Her mother was no ally, eager to have her daughter gone so she could resume the bohemian existence she'd squandered by marrying the prosaic Herbert Delaney.

And so, in the September of her fourteenth year, Carrie found herself being driven north. Austere New England was alien territory to her. Her first few weeks on campus were pure misery. The school's buildings didn't help; all that massive stone and dark wood made the campus feel like a prison. The foliage of the surrounding Berkshires was equally hostile, full of gnarled trees that were home to skunks and mosquitoes and actual bears. Even the topiary in front of the administration building was intimidating, formed into the severe date of the school's founding, 1797.

But October came and the leaves changed and Carrie began to shed her awkward loneliness. She latched on to a group of fellow New Yorkers who inhabited a sardonic corner of the dining hall. And then there were the boys, not her pimply freshman classmates, but upperclassmen, with their letter jackets and driver's licenses. Once they got a good look at Carrie's long legs and feathery hair, they began to pay attention. Even if nothing would happen with this fourteen-year-old now, these future bankers and CEOs already had a nose for a good investment. They knew that just a few semesters could make all the difference with a girl her age. They were willing to bide their time.

Quint played no part in any of this. For the first few months of school no one really knew he was around. As one of a small number of day students he was already at a severe social disadvantage, missing out on the nighttime world of bongs, clandestine romances, and slouching study groups. He would simply appear on campus for the first class and disappear after sports. He was good-looking enough but also clearly out of the flow of fashion, his Oxford shirt and chinos too neat and clean, his lace-up leather shoes at odds with the sandals and clogs worn by the boarders. And his hair was far too short. Even his extracurricular activities kept him apart; his obligatory fall sport was cross-country, and by all accounts he was a loner even among that group of misfits.

The only place left for him to make his mark was in the classroom. If he was easy to ignore in the cafeteria or on the Frisbee-crossed quad, it was impossible to miss him there. Word soon got out that there was a *very* smart boy on campus. Carrie's classmates might have gone to extraordinary lengths to affect academic indifference, but just about everyone knew what was expected of them. Report cards were sent directly home to Fairfield County and Back Bay and the Upper East Side, where the reckonings might be rare, but they could also be harsh. Even by these elevated standards, Quint was a highflier, justifying the full scholarship he was rumored to have received. Test results were posted back then, British-style, on pocked hallway bulletin boards. His name was consistently at the top. Everyone could see in the eyes of the veteran teachers that this young man with the confident smile and intense manner was a rare bird.

He became the object of occasional gossip. Nobody knew where he was from. The prevailing rumor was that he was the child of a minor administration functionary, someone in admissions or development or even—this was said with horror—physical plant. When confronted about his background, he was tantalizingly vague. Unlike the other day students, he never invited anyone home for the weekend. Of course, he wasn't known as Quint then. He was just Wendell Manning V. Later people thought his nickname was the inevitable product of a native-born DWA, Princeton, and Wharton pedigree. The truth, however, was that it was given to him by some ironic upperclassmen during that first year at the school, a passing joke that grew serious, like everything else awkward about him. To Carrie, he was never more than the vaguest presence in that freshman year. Her mind was decidedly elsewhere. She had a sort of boyfriend, a junior named Dwight Hanes; she'd inhaled her first chewy lungful of hash smoke. Her mother was nowhere in sight, and the rough edges had been polished off her father's memory. She had no reason to be interested in some brainy day student.

But then, at the beginning of her second year, he began to talk to her. It happened during biology class. She was so astonished by this turn of events that the first few times it happened she pivoted away from him. But he was undaunted. One day she found him walking beside her as they left the science building, speaking to her with a distinct local twang. There was no ignoring him now.

"What?" she whispered urgently, having in her panic failed to understand him. "What are you saying? Why are you talking to me?"

He wanted to be her lab partner. She didn't know what he was talking about. She'd heard nothing about this. With typical prescience, he explained that the biology teacher would be making an announcement in the next class. Her first instinct was to turn him down, but then she figured out this might be a shrewd move, his perfect scores and confident answers certain to jack up her low C average. So Carrie shrugged and said the words that sealed her future.

"Sure. Okay. Why not?"

At first, he really did seem to want to be nothing more than her lab partner. For the first few lessons he did all the work, an arrangement that suited her fine. Petri dishes, sprouting sweet potatoes, all that gooey organic stuff: He could have it. Carrie watched in fascination as he worked, explaining what he was doing in a patient voice, with its hard local vowels and uncanny practical intelligence. But the teacher caught on—pretty girl, studious boy, this wasn't exactly new—and so Quint had to delegate tasks to her. He'd watch her closely, touching her hand occasionally when it needed guidance. She hadn't noticed his fingers until now, so long and agile. Her class average shot up to an unprecedented B. His remained an effortless A+. Carrie began to relax around him, although conversation remained confined to the task at hand. Outside of class she would grant him nothing more than a sober nod if they happened to pass each other, nothing at all if she happened to be with anyone else.

And then came the frog. Carrie knew this was coming but had chosen not to think about it until the day they arrived in class to find their viscid little victims lying belly up on ominously stained boards. She was stunned to discover that the frog was still alive, though for some reason it appeared to be incapable of doing much more than breathing. She couldn't stop looking at those unblinking eyes as the teacher explained that they were to slice open its midsection and observe the dying function of its cardiopulmonary system.

"Clearly," she stage-whispered to her partner, "this isn't going to happen."

Quint merely smiled.

"But why is it just lying there?" she asked. "Why isn't it hopping away?"

"It's been pithed."

"What?"

"Its spine has been severed. Mr. Murray did it before class."

"I pegged him for a sadist."

Quint picked up the scalpel.

"Wendell," she said, smiling nervously, "what exactly are you doing? We don't know anything about this frog. He could have all these little froglets waiting for him to come home from work."

"Tadpoles. And it's a she."

Carrie looked at the pimply pale expanse of the frog's exposed underside. Now how the hell did he know *that*?

"If you kill that frog, it will haunt you until your dying day."

"Okay," he said. "You do it."

"You have *got* to be kidding."

"Come on." And then he looked at her in a way no one had ever looked at her before. It was a look of total recognition, the sort of recognition that can only come with honest to God love. "You know you want to, Carrie Delaney."

"Excuse me?"

"You'd like to feel what it's like to kill something. This will probably be your only chance. At least I hope it will be."

"I have to find out he's crazy at the exact moment he's holding a weapon."

"Don't worry," he continued. "Everybody wants to do it."

He wasn't kidding. From around them came the sound of disgusted slaughter.

"I'll help you."

She looked back at the frog. It was waiting. Pithed. And then something infinitely strange happened, something that to this day still amazed her. She found herself wondering what it would be like to feel the irrevocable progress of the blade through that repulsive skin. Where was this terrible thought coming from? Who was this boy that he could make her think such things? She took the scalpel from him and held it the way she imagined you were supposed to hold scalpels.

"This is the point where Carrie loses her lunch," she said as she placed it over the frog.

And then his hand was on top of hers, those long, agile fingers gently controlling her. He pressed down gently, causing her to bring the blade in contact with the frog.

"Go on," he said.

The knife was very sharp. The flesh puckered, revealing a gray internal stew, some of it churning sluggishly. Carrie felt her gorge rise. But the nausea soon passed, and to her surprise, she didn't feel faint.

"Now what?" she asked.

"I think we're supposed to remove the heart."

She finally freed her hand from his. She handed him the blade.

"There *are* limits," she said.

Two weeks later he invited her to his house for dinner. She agreed, grateful for the B, but also remembering the warm, covering feeling of his hand on hers. The deal was that they would meet at five by the student union. He said nothing about where he lived or how she should dress. She decided to wear the unofficial DWA uniform, a denim dress and a sweater.

"You look nice," he said when they met, not looking at her.

He walked her across the campus toward the physical plant. They stopped alongside the service road that led to one of the campus's back entrances just as a white van pulled up.

"Careful," he said as he opened the side door. "It's a mess."

Carrie entered the van and slid across a bench seat patched in several places with electrical tape. The floor was a jumble of newspapers and plastic bags and snipped wire bands. The person who turned to greet her was obviously Quint's mother, with the same intense blue eyes and jet black hair, though her face was much longer than her son's, anchored by an absurdly large jaw. The teeth structuring her smile were slightly overlapping but scrubbed white.

"Hello, Carrie," she said, her voice flat and local. "I'm Gloria Manning."

Carrie smiled back, words having abandoned her.

"Well, I can certainly see what all the fuss is about," the woman said merrily. "You truly are one of the Lord's gorgeous creations."

Carrie was acutely embarrassed on Quint's behalf, though he seemed unfazed by his mother's words. It was a few short miles to his home, a hunter green farmhouse with a carport on one side and a small screened porch on the other. There was a long, sloping front lawn currently occupied by a man on a rider mower. He was making neat diagonal lines of alternating hue. Carrie guessed this had something to do with the direction of the cut, though she couldn't be sure. She'd never lived anywhere that had a lawn.

What really captured her attention were the evergreens. Acres and acres of them, covering the gently sloping property all around the house. They were sectioned by a grid of meandering dirt lanes. The trees in some of the zones were only a few feet tall, while others were normal size. A few of the patches were filled with neat rows of stumps.

Wendell Manning V lived on a Christmas tree farm.

The house smelled of lemony furniture polish. Gloria Manning went into the kitchen to make dinner; Quint led Carrie into the living room to listen to music. He put *Blood on the Tracks* on a contraption that could only be described as a hi-fi, teak wood and a creaking lid, speakers hidden by rough thatched screens. During lulls in the music she could hear the buzzing of the mower moving back and forth across the lawn. He told her about his family, but she got the feeling it was only because they were at his house. He had a younger brother, Warren, who was at a school for kids with Down's syndrome. His mother woke up very early to distribute newspapers to delivery boys throughout the county. His father had a job in a lumberyard; he used to work in the mill, but there had been some sort of accident, and now he was in charge of shipping. At Christmas everyone sold the trees. As he spoke, Carrie was struck by his lack of self-consciousness at these modest circumstances, though later she would understand this casual attitude stemmed from the fact that he'd already left this family. He was like a tour guide, walking her through a part of his life that would soon be over. His quaint beginnings. Me, when I was Wendell.

Dinner was served, a smoking meteor of beef, baked potatoes wrapped in tinfoil, green beans smothered in Campbell's cream of mushroom soup. Iced tea in a big glass pitcher with sunflowers painted on by Gloria. Smelling of gasoline and turf, Quint's father arrived just as they sat down. Cut grass adhered to his thick forearms like a pelt of green hair. He washed his hands in the kitchen sink and nodded distantly to Carrie when Quint introduced them. She couldn't see any sign of the injury Quint had mentioned and later learned that it wasn't his father who had been hurt, but a coworker whose arm had been sliced off. Gloria Manning led them in prayer and then proceeded to talk through the remainder of the meal, the only interruptions being Carrie's terse answers to her occasional questions. Quint's father said precisely nothing through the entire meal.

After the Neapolitan ice cream and fresh blueberries her future husband took her for a walk amid the trees.

"What's the name of these trees, anyway? I mean, other than Christmas."

"Blue spruce. Weren't you paying attention during bio?"

"I didn't have to pay attention," she said, hooking arms with him. "I had you."

His cheeks reddened, and Carrie realized that she could wind up loving this character if she weren't careful. They arrived at a pond at the back edge of the property. The mosquitoes weren't too bad, and so he took her out in a small rowboat he'd floated the previous summer. As they cut through the scummy water, he pointed out a pair of bulbous eyes, barely breaking the surface.

"Where's my shiv?" Carrie asked.

"That's a different kind of frog."

"Yeah, I know: It's alive." They drifted for a moment. "So how did you know I would do that?"

"I know all about you," he said without hesitation.

It was the sort of thing kids said to each other all the time. Ouija board bullshit. But this was different. He meant it. What she'd suspected for the last few months was true. He was in love with her. No one had ever really loved her except her parents, and there was so much complication and corruption in that love that it was nothing like this. And then she had what her English teachers would later describe as an epiphany. The boy sitting across from her wasn't strange at all. It was Carrie who was strange; it was the other kids with their rivalries and their tribes who were odd, alienated from one another and their own stunted selves. Wendell Manning V was exactly what he was meant to be, utterly confident and perfectly complete. He was only biding his time. Youth was just an unfortunate prelude, something he was never meant to enjoy. It was just an accident that he lived in a modest house with ordinary parents and a stricken brother. An accident he was bound to rectify.

So when he let go of the oars and leaned forward to kiss her, she had no choice but to let him. The boat rocked with his motion, and she was startled, so he steadied it with his agile hands before placing them on either side of her head. They kissed until she wondered what was going to happen next. It could have been anything. She felt, well, pithed. His mother settled the issue by calling to them from the house. It was time to get Carrie back to school. Quint rowed them to shore. It didn't take him long, just a few steady strokes, to get them where they were going.

Now, as she neared the end of Federal, the thought that he'd been able to see it all back then suddenly wasn't so comforting. It made her sad to think that she'd spent so long living without surprises.

She wondered if the next twenty-five years would be the same. She couldn't imagine what that would be like. But maybe this was something Carrie should start accepting: that just because she couldn't imagine her fate didn't mean that it wasn't headed straight for her.

She reached the arterial turns at the beginning of Orchard, a series of tight oxbow bends that separated the plateau where she lived from the rest of the town. There were no houses here, just tall trees that loomed over the narrow shoulder and thick guardrail. She hated this stretch, its perilously tight bends, the side roads that could disgorge merging traffic without warning. And then there were the joggers and bicyclists, using the road with an arrogance she could never understand. Usually she crawled up at thirty miles per hour, fully expecting a UPS truck to slam into her at every turn. Today, however, she pushed the Lexus hard, letting the car sway up the hill, enjoying the slightly out-of-control feeling.

Her mobile phone rang just after she reached the top.

"I got your message," Jon said. "I spent the night in the city."

Carrie wondered if he'd been with a woman. Not that it was any of her business.

"So how was the banquet?" he asked.

The banquet. It seemed like months ago.

"A rare loss for the home team."

"Oh. I'm sorry to hear that. Or should I be sorry to hear that?"

"Maintain a lofty neutrality. Look, Jon, there's been—something's come up. It looks like we're going to have to put the series on hold."

"On hold?" His voice was surprised and alarmed.

"Yes."

"Do we know for how long?"

"Nobody's sure. Jon, look, there's a chance it's going to be, you know, this is it."

"Jesus."

They shared a disappointed silence as Carrie neared her house.

"What I was thinking was that we could get together for one last board meeting. Sort of to go over things."

"Well, yeah. Sure."

"Friday?"

"Friday will work." He laughed quietly. "Guess what? I finally got my hands on *Cat People*."

"The Simone Simon one?"

"Of course. Maybe, I don't know, we can all watch it on Friday."

"Okay," she said. "That would be good."

Carrie hung up just as she pulled into her driveway, the gate swinging open automatically at the approach of her car. Trust Jon to come up with a good way to end the whole wretched business on a positive note. Friday she'd make the Garden Film Society board dinner, and they could all watch Simone Simon driving men crazy. And that would be the end of it.

Shannon hated Monday afternoons. Ian's sessions with Ronnie ended at four, and there was no telling his frame of mind when he emerged. Sometimes he'd be bursting with energy; at others he'd be moody and withdrawn. It would usually take her the remainder of the day to bring him back around from the bad memories Ronnie would stir up, especially if she forced him to talk about his mother's death. Shannon would wait for him in a pay and display parking lot behind Totten Savings, close enough to Ronnie's office for him to walk there in just a few minutes. She liked to get there early so they could be together right away. Today she'd come directly from school, even though that meant she would be waiting for him for the better part of an hour. Jamie wanted her to go with him to a swimming party some seniors were having, but putting on a bathing suit in front of those vultures was inconceivable. The boys would ignore her and the girls wouldn't. It was typical of Jamie to be going, even after what happened at the banquet. Despite his humiliation, he was still intent on proving what a good sport he was. But that was Jamie. Always trying to make the grade. Always trying to be the boy his father wanted him to be, then drinking himself stupid when he understood it would never happen. Shannon had tried to get him to stand up to Quint and tell him that maybe he didn't want to get straight As and go to Duke and intern at some stock brokerage. But Jamie didn't have the strength to face down his father. Instead, he would do as he was told, then go drinking with his moron friends to forget what a coward he'd been. It would be like this until the day he died. Fraternity rushes and job interviews; bosses and partners; a needy wife and kids of his own to turn into perfect little Mannings.

A meter maid puttered by in her golf cart, giving Shannon the eye. Technically, she should have paid a dollar for a windshield sticker, but the smallest she had was a five, and she didn't feel like going off to break it, especially with her dad haunting the coffee shops on Federal. She checked the time. Not long now. Although Mondays were always bad, she dreaded these days in particular, when Ian and his uncle had their joint sessions. The combination of Ronnie and David could drive Ian into a deep toxic funk. He'd emerge from them even more troubled than usual, oblivious of Shannon's soothing words or even her touch. She hated the fact that there was this part of him that she couldn't affect, a secret warren of emotions she couldn't understand. She consoled herself with the thought that it would be over soon. Ronnie would stop working, and Ian would be rubber-stamped out of the system. They'd be eighteen and free to do whatever they wanted. Until September, anyway, when the world would once again try to pull them apart. Although Shannon was starting to think that might have to change as well.

It would be so great, finally being able to tell people. Ronnie would have to face the fact that Ian's therapy had been a sham, that Shannon had been the cause of his happiness. This was something Shannon knew from hard experience, having endured her own brief therapeutic spell when she was in eighth grade. It had happened during the worst period in her life. She seemed to have only two moods back then: rage and depression. Her father now jokingly referred to the time as the Hat Years because of the thick wool cap Shannon had taken to wearing everywhere, despite the nasty remarks of her classmates and Drew's gentle requests that she might want to let people see her pretty hair. Ronnie, recently on the scene, had started suggesting that there were things that could be done so Shannon wouldn't have to feel so bad all the time. Finally, a firebird she'd penned a bit too strenuously into her forearm had become infected. A small draining procedure was required at the doctor's office; a course of horse pill antibiotics prescribed. That night Ronnie convened an informal summit around the dining room table, suggesting she might want to talk to a colleague. Shannon, scratching at the edges of the gauze bandage, stubbornly refused. But her father insisted, defying his daughter for once. She needed help and she was going to get it.

And so she started seeing Dr. Gladwell, a tall man with an elongated head and a deep, sleepy voice. He wore frayed cloth ties and New Balance shoes, and so of course he became Dr. New Balance. He half listened to the answers he pried out of her during the first session, his pen moving over his clipboard in a way that suggested he was ticking off boxes. Little of use came back from him. Just obvious questions about her mother. There was no advice, no strategy for dealing with her anger and confusion. Nothing about this new woman her father had brought into their life. Shannon was later to understand why: He wasn't a psychologist like Ronnie, but an actual psychiatrist. For him, drugs were the remedy to every problem. Finally, he wrote her a scrip for some mild antianxiety pills. And truth be told, Shannon actually began to feel better. A *lot* better. She stopped waking up in the middle of the night with her heart pounding; she stopped making late-night hang-up calls to her mother's number in Oregon. She even took her SSATs and attended the interview at Country Day. To her father's delight, the hat came off and was buried deep in the hall closet. It took several shampoos, but the lopsided wave in her hair soon vanished as well.

But then Shannon discovered that Ronnie was secretly involved in her treatment. Suspecting that something was going on when her stepmother started moving to other rooms to take calls, Shannon had listened one night through the door of the master bedroom. She couldn't believe what she was hearing. Ronnie was speaking to New Balance. About her. Shannon was the one to call the next family summit. Ronnie maintained that she'd only observed in her role as a parent—*a parent!*—that Shannon was becoming a bit too lethargic and the meds might possibly be lowered. Although Drew meekly took his daughter's side, he wouldn't go so far as to agree that she stop seeing New Balance. Instead, he extracted a promise from Ronnie that she would no longer discuss Shannon's therapy with her colleague.

Shannon refused to accept this feeble compromise. And this time she had leverage: her recent acceptance at Country Day. Unless she was done with New Balance, she would refuse to attend her father's precious private school. If they tried to force her, even if they physically transported her, she'd just sit there, stoic and immobile, until they flunked her out. In the end her father sided with her. His ambitions for her were too deep to let her remain in the public system, with its gun rampage drills and nacho machines. Shannon's therapy was over. Ronnie protested, but there was nothing she could do. Final authority belonged to Drew. For once he exercised it.

And so it was over. No more pills, no more New Balance. Shannon could feel herself slipping a few times but refused to give way to the siren call of missed meals and daylong tantrums. She had an incentive now: proving Ronnie wrong. And so she fought and fought, and by the end of the summer she had won. The wool hat stayed buried amid the ski goggles and deflated tennis balls; she was getting up early every morning for her camp counseling job. There were no more inky gouges in her skin; no more binges on the Costco-size boxes of Peppermint Patties. She'd beaten them all.

Of course, three years on, Shannon could see that she had been too hard on her stepmother. There was no malice in what Ronnie had done. She really did believe that pills and New Balance were the route to happiness. But that didn't change the fact that it was all a big con, this teen crisis thing. Shannon saw it every day, the way her classmates manipulated adults with syndromes and conditions that were nothing more than camouflage for laziness and selfishness. Tatum Shapiro, for instance, would use her weight to blackmail her parents, shedding pounds after every confrontation, then regaining them when things broke her way. During the SATs a clear minority of students had downed pencils at the end of regulation while the rest beavered on, armed with permission from their family doctors, as if time could put in what nature left out. Most days the late-morning line outside the school nurse's office for pill distribution snaked around the corner. Meanwhile, the truly wasted kids kept out of sight, huddling in their rooms, music turned up and smoke leaking from their nostrils, their minds full of things that Shannon's classmates wouldn't understand in a million years.

Ronnie was nothing more than a well-meaning part of the whole absurd system, encouraging kids to wallow in self-pity when they should be working out their own problems. Although Ian understood this—it was what all those anarchy books he read were about, after all—for some reason he still let her get to him, stirring up memories and emotions that he should have kept far beyond her reach. That was what was so frustrating about Monday afternoons. Shannon worried sometimes about how seriously he took his sessions with Ronnie, taking advice to heart that he should have dismissed immediately.

Suddenly the passenger door opened, and there he was, sliding into her car. Shannon's fears were confirmed when she saw him. His eyes had an impenetrable, marbled sheen. His knee began to fibrillate; his fingers drummed the padded dashboard in front of him. She leaned over to kiss him, but he pulled away.

"What did I do, exactly, that I have to take this constant shit from everyone?"

She didn't like the sound of this. Everyone included her. She put her hand on the back of his neck. His muscles shimmered with energy, bad energy, the sort of thing you'd feel in a downed power line if you were stupid enough to grasp it.

"Ian . . ."

"Nothing," he continued, answering his own question. "I didn't do anything except get born to a mother who got cancer. And now I'm getting all this *pressure*."

"What happened?"

"It was my uncle. He got into this big argument with her."

"What about?"

"North Carolina. She's like, I don't think it would be a good idea for Ian to experience that kind of radical change. But my uncle's not even listening. He's just getting mad at me for divulging his big secret plan."

"So what happened?"

"He lost it. Walked out." He shook his head. "He's going to keep af-

ter me about this bar thing until I give in. You don't know what he's
like."

"But it's *your* money. And it's your house. Or it will be soon."

"So what am I supposed to do? Kick him out? He's spent the last
three years looking after me, Shan. He's my mother's brother. I can't
do that to him."

Before Shannon could answer, there was a sharp noise just inches
behind her. It was the meter maid, rapping on the car window with a
thick furrowed knuckle. Her face loomed like something at the wrong
end of a fisheye lens. She had no eyebrows, just oily beige crescents
daubed above her thyroidal eyes.

"What?" Shannon asked through the glass.

"You need a sticker if you're going to park here."

"I'm not parking."

"You've been here for over five minutes. That's when standing turns
into parking."

"What, you have a rule for this?"

"You need a sticker, young lady."

It sounded as if the conversation were taking place underwater.

"Can we please have a couple minutes to finish our conversation,
ma'am?"

"Either get a sticker or I write you up."

"All right," Shannon said. "Jesus."

She reached for the key but before she could turn the motor over,
Ian was out of the car. It was amazing how fast he was moving, dipping his shoulder to make the tight corners at the front fender. He
stopped just a few feet from the woman.

"What is your *problem*?" he asked.

She took a half step backward.

"We're just sitting here talking," he continued. "This is public
space. This is common land."

"This is a pay and display lot, sir."

Ian laughed incredulously.

"Pay and display. That sums up this whole fucking society."

The woman's face changed. She reached into her back pocket. For
a terrible moment Shannon thought she was going to pull out some

instrument of contemporary law enforcement, a Mace-spewing aero-
sol or a Taser. But it was only her ticket pad. She ostentatiously
turned her back on Ian and began to walk toward the rear of the car.
He watched her, his face growing even darker. Shannon couldn't understand what she was seeing. This wasn't Ian. He wasn't violent. He
wasn't capable of menace and confrontation. But the meter maid
wouldn't know that. Shannon had to do something or the police
would be called. She got out of the car, blocking his way with the door
just as he began to move forward.

"Ian," she said softly, her face close to his, "let's just go."

He wouldn't meet her eye, ducking and darting his head around
hers so he could see the woman.

"Look at this corporate lackey. She's actually writing you up."

"Ian, listen to me—*it doesn't matter*."

He still didn't seem to be registering her words.

"Do you want her to call the cops?"

That worked. Mention of the police changed everything. The rigid,
impenetrable sheen vanished from his eyes, allowing them finally to
focus on Shannon. The urgent anger that had possessed him a few
moments earlier was gone, so abruptly and absolutely that it was impossible to believe it had ever been there. The old Ian was back,
peaceable and ironic, capable of grasping the absurdity of this woman
with her fake eyebrows and sputtering little go-cart. He gave a brief,
bewildered laugh.

"Yeah. Okay."

Shannon waited for the woman to finish writing the ticket. She
might still call the police if they drove off. Once they were free Ian
said they should go straight to his house; his uncle would be working
until midnight. He apologized several times on the way home, saying
it had been stupid to let things get away from him like that.

"So why'd you do it then?" Shannon asked gently.

He didn't answer for a long while, staring out the window with a
bewildered smile.

"I don't know," he said eventually. "It was weird. It was like I was
watching myself do it or something."

"It's my fault," Shannon said, not wanting to press him after what he'd been through at Ronnie's office. "I should have just got a sticker."

They went straight to his bedroom. She could feel residual tension in his muscles as they slid between the sheets, but that went away after a few minutes of kissing. And then they were doing the thing that erased all the badness and complication. The energy was still in his body, but it was all good now. Time went away; the world went away. It was just the two of them, doing the only thing Shannon could bring herself to care about these days: being close.

When they were done, she began to think about the incident at the parking lot, deciding it was the result of his uncle's pressure on Ian to join him in this ridiculous North Carolina scheme. The situation was going to get worse unless she did something about it.

"Hey, Ian? I was thinking. About your uncle. Why don't you just, you know, cut a deal with him?"

He turned to her.

"What do you mean?"

"Tell him you'll give him some of your mom's money so he can buy his bar. But you're going to keep the house and the rest of it."

"I don't know. I think he wants us to stay together. I think he still feels responsible for me."

"Come on, you're not fourteen anymore."

Ian didn't say anything to this. She could see that he was waiting to hear what she had in mind.

"Offer him like a third. He's *got* to think that's fair. I mean, you're not going to live with him forever, right?"

"God. No. I mean, he's a decent enough guy, but he's not exactly somebody you want to live with."

"Then this would be the perfect time to make the break."

"He might go for that," he said after a long silence, though there was little conviction or excitement in his voice.

"And there's something else I was thinking." She took a deep breath, knowing that once she said it, there would be no turning back. "Ian, I'm going to bag Oberlin. I think I'll take that place here at the university instead."

He turned to her. She could feel him watching her in the darkness.
"Really? You're going to stay?"

"Yeah. Really."

"God, Shan, that's amazing. But wait, what will your dad say?"

"He'll probably be glad to save the money."

"This is . . . I was starting to think, you know, since you were going to Ohio I might as well do this North Carolina thing after all."

"So you're going to talk to him about it? Offer him this deal?"

He didn't answer right away.

"Ian?"

"Yeah," he said softly. "Definitely."

Later Ian went to the kitchen to organize dinner. She fetched her clothes and carried them to the bathroom. Like everything in Ginny's house, it was cheap and cramped. It was also a mess. Watermarks stained its surfaces; formations of dried shaving cream and calcified toothpaste surrounded the sink. The exhaust fan labored mightily but couldn't cut that sour male aroma. She took a quick shower. When she turned off the tap, there was the usual shudder within the house's thin walls. She dressed quickly, eager to talk to Ian about what they'd just decided in case his confidence was faltering. As she neared the kitchen, she heard him speaking. So much for organizing dinner: He was ordering a pizza. She didn't hear the other voice until she'd stepped through the door. The person speaking sat at the kitchen table. His back was turned, but there was no way Shannon could escape. He must have seen the change in Ian's face because he spun around.

Whatever mental images she'd conjured of David these past few weeks vanished as he rose to greet her. He was much better-looking than Shannon would have guessed, with sharp eyes and a long, thin nose like Ian's. He was sort of short, but lean and fit in his black suit, with big hands and raised veins that suggested considerable strength. He had long brown hair and an abundant mustache. Shannon could imagine women being drawn to him, then coming to regret that attraction. He was younger than she'd anticipated; the word *uncle* had always brought middle age to mind, but he appeared to be in his early thirties.

"You must be Ian's girl," he said, a hint of the South in his voice.

"Yeah," Shannon managed in her for-adults voice. "Yes."

He paused, as if expecting more, then extended a veined hand.

"I'm Ian's uncle David. I expect you've heard all about me."

8 It was a point of pride for David that he had never once called in sick during his nine months at Camelot Coach Service. He'd worked through it all. The high fevers and the clenching lower back; the headaches stoked by the piercing beams of approaching traffic. He'd driven through public holidays and ice storms and that spell when some crazy junkie in a thousand-dollar Italian suit was pistol-whipping area livery drivers. It didn't matter how he felt. Good or bad, David always drove.

But tonight he wasn't sure he could spend eight hours ferrying strangers. He had to talk to Ian. He'd thought about grabbing him as he left Traynor's office but decided he should cool down before they talked. So he drove over to Camelot's headquarters, a restored Sunoco station in Dresden. Hamed and Jack were both in the office, their zip-booted feet up on their twin desks, murmuring to each other in illicit undertones. They shut up when David walked in the door. As if he didn't know all about their little schemes, the tax dodges and drug runs and "cousins" from Cairo. Jack smiled his jackal's smile; when the moron had decided to choose an American name to replace his unpronounceable Egyptian one, he'd opted for his hero, Jack Nicholson, an actor he actually believed he resembled in some way other than a propensity for fatting up.

"Got a package delivery," he said in his leering voice.

"No, thanks."

"When you gonna get with the program and make some real money, my man?"

Here we go again, David thought. A few months ago he'd made the mistake of mentioning to another driver that he used to deal a little, and now everybody on the lot thought he was Pablo Escobar.

"Could you speak a little louder, Jack?" he said. "The wire is in my Jockeys, and I want to make sure the guys in the van are getting everything down."

Hamed pursed his lips, and Jack started making censorious noises, neither of them seeing the humor in wiretap jokes. Not that David gave a damn. They would never fire him unless he started missing shifts. He was reliable and he spoke English and he would work anytime. All he had to do was hold on a few more months, and then he would never again have to take orders from anyone.

"David, come on, we need a serious business favor tonight," Hamed said.

"What can I tell you? I carry human beings from here to there. I don't do packages. You know that about me."

"Lot of money in it."

"There's a lot of money in a lot of things," David answered. "This is America."

It wasn't until he was on the road that he finally allowed himself to think about what had gone wrong at Traynor's. He should have known that it was going to be a difficult session the moment she asked to speak alone with him. Tea was offered, and David accepted, wanting to be agreeable, even though he remembered its tasting like wet straw. Traynor soaked two bags in mugs emblazoned with wildfowl taking flight. He took comfort in the sight of the doctor's advancing pregnancy.

"So," she started, "what I'd hoped to speak with you about today were some strategies for Ian's continued care after he's through here."

David felt a faint stirring of alarm.

"Continued care? I thought you said he'd made good progress."

"He has. I think we've dealt with his substance problem very well. What I was hoping was that I could give you the name of a psychiatrist and you could set up a meeting between him and Ian."

"Well, um, would that be part of our deal here? I mean, in terms of Ian's parole?"

"Oh, no. This would just be, well, think of it as a checkup."

"Wait, is there something wrong with him?"

She took a thoughtful sip of her tea.

"We've recognized that Ian's drug use was a means of dealing with grief over his mother's death, but I think there's also a possibility that it was a form of self-medication for handling some deeper issues as well."

"What kind of issues?"

"I'm not really qualified to make those sorts of assessments, Mr. Warfield. That's why I wanted him to see this psychiatrist."

"Wait, that's where I'm getting confused. Aren't *you* a psychiatrist?"

"No, I'm a psychologist. A psychiatrist deals with a different array of concerns."

David looked down into his mug. A few oily green leaves were floating on the brackish liquid. He got it now. The cop led to the lawyer who led to the judge who led to the psychologist who led to the psychiatrist. The big legal merry-go-round, all of it funded by David Alan Warfield.

"Okay," he said. "Absolutely. Only the best for the kid. You know my policy."

She smiled as she wrote on a piece of headed notepaper. David put it in his breast pocket as she went to get Ian, figuring he'd have the good grace to wait until he was at home before shredding it. Ian shot him a quick look as he entered. David gave him a terse nod, letting him know that it was all right.

"Right," Dr. Traynor said as she carefully lowered her swollen body into her seat. "Now, I think we might profitably spend today talking about strategies for helping Ian deal with turning eighteen. I understand a fairly big windfall is about to come his way?"

David nodded warily. Ian remained perfectly still.

"And Ian has mentioned that you were thinking about going into some sort of business together. A bar and grill in North Carolina?"

Stunned that Ian had been talking to her about this, David turned to his nephew.

"Well, it's an idea we've been kicking around."

"What I'm thinking we might explore," she continued, "is whether Ian really needs that sort of major change at this point in his life."

"There wouldn't be any major changes for Ian except his zip code. I'd handle the tough stuff. He'd just reap the rewards, so to speak."

"But do you really think a bar and grill is a good environment for him, given his past history? I mean, he wouldn't even be twenty-one."

"Well, okay, you say it like that, then obviously your answer is no. But it's not like I'm going to have him slinging drinks or bouncing the door." David smiled. "You should see this place. It's not your basic beach bar. There's no jukes or wet T-shirt contests or sports TV. The customers are locals and your better sort of tourists. And there's music, people playing traditional instruments. Folk songs. Sea shanties."

Traynor nodded in affable confusion. She still wasn't getting it.

"Look," David continued, "all I'm talking about is putting Ginny's money into something that will provide Ian with security. This place is an incredible investment."

"How about an education? Wouldn't that be a good place for the money?"

"No, you see, an education is part of the whole deal here. We could use the proceeds . . . there's a college in Wilmington, and if he doesn't like that, they're all over the place down there. They got the— what's it called?—the ACC."

"Ian? Maybe this would be a good time to talk to your uncle about some of the things we've been discussing."

Been discussing. Perhaps David should have paid closer attention to what his nephew was getting up to on these Monday afternoons.

"I don't know," Ian said. "I just . . . I don't know if I want to sell Mom's house."

David sat perfectly still. Four short days ago Ian had promised to think seriously about the idea, making it seem like 90 percent of a yes. And now it was as if he'd already decided against it without even having a real conversation with David.

"Ian, I've explained to you . . . this is a golden opportunity."

"For you."

"No, not just for me." Ian didn't respond. "Look, if this is about your girl . . ."

For the first time since they'd entered the office, Ian's expression came to life. He looked up at David, then at the doctor, then back at the floor.

"It's not about that," he muttered.

"Is there a girl?" Traynor asked brightly. "Are you involved with someone, Ian?"

"No. Not really."

David was tempted to call him on this lie, though that would be a mistake. He needed Ian on his side.

"I think what Ian is asking for here is to have a bit more say in decisions about his future," the doctor said after a long silence.

"But what exactly are you suggesting he should do? Stay here working at his crummy job? Maybe start running again with those jokers over at Gryphon Games?"

"I think that you should both be comfortable with any decisions that are made."

"But this is the only thing that's on the table."

"Perhaps then we should use the remainder of our time here to come up with some other ideas."

Other ideas. He'd been a fool not to see what was going on here from the first. She was trying to talk Ian out of going to North Carolina.

"Look," David said after taking a long breath, "I know it might seem to you like I'm not the best person to be making decisions for Ian just now. I mean, I'm not gonna sit here and say I didn't make mistakes when I first started. But come on. You take a guy, never been married, no kids that he knows about, you give him a mixed-up thirteen-year-old boy to look after, mistakes are going to be made."

"Mr. Warfield, honestly, no one is trying to place a negative light on you here. I think you've done extraordinary things with Ian. I really do. I just think we should all be sure that his future interests are at the center of any plans that are made."

"Well then, we're all set. This Cove, this is perfect for his future."

"But don't the both of you have to agree for that to be the case?"

"Sometimes one person can see what's right for another without the second person knowing it." He gestured around the office. "I mean, isn't that what this is all about?"

Traynor shifted uncomfortably in her seat.

"I supposed my real concern is that Ian not experience too much pressure or disruption at this key time in his life."

Pressure. Disruption. So there it was. She thought he was bad for the kid.

"You know," David said generally, addressing a mythical fourth person in the room, an impartial judge who would be able to see his point of view, "I'm here because I have to be. And I'll take ten kinds of crap if it'll help Ian. But I will never admit that I am bad for him. Maybe I was once, but that's over with. I work twelve-hour days and have exactly no personal life right now because I'm paying for my mistakes. This move to North Carolina is the right thing. And the truth of the matter is, yes, I *am* the one who has to make that call. Because once you guys sign off on him, he's alone again."

"All right then," Traynor said, undeterred, seizing on exactly the wrong thing. "Let's talk about some of those mistakes, as you call them, and see if we can look at this current decision in the context of—"

"Look, I plead guilty. I screwed up. But that's not happening anymore. That's dead and buried."

"Nothing is really dead and buried, Mr. Warfield."

"My sister is," David said as he stood. "Which leaves me. Not you. Not the courts. Just me."

"Mr. Warfield, please—"

But it was too late. He was on his feet. There was nothing left to do but walk out of the room. The session was over.

His suspicion proved correct. Work wasn't going to happen. He decided to call it quits after his first client. He had to get home and find out what Ian was thinking. He'd been a fool to lose his temper with Traynor. A waste of precious time. He was visiting Carolina in four days, and he had to know that the boy was on his side. Jack and Hamed were gone when he dropped off the car, which meant that, technically, he was leaving work without permission. But he couldn't concern himself with that now. His route home took him by the dental practice where Ginny had worked, a windowless building with a big molar-shaped sign out front. At least *she* would understand his motives. She'd know what he'd given up to raise her son. His poor sister. What a rotten hand she'd been dealt. First what their father had done to her and then the cancer. It had been almost a year since they'd last spoken when she called with the news. There was an urgent hush in her voice, so quiet that at first he thought she'd called to say she had the "answer."

"To what?" he asked.

But then she repeated herself and he understood. It had started in an ovary, and now it was in her liver, which meant that the show was over. David was genuinely aggrieved by the news. He'd always had a soft spot for his sister.

"Remember what we talked about, David? Hon? About Ian?"

He remembered. During a brief visit to Connecticut a few years earlier—shameful to say, he'd come to borrow money—she'd asked if he'd look after her son if anything happened to her. Sure, David said, that freshly signed check in his hand, figuring nothing was going to happen to Ginny. She went to work and then she came home and ate. Nights off, she got together with the girls at Chili's and ate. If she was a man, her heart might give out, but women could carry fat right to the end of the line. But now this. Cells were going haywire in her big body, and no one could stop them.

"There's money, David," she said, sensing his panic. "I took out a policy. A big one. They gave me a good rate because I don't smoke. And the house. The mortgage is insured as well."

So it was good-bye, Florida, a move he was thinking of making, anyway. Tib was already gone after that spell in the county jail, and it just wasn't the same at the Windjammer without him. David arrived in time to watch his sister die. She'd lost so much weight that it was hard to tell she was the same person. After all those years of trying, Ginny had finally found a diet that worked. She was weak and sleepy, but the part of her mind that made her a good mother was stubbornly holding out until she knew that her son would be looked after. She was full of advice and regulations about what the boy could eat, what time he should go to bed, the amount of television he could watch. And then they moved her to the hospice section and a morphine drip was opened. David and Ian cut back on the visiting, since there was only so much time you could watch someone lying unconscious. Finally, the phone rang one morning while he was getting out of the shower, and that was it for poor Ginny. It wasn't until after the funeral that he found out about the trust. She'd neglected to mention that in all her advice. As guardian David would be entitled only to his sister's tightfisted version of what was enough to keep the household running. Still, there was a promise of a big payoff down the road—provided he stuck around. Besides, if David didn't take care of Ian, then it would be foster homes for the kid, which had a tendency to create drug abusers, petty criminals, and born-again Christians. He couldn't do that to blood.

At first, his relationship with his nephew was simple enough. Ian, stunned by his mother's death, was nothing like the other teenage boys David had known, scrawny lying terrorists with a craving for sex, speed, and random violence. He was a genuinely sweet kid. Mornings David would drop him off at school, where evidently he was no trouble at all. At night there was dinner—Ginny had bought a microwave after her diagnosis—and then television. The bed-wetting was a problem, but he bought some plastic mattress covers, and Ian understood that he was expected to deal with the mess himself. David would look after the boy, but there were limits.

Meanwhile, he had to figure out what he was going to do with himself. He tried to find work at Foxwoods, but they were hiring only janitorial. He considered driving limos, his mainstay in Miami before he moved to Daytona, but then he wound up in conversation with the manager at Bill's Tavern. Although David had vowed never to work in a bar again, it proved to be good work; busy, but lacking the undercurrent of violence and sexual chaos he'd come to hate down in Daytona. The customers might wear ripped jeans, but their haircuts and manners made it clear that they had important jobs and onerous mortgages. The only time he ever had to call the police was when a guy who couldn't have been more than forty dropped dead of a heart attack while standing at a urinal.

The problem was what to do with his nephew. After returning a few times to the haunted wreck Ian became after an evening passed in the company of his mother's ghost, David knew he would have to make other arrangements. Full-time sitters were very hard to find, and when he finally did track one down through a Federal Street agency, it turned out she would cost him half his pay. He talked to the trust people at Totten Savings, but they were hard-nosed about it, suggesting he work more reasonable hours.

In the end, he decided simply to bring the boy with him. There was an empty office next to the manager's. The idea was that he could do his homework, then watch the small television David bought him at a pawnshop. Most nights he'd fall asleep on the small sofa, and David would carry him to his car, his body warm and slack. Although David brought in one of those waterproof sheets, Ian never wet the sofa. That only happened in the hours just before dawn, when the dreams were the worst.

Ian eventually developed an interest in comic books, not the bright superheroic ones of David's youth, but dark, twisted things like *The Crow* and a truly scary series about evil puppets. He bought them at Gryphon Games, a store on Federal that sold hobby figurines to boys who were a little too old for that sort of thing. The guys who ran it had the same ideas about hair styles as the members of the Skynyrd tribute band back at the Windjammer. Ian started doing some drawing of his own, using the backs of surplus paper place mats. At first he copied straight from his books, though he was soon filling one page after the other with his own people. David's favorite was one about a group of kids who lived in a hidden world they could access only through secret doors at the bottom of their parents' swimming pools. To his untrained eye the boy had real talent.

The months stretched on, David relaxing into the rhythm of a life he'd never imagined for himself. He had a few short affairs with women but nothing real; he'd party sometimes with guys who worked at the bar, though just as often he'd spend time with his nephew. Ian began to miss a lot of school to hang out with the Gryphon Games crew, though David didn't have the time to play truant officer. A new cook was hired at Bill's, a Russian named Pavel, and after they got to know each other, he told David he had a connection in Coney Island who could supply them with some exceptional bud. David was wary at first, though the yuppies at the bar were constantly asking where they could score. He told Pavel that he would help him out on the condition that they didn't get greedy. Never more than an ounce at a time, and nothing but pot. Pavel shrugged in that way Russians had. And so David began dealing to regulars, grossly overcharging them, denying anyone who didn't look totally cool.

For the first time since moving to Connecticut he began putting money away. Ian started reading strange books by foreigners, many of which seemed to involve the dubious notions that money was not important and laws did not have to be obeyed. He was also getting very serious about his drawing, spending long, secret hours bent over his pads, no longer so eager to share his vision with his uncle. David could tell he'd begun smoking dope himself, detecting the telltale red-rimmed eyes and woodsmoke aroma. The squirrelly stashing habits. David made some token efforts to talk him out of it, though he remembered how it went when you were that age. If Ian wanted to get high, then he was going to get high. Besides, given his current sideline, who was David to talk? And there was something else, something that he didn't really admit to himself until after the arrest. Ian was a lot easier to look after when he was smoking. All that teenage bullshit—the occasional tantrums, the black moods and locked doors—was smoothed out into something agreeable and slightly dopey. So he made a deal with his nephew. He could use—provided he got his stuff from David. Ian agreed; who wouldn't? David gave him a small bag at the beginning of the week and even bought him papers and a pipe, since the paraphernalia laws were so tough. In a fucked-up way it was the responsible thing to do.

And then, last summer, disaster struck. It was the Dresden cops who got him, spotting the joint he was smoking despite David's warning that he should never light up in the car. Ian had panicked, leading them on a five-minute chase, during which one of the cruisers damaged its front end after missing a turn. When the call came, David briefly contemplated a quick return to Florida, though he couldn't leave the boy hanging like that. So, convinced that there would be a pair of cuffs waiting for him as soon as he stepped through the door, he drove down to the Dresden Police Station, a run-down brick building that was nothing like the new headquarters in Totten.

But Ian did not betray him, despite pressure from the cops, who were mightily pissed off about that damaged cruiser. They'd tossed him into an adult cell for the night, even though they could have easily held him as a juvenile. But all Ian would say was that he'd bought his drugs from a stranger in the Cumberland Farms parking lot. Of course, the cops had strong opinions on the subject, so after warning Pavel, David quit his job at Bill's and purged himself of everything even remotely resinous. But there was nothing they could do without Ian's testimony. Remembering his mother's words, he had stood by his family.

"I'm not going back there," was all he said when they let him out the following morning. "I am *not* going back. I'll fucking kill myself before I do."

David tried to get him to say what had happened, but Ian retreated to his room for long periods of silent drawing. David searched the yellow pages for a lawyer, choosing the guy in Hartford with the biggest ad. He explained that since Ian was under eighteen and it was his first arrest, there was a good chance he could stay out of jail.

"We're going to have to pay to fix that cruiser," he said. "And your nephew should offer to undergo counseling for the drugs."

"Where do we sign up?"

It wasn't that simple. The state of Connecticut wasn't in the business of providing free counseling. David would have to organize it himself, bringing it to the judge as a done deal. Traynor was the only one with an opening. She would take insurance, which would have been nice if David had any. Since there was no way the trust department at the bank was going to pay for this, it would have to come out of his own pocket, just like the bond and the body shop and the lawyer's fees. But it was a small price to pay for the loyalty his nephew had shown him.

Convincing Ian was no problem. He would have done anything to stay out of jail. His fear of being locked up was so intense that David knew something bad had happened during those sixteen hours he spent in the Dresden Police Department's basement. He finally got him to tell his story. It turned out he'd been put in holding with three other men. There were two drunk drivers and an elderly black man who were eventually released, leaving Ian with a short, hairy guy who looked like a troll. Once they were alone the man began to talk. He was friendly at first. The cops came down to check on them once or twice, then let them be. They were still angry about their cruiser. The troll stopped talking, and Ian started to nod off on the narrow aluminum shelf that was supposed to be a bed. But then the other man walked noisily over to the communal toilet, a reeking aluminum volcano that sprayed filthy water every time it flushed.

"Come on over here," he said.

Ian didn't know what to do.

"I'm not going to ask again."

Terrified, Ian walked over, seeing now that the man had taken out his thick purplish cock. He nodded down at it.

"Hold this while I piss," he said.

Ian laughed nervously, and then he stopped laughing when he saw the man's expression. He lightly grasped the purple cock, holding it steady while the stinking piss jetted from it into the bowl.

"Shake it," the man said when he was done.

This happened twice more that night. Nothing else; the troll never even put a hand on him. He was asleep, curled on one of those hard shelves, when the police came to take Ian to his hearing. Ian was too ashamed to tell them what the man had done.

David sat still for a long time after Ian finished speaking. And then he reached out and put his hand on the back of his nephew's skull. He hadn't really touched Ian since those nights he'd carried him sleeping from the office at Bill's.

"All right," he said. "All right."

He went to the public library and found the newspaper for the day after Ian had been picked up. It printed police logs for all the towns in the county. There were six arrests in Dresden. David was able to narrow it down to two potential names after dismissing the women and those DUIs. Darius Carter, who was picked up for violation of a spousal abuse order, and Raymond Wayne Athey, Jr., who had been arrested for larceny under $250. The paper listed their home addresses. David drove by Carter's apartment first and was greeted by a sleepy, perplexed black man. Which left Athey. He lived in a small neighborhood of densely packed little houses, cheap bars, and auto supply shops. David didn't have to knock on a door this time. A man perfectly matching Ian's description stood opposite the address the paper had given, holding forth to a Hispanic gentleman working on a motorcycle. Athey couldn't have been more than five-four, with thick shoulders and bowed legs. He really was a troll. His massive right hand encompassed the Rolling Rock he was drinking. David pictured his nephew's thin fingers on the man's cock and wanted to get out of the car right then and there. But that would be reckless. He had already done enough that was reckless.

He went back that night, parking three blocks away in the half-full lot of an Italian family restaurant. He'd bought a heavy monkey wrench at Home Depot just for this purpose, something no one would think was a weapon. Except Raymond Wayne Athey, Jr. He wore his old work boots as well. It was a quiet, normal night; he could hear voices from the houses, the tinny sound of televisions. Athey's home was lit up, and David wondered if there was anyone else inside. For some reason he'd assumed there wouldn't be. But it didn't matter. This still had to be done.

He walked along the tilted fence bordering Athey's driveway. Behind the screen door at the side of the house was a small, empty kitchen. David checked—the door was unlocked—then stepped back into the fence's shadow to wait. Bugs clicked against a pale bulb above the door. Somebody laughed a few houses away. A siren, a plane overhead. And then Athey came into the room, speaking on a cell phone. He was wearing a ratty blue robe and no shoes. He balanced the phone between his shoulder and his ear as he began to organize a bowl of Cheerios. David stepped up to the door, waiting until both Athey's hands were occupied before pulling it open.

"Springfield," he was saying into the phone. "No, Massachusetts."

He turned in time to take the first blow on his left ear. He dropped everything, the bowl and the phone and the cereal carton. But he didn't fall, that low center of gravity keeping him on his feet. Fearing another blow to the head might kill him, David grasped the wrench like a police baton—one hand on either end—and pushed it against the man's neck as he hooked a foot behind his right ankle. Athey went down hard, his head banging on a cabinet door. He tried to pull himself up on the counter, and David hit the side of his elbow with a short blow that sent him back to the linoleum. His robe had fallen open, revealing a thick, hairy body. A big, fish-shaped cock followed the contour of his pelvic bone. David saw his nephew's pale hand on it.

"Ray?" a voice from the phone asked. "Dude?"

David slammed the wrench down on the phone. Athey was lying still, holding his injured arm, waiting for the next thing to happen. David breathed a few times and then kicked his boot up between the man's legs. It was like the jellyfish he and Tib would stomp on the beach while walking home from work back in Daytona. That squat troll body shriveled. David kicked him five or six more times, feeling the same liquid give. Athey made sounds, and then he stopped making sounds. David fought the temptation to say something. He turned and walked away, his work boots crunching Cheerios.

There was a Honda parked around back when he arrived home from Camelot. Ian's girl. David pulled next to her and cut the Chevelle's engine. He hesitated, wondering if barging in would be such a good idea. Up until now he'd played along with Ian's unspoken desire that he not meet her. But David had to talk to his nephew. Carolina was four days away.

He was at the table, eating potato chips with one of the out-of-date dips they let him bring home from his job. At the other end of the house the shower stopped running with its usual shuddering clang.

"I thought you were working," Ian said, trying to hide his alarm.

"Somebody else can do the driving tonight." David pulled out a chair and sat across from him. "Don't worry. I'll behave."

Ian managed a nervous half smile.

"Look, bud, I'm sorry about what happened earlier."

"No, it was my fault, Uncle David."

This stopped David in his tracks. It was rare for Ian to call him uncle; rarer still for him to apologize.

"I mean, I was thinking," he continued. "We can definitely make this North Carolina thing work."

David couldn't quite take in what he was hearing. Just a few hours ago the boy had seemed dead set against the idea.

"So what was all that back at Traynor's office?" he asked.

"I don't know. She just, I don't know—she can get your head turned around."

"Tell me about it."

Ian's words were beginning to register with David. He was on board. But before he could speak, he heard something behind him. The girl. She wore no makeup, and her hamster's nest of wood-colored hair hadn't seen a brush in a while. She was tall and seemed to possess all the usual curves, though it was hard to tell because her body was camouflaged by a loose sweatshirt. One thing was certain: If she had it, she certainly wasn't putting it out there. But she had big, lively eyes and a mouth that was the sort of thing a boy wouldn't mind kissing.

Her name was Shannon. David liked the voice, the soft undertone, the lack of helium shrillness. She showed some class by looking him in the eye and confidently answering his questions, the first being where she went to school.

"Country Day?"

"I tried to get Ian in there a couple years ago, but they were full up. Supposedly."

"He's not missing anything."

"Still, it would have been nice to have a choice."

"That's true," she admitted, her neck reddening slightly.

David smiled at her. This girl really was all right.

"So what is it your father does, Shannon?"

"He sells houses."

"And does your mother do that as well?"

"My mother lives in Oregon."

"Oh? Divorce?"

She nodded.

"Well, then, that's something you and Ian have in common. Motherless children, as Mr. Clapton says."

And then, to David's astonishment, she reached her hand out and gently covered Ian's.

"We have a lot in common."

David stared at her, then looked at his smiling nephew. He was puzzled. First Ian had said he'd be willing to move to North Carolina, and now he was acting as if he'd found the love of his life right here in town.

"So, who wants some dinner?" David asked. "It'll be my treat."

PART THREE

The duct men arrived just after eleven. Their white van passed beneath the sign at the corner of Federal that had recently been modified by some clever vandal to read RES ENT STREET. Three workers piled out, moving with the crisp detachment of soldiers as they changed into their papery white jumpsuits, particle masks, and protective goggles. Watching from a front window, Drew wondered just what sort of toxic matter they expected to find lurking in the walls. As if to answer, they unloaded a long-snouted vacuuming apparatus, a thick-wheeled contraption so heavy that it had to be lowered by a mechanical lift. They walked the machine carefully up his crumbling steps, passing it through the front door with an urgent, grunting choreography. The hall's slats groaned beneath the unexpected weight.

Goggled eyes stared at him. The duct men were primed for biocide.

"I guess you guys know what to do," Drew said, trying to remember how much this was going to cost him.

They started in the living room, attacking the metal grillwork with rubberized crowbars and power screwdrivers. Drew watched in bleak fascination as they probed the house's cavities with flashlights, muttering darkly to one another, speaking the language of mold. They moved in the jerky, otherworldly fashion of astronauts. Hiring them had been Ronnie's idea. Although Anne had organized a similar treatment when she was pretending to live here, evidently a decade was an aeon in the evolution of microorganisms, allowing for any number of toxic generations.

Once the men were working Drew resumed the lonely task that had occupied him all morning, wandering from room to room, trying to figure out how he was going to tell Ronnie that they had to sell their house. Putting it on the market was his only realistic chance of getting his hands on enough money to pay his debts. There was nothing else he could sell, nothing else he could borrow against. He'd already stripped Hagel & Son bare. No. 33 Crescent was the sum total of his worth. It was the only way he could keep the bank from coming for him.

The actual sale would be no problem. The house was a real prize, built in 1895, when people knew how to make houses. Drew had become its unexpected owner on that bleak morning thirteen years ago when he woke to the news that his parents had been killed in a car accident on a ski trip in Vermont. They'd been out to a late dinner; his father misjudged a turn; a sugar maple awaited them at the bottom of a steep decline. The twin webbed puckers on the windshield Drew saw when he went to deal with the car told the whole story: His parents hated seat belts. As their only child Drew got the house. He and Anne and baby Shannon were subsumed by the place. Five bedrooms, a big attic ripe for conversion, a concrete basement that had remained miraculously free of damp through a century of rain and thaw. Pocket doors and ornamental mantelpieces. The ceilings were eleven feet high, and the recently burnished wood floors went on forever; there was even a butler's pantry. The peaty garden patch out back automatically yielded rich vegetables each summer. There were still problems, most notably an occasional lack of pressure from the town's mains and a knob and tube electrical system that would soon need to be updated. And of course, the fresh coat of paint every six or seven years. But these were easily offset by the house's beauty and its proximity to the town center. No. 33 Crescent was a prize. It could be sold for top dollar.

Ronnie would be heartbroken. She loved this house. In the past five years she had made it her own. Much of the money that had gone into fixing it up had come from her practice. Walls had been stripped of paper; chintzy 1950s fixtures replaced; the old wall-to-wall carpeting torn up. And Ronnie had many more plans, especially for the attic, which was to become a place for the twins. There would be a media center—no cable, just a DVD player for educational programs—a tumbling zone, and a small library. Exposed beams from which mobiles could be hung; wall-lining storage cupboards. An advanced air filtration system to take care of the clouds of verminous dust the old house occasionally discharged. The designs were in hand; Phil Ferris was set to begin work in September, his 50 percent start-up fee to be paid, supposedly, by that equity credit line. All of Ronnie's dreams for her children were located here. The first steps and birthday parties; the predance photos and postgraduation dinners. This was her house as much as Drew's. And even if she agreed to give it up, selling would create as many problems as it solved. After settling the credit line and his other debts, Drew would walk away from the transaction with next to nothing. There was no way he could buy another house like this in Totten Crossing. Even the bland suburban split-levels up near Dresden would be beyond his means. They would have to rent a town house or even an apartment, unthinkable with babies on the way. Either that or move somewhere rural and chilly, New Hampshire or upstate New York, where they knew no one and had no work.

A seismic shudder erupted just as he stepped into the upstairs bedroom he used as his study. The mold machine was operating, gulping badness from the walls. The incredible noise was amplified by the cavernous ducts. Drew took a box of shortbread cookies from the bottom drawer in the roller desk and dropped into the old leather recliner that dominated the room, an almost organic entity that emitted a strangely compelling odor of decay every time he worked the foot-long lever. It was his father's favorite chair. He'd spent countless hours in it, reading Trollope or the *Times*, laughing into the phone, perfectly content to be exactly where he was. Drew couldn't afford to be so relaxed. He had to think of something before his fate was taken out of his hands. Andy Starke had been after him twice already this week. The first message on Tuesday had been anxious but friendly; yesterday's, ominously chilly. Drew had come straight home after work, hoping Starke wouldn't try to pay him a visit here. Fortunately they hadn't reached that point. Yet.

He worked the lever and eased himself back, wondering how his father had done it, getting through the day without ever raising a sweat. Stress was as foreign a concept to him as pederasty or vegetarianism. He must have had the usual setbacks, but he never let them affect his rolling good cheer or sly sense of humor. It was an outlook he'd tried to pass on to his son. As the machine rumbled downstairs, Drew thought back to one lesson in particular, a summer afternoon when he was eleven. He'd just returned from tennis when his father called to summon him to Federal. Drew hurried over, anxious to make a few dollars planting a FOR SALE sign or mowing a lawn. He found Walt in a rare state of solitude, skimming over a purchase and sale agreement. The job was a big one; he wanted Drew to collect rent money from one of his tenants on Jefferson Street and then deposit it in Totten Savings. The man's name was Otis Winter. He was expecting the visit.

"Oh," his father said as he turned over a deposit slip, "and look out for his dog."

Drew's mind was filled with visions of slobbering jaws and merciless black eyes for the entire bike ride over. The house turned out to be a dingy two-fam, a property Drew sold twenty-five years later to pay his gathering debts. He had hoped to see an envelope clothespinned to the mailbox by the front door, but there was nothing. He leaned his bicycle against the chain-link fence and searched for evidence of the killer dog, his heart sinking when he saw the massive assemblages of calcified shit scattered around the weed-strewn yard. He briefly contemplated riding back to town and telling his father that there was no one home. But his visit was expected. So he removed his bicycle chain with its dangling Yale lock to use in case of attack, then pushed open the suitably creaky gate. He waited, ready to bolt. But there was nothing. He leaned back toward the street as he walked to the front door, like a base runner facing a pitcher with a quick pickoff move. When he knocked, he expected explosive barks, the clicking scrabble of attacking claws on linoleum. But all was quiet.

And then he heard the panting. The dog had somehow got behind him. It was huge, on the verge of moving from the canine category into the realm of horses and bears. Drew knew that the weapon he'd brought was useless; it would do nothing more than enrage this beast. Prickly shrubs barred escape to either side; the door behind him remained shut.

It took a few seconds for him to understand his father's joke. The dog was ancient. Scabbed, arthritic, covered with graying hair. Its cloudy eyes took in the visitor with epic indifference, reinforced by a squeaking yawn that revealed a yellowy row of teeth. It gave its tail a single shake and then limped off in search of shade.

The door opened behind him. Otis Winter proved, if anything, more aged than the dog. He held a wrinkled envelope in his wrinkled hand.

"You Walt Hagel's boy?"

Drew nodded dully. The man turned over the envelope. Drew could feel the thick, papery softness of the considerable currency within.

"Tell your dad I said howdy-do."

Deeply embarrassed that he'd fallen for his father's joke, Drew pedaled away at top speed. It wasn't until he was inside the bank that he realized disaster had struck: The envelope was no longer in his back pocket. His panic gathering, he raced back to his bicycle and retraced his route, scouring every inch of road. But the money was gone. He recalled the envelope's soft thickness. There had to be hundreds of dollars inside. And he'd lost it.

He was in tears by the time he reached the office. Male voices and soft laughter sounded inside. Somehow, he managed to open the door. His father sat behind his desk, facing two strange men, who turned to look at Drew, smiling, because people always smiled when they were in Walt Hagel's company.

"Andrew, what is it?" his father asked.

He walked up to the desk and told him, the words coming out in one breathless torrent. As he spoke, his father's eyes traveled from one man to the other. Drew's story ended, and he started crying again.

"Drew, stop that now. Hey, come on. You know how much money was in there?"

Drew shook his head, dreading the answer.

"Thirty dollars." He turned to one of the men. "The old coot pays me with ones. I haven't raised his rent in twenty years. I just can't bring myself to do it."

The others murmured in wry acknowledgment of the onus that decency places upon honorable men. Drew sniffled, too young to understand that all had been forgiven.

"Tell you what," one of the men said.

He pulled out his wallet and removed a ten, which he slapped on the desk as if he were stubbornly betting against the odds. The second man followed his lead, tossing down two fives. Drew's father completed the transaction. Thirty dollars rested on the desk's polished surface.

"It's only money, Drew," his father said. "Never let losing money get you down. Now go put this in the bank before one of these chiselers changes his mind."

Drew collected the cash and put it in his front pocket, making sure this time to keep his hand on it until he was standing in front of the teller.

The howling stopped, followed by the rumble of the machine being dragged across the front hall. There was more rattling of grilles and terse strategic discussion, and then the ruckus started again. So. Bottom line. He had to get his hands on $250,000, because the moment his file went to Collections and they understood what he'd done his loan would be called in. He figured it would be another week before that happened. And then there would be certified letters and 8:00 P.M. calls and stern raps on the door. Ronnie would find out. It was all so ridiculous. He was a resident of the wealthiest state of the wealthiest nation that had ever existed. He was still young enough to play three sets of tennis; he had a bachelor's degree from an accredited university and owned a business. A quarter million dollars. These days it was nothing. Third-rate Flemish paintings sold for ten times that amount; leading actors received it for two days on the set. A decent relief pitcher pulled down as much for a road trip. There had to be a way. And yet if there was, it remained a mystery to Drew.

Equally bewildering was Quint's role in all of this. How could there be no dividends? How could he have permitted such a loss? Drew understood risk. He'd heard the muttered coda of the television commercials; he'd read the fine print at the bottom of the *New Yorker* ads. But Quint was supposed to be immune from all of that. Otherwise, he would have never paid so much for the banquet table; he wouldn't be subsidizing the Garden. He wasn't some high roller, some pump-and-dump artist. You could trust Quint Manning. He didn't lie; he didn't take shortcuts. And he'd seen the way Quint played tennis, relentless and fastidious, hitting everything toward the center of the court, keeping the ball in play, never risking one down the line unless it was dead certain to go for a winner.

The tennis court. Drew's portal into the secret world of WMV. The simple act of pairing with another man to win games. It had started on an unusually warm Saturday last March, as he was dropping off Shannon so Carrie could take the two kids into Manhattan. Of course, it wasn't the first time Drew had seen the house on Orchard, but his sightings had always been from a distance, where it appeared little more than a series of large, slate gray boxes joined in a seemingly random configuration. Up close, however, it turned out to be a real home, surrounded by toys and noise, shucked clothes and splayed paperbacks. The formidable security gate had opened automatically, almost apologetically, admitting Drew to a broad forecourt where nearly a dozen cars were parked, Audis and Mercedeses and a vintage Porsche. Carrie stood near a corner of the house, listening with languid patience as a gardener pointed to an unruly clot of vine that had begun to overwhelm one of the sheer walls. Drew recognized her from school functions—she was not easily forgotten—though they had never actually met. She came over after noticing his car. Drew cut the engine and got out, much to Shannon's alarm; his daughter was still young enough to think she could deny having parents.

"Jamie's in the basement killing zombies with his brothers," she said to Shannon after Drew introduced himself. "Just follow the sounds of the plasma gun."

They watched her walk into the house as if she owned it.

"That is one great kid," Carrie said.

Drew nodded helplessly, having nothing to say in response. He had yet to meet Jamie.

"Are you rushing off somewhere?" she asked, shading her eyes. "Would you like a Bellini?"

"Isn't he a painter?"

"Wine coolers for the pretentious," she said. "Thisaway."

He accompanied her around the side of the house. His first thought when he saw the backyard was that he knew people lived like this; he just hadn't seen much firsthand evidence of it. The great sweep of perfectly tended lawn, the slate-lined pool covered by a low blue mist, the tennis court with its tidy little hut. Four men played, watched by several others on a hedged patio. There was something strange about the scene that took Drew a moment to figure out. The court had no surrounding fence. Balls littered the lawn all around it, light green interruptions of a perfect field of darker green.

"There's no fence," he said, a little stupidly.

"It would ruin the view."

Carrie's tone was neutral, leaving him to guess if this had been her decision or someone else's. Drew counted eleven men as he approached. His age or younger. Ten white guys and Godeep Mahabal, who was running his flustered-looking opponents ragged with drop shots and topspin lobs, smiling pleasantly at their curses every time a ball spun dead in the clay. The seven men who weren't playing held glasses of peach-colored liquid. One of them detached himself from the group. Quint. Drew recognized him, too. He was a few inches shorter than Drew, with dark hair and intense blue eyes. His black tennis shirt bore the logo of a conference in which the term *Strategic* figured prominently.

"This is Drew, the wonderful Shannon's father," Carrie announced.

"She's a lovely girl," Quint said, his expression somehow warmer for the absence of a smile.

They made small talk for a while, leading to the inevitable question.

"So what is it you do, Drew?"

"I'm in real estate. I have a brokerage here in town. Hagel & Son? I'm the son."

"Oh, right. I've seen the signs."

"Ask him," one of the men called in a hard British accent, the sort that suggested gray terraced streets and soccer stadium thuggery. "He looks likely."

Quint turned slightly, entertaining the notion, his eyes still on Drew.

"Do you play? Our twelfth guy is a no-show."

"Douche bag's a permanent no-show," someone else muttered.

Although it had been years since Drew played an actual set of tennis, there had been periods before that when he had done little else. At Totten High, he'd won the county championship his senior year and made it to the quarters in the States, beaten by a guy who later went on to push Vitas Gerulaitis to five sets. At UConn he'd never made it past number three singles, but he had still played for a good two hours every day, after classes and often when he should have been attending them.

"Not in these clothes," he said, gesturing to his paint-splattered jeans and his Pep Boys T-shirt.

"We got stuff," Quint said, looking at his wife.

"The question is, do you have the *heart*?" Carrie said with a weary smile.

"Yeah, sure. I got game."

Carrie took charge of his transformation. She led him into the hut and stopped in front of a large chest of drawers. Next to it was a closet stuffed with old rackets and dozens of tennis ball canisters. The walls were covered with photos of the Manning family at play.

"So what are you, about a thirty-four?" Carrie asked as she rooted through a drawer large enough to hold an average corpse.

"During the Reagan administration," Drew said. "The first one."

She smiled but didn't look up.

"I'm afraid you've stumbled into the valley of the flat abs," she said. "Hold on."

She'd found a surfer's bathing suit, navy blue with yellow whorled designs on the side. She held it up, an antic smile on her face.

"Works for me," Drew said.

"You want a shirt?"

He plucked at Moe, the central Pep Boy.

"What's wrong with this?"

"*I* think it's perfect."

There was a locker room where he could change. To get to it, he had to pass through a galley kitchen where the gilded necks of champagne bottles emerged from an ice-filled sink. After dressing Drew chose a racket, took a deep breath, and stepped outside. The men shot quick glances at his costume. A short, angry-looking guy, panting and sweating from the court, pointed at Drew's T-shirt.

"Hey, I capitalized those assholes," he said.

Quint introduced Drew around. The others were all polite enough, but also reserved, as if they were conscious of a downside of being friendly with a stranger. It turned out that this was a regular event and Quint's usual partner had just this morning made it clear that he would no longer be playing. There was considerable dark commentary about him. The man had broken some code that forbade business from spilling over into playtime. So Drew was teamed with Quint. They were in the next match.

Drew soon determined that all the players were late arrivals to the game, expensively taught and ferociously competitive, but lacking that inner knowledge that could be gained only while young. In his prime he would have mopped up, but twenty-five pounds of flab proved a good leveler. They lost the first three games largely on Drew's errors, scraped by in the fourth, lost the fifth, and then won the last five games to take the set when Drew finally found his touch. At some point Shannon appeared with a boy whose looks strongly favored Quint, though they were softened somewhat by his mother's beauty. The legendary Jamie. Drew was briefly aware of his daughter's mortified expression as she watched him scramble around the court in his oversize trunks, though he was too wrapped up in his match to pay her much attention. When it was over, Drew collapsed in a shaded chair, drenched in sweat, his muscles cramping. Carrie looked at him from the table where she'd been watching her husband play. She was wearing a big straw hat and sunglasses. She could have been an advertisement for, well, anything.

"Would you like to try a Bellini *now*?"

"Maybe I should have a few gallons of water first."

She brought him a big bottle of Évian and the drink, which turned out to be champagne and peach juice. After launching a general farewell—Drew got the feeling she wasn't especially enamored of her husband's crew—Carrie went off to take the kids into the city. As he waited for his next turn on the court, he tried to follow the fast and furious conversation. Though he understood little, he nevertheless felt strangely elated to be here. An hour later he was on the court again, making fewer mistakes this time out, the old skills returning. They won their second match six-two.

"You want to do this on a regular basis?" Quint asked him as the men gathered for a last drink before heading off for lunch. "See how long we can stay undefeated?"

Over the next few months Drew powered up Orchard's narrow arterial turns every Saturday morning. After daylight savings they played on Wednesday evenings as well. Most of the time he partnered with Quint. Carrie appeared infrequently. The refreshments were usually handled by a Haitian maid who ignored the tennis with Olympian disdain. On the few occasions they were short a player, Jamie would join them, teaming with his father. Drew detected some real talent in his strokes, though he had a tendency to choke, perhaps because Quint, usually a model of on-court graciousness, was extremely hard on the boy. He rode him after every error in a quiet, insistent voice that would have driven Drew to homicide if his own father had used it on him. Jamie would become surly and dejected; they'd lose matches they should have won easily.

Most of the time Quint teamed with Drew. They became unbeatable. Drew would take up a position at the net, usually on the left side, his bulk and reach forcing the opponents to play everything deep, while Quint's metronomic, unflappable forehand sent back shots that landed just inside the baseline. Finally, inevitably, their opponents would make an error, and Drew would pounce, volleying the ball into the unprotected expanses of the Mannings' lawn. Even though their tactics soon became obvious, there was nothing the other players could do.

"That," Quint said when this was pointed out over postmatch

beers, "is the perfect strategy. Utterly transparent but still unstoppable. So strong that you don't even have to hide it."

This was something Drew had missed since things had gone bad with Anne. A feeling of camaraderie with other men. Ronnie was wonderful, a godsend, but there wasn't a lot of male fun on offer with her; certainly not the sort of good times to be had at Quint's court. Drew hadn't known how much he'd missed this, just hanging out, filling a few hours with hard games and lazy banter. There was one recurring moment that he prized above all others, when he would huddle with Quint at a pivotal time in a game to decide how they would play the upcoming point. Drew would stand with his back to the net, a wall to their opponents, and Quint would lean forward slightly, averting his head, his voice low as they'd decide how to play the next point. And then their eyes would hold, sealing the deal before they took up their positions.

Off the court, however, Drew continued to feel like an outsider. He smiled knowledgeably but contributed nothing to the big, cagey talk. Occasional newcomers would ask him what he did and then nod neutrally after his answer before moving on to the next topic. He soon began to inflate his notional worth, using phrases like *holdings* and *limited partnerships* instead of *two-fam* and *Fannie Mae*. And still he had no idea what these men were talking about. Like spies or gangsters, they had a knack for omitting key nouns from their sentences. What he did understand was that the markets they spoke about had nothing to do with the Dow or the NASDAQ. The word *derivative* was often used. And there were others. *Directional. Convergence.* And his favorite: *stochastic*, a word he didn't understand even after looking it up in two separate dictionaries. One thing he did understand was that Quint was the calm center of it all. Even if he didn't say anything, his response—a guarded smile, a skeptical slant of his head— was duly noted and often conclusive. Although Drew typed his name into numerous search engines, all he could discover was that his publicity-shy hedge fund was rumored to provide astronomical returns. He stumbled on the 44 percent figure in a posting on some newsletter's bulletin board, hearing it confirmed courtside a few times after that.

It was early May before he got up the nerve to make a direct approach. They were having a postmatch drink and talking about the area's skyrocketing property values, Quint speculating that Drew must be doing very well.

"Well, I don't run it up the flagpole, but it's been quite a year," Drew lied. "In fact, I've got some extra cash floating around I need to park somewhere."

"Extra cash," Quint said, grimacing agreeably. "Man, do we hate extra cash."

"That's what I was going to talk to you about."

Quint looked at Drew. There was no turning back now.

"I was wondering, you know," Drew continued, "if I might be able to take up a position at WMV."

His question cast Quint into silence, and Drew was briefly terrified that he'd violated an unspoken code, that his days as a doubles partner were over. But just then there was a yelp up by the house, his daughter's delighted voice as she grappled with Jamie on a deck chair near the sliding glass door. After a moment the young couple began to kiss, though Shannon cut it off when she realized they were being watched. Drew turned back to Quint and saw that he'd seen them as well.

"Let me see what I have," he said.

The call came a few weeks later. By the middle of June he was invested. After that, Drew thought he could detect a subtle change in the attitude of the tennis crew toward him. Silences would no longer descend when he came out of the hut. Arcane references were explained to him more often; there were questions directed at him about area property. Drew and Ronnie were invited to dinner parties on Orchard and to Carrie's big fund-raiser at Totten Arts. There had even been talk of going down to their place in Aruba over the Christmas break, though Ronnie's discovery of her pregnancy made travel impossible. It was just as well, since a few weeks before Christmas Shannon had shocked everyone by breaking up with Jamie. The invitations from the Mannings dried up for a while, a spell of silence that had ended with the banquet invitation. And Quint had mentioned that tennis would be starting up again soon. Drew was beginning to think he would once more be able to experience the courtside talk and the allowable midday booze, those moments when he'd come off the clay after a victory to collapse into a chair and think that this was the sort of place a man should be.

But this had all vanished at Capital Park on Monday. It was as if the past year had never happened. The tennis and the parties and the banquet. It couldn't be right. There had to be a remedy. As he thought about it now, he could see that it was his fault, a simple miscommunication stemming from his numb silence in the office. He had been wrong to stumble away without drawing on the reserve of good feeling created during all those victorious matches. He should have put it on the level of friendship. After all, Quint had no reason to know that he wasn't like the others, unable to let his money ride for another year.

The house had grown silent. Drew levered himself from the chair and went downstairs. The men were in the front hall, retracting the behemoth's snout. Its articulated body smoked and gargled.

"You're good to go," one of them said, handing Drew an invoice.

He wrote them a check, further depleting his account. As he watched the van pull away, Drew understood what he had to do. He would go back to Quint and tell him the truth. It was that simple. He'd tell him what he'd been too shocked to say on Monday: He could not afford to skip a dividend. Once this was understood, they could devise some sort of advance on the money Quint had assured him would be coming next year. Just enough to tide him over. These sorts of unorthodox arrangements were hatched all the time. And he wouldn't go to the office. That would make it too formal. Instead, he'd drive up Orchard tomorrow morning. They could work something out, maybe even hit a few balls afterward, now that the weather was turning nice.

10

Ian wasn't in his usual place. Normally, they met in the alley behind Earth's Bounty, but when she pulled in, there was no one around. After waiting a few minutes she got out and tried the steel door. It was locked, so she walked around front, confused now, because there was no way he could have forgotten she was meeting him. An underlying odor of yeasty decay greeted her as she entered the supermarket. She made her way past banks of gleaming, perfectly stacked fruit, stopping at the end of a canyon of California wine. What she saw confused her even more. Ian was still behind the deli counter. But he never worked overtime. And there was something else. While he usually moved slowly, doing the bare minimum to get through his shift, he was now working with feverish absorption, loading and weighing the plastic tubs with elaborate care, operating the slicing machine with almost comic speed.

Shannon approached the counter. His eyes were strange, as if they were focused on a point far beyond what he was doing. It took her a moment to get his attention. He seemed confused to see her, as if he'd forgotten they were meeting. But that was impossible. She shot him an inquisitive smile, and this finally snapped him out of his work trance. He smiled sweetly and began to untie his apron, telling the woman working with him that he was leaving. Shannon went back through the front entrance while he clocked out. He was waiting for her in the car, a silver foil tray at his feet.

"So what was that all about?" she asked after a long kiss. "You looked like some kind of crazed deli robot."

"Lost track of time," he said.

He remained loaded with energy on the way home, bouncing around the front seat like a cricket in a jar, unable to keep his hands off her. At the house he could hardly wait to get her into the bedroom. She had to slow him down a bit at first, but before long it was what she'd been daydreaming about ever since he'd told her his uncle was going away for the weekend. When they were done, she wanted to lie with him for a while, touching and talking, but he was immediately on his feet, snatching a pad from the general chaos on his desk. He selected a pencil and whittled it down with the Browning knife she'd bought him as a surprise a few weeks earlier. It cost fifty dollars and had a blade so sharp that it frightened Shannon just to hold it. But Ian handled it with an almost reckless confidence, soon dusting his naked thigh with wafer-thin shavings. When he was ready, he spun his desk chair and perched naked on it, staring at her body.

"What are you doing?" she asked in alarm.

He began to pass the pencil over the paper, not touching it, just making shadows of the lines he intended to draw.

"Ian . . ."

She reached for the covers, but they had all been swept to the floor, so she raised her hand, like someone trying to block a camera's lens.

"You're just so beautiful."

"I'm not. I'm fat and ugly."

His hand stopped moving.

"Shannon, do you know how much I want you all the time? Let me draw you. Please."

She let her hand fall, surprised to find herself wanting this.

"You're not going to show it to anyone, right?"

"Who am I going to show?"

He worked faster than usual, his eyes traveling over her body, his hand moving smoothly over the page. She wanted to speak, but everything that came to her mind felt wrong. So she focused on his eyes as they passed rapidly over her. After a while she could just about feel his gaze on her skin, light but tangible, like a soft breeze. When he finished, he pulled back his head to examine what he'd done, his expression critical but also satisfied.

"Let me see."

He tore the paper loose and offered it to her without hesitation. It was amazing. He'd never drawn so well. It looked exactly like her, the body she'd spent so many hours viewing unhappily in mirrors, the long face and wild mop of hair. There was no attempt to prettify her, to make her thighs thinner or her nipples smaller; he'd even included that small mole on her hip. It was completely honest. And in that honesty there was desire.

"Come here."

She draped them in the blanket. Ian reached up to put on some music, the university station, and they listened without talking, letting their thoughts run. This was what she'd been dreaming about all week. Being totally alone. Finally, he stretched and said he was going to warm up the spinach lasagna he'd "liberated" from Earth's Bounty.

"Wait, you *stole* it?"

"Property is theft," he said as he got out of bed. "Pasta for the people."

She laughed quietly, though she didn't like the idea of his getting caught. She went to take a shower. There was a moldering towel stuffed in the rack, the one his uncle used. It reminded her how glad she was that he was away. Monday's dinner had been an ordeal. They'd gone out for pizza, and David had made a point of paying from a wad of cash held together by a gold-plated clip, as if he were some high roller and not a limo driver living off his sister's insurance money. He mostly talked about himself, drawling tales of his wild days in Florida. Shannon parried his questions about her family and her plans for the future, careful not to give him anything that might connect her to Ronnie. It wasn't until the end of the meal, when Ian went to the bathroom, that David got to the point.

"So you understand about Ian, right?" His voice was suddenly stern. "You know he's had some trouble in the past?"

"I do," Shannon said. "It's not a problem."

His eyes were locked on hers.

"The important thing is that he steers clear of bad influences. There's been a lot of that in his life. Those retards from Gryphon Games." He managed a cool smile. "Not that you're one. A bad influence, I mean. I can tell that right away."

"I'm not sure . . . wait, what are we talking about?"

"We're talking about looking out for Ian's best interests."

Shannon understood. The topic was North Carolina. He was sounding her out to see if she was against the move. Although a dozen sharp answers shot through her mind, she decided to play dumb. David looked like the kind of guy who liked women that way.

"Well, yeah, we all want what's best for Ian."

"My point," he continued, crumbling a section of burned crust into charcoal powder, "is that even though Ian might be about to turn eighteen, he still has a lot of growing up to do."

Not with you, Shannon thought as she nodded.

"So what did you think?" Ian asked when they spoke on the phone later that night.

"I think the money you're giving him is going to be well spent," Shannon said.

She stepped dripping from the shower and opened the closet's cheap louvered doors to find a towel. Something caught her eye: a neatly folded terry-cloth robe, pink with floral trim. His mother's. Shannon put it on; she could have fit another complete person inside it. But it smelled good and was as soft as a young animal. She tied the belt and went into the kitchen. Ian waited for her at the table. He'd lit some candles. The lasagna was on the table, steaming and bubbling from the microwave, reminding her of how hungry she was. After a few mouthfuls she became aware of his stare. He was smiling, something on his mind.

"What?"

"Shan, listen . . . about this college thing. I was thinking. You should live here instead of a dorm."

Whoa, Shannon thought. Where did *that* come from? She hadn't said anything about moving in together. But he was off before she could answer, his gaze locked on a flickering candle. His eyes had that same looking-beyond quality she'd seen at Earth's Bounty. It was hard to tell if the light in them was reflected from the flames or coming from somewhere within his brain.

"It would be great. We'd be completely free. Just the two of us."

"Ian, this isn't exactly what I had in—"

He didn't hear her. His headlong talking continued.

"You could go to classes and I could work during the day and then people could hang here at night. But we'd be in charge, and so if we wanted to be alone, all we'd have to do is tell people to give us some—"

"Ian. Whoa."

She'd spoken a little louder than intended, but she had to do something to stop the flow of his speech. He finally took his eyes off that flame.

"I . . . let's just take this one step at a time, all right? I mean, it's going to be a big deal for me changing schools as it is. I don't want to give my dad a heart attack."

"But I thought it didn't matter what your father thinks."

"It does if I want someone to pay my tuition."

"But *I* can do that."

"Ian, come on, I don't want you spending your money on that."

He was genuinely confused, as if Shannon were the one who wasn't making any sense here, as if she were the one whose mind was racing around like a kite that had slipped from its owner's grasp.

"We'll still be together practically every night," she said. "It's just . . . I think we should just take this a bit slower."

He continued to look at her in confusion.

"I'm not saying it isn't going to happen, all right? It's just better for now if I get a room. Just to keep people off our back. All right? Ian?"

"You're right," he said, finally relenting. "I just want us to be together."

"Me, too. Don't ever think I don't."

They lapsed into an uneasy silence. Shannon felt bad about shooting him down, though she was a little bit angry with him for racing ahead of her like that, forcing her to make another important decision so soon after her first one, and then retracting his plan at the first sign of opposition, as if he hadn't been serious in the first place.

"You mad at me?" he asked.

"Of course not," she said, letting it go, not wanting to spoil their weekend.

They said little for the rest of the meal. Just as Shannon finished, her cell phone rang, chirping from her bag on the Formica counter.

"Let it go," he said.

She was about to agree, then remembered Ronnie. She couldn't let her father face some endless waiting room torture session on his own. At first, it was hard to tell who it was. There was an oceanic swell of noise, punctuated by the rhythmic thud of a background bass. And then a vaguely familiar voice spoke her name. Madison McNabb. This was not good. Shannon had told her father she would be sleeping over at the McNabbs' after the big party. She hadn't bothered to square this with Madison, since that would mean actually talking to Madison.

"Why are you calling?" Shannon asked. "Has my father been trying to get hold of me?"

"Your father? It's *Jamie*. He's *losing* it. He's puking all over my party and he broke a"—her voice briefly faded—"and my mom says he'd better get his ass out of here but there is no way he can drive and so we called his house but"—another fade—"he wants you to come pick him up—and where *are* you, anyway?"

Shannon did not want to do this. But she also understood the trouble Jamie would get into if his parents had to fetch him drunk. He'd lose his car for the summer. He'd be grounded. No tennis camp or trips to Block Island with his posse. Quint wouldn't mess around about something like this.

"All right," Shannon said. "I'll be right over."

She explained the situation to Ian.

"You don't have to come," she said. "It'll take a half hour."

"You might need some help. Besides, I'd like to meet the famous Jamie."

Shannon hesitated, thinking this might not be a good idea. She'd managed to keep Ian away from the rest of her life so far. But they'd already had one disagreement tonight, and she didn't want more friction. And it wouldn't matter if Jamie found out about Ian. She could keep Jamie quiet.

The McNabb house was a simple ten-minute drive away, down Totten Pike, then left on Shaker Road. It was set back several hundred feet, at the end of a twisting driveway lit by hooded carriage lamps. The familiar cars of her classmates spilled out onto the street. Shannon would never get a place up close. She drove up to the house, anyway, figuring it wouldn't take long to extract Jamie. The cars lining the driveway were parked carefully. That was one good thing about her classmates. They certainly were civilized, even when they were being wild.

And then reflectors were blazing directly in front of her. She had to hit the brakes hard to avoid smacking into the car. It was Jamie's Wrangler, parked right in the middle of the driveway. Cars flanked it tightly on either side, meaning that he had completely choked off the escape for the vehicles lining the circular drive in front of the house. Beyond it, the McNabbs' massive mock Tudor was alive with light. A steady mechanical beat emerged from deep within.

"Nice car," Ian said.

"It's Jamie's. Look, Ian, it's probably better if no one knows you're here, all right?"

He nodded distantly, his eyes still on the Wrangler. When she opened the McNabbs' front door, there was a gust of noise and odor, something sweet, like burned sugar. Madison's mother was some sort of interior designer, and every inch of the house was crammed with art and furniture. Mr. McNabb was long gone, having moved out to L.A., where he was a lawyer for sitcoms now instead of soaps. He was the one who had helped Madison get *Soul 2 Seoul* on MTV.

A small group of juniors slouched in the front room, sipping at Nalgene bottles. None knew Jamie's whereabouts. Shannon walked toward the back of the house, sidestepping a fat Lab that sniffed listlessly at her crotch. The music was coming from a big dark den crammed with kids. Some of them were dancing, though most simply swayed as they shouted at each other over the music. Jacob Hsu noticed her. She beckoned him into the hallway.

"Do you know where Jamie is?"

Jacob gave his head a wistful shake.

"Jamie's out of control."

"Okay, but where is he?"

Jacob shrugged. She went through to the kitchen. There were several big aluminum tubs filled with melting ice and soft drinks on the floor; the table was covered by plundered trays of snacks. She threw open the sliding glass door and was almost bowled over by a boy stumbling blindly toward her. Matt Petrillo, looking as if he'd just witnessed some unspeakable event. His face was clenched in agony. Tears and snot covered his cheeks and chin; primal noise gurgled at the back of his throat. Stephen Dulea followed closely behind him with a Hi8, filming Petrillo as he staggered across the kitchen and dunked his head into one of the tubs.

Three other boys were laughing on the deck. Jamie's crew. One of them dabbed at his swollen eyes with a fat wad of paper towel. Another held up a small metal canister as if he were going to squirt it at Shannon. Pepper spray. She didn't flinch.

"Have you guys seen Jamie?"

"Jamie's wasted."

"Thank you. Now do you know where he is?"

They didn't answer, turning their attention back to Petrillo as he stumbled out the door, water streaming from his short black hair. He was pointing at one of the other boys. Next. Shannon walked to the edge of the deck. Light from the house illuminated the kids gathered on the high jump mat Madison's father had bought after her younger brother took up the sport. He'd recently quit to play Ultimate Frisbee, and now they had this foamy monstrosity in their yard. Shannon didn't see Jamie. She went back into the house, trying to remember the layout from when she and Madison had been friends. There was a small study off the kitchen, the sort of space where a wanton guest might be dumped. The door was half open, and so she pushed it open. Inside, Diane McNabb sat on a small sofa with Jesse Schoenbrum. Her tan legs were folded beneath her skirt, her varicose veins a color similar to the Vedic ankle tattoo they ran into, like little twisting blue feeder streams. Her arm was propped on the back of the sofa, allowing her fingers to play through her frosted hair. Jesse, the poet, had a wounded, confessional look in his eyes. There were rumors that Diane had been sleeping with one of her son's college friends. Whenever Shannon missed having her own mother around, she thought about Madison and felt momentarily better.

"You've come for Jamie," she announced when she saw Shannon, her orthodonture glinting in the room's harsh light. "We tried to call his house, but there was no answer. My idea was to call the Mahabals, but Jamie demanded you. You have to understand, he can't stay here in the condition he's in. There's been breakage."

Jesse, who was just the sort of idiot an older woman would hit on, nodded in stern agreement. Shannon was tempted to tell her that *she* hadn't brought Jamie here; that *she* wasn't the adult letting kids get wasted while she seduced someone who was by definition young enough to be her son. And then, of course, there was the fact that Jesse was about two years away from figuring out he was gay, although a roll in the sack with Diane would move that date up considerably.

"So where is he?" she asked instead.

"Upstairs in the guest room. Madison's up there. She'll show you."

It was hard to get past the people sitting on the stairs. Why do people always sit on stairs at parties, Shannon wondered, but never anytime else? There must have been two dozen empty chairs in the house, but here they were, like so much folded laundry. They stopped talking to watch her pass, making as little space as possible. Madison was perched on the California king in her room, among her famous stuffed animal collection. Other girls were spread out among the animals. Her entourage. It had been two months since the ten-minute video diary of her unsuccessful trip to find her birth mother in Korea had aired, but she was clearly still riding high on the wave of adulation.

"At last," she said when she saw Shannon, flinging aside the unicorn she clutched to her stomach. "He's *ruining* my party. This is just to get revenge on me for winning the Carswell."

"But where's Jazz? Why didn't you call him?"

"He's at his brother's birthday. Besides, I figured you wouldn't be busy."

There were snickers. Shannon refused to rise to the provocation. The guest room was at the end of the hall. Madison led her as far as the door, talking over her shoulder.

"My mother says she's liable if she gets caught with a drunk kid in the house. *And* he broke a Kampuchean urn."

"Half the kids here are drunk, Madison. The ones who aren't stoned, I mean."

"Not like *this*," she said, flinging open the door.

Shannon turned on the light. Jamie lay perfectly still on the bedspread, one arm across his chest, the other dangling off the edge of the mattress. Someone had stuffed monogrammed hand towels beneath his head, like packaging for a fragile shipment. Air moved wetly through his slack mouth. Shannon crossed the room. There was a trail of something clear and crusty running across his cheek. A vague bilious odor emanated from his body. She wondered how they expected her to get him down the steps. There was no way she could summon Ian, and she doubted the wrestlers would be much help. They'd probably just want to light his shoes on fire and film it.

"Could someone turn off the lights?" Jamie said without opening his eyes.

"Jamie, it's me."

With great effort, he managed to crack open one eye. And then he seemed to fall back asleep. This was how Jamie got.

"Jamie?"

"Present."

"Get up."

He raised himself onto his elbows.

"Tell me if you're going to puke."

"Already puked," he said affably.

She helped him to his feet and walked him down the hall, feeling like a prison guard in one of those death penalty movies. The chatter in Madison's room stopped as they passed, then resumed with a new charge of censure. The prospect of projectile vomit made the people on the steps more amenable to making way.

"Wasted," someone said.

Jamie raised a hand in regal acknowledgment. Shannon got him through the front door, then released him with an angry little shove. He followed some drunken radar to his Wrangler, propping a forearm on one of its thick protective bars, then placing his head on his arm. His eyes were closed; he looked woozy.

Shannon joined Ian, who was leaning against her car, watching the drunk boy.

"So what's the plan?" he asked.

"We take him home and pour him on his front porch. Ring the doorbell and run."

"What about his car?"

"He can pick it up tomorrow. His dad can buy him a new one."

"I thought the idea was that his parents didn't find out he was drunk. Besides, if we leave the Jeep here, no one can get out."

As usual, Ian was right.

"I'll just leave his keys in it," she said. "People will figure out what to do."

"Come on. You can't leave keys in a car like this."

"Nobody's going to *steal* it, Ian."

He shot her a skeptical look. It was one of those exchanges that reminded her what different worlds they came from.

"Look, let me dump it on the street," he said. "He can get it tomorrow."

"Can you even drive a stick?"

"Shan, my uncle taught me to drive in his Chevelle."

She figured there wouldn't be any harm in this.

"Yeah, all right. Stay here and let me get the keys."

As she approached the Wrangler, she saw that someone had emerged from the house. Jacob Hsu. Shannon turned back to warn Ian, but he had already stepped back into the trees. Before she could reach the Wrangler, she saw that Jamie was pulling his keys out of his pocket.

"Jamie, what are you doing?"

"Not leaving my car here tonight."

Clearly, no amount of Heineken could obliterate his instinct for self-preservation. He finally worked the keys free.

"Jamie, come on. Hand over the keys."

He smiled in amiable defiance, holding them above his head. Jacob was approaching.

"You guys need some help?" he asked. "Shannon?"

"Jacob, my man," Jamie said before she could answer, his keys still dangling above them. "Let me ask you something. Do you and your robots ever, you know, get jiggy widdit. I mean, you bundle a little wetware into those suckers?"

"*God*," Jacob said.

"Jacob, I'm sorry," Shannon said. "He's just drunk."

"You wonder why people are sick of you and then . . ."

Jacob shook his head, unable to summon the appropriate grammar of indignation. He turned and walked quickly away down the driveway.

"That's great, Jamie. You're well on the way to becoming a total jerk. All you have to do is register Republican and the package is complete."

"I was just messing with him."

"You just mess with everyone. Now are you going to give me the keys?"

"Gotta get the car home."

Shannon saw that this could go on all night.

"All right, look. If I get someone to bring your car, will you let me drive you home?"

"Who?"

"Stephen or Matt. They still seem relatively sober."

"Cool."

Shannon stepped forward, grabbed Jamie's shirt, and pulled him none too gently back to her car. He smiled stupidly and let himself be led. She opened the door and guided him inside, letting his head fall back against the seat. His eyes closed again in that heavy-lidded way of drunk people. He was being taken care of. This was why he'd insisted they call Shannon. She knew how to keep him out of trouble.

"Keys. Jamie?"

He held them out for her to snatch. Shannon looked back at the house, regretting her promise now. Finding someone sober enough to drive the car would completely ruin an already compromised night. Whoever drove up to Orchard would need a ride back here. Which meant she'd have to leave Ian standing in the woods so the driver wouldn't see him.

She decided on a different plan. Ian would move Jamie's car to the street, and the three of them could ride up to Orchard together. If Jamie woke up and saw Ian, then so be it; she'd blackmail him to secrecy. And then, in the morning, she'd drive over to Orchard early and bring Jamie back to pick up the Wrangler. If his parents saw what was going on, she'd tell them that it had been her idea to leave the car behind when they'd gone on to another party. They'd have their doubts, but they would also have to trust her. Carrie liked her too much and Quint was too polite to accuse her of lying. Provided she could get him in the front door undetected, Jamie would be all right.

She walked over to Ian.

"All right," she said, tossing him the keys. "Dump it at the end of the driveway."

He looked at the Wrangler, his eyes widening a little.

"Excellent."

Jamie dozed in her car, leaning against the door, smiling contentedly. She poked his shoulder. He didn't move. She poked him again, harder. This was good. He wouldn't know they'd left the Wrangler. Backing up the length of the driveway wasn't easy, especially with the Jeep's taillights shining in her face. But she made it without dinging any cars, pulling clear across Shaker to wait for Ian to emerge. He was wavering slightly as he reached the edge of the driveway, moving a little too fast for her liking, though he pulled next to her without difficulty. He was smiling broadly. His eyes once again seemed to be looking straight through the world. The Wrangler's mighty engine gunned in that familiar high rpm whine and there was a grinding of gears and then it leaped ahead of her like a particle in a subatomic reaction. She watched in confusion as Ian passed several perfectly good parking spaces. And then she understood. He was going to drive all the way up to Orchard. Shannon raced after him, catching up just as he reached Totten Pike. She thought about passing him, trying to corral him and get him to go back, but he had already turned onto the main road. She followed, uncertain what to do. If he was pulled over, it would be up to her to explain that he was only helping out a guy who was too drunk to drive. At least she had the evidence snoring right beside her. She checked the speedometer. He was keeping it at forty. Maybe she was just being paranoid. No one was going to bother them as long as they kept it slow and easy.

She looked over at Jamie, cocooned in the silky knowledge that somebody was looking out for him. He seemed as pathetically helpless as a baby, an impression reinforced by the slightly rancid odor coming off him. It was hard to believe she'd ever thought he was strong. Before she got to know him, she considered him a rich, pleasant, unimaginative boy who didn't have to worry about being popular or getting into a good college. But then, last winter, they were paired in Giving Back, the school's community service program, and Shannon discovered that Jamie Manning was very different from what she'd expected. They were assigned to spend Monday afternoons with a shut-in widower named Sebastian Rickey. Although Shannon feared she would have to do all the work, Jamie turned out to be wonderful with the old man, happy to listen to his vague memories of playing minor-league baseball, reading to him from a moldy collection of *Reader's Digest*s. Rickey would invariably fall asleep before the end of each story, leaving Jamie and Shannon to talk. His sensitivity and his sense of humor surprised her. She remembered one conversation in particular. Jamie had been reading a story about human cannibalism after an Andean plane crash. Rickey had dozed off just as the flesh was being consumed, his cracked lips parted in a grimace, his withered chest snatching at oxygen.

"Do you want me to keep going?" Jamie asked, holding up the book.

"Isn't it kind of obvious what happens?"

"Would you do it?" he asked after a long silence.

"Do what?"

"Eat somebody if you were starving to death."

"God, no." She looked at his pensive face. "Why, would *you*?"

"Only if it was someone in my family or a really close friend. Or a girl I loved."

Shannon started to laugh but then realized he wasn't kidding.

"You're serious?"

"Well, if you ate a stranger, it would be like you were, I don't know, violating them or something. But if it was my parents who were dead, I'd know they'd want me to survive. I mean, I'd definitely want them to eat my flesh instead of letting it just rot."

Shannon stared at him in utter astonishment and wondered how the sweetest, most sensible thing she'd ever heard a boy say could also be among the most disgusting. She soon decided that Jamie's bland self-confidence was just as much an act as Jesse Schoenbrum's rebelliousness. He told her that he didn't really want to work on Wall Street or go to med school; he admitted that his high class rank and captaincy of the squash team meant little to him. He didn't know what he wanted to do when he got older; he just didn't want it to involve all this *pressure*.

They began to meet away from Rickey's house, cutting study hall to go to Starbucks, doing homework together in his room. Soon they were together. Their classmates were shocked, but Shannon believed that Jamie was ready to leave behind the Springsteen poster and drinking buddies and, most of all, his father's control. She lost her virginity to him on an April afternoon when they were the only ones in his house, Jamie terrified the whole time that he was hurting he They soon got better at the lovemaking, though he remained gent than she'd have thought a boy could be.

As they grew closer, Shannon began to understand the stren Quint's hold over his son. She pressed Jamie about standing u father. He always agreed, and for a while she thought he mean that summer's planned mutinies—his refusal to attend te and an intensive weeklong SAT workshop—were aband long talks with Quint. Afterward he would disappear w friends. That was what finally finished them. The drin ginning of their senior year he was getting drunk n ten. He would drag her to parties, then leave her he attacked the keg. If she confronted him about it, he'd accuse her of nagging. She got tired of sneaking him up to his room so his parents wouldn't know he'd just downed ten beers. He stopped confiding in her, aware that she would only give him advice he didn't have the strength to follow. Worst of all, the tenderness began to fade from their lovemaking. He was too abrupt at the beginning and eager to slip her embrace once they were finished. Shannon knew that she had been wrong. She could never change Jamie.

He seemed genuinely confused when she broke it off. He really wanted to stay her boyfriend. But she knew she was doing the right thing, just as she'd known when she stopped taking the psychiatrist's pills. And so she held her ground, no matter how much he promised to break from Quint's influence. Though it didn't take long for him to let her go. That was the thing about Jamie. He would never grasp. He didn't know how. If that was what she wanted, then there was nothing he could do about it. It was just a shame, though, because he really liked her.

understood that she'd lost touch with the Wrangler just as
ched the arterial bends at the bottom of Orchard. After a
tutter it had just vanished. It took her a moment to un-
happening: Ian had dropped the car into a lower
advantage of all that power, those four wheels
often did the same thing. She knew better
road narrowed as she climbed; familiar
the bends a bit too fast, causing Jamie
to rest on her shoulder. It took her

gler at the top of the hill.
ing for her to pass so he
a little beep and then
didn't pull right out.
he headlights shimmer.

The security gate swung open automatically at her approach. There was a car she didn't recognize parked in front, although this was not unusual; the Mannings' forecourt was always full of strange cars. Ian pulled in behind her, slotting the Wrangler into one of the sheltered spaces.

It took her a few stiff prods to rouse Jamie. She frog-marched him to the front door. The light came on, but it was only the alarm system. She remembered his keys and went back to get them, leaving Jamie swaying on the porch. Ian had moved from the Wrangler to the passenger seat of her car. The intruder light didn't reach his face; it was hidden in shadow.

"Keys," she said through her open window.

There was a brief pause before he handed them to her.

"Ian?"

He turned them over. Shannon hurried back to Jamie, still swaying contentedly, his eyes shut against the rude light. She opened the door and stepped into the front hall. The house was quiet.

"All clear," she whispered. "Go right up to bed."

Jamie saluted. She dropped the keys in his shirt pocket and then propelled him with a gentle shove, shutting the door as quietly as possible behind him. It was still unlocked, but there was nothing she could do about that. If he got home-invaded, it wasn't her fault. She'd done enough for him for one lifetime.

Eager to get them back to Ian's house, she walked quickly back to her car.

"So I thought you were just going to park it on Shaker," she said as she gently pulled the door shut.

Ian didn't answer. Shannon decided to let it go, taking his silence as an apology for driving the Jeep all the way back. They still had the rest of the night and a good part of tomorrow to be alone; there was no reason to spoil things with a fight. She reached to turn the key in the ignition, but his voice stopped her.

"Shan, wait." It sounded as if he were speaking from very far away. "You saw that guy, right?"

She looked across the car. She couldn't see his eyes in the shadow.

"What guy?"

He gave a hollow, nervous laugh. His voice still seemed very far away.

"Back on the hill. That guy on the bike. He just came out of nowhere. Right in front of me. I swerved but . . ."

He didn't finish the thought. Shannon tried to remember seeing someone back on the turns, but there was only empty road and darkness.

"You saw him, though," Ian said. "I mean, he was okay, right?"

11 It would be only Jon tonight. Don White had left a message that morning; his brother had suffered a stroke, and he would be flying to Tempe on the next flight. Myra Carter-Scheine had sent her regrets yesterday, explaining that a dinner obligation she thought she could change was proving intractable. Carrie phoned Jon, offering to reschedule. But he was still eager to do it. She knew this wasn't a particularly good idea, given what she'd recently been thinking about him. But a spell of resentment accompanied the thought. Why shouldn't she be able to see a friend? She'd agreed in the end, reminding him to bring *Cat People*. They could have dinner together, since Carrie's family would be abandoning her. The boys would be out all night; Dillon and Nick were going to the Mahabals' directly after school for Aninder's birthday sleepover, while Jamie would be crashing with Steve or Matt after the big party at the McNabbs'. And Quint was staying in New York for the night, then returning first thing Saturday for a tennis meeting at the house with lawyers representing some of his larger investors. It was either Jon or eating alone. Not exactly a difficult choice.

In the afternoon she drove into town to get something to cook. Being male, Jon would expect actual food. She bought some fresh grouper at the fish market but made it only as far as the parking lot at Earth's Bounty, scared off by the usual preweekend rampage. She didn't have the heart for the vegetable aisle tussles, the rush-hour clot at the checkout lines. There would be something to go with the fish.

Saffron rice, since Sonia Mahabal had recently given them a vial of those precious red-gold threads after returning from a visit to India. At home, Carrie spent a half hour pulling the big brush around the clay court to get it ready for Quint's men. When she was done, she took a long bath to clean off the red grit that clung to her wrists and ankles and neck. The big glass of pinot blanc she downed while soaking in the hot water shot straight to her head. That was good. She wasn't especially interested in thinking about what was going to happen in the next few hours. She put on a loose flowery dress and some sandals. It was well after seven by the time she got to the kitchen. She poured herself another glass of wine and searched the Sub-Zero for something to accompany the grouper and rice. A salad looked possible. She took a census of the numerous tubs and resealable bags. Much of it had to be consigned to the waste disposal, but there was enough to cobble something together. Radicchio, shredded carrots, pine nuts, crumbling feta. She chucked everything into the big teak bowl custom-lathed by happy peasants somewhere and then examined the long row of ten-dollar bottles of dressing on the rack inside the fridge door. Raspberry truffle. Balsamic almond. Cactus mango. Cactus, she thought. Good God. She wondered what was next. Fish gill chutney. Badger gland smoothies. Soon the human mind would run out of products to invent, and that would be the end of time. No heavenly fire or galloping horsemen; no mushroom clouds or incurable plagues. Just a terrible realization that there was no longer anything new in the shops. She chose the balsamic almond and took another long drink of wine.

Jon's arrival was heralded by the hollow thud of a slamming car door. As was his habit, he raised his eyebrows in a slightly ironic greeting when she opened the door. She led him into the kitchen, and he perched on an island stool. She pulled the bottle of wine he'd brought from its wrinkled paper skin. Shiraz, wrong for fish, and she'd already invested heavily in the pinot blanc. So she poured him a glass of that, then emptied the dregs into hers.

"Are you hungry?"

"Starving. I've been working all day."

"Oh, yeah? What on?"

"Third act."

"You know, you're going to have to let me read this one day."

"One day."

She got the grouper going. The saffron-soaked basmati was already done, sealed tightly, warm on the warming thing at the back of the range. She dressed the salad, then levered some of it into a bowl and handed it to him.

"So how are you doing, Carrie? You seem all right, considering."

"I don't know. I'm still kind of numb about it."

"So what exactly happened? I thought the funding was all set."

Carrie had to choose her words. Quint wouldn't want her divulging to anyone that WMV was in trouble.

"Mold."

"Yikes."

"The term *systemic* was used. The situation might not be salvageable. Mold experts are caucusing."

Jon bought this. There had been several black mold catastrophes in the area: condemnations, demolitions, some property even burned in witchy public conflagrations. She watched him as he flipped and sorted the food with his fork, studying the angles of his face, the oblique junctures of cheek and jaw, the dense patterns of his hair. It was a nice face. She briefly wondered what it would be like to kiss. He continued to eat, oblivious of her scrutiny. It always amazed her how rapidly men ate. She took another sip, finishing her glass, the familiar fog beginning to descend. She pulled a second bottle from the glass-fronted drinks fridge. A case had arrived a few days earlier from one of Quint's clients, probably somebody who hadn't yet got the bad news. She couldn't remember what she'd done with the corkscrew, so she got another one from the corkscrew drawer. After she fumbled with it for a moment, he took everything away from her. As he opened the wine, she looked at the fish under the grill. Done. She served it with the rice. She'd completely forgotten a vegetable. Welcome to Carrie's world.

"Well, cheers," he said, holding up his glass.

They ate. It was her first food of the day.

"So where is everybody?" he asked. "Usually, I come over here, it's like Grand Central."

"The boys are out being boys. Quint is working in New York."

"That man seems to work an awful lot."

"*Awful* being the operative term."

"I've always wondered," Jon said after a moment. "Do you understand any of it?"

"Any of what?"

"WMV. What goes on over there. I tried to look it up once online but didn't get past the title of the first article. 'Manning's Drastic Stochastics.'"

Carrie shrugged, picturing him checking on her while she was doing the same to him. We've all become digital Peeping Toms, she thought. Just type a name into the search engine, and see what mysteries are revealed.

"I guess I sort of understand," she said. "When I was in high school, they had this course. Physics for poets. Well, that's me. I get the concepts but can't do the math."

"But it's not just your run-of-the-mill brokerage."

"That it isn't."

Quint would kill her if he knew she was talking about this. But then again, Quint wasn't here.

"So what is it? They launder money for the mob?"

"I wish. At least then visiting clients would be *fun*."

He was waiting.

"Okay. It's a hedge fund, right? As in hedge your bets? Spread the risk? The theory is, you give them your money, and they bet some on black, some on red, so you win no matter where the ball ends up. Markets go up or down, you win."

"Sounds reasonable."

"Yeah, well, that's only half the story. Some firms, of which ours is most decidedly one, are a lot more into the red than the black. If you're certain you know where the ball's going to wind up, there's no reason to hedge your bet."

"But how would you know that it's going to be red?" he asked.

"You do the math. You see, Quint is an extremely rational person. And he thinks that because he's rational, everything else is, too. Especially markets."

"Contrary to all evidence."

"Okay, look. Just because a market is acting crazy doesn't mean there aren't rational reasons behind it. So what he does is figure out where it *should* be and then bet that it will get there in the end. So if he sees that, I don't know, Turkish government short-term bonds are priced too steep, he'll make a wager that they'll go down."

"And this works?" Jon asked.

Carrie gestured to the house around them.

"Sorry," he said. "Duh."

"It's called shorting volatility. I've always loved that term."

"It sounds like a riot at a midget wrestling match."

She laughed and then took another sip of wine, realizing once again that Jon was the first man to be able to make her laugh in a long, long time. He was really doing a number on his grouper. It was almost gone. The rice, too. Carrie had succeeded in dismantling her fish without actually ingesting any of it.

"So what's it like, Carrie?" he asked, not looking up from his plate.

"What?"

As if she didn't know exactly what he meant.

"People say you guys have like thirty million bucks."

"We don't have that much," she said quickly, too quickly, surprised by how close he was. "I mean, a lot of it is funny money nobody gets to touch. And who's talking about how much money we have, anyway?"

He waited for a proper answer. She sighed.

"What's it like? I don't know. Who can say what their life is like? I mean, it's your life. The one you wound up with. As opposed to all the other ones you had your eye on." She took a long drink of the wine. "What's it like? It's safe. You know? Incredibly safe. Doesn't that sound awful?"

"Not if it's what you want."

"It's what I *wanted*, that's for sure." The wine was doing its trick. The words were just coming. "I mean, when I got back together with Quint, I was coming seriously unglued. Not like Zelda or Frances or anything."

"No Aimee Mann sound track."

"It wasn't something I could step aside from every now and then and say, 'Hey, this is fun, check it out, everybody, I'm losing my shit, don't I look *cool*?' It was very, I don't know, lonely. It was nothing you'd notice. You'd have to be paying attention. Not that anyone was. Except my mom. And she was loving it, every fucking minute."

"*Back* together?"

It took her a moment to understand what he meant.

"Oh, right. Yeah, we'd dated for a while in prep—in high school. Then I went off to drama school to be fabulous. We got back together during my postfabulous epoch."

"When was this?"

Dinner was over. Jon had finished his food; she'd never really started hers. She took another long sip. Her glass was almost empty. He poured this time, both glasses, mostly hers. Carrie was aware that she was performing. But that was all right. It was Friday night, and there wasn't anyone around except Jon, sweet Jon.

"After I washed out of drama school. I was living with my mother on the Upper West Side. Quick footnote about my mom: She was batshit. The woman wore kaftans, all right? She thought she was an Upper West Side bitch diva, but she was just a sloppy drunk who inherited a co-op. Anyway, I'm living with her and doing all that questionable early eighties New York shit. And then Quint returns."

Jon was watching her closely now. There was that quality she'd been seeing in his eyes recently. Desire. And for the first time he wasn't trying to hide it. What are you doing? she asked herself.

"I think he liked the fact I was such a wreck."

"It gave him the upper hand."

"No, that's not it, really. He always had that. Anyway, then I was pregnant with Jamie, way before I wanted to be pregnant, but what the hell, I thought. God, did I love it. Being pregnant. Having a little baby. We'd spend hours just lying in bed. I'd read him books and dream about what he'd be like when he was bigger." She shook her head. "And here we all are, a mere two decades later. Bigger."

"Here we are."

"Who'd a thunk it?"

"But it's not so bad. At this precise moment."

She looked at him, thinking what an incredibly nice thing that was for him to say.

"You done?"

"That was great."

She picked up the DVD and used it to gesture for him to follow. "Showtime . . ."

She was a little unsteady as she led him through her house, past the library and the living room and Quint's office. She passed a mirror and hazarded a look. Her pupils were the size of buckshot. And then it was down to the screening room, its chairs and sofas and big pillows arranged in the deliberate random fashion Carrie favored. She'd initially considered building an honest to God twelve-seat cinema, but the idea of the Manning clan watching *Lawrence of Arabia* as if they were seated in the first-class cabin of a 747 proved a bit much. This was back when the idea of their gathering to watch something other than Duke or *Die Hard* was still a possibility. Carrie didn't like to dwell on the plans she'd had for this room. It was the place she was going to turn her children on to movies, to soften and civilize them. Jamie in particular, back before she'd lost the battle for his soul. She had fantasies about him gathering here with his unusual edgy friends, watching everything from *Godfather II* to that bootleg Karen Carpenter thing, the one with the Barbie dolls. Gradually developing a passion for films that would lead to school projects with the Hi8 they gave him for his fifteenth birthday and he never once touched; an internship in New York with Spike Lee or Good Machine. Film school at NYU. Quint getting together the funding for that first feature. But instead, it was racquetball and kegged beer and AP math, the ballistic Wrangler and the girls who would no more sit through a foreign film than work at Taco Bell. Carrie had foolishly allowed hope to be revived during his time with Shannon, not that he would become a filmmaker but at least be something other than this package of preordained American male perfection. Though she'd learned her lesson by now. You couldn't dream for other people. Not even your kids. Especially not them.

She put the DVD into the machine and turned around to the unaccustomed sight of Jon on the sofa. Before, he'd always taken the chair just to the sofa's left, while Carrie sat in the one to its right, leaving the oldsters, Don and Myra, to occupy the long sofa, effectively desexing a room in which uncircumcised Eurococks or ochernippled Latin breasts were apt to appear on-screen. But now there he was, looking up at her, his eyes narrowed slightly in what she understood to be an invitation. Or challenge. Or that dangerous place somewhere between the two. So she had a choice. She could sit in her usual chair and they could watch the film and then he would go home and she'd stumble into her bed and they would probably never see each other again. Tomorrow she could wake up in time to greet her husband and the squad of horrible men who trailed behind him; she could ask the boys about their nights and smile tightly as they grunted at her. Or she could sit on the sofa and see what happened. Red or black, Carrie Manning. Make your choice. No bets hedged tonight.

She chose the sofa, folding a leg underneath herself as she sat, catlike.

The movie played, the usual progression of sound and shadow that tonight she found impossible to follow. Her mind was reeling from the wine and the thought of what was about to happen. She didn't know how much time passed before she felt a disturbance in the taut understructure, a shift of mass in her favor. She turned her face to take his kiss, but he'd stopped a half cushion away. It was there on his face, though: desire laced with just enough fear to make her want him. She narrowed her eyes quizzically, and then she felt his hand, landing softly on the inside of her thigh, just above her knee. Okay, she thought, closing her eyes. This will work. He moved up her leg, brushing the skin, so light and gentle that he broke contact a few times. She unfurled her leg, and then his hand was there, cupped beneath her, turning slow gyrations. A finger rose, and Carrie fell back into the cushions. He was beneath her panties, tiny bones moving in sly conjunction, sifting folds and declivities. And still he wasn't touching her in any other way. It was just his hand. She lifted her legs so that her heels were perched on the edge of the cushion. There was a movie on the screen, but all she was aware of now was that tiny intersection of her body with his. He got a bit ahead of himself, and she had to slow him down with a gentle tap to the back of his hand, but after that he knew exactly what to do. Time either passed or it didn't, until she could feel the great swell of electric warmth passing through her. Her mouth was wide open and there were sounds coming that were hers and still he didn't touch her with anything other than his hand.

Frantic motion: He was taking off his clothes with his one free hand. She reached out to help, but it was a futile, blind gesture. The phone began to ring. There was no way she was going to answer it. Finally, he grabbed her behind the knees and spun her until she was laid out on the sofa. She reached out, and there it was, different from all the others but also the same, that strangely compelling combination of vein and flesh.

Flesh.

"Jon, wait."

"No, okay, I've got . . ."

She released him, keeping her eyes shut. There was the sound of purposeful motion in front of her, the rubber dance, a ruffle of shucked trousers, an elastic scroll and snap. And then he was there again, right there, moving inside her without any help. She put her hands on his back, his shoulders, everywhere. His body was lean, but there was something formless about it as well, as if he'd once been fat. She raised her head to kiss him; she'd had enough of this not kissing. She could taste the almond and wine on his tongue. Soon the currents were running through her body again, a much higher voltage this time, and then she could feel his back muscles stiffen, the arc of his spine. He pushed his face down into the cushion next to her, and he didn't seem to breathe for the longest time. Sweat was coming through his chest. They kissed, and then after a while he rolled off, slipping into the space between her body and the back of the sofa, his head propped on a pillow that had been mashed into the corner.

There was more writhing and snapping as he removed the condom. She turned her back to him so he could sort himself out. When he was done, he pulled her closer. She could feel his naked body all along hers, damp in some places, dry in others. The movie was over. The screen was a deep, neutral blue.

"Carrie, that was great."

"Yeah, he was a pretty good director. Underrated."

She closed her eyes and was overwhelmed by wine and darkness. A strange fugue state followed: not sleep, more like what she imagined hypnosis to be. She let her mind drift, and after a long meandering voyage it arrived at the realization that she'd just betrayed her husband and it didn't feel like anything at all. And then this last thought slipped away and real sleep came.

The next thing she knew his body was passing over hers, and then there was another dance, this one even more frantic. She opened her eyes. Jon's bald knees were directly in front of her face.

"What?" she asked.

"I think somebody's home."

It took her a moment to register the magnitude of the words he'd just spoken. She was lying naked on the downstairs sofa, a swampy patch under her right hip, a slightly engorged, unhusbandly penis within arm's reach. Somebody's home.

"What time is it?"

"Before midnight," he said, dressing swiftly.

She sat up, crossing an arm instinctively across her breasts. He started to say something, and she held up her free hand to silence him. At first there was nothing, and she was beginning to suspect he'd been mistaken when she heard the pressurized movement of water down through the house, followed by the sound of heavy footsteps near the kitchen.

"Okay," she said, her mouth dry. "It's Jamie."

She located her panties and slipped them on. Jon finished dressing and then stood in the television's blue light, awaiting orders. They weren't making eye contact. Carrie knew she had to decide what to do. Jamie would have seen Jon's car, so there was no reason to pretend he wasn't here. But this wasn't necessarily incriminating. Jon was always coming over. That was it, then. She'd pretend they'd watched a movie, which they sort of had done. Or that they *were* watching a movie. That was better. That way she could get Jamie into his room before spiriting Jon the hell out of here.

"Just wait here," she said.

She went upstairs and headed toward the kitchen, pausing in front of one of the darkened mirrors to check that she wasn't in too great a state of disarray. The dirty plates and glasses were still on the table. The two empty wine bottles. Her son stood in front of the open fridge, frozen in some sort of appliance rapture, his head dipping forward in a loose liquid rhythm, his hooded eyes struggling to remain open.

"Jamie?"

He looked up, baffled, as if the voice had come from some point above the Sub-Zero, an angry household god speaking his name. She hit the lights. He reacted as if it were a sheet of flame.

"Wow. Harsh."

He turned to her, his drunken eyes flexing in surprise. Carrie used the rheostat to dim the light considerably, wondering if she should have checked herself a little more closely in that mirror.

"What are you doing home?"

"I thought you were in bed."

"Didn't you see . . ."

There was no reason to finish the question. He hadn't seen Jon's car. Or, if he had, he hadn't registered that it was distinguishable from the shrubbery.

"Dad here?" he asked in sudden alarm, looking over her shoulder.

"He's in New York. Jamie, where are you coming from?"

"Madison's party."

"Like *this*?"

"Like what?"

"Jamie, how did you get home? Tell me you didn't drive home like this."

"It's cool," he said.

"It most certainly is not cool. You've been drinking."

"A couple beers. They tried to call you. Where were you?"

"Jamie, answer my question. Did you drive home like this?"

"Shannon gave me a ride."

"Shannon? Where is she?"

He shrugged. Gone. He turned, letting his motion shut the fridge door, sending a cool wave over Carrie. He walked away from her with great inebriated dignity.

"Jamie . . ."

But he was already gone. Carrie didn't know what she would have said if he'd hung around. And then she remembered. Jon. For the last sixty seconds she'd somehow managed to forget about the man she'd just had sex with. She waited until Jamie reached his room, then went to the basement steps. He was lurking at the bottom.

"Is everything all right?" he asked when he joined her.

"Yeah. Look, you'd better go."

She walked him to the front door. There was an awkward moment when it looked as if he might try to kiss her. But Jamie's unexpected arrival had spooked her. She was already pulling away from him. Carrie's big adventure was definitely over.

"Can we—" Jon said.

"Look, I'd really . . ."

"Okay. Sure."

Intruder lights lit the way to his car. She was about to shut the door but was stopped by an unexpected sight, reflectors seeping through foliage where there should have been emptiness. She stared at the red glow, then walked out into the forecourt to get a better look. It was Jamie's Wrangler. Carrie didn't understand. If Shannon had driven Jamie home, then how had the Wrangler wound up here? Unless someone else had driven it. But Jamie hadn't mentioned anyone else. He'd said Shannon.

"Carrie?"

Jon was watching her from the side of his car. Once again her concern about Jamie had crowded him out of her mind. She smiled at him so she wouldn't have to explain what she was doing. He returned her smile and walked over to her to place a hand on the side of her face. He thought she'd come out for more. He leaned forward and kissed her. It was nothing like how it had been in the basement. She

pulled back after just a second, gesturing with her eyes to all the surrounding light.

"This isn't—"

"Are you going to call me or should I?"

"I'll call you."

She watched him get into his car and drive off, then hurried back
inside. She found a hairbrush and went to straighten herself up in a
kitchen mirror, looking very much like a drunk woman who'd just
been fucked. The face Jamie had just seen. At least she could take
consolation in the fact he was probably too smashed to notice. If *consolation* was the word. Her head was pounding as she climbed the
stairs. Jamie's door was locked. She knocked and there was no answer
and so she knocked louder. Nothing. She could find the key and force
her way in, but there was no reason. Even if she could wake him, he'd
be less coherent than he was in the kitchen. Answers would have to
wait until the morning.

Mortified that Jamie might have driven home in this condition, she
walked slowly back downstairs. She didn't know what she was going
to do. She certainly wouldn't tell Quint. He would go berserk. The
very least he would do was ground him for the whole summer, no
questions asked, leaving her stuck with this caged animal of a son
who hated her for not shielding him from his father's wrath. On the
other hand, if he'd really driven home like this—the thought terrified
her. Something had to be done.

She paused at the bottom of the steps. Why did she have to decide
about these things? Why was it left to her? She wanted nothing more
than to climb into bed. But there were things that needed to be done.
Quint would be arriving early in the morning. She went back down to
the basement and removed that swampy slipcover, consoling herself
that at least she'd ordered ones that could be easily cleaned, even
though the offending substances she'd anticipated had been root beer
and popcorn grease. She removed the other two as well and tossed
them and her panties into the washing machine. She poured in most
of a jug of detergent and hit the button. There was a great noisy cas-
cade, the water that would erase it all.

And then she remembered. The condom. Jon had used a condom.

What had he done with it? She recalled his taking it off on the sofa but had no idea what he'd done with it. Surely, he'd disposed of it after she'd gone upstairs. Unless he'd forgotten, leaving it for her sons to find. She hurried back into the screening room to check the carpet around the sofa. Nothing. She looked in the sofa itself, pulling up the naked cushions, inserting her hands into the gaps, finding calcified food and small change and little plastic men, but no slimy used sheath. She got down on her knees and checked beneath the sofa. But it wouldn't be beneath the sofa. Unless it was. She saw the shadows of objects. More plastic men, ice-cream wrappers, a beer can. But no condom.

Carrie raised herself to her knees. Settle down, she told herself. Jon wouldn't have left a used rubber on the floor. This was Jon. But where would he have . . . The bathroom. She pulled herself to her feet and hurried to the adjacent bathroom. The garbage can was empty. Which meant he'd flushed it down the toilet. But this toilet could be tricky. She imagined its coming back up like the bloody rags in *The Conversation*. She'd have to call him to be sure. But she didn't want to call Jon, especially to ask him whether he'd managed to clean up after himself.

Quint would be home in eight hours.

She rushed back to the sofa. Maybe he'd thrown it. Yes, maybe he'd swung it over his head and then slingshot it across the room in triumph. I . . . just . . . banged . . . Carrie . . . MANNING! Maybe it was sticking to the wall like those umbilica in *Eraserhead*. She looked around, and of course, there wasn't a used condom stuck to her wall. And why the hell was Jon bringing a condom to her house, anyway? She sat in the chair where she usually sat, at least on the nights she didn't cheat on her husband. All right. Get it together. Jon had flushed the rubber down the toilet. It was currently making its way toward wherever the sewers of central Connecticut emptied. He's gone and everything down here is clean, or will be clean when the washing machine stops. Nobody will know anything. Relax, Carrie told herself. You've *gotten away with it*. The thing to do now is stop panicking and get back upstairs. Take care of business there and then get some sleep. Your husband will be home in a while.

Your husband.

She took a deep breath and climbed back to the kitchen. The empty wine bottles went into the recycling bin in the garage, the plates in the dishwasher, the uneaten food in the disposal. This was good. European machines were her friends. The house was taking care of itself, erasing what had happened. Before leaving the kitchen, she noticed the message light on the answering machine. She hit the button, conjuring a self-righteous, too-familiar voice, buffered by party sounds and static.

"This is Diane McNabb calling. It's Friday night at . . . nine something. Could you call me if you get this? It concerns your son."

Fucking Diane. Now she'd have to be dealt with. Carrie erased the message and took one last look around. Satisfied, she armed the system and then headed back up the steps to go to bed. She paused at her son's door. It was silent inside. Why would Jamie be awake? He had his mother to look after him. Besides, she still couldn't think of what she'd say to him. In fact, she couldn't think of anything. She headed to her own room. It would be morning soon; she'd think then.

PART FOUR

12 It was hard to know the right time to head up to Orchard. He didn't want to do it too early; the meeting was going to be complicated enough without rousing people from bed first thing on a Saturday morning. But if he left it too late, the family would have already dispersed. Sometime around ten would probably be best. The Mannings would be wide awake, but not yet about their business. He'd be able to have a few minutes alone with Quint. They could sit on that big patio with a cup of coffee and sort this thing out before lunch. Drew was sure of it.

It had already been a long day. He'd been up since five-thirty, awakened by Ronnie's groggy shuffle to the bathroom. It was her third trip since going to bed, her bladder now under comprehensive siege from the pressure of the twins. Nights had become a trial for her. It was getting harder for her to find a comfortable position in bed; she was hungry, but food disgusted her. And the room's climate was a problem, too hot without air conditioning but too drafty when Drew switched on the wall unit. By the time the sun shouldered through the drawn curtains, he understood that there was no way she would be able to work for three more weeks. Soon she would be home for good. Once that happened, his secret would be impossible to keep.

To pass the time until his meeting, he dedicated himself to looking after her. He made her some herbal tea and arranged the pillows and massaged her bloated feet. Once she was as comfortable as she was going to get he pulled up a chair and began reading to her from his father's musty old copy of *The Moonstone*. Ronnie loved to be read to; it relaxed her without stoking her toxic headaches. Things were certainly hotting up in Yorkshire. Rachel Verinder was in peril, but Sergeant Cuff was on the case. Drew was able to lose himself in the narrative, though at one point he looked up to catch her worriedly probing her taut belly.

"Ron?"

"Keep going," she said, determined not to give in to the doubt and fear moving through her.

He left home at half past nine, giving himself enough time to stop at L'Oeuf Splendide for a smoked ham croissant and a cup of strong coffee. As he ate, he went over what he was going to say to Quint. His appeal would be direct. Subterfuge would be wasted. He would first admit that he had been wrong to join the fund. Quint's warning, while difficult to take seriously, had nonetheless been explicit. Drew should not invest money unless he could afford to lose it. And yet that was exactly what he had done. There was no disputing that he alone was to blame for his current mess. But that still didn't change the fact that he needed his money back.

His plan was simple. Not much more than a sketch of a plan, though Quint could fill in the details. Drew would propose that WMV pay him a sum equal to his original investment as a sort of advance against the future profits Quint had talked about Monday. And then, next year, when Drew's placement recovered, Quint could have it all, the original money plus any future dividends. Although in the short term WMV would be down, the fund would come out way ahead in the end, reaping the yearly profits Drew had been dreaming about. It was an unorthodox agreement, but that was the point of Quint's fund. They were unregulated; they could do whatever the manager decided. Of course, this would mean that Drew would be back where he started, though given what he'd been experiencing since Monday, that wasn't such a bad place to be. This wasn't his world. He didn't have the stomach for it. From now on he'd stick to hard work and prudent planning. His father had often said that the problem with shortcuts was that they tended to run close to the edges of steep cliffs. As usual, the old man had been right.

People dashed in and out of the restaurant, picking up bread and coffee, something sweet for the kids. Most were young and casually well-to-do, busy with home improvement schemes and youth sports. A few faces were vaguely familiar, but most were strangers. Which was all wrong. He should know these people. They should be detouring to his table for small talk with the man who sold them a slice of their futures. But Drew, stunned by Anne's departure, had been sleepwalking during the period they arrived. He'd let it all drift, convinced that buyers and sellers would walk through the door just as they had for the last thirty years, that the rentals would keep ticking over, providing a steady flow of cash. His father had gone through slack periods, but he'd always managed to survive. Hagel & Son would keep him going until he was ready to get back in the hunt.

The problem was that Totten Crossing had become a very different town during that time. Its location just beyond the commuter belt had become a draw. Businesses began to relocate to the area; people who worked in the city were able to justify the long commute by spending two, three days a week in their hooked-up homes. The sleepy real estate market boomed. The moribund local Century 21 bureau started hiring extra staff; RE/MAX opened up shop in Dresden, and Coldwell Banker snapped up the Hanratty brothers, previously Drew's only rivals. Listings that were once his business's birthright would be hotly contested. The purple and white Hagel & Son signs began to disappear, like some bright harmless weed being slowly eradicated.

And then PMG arrived. It came just as Anne was getting ready to go. The Property Management Group. It had materialized from nowhere, its birth heralded by a big spread in the local paper as well as something in the *Hartford Courant*. Four women on the cusp of middle age who claimed that they were going to "bring modern sales techniques" to the area. Drew initially saw them as a bunch of bored housewives playing at business, like Carrie Manning with her cinema. The Post-Menopausal Gals, he dubbed them. It would have been funnier if they hadn't managed to corner the local property market in the space of two years. Drew hardly knew what hit him. They hustled; they speculated; they offered clients financing from European banks and developed a Web site with 360-degree home tours. They even stole listings, something unthinkable in his father's day. The partners themselves were rarely seen at the properties they listed. Instead, they used eager young "showers" to do the legwork that had been Walt Hagel's stock-in-trade. They soon destroyed all competition. It was as if the Lakers had started playing in a suburban high school league. Coldwell Banker closed up shop; Century 21 cut way back. No one could touch them. Drew knew he had to change the way he worked. He began posting target lists on the back of his office door; he told Janice to bar him from leaving for the day until he'd done some real business. It was tough. He'd chase a listing, giving it everything he had, only to have a Property Management sign appear in front of the property a few days later. But still, he was making enough to keep everybody comfortable. He might never be able to beat PMG, but at least he was still in its league.

And then Anne left. Even now, with everything Ronnie had taught him about dwelling on the past, he found it impossible not to blame his first wife for the failure of his business. Her betrayal had been so comprehensive, so absolute and unexpected, that it made everything else seem a waste of time. Of course, he'd been a fool not to know she was screwing Timothy Purdy, the slouching ironic moron she'd lived with before Drew met her. There were abundant signs, the grudging marital sex and the painted toenails and the sudden need to put in extra hours at her hated consumer affairs job at Aetna. And then there was the utterly bogus awakening of her spiritual side. Pretending to take Bikram yoga, returning from the hot studio flushed and in need of an immediate shower. The weekend "mindfulness retreat" up near Great Barrington with the Vietnamese Zen master that turned out to have been spent with Purdy at a B and B. Worst of all, most subtle but also most blatant, was the bumper sticker that appeared on her Stanza: "Don't Postpone Joy." Drew, the fool, the optimist, had taken it as an affirmation of her contentedness with the life they'd made, when a more accurate translation would have been some combination of "I'm with Stupid" and "Hasta la Vista."

And then there was what she did to Shannon. He would never forget the moment at the Relation Shop when Tina, their mediator for family transitions, made it clear that Anne was going to cede absolute custody of their little girl. Drew turned on his wife in astonished rage. For the only time during these torture sessions, she would not meet his eye. He shouted; he swore; he almost clocked Tina. But Purdy didn't want a child, and so neither did Anne. Drew finally stormed from the office, dismissing the mediator and carrying on the remainder of their breakup with high-billing lawyers who had no interest in workshopping this family transition.

It was then that things came unglued. Drew simply gave up. All those resolutions to do better seemed like sick jokes. He started to leave the office earlier and earlier, stopping at Bill's to prepare himself for another endless evening looking after his miserable daughter. Debts would come due, and he'd sell off another chunk of land. He knew this was wrong; he knew a reckoning awaited him. But Anne's betrayal had downed a vital link within him, the wire that joined his understanding that a distant crisis loomed with the action needed to avert it. There was always enough to get by, and with his life in ruins, getting by was just fine.

Then he met Ronnie, both of them eating lunch alone on Federal. Adjacent tables. She was new to the area, bright ginger hair and that tiny body. She'd just earned her doctorate from the university after escaping a five-year entanglement with a coke-addled sportswriter up in Worcester, a tempestuous and humiliating marriage she rarely spoke about. She needed someone steady and kind and edgeless; mostly, she needed a man who would always respond to her gentle care. With her, his indifference soon vanished. But while Ronnie could pull his soul out of its slough of despond, it was too late for his business. PMG ruled. The only listings he could bring in now were cheap bungalows and rickety frame houses. His company's capital reserves had been squandered. There was nothing left to invest when he saw a good thing. He even had to sell his office to PMG, renting it back from it at a ruinous rate. There was just enough coming in to pay the school bills and the costs of running the big house on Crescent, enough to keep doing the only thing he'd become good at since Anne left him: maintaining the aura of easy prosperity that was the last vestige of Walt Hagel's inheritance. To his friends and neighbors, Drew continued to project the image of relaxed prosperity. He even let on to Ronnie that he was doing far better than he was. He'd been weak for her once, and he couldn't allow himself to be weak for her again. She might be a psychologist and in some ways a saint, but he knew from bitter experience that too much pity would eventually lead to contempt.

He worked and he worked. He wasn't greedy. He didn't want riches. He didn't want a Z3 or first-class tickets or a weekend place at Killington. All he wanted was enough. But enough wasn't what it used to be. You needed a whole lot more to have enough these days. He'd get up in the morning and slip on that day's sports coat and go down to the office on Federal and get his ass kicked. He'd fight the good fight, and he'd lose. Nothing came of the long hours and dogged effort. And yet still no one knew, except perhaps the ladies at Property Management, and they weren't talking. For six years Hagel & Son registered utterly bogus profits. Early last year the final outpost of his father's empire had been abandoned: Otis Winter's place. The reckoning should have come soon after. His confession to Ronnie; the demise of Hagel & Son; his search for a new job. But then on a warm March morning he took Shannon over to her boyfriend's house and was asked to join a tennis game. Enough, like the weak volleys of his opponents, was suddenly within reach.

Traffic was bad in town, though it thinned as he made his way up Orchard's sharp turns. Drew slowed, on the lookout for joggers and dog walkers and kids on bicycles. He slowed to pass a few official-looking sedans parked halfway up the hill, bracketed by the burned stubs of flares: yet another accident on this bad stretch of road. The Mannings' elephantine gate was already swinging out as he approached. Thinking it was opening for him, Drew pulled into the center of the drive, only to be confronted by the sight of Carrie's Lexus powering straight for him. He jerked his car to the right and hit the brakes hard, then gave a self-deprecatory little wave as she pulled up next to him. They both rolled down their windows. She looked tired, her usually luminous skin bloodless and papery. Her eyes traveled momentarily down to his chin.

"You here to play?" she asked.

"Play?"

Her smile diminished, becoming the sort of smile you would flash a stranger.

"Anyway," she said, "I'd better run."

He began to inch forward, but she was speaking again.

"Oh, Drew? Could you ask Shannon to give me a call?"

"Sure. Should I tell her why?"

Carrie was about to answer but for a second time stopped herself. "She'll know."

She drove off without another word. Drew watched her in his mirror, wondering what she wanted with Shannon. He thought about his daughter hooking arms with Jamie after the banquet, all the time she was spending with him recently, the trips to the beach and the evening study sessions. Maybe they were getting back together. Maybe everything was set to return to the way it had been last summer.

And then he looked back out his front windshield and saw the cars. There were at least a dozen; some he thought he recognized from last summer. Carrie's question now made sense. The tennis game was back on. Drew sat perfectly still for a long while, unable to understand why Quint hadn't called. They'd talked about this at the banquet. Maybe he'd been trying to get Drew at his office, leaving messages on the machine he wasn't checking for fear of dealing with Andy Starke. Perhaps he'd called just now, while Drew was at the restaurant.

All at once Drew understood. Quint hadn't called because he was embarrassed about Monday. That had to be it. He put his car in gear and parked in the first available slot, even more determined to settle this thing. He caught a glimpse of himself in the side mirror as he started to get out of the car, noticing some large, weightless flakes of croissant on his chin. They'd been there when he was talking to Carrie. It was what she'd glimpsed but had been too polite to mention. Drew collected them with the wetted end of his finger and ate them. As he walked around the side of the house, he could hear the pock of struck balls and the rasping voices of men at play. He'd been mistaken up at the driveway, it was a different crew from last summer. A few saw him approach but didn't make anything of it. Mahabal and Quint were standing together in the shade of the hut's striped canopy, away from the rest of the men. They were speaking privately, watching and not watching the game. There was a new tension in the air. No jokes, no smiles, no exotic drinks. Mahabal saw Drew and said something. Quint's expression remained neutral as he turned to look. He didn't move, waiting for Drew to come to him.

"Morning," he said, his voice friendly enough, though Quint's voice was always friendly.

Drew's nod was intended to encompass both men.

"Sorry just to drop in like this," he said.

Quint waited, offering nothing in return.

"Could I have a word with you?"

"We're kind of busy here, Drew. We're about to go into a meeting."

"I just need a minute."

Quint turned to Mahabal.

"Let me know the second they call."

He gestured for Drew to follow him into the hut. Although there were plenty of chairs scattered around, there was no question of either of them sitting. Quint waited for Drew to speak, his expression neutral.

"Look, Quint, we need to talk about my placement. I think we were . . . I think there's been a lack of communication."

"A lack of communication?"

"It's entirely my fault. I should have been clearer about this money. Thing is, I can't really afford to lose it."

"Drew, I think I was clear about the level of risk involved."

"Yes, but I never thought—I mean, that wasn't supposed to happen."

Quint looked down at the toe of his tennis shoe, which he'd begun to scrape back and forth across the all-weather carpet. The men on the court had stopped playing. They were gathering on the patio now, toweling off, getting ready for something. Impatient questions were being fielded by Mahabal.

"Obviously, it wasn't in the plan," Quint said, choosing his words.

"But as I said on Monday, there's every reason to think this setback is temporary."

"Yeah, but . . ." Drew wasn't making himself understood. "We can't just leave it like this. That's what I'm trying to say. We have to hash out another arrangement."

Quint's eyes flashed toward Mahabal, who was standing just outside the door.

"Drew, I don't know where you're going with this, but if you're talking about a lawsuit, you and I really shouldn't be having that conversation."

"Nobody's talking about a lawsuit. I just thought there might be some way I can get my hands . . . look, all I want to do is break even."

"Break even?" Quint asked, genuinely perplexed at the notion.

"What I was thinking, you could, you know, advance me, just, you know, my initial investment. And then when the fund recovered you'd already have my money, and that could be your repayment. I mean, you said yourself that it was going to bounce back. You could keep that. No matter how high it went."

"That's not how it works, Drew. If I did that for you, then I'd have to do it for everyone. It would bankrupt us."

"That's the thing, though. I'm not like everyone."

"What do you mean?"

"That money, it's all I had. If I don't get it back, I'm in . . . trouble."

"But you filled out the accredited investor forms. I have them at the office."

"They weren't entirely, you know, that wasn't the whole story."

Quint's face froze. Drew understood immediately that he had completely miscalculated the situation. Suddenly the tennis and the banquet and the kids meant nothing.

"Hold on, you lied on the form?"

"No, come on, I didn't *lie*. I just, you know."

"Drew, the SEC has established those requirements for very specific reasons. If you've played fast and loose with them, then that's fraud."

"Wait—"

"And I have to warn you—I mean, if you want to pursue this, I can

have Godeep revisit those forms with an eye toward their legal ramifi-
cations."

This was going all wrong.

"Look, I think we're getting turned around here—"

Quint held up his hand, showing Drew his smooth palm, his thin
splayed fingers.

"Drew, I'm stopping this conversation. You've left me no choice
other than to redeem your money at its current level. I'm going to
have a check cut for the balance of your placement and delivered to
your office next week."

"Quint . . ."

"Drew, our business is over."

And then, without another word or gesture, Quint turned away
from him. Mahabal had moved into the doorway. He was holding up a
cell phone. Quint walked across the hut and took it from him. After
taking a deep breath, he held it to his ear.

"Okay, go ahead," he said into the phone.

He listened, his back still to Drew. Mahabal watched him; the men
on the patio were trying to see as well, though Quint had moved to a
corner, where he was invisible to them.

"Is that it?" he asked.

After several more seconds he cut the connection without another
word, lowering the phone and tapping it against his thigh. He looked
at Mahabal and gave a quick nod.

"Right," Mahabal said, clapping his hands like a schoolmaster.
"Shall we start?"

Quint was still standing alone in the corner of the hut, his back to
everyone, surrounded by wicker furniture and photo arrays of his family. There was something bereft about him; his normally flawless
posture seemed to diminish. And then he sensed Drew's continued
presence. He turned and their eyes met.

"You should go," he said, his voice flat. "Now."

The men had begun to enter the hut. A few of them shot Drew
quick, unhappy looks. Quint was right. He should go. He took a step
toward the courtside door, though he wasn't sure how he would make

it past the men jamming the small opening. He remembered there was a door behind him, leading directly to the lawn. It took him a few seconds to figure out the lock, but after that there was nothing in his way.

He stopped at Subway on the way home and ordered a meatball sub. It wasn't too much more for the whole meal, so he got a large root beer and a bag of chips as well. He downed them quickly, finishing everything by the time he got home. He checked his face for crumbs this time, then slotted the cup and wrappers into an already full trash bag at the side of the house. It was just after noon. Ronnie was in the kitchen, looking through the paper and drinking a large mug of her Mother's Friend. She looked up as Drew sat heavily across from her.

"You all right?"

"Yeah," he said. "Fine."

Bitter steam from her cup wafted across the table toward him. This, of course, would be the time to confess. He'd been greedy; he'd been a fool. He'd ask her forgiveness and swear he'd set it right. Whatever it took. He'd work twice as hard. He'd sell his company to Property Management and take a position with it. Get a second job. They'd have to jettison things, one of the cars, some of the old furniture. He'd speak to Shannon about Oberlin, a deferral or maybe even a transfer to the state university. If his wife and daughter were with him, they could scrape by. Because Quint had no intention of doing anything for him. Quint had *dismissed* him. It was just another deal to him, one that went bad, hedged by all the others that spun gold. He was already on to the next trade. And then there would be one after that, and one after that.

Drew looked at his wife and knew he couldn't do it. He couldn't tell her.

"Shannon back?" he asked.

"I haven't seen her."

"Did she call?"

"Not to my knowledge."

"That's sort of strange, isn't it?"

Ronnie shrugged. It had been a long time since she'd allowed herself to speculate about Shannon's behavior.

"You hungry?" she asked.

"Yes," Drew said, knowing he shouldn't be.

"There's some turkey breast. I'll make you something."

"No, I'll do it. *You* want something?"

She shook her head at the impossibility of food. He made himself a sandwich, shielding the cutting board from his wife as he coated the bread with a thick skin of mayonnaise. He ate joylessly, the food tough to swallow with those meatballs still resident in his gut. He flipped through the paper but couldn't focus on anything. The front door opened. Shuffling feet, and then his daughter appeared in the kitchen doorway. This was unusual; she normally bolted straight upstairs. She looked tired, though Drew put that down to a night with her friends.

"Were there any calls for me?" she asked, her voice slightly breathless.

It was a strange question. Shannon had a cell phone. No one called her on the house line.

"No," Drew said. "Are you expecting something?"

She shook her head, sullen now, having made all the contact she intended. She nodded at the disorganized mass of newspaper on the table.

"Are you done with that?"

Before Drew could answer, she had collected it and was gone, her feet pounding up the old steps. Ronnie's ginger eyebrows rose slightly, but she said nothing.

"That was weird," he said. "Wasn't that weird?"

"Sweetheart, if you're worried about your daughter, you should *talk* to her."

She was right. There was no reason to sit down here and speculate. Shannon was right above him. His wife was right across from him. Everything was so close, waiting to be dealt with.

He heard her voice as he reached her door and paused to listen.

She was speaking with the flat, slightly exasperated pitch of someone dealing with an answering machine.

"Jamie, this is me. We've really got to talk about . . . oh, never mind, I'm coming over."

Drew knocked. It took her a while to open the door. She'd changed her clothes, cargo pants for jeans, one sweatshirt for another. Room odor wafted past her: scented candles, sandalwood and patchouli. Up close she looked even worse than she had down in the kitchen. Her eyes were puffy, as if she might have recently been crying.

"I was just wondering what was going on. You seem . . . upset."

"Nothing," she said, managing a feeble smile. "Just tired."

"You have fun last night?"

She nodded, then shrugged, then turned away, presenting him with her profile. Her mother's profile. Her eyes were fixed on some vanishing point within her room.

"Look, Dad, I'm sorry, but I really have to get going."

To Jamie's, he almost prompted.

"Can we . . . we'll talk later, all right?"

"Okay," he said.

Ronnie was still in the kitchen when he returned.

"Everything all right?" she asked.

Drew nodded absently. A few moments later Shannon's feet sounded on the steps. She went out without saying good-bye. It wasn't until the door had slammed that he realized he'd forgotten to pass on Carrie's message. But there was no reason to go after her. She was already heading up there.

13 Shannon had expected to see police cruisers on Crescent when she arrived; officers locked in grave conversation with her father and Ronnie in the kitchen, all of them turning in slow motion as this lost and wicked girl stepped through the door. But it was the same old scene, her stepmother bloated and uncomfortable, her father chewing mechanically. When he came up to her bedroom a few minutes later, she was momentarily tempted to tell him the truth. But that would mean betraying Ian. She'd promised not to say anything unless he agreed. And she wouldn't break her promise to him. Whatever else was going to happen today, that was the one thing she would control.

Last night it had taken her a while to understand that something was wrong, that Ian was trying to tell her that he might have hurt somebody. Finally, however, his words began to make a dreadful sense.

"I was downshifting when I came out of one of the turns and the car sort of jumped and all of a sudden this bicycle was right there," he explained, his face still hidden in the car's shadow. "I didn't even see him until he was next to me."

"I don't—did you *hit* him?"

"I just sort of scraped by him . . . I think . . . maybe I clipped him with one of those roll bars. It's hard to tell with all that shit on the car. But you would have seen him if he went down or anything, right?"

"Jesus. Ian. We have to go back there."

"What?"

"If you think you knocked somebody over, we have to go back."

"Come on, Shan," he said. "You would have seen something."

"I could have missed it. I was dealing with Jamie, and I could have missed it."

Neither of them spoke for a few seconds. Shannon was waiting for something to happen that would make her better understand this. But there was just the darkness and the silence and the familiar mass of the Mannings' house looming over them.

"Ian, some guy could be lying there," she said finally. "Right now."

"What if he is? What if he is and he recognizes me?"

"He won't recognize you. We're in a different car."

"I barely . . ."

His voice trailed off. Shannon knew they had to go back right away. A man might be hurt. She started her engine and drove through the gate, so fast she almost banged into it before it could open all the way. As they raced back down Orchard, she kept hoping to see a man on a bicycle, pedaling furiously, eager to tell somebody about a fool in a Jeep who'd almost killed him. Ian was searching as well. But the road was empty. They soon entered the turns, following the road's twisted logic back to town. It was so dark and empty that Shannon was briefly able to believe that nothing had happened, that the reason she hadn't seen anybody was that the rider turned off into one of the side streets before she could reach him.

And then she saw the cars, stopped in a place there was no reason for them to be. There were three of them, the closest and the farthest facing uphill, the middle one pointing down. A pale matrix of headlights illuminated the surrounding trees. Hazard flashers worked, listless and urgent.

"Oh, shit," Ian said, sinking into his seat. "Oh, fuck."

She slowed down.

"Shan, what are you doing? Drive, drive."

But she pulled to the side of the road, stopping directly across from the other cars. Ian sank deeper into the seat, shaking his head, no longer able to look. Three people stood in a bright box of light between the opposing cars. They were looking down at two men. One of them squatted at the head of the other, who was lying next to the corrugated post of the guardrail. The squatting man's hands hovered over the other's shoulders, as if he were measuring him. Shannon couldn't see the fallen man's face, though his legs were bare and there were reflective chevrons on his vest that glowed in the conflicting headlights. He wore fingerless gloves; his left hand was moving, swatting lazily at the air, as if he were telling a story. Which meant he was awake. He was talking. That was good. But it was also bad, because if he was talking, then he might be telling them about this lunatic in a Jeep. A racing bicycle lay just downhill from him, its front wheel sticking up, the ram's horn handlebars balanced on the road.

"Shannon, let's go," Ian said, his voice sounding like something projected by a failing amplifier. "People are here. Help's on the way."

"Ian, I have to see."

He looked at her helplessly. Shannon opened the door and got out. She paused by the car, but the light was patchy and people were in the way, and she knew she would have to get closer. As she crossed the road, she thought she could hear a siren, though the sound was immediately swallowed by a burst of wind through the trees. Not yet ready to look at the cyclist, she examined the people who had gathered. The squatting man was heavy-thighed, with a big drooping mustache. He was frowning, in charge but not happy about it. There was a young woman, holding a phone to her ear, who moved farther up the hill as Shannon approached. And there was a couple, old enough to be somebody's grandparents, standing uneasily in front of a Volvo, the only car parked downhill from the cyclist. The man jangled keys, waiting for someone to give them permission to leave.

Shannon finally allowed herself to look at the cyclist. That arm was no longer swatting the air. It had settled back on the blacktop, his hand clenching and unclenching. He wore a cyclist's knee-length pants, and beneath his vest of chevrons there was a skintight shirt covered with colorful decals. His helmet was lying flat beneath him, like a bowl for his head. His face was plainly visible now, sharp-featured, a coating of stubble on his cheeks and chin. His eyes snapped open just as Shannon looked at him, staring up into the bug-strewn light, but almost immediately they started shutting again, the lids moving very slowly. There was a long, dirty scrape along his left knee, though in the patchy light it was hard to tell what was blood and what was road grit.

Shannon looked away. The old couple watched her. There was something complicit in their expressions, as if they were trying to enlist her in their desire to get away from here. The breeze diminished, and now there was the unmistakable howl of an approaching siren. The girl with the phone walked back over to them when she heard it. She wore a convenience store smock and no shoes.

"Somebody's *definitely* coming now," she said.

The Volvo people said something about moving their car. They started it up and drove off, backing a long way down the hill before pulling a rapid U-turn. Their lights swept over Shannon's car, and she caught a quick glimpse of Ian's face inside, watching her, terrified. The girl with the phone had seen Shannon and came over to her. Her naked toenails were painted black. The man with the mustache looked up at them, his hands still frozen above the jogger's shoulders.

"What happened?" Shannon asked.

"I think he fell off," the girl said.

The man with the mustache shook his head.

"Somebody hit him."

"Really?" Shannon asked. "Who? Did he say who?"

The man shook his head. The cyclist's eyes clicked open, but he wasn't hearing what they were saying. His pupils once again fixed on the dark sky for a long moment before slowly starting to shut, their motion reminding Shannon of a collapsing parachute.

"I just found him like this. Almost hit him myself. It's a good thing he's wearing his vest." He looked back down at the man, whose eyes had finished closing. "Well, not a good thing, but you know."

"He's in shock," the girl with the black toenails said. "Don't you think?"

"He whacked his head pretty good," the mustached man said. "I'm thinking it was on the guardrail. A helmet's not going to do anything about that, the angle's right. Well, not right, but . . ."

Flashing lights appeared around the curve beneath them; the policeman had turned off his siren for the last part of the drive. He parked where the Volvo had been, his pulsing light illuminating Shannon's car, though Ian's face was no longer visible. Shannon recognized the officer as he got out of the car. He'd come to Country Day a few months ago to talk to the girls about rape prevention. You kicked; you screamed; you ran like hell. He looked at everybody in that disappointed way police have and then went up to the cyclist, staring down at him critically, as if he were the one who had done something wrong.

"Is he with it?" the cop asked loudly.

"He's breathing. His eyes'll open if you give him a minute."

"Has he said anything?"

The man with the mustache pulled his hands away from the shoulders; they were like moorings being released. The cyclist's eyes remained closed.

"He's groggy."

"Sir, an ambulance is coming," the policeman said, his voice still ridiculously loud. "Remain still."

After understanding that he was not going to get a response, he took a quick, unhappy inventory of faces.

"Did anyone see what happened?"

The girl and the mustached man shook their heads. The cop's eyes came to rest on Shannon. There was nothing stopping her from telling him the truth. She could say it any way she wanted. She could explain how Ian had only been keeping someone from driving drunk. But then the cop would want to talk to him. He would demand a driver's license. Ian would have to sit in the back of the cruiser while they called in his name. The story suddenly seemed unlikely, with Jamie gone and the Wrangler parked safely. Ronnie would find out everything. The probation officer and the judge would get involved. They would be finished.

She shook her head. The cop looked unhappy with her answer, but this was just his manner. Another siren was sounding now, mixing with the first cruiser's idling engine and the wind in the trees. Cars passed, slowing down to look. They'd be sending fire trucks and ambulances and more police, overreacting the way they always did. If she hung around any longer, she might get boxed in. Somebody would see Ian and want to hear what he had to say. They'd know it was him;

he was too sensitive to be a good liar. She looked one more time at the cyclist. His eyes popped open and then began their tortuous closing. Shannon wished he'd just fall asleep. There was no reason for him to struggle like this. Help was on the way.

"Sir, can I move my car?" she asked the policeman.

"Yeah," he said, not looking at her, his eyes fixed on the injured man's face, as if he were finally figuring out something about him. "Yeah, you'd better."

She walked rapidly back to her car. Ian had slid down so far that he was almost lying on the seat. He was staring at her, his face looking even more terrified in the strobing police light.

"What?"

"He banged his head. But he's awake."

"So we can go now, right?"

Shannon knew it wasn't right to leave. But she had to get away from the flashing lights and the man's closing eyes. She had to be somewhere where she could think.

"Yes. We can go."

Familiar sights on Totten Pike were now full of menace. The abandoned Sunoco station and the house that still had its Christmas lights; the stop sign with the words *Making Sense* sprayed at the bottom. As she turned into the driveway, she was certain the police would be waiting for them, although the house was exactly as they had left it, a few lights switched on inside, the yellow bulb burning above the back door. There were dirty plates in the kitchen, and one of the candles still flickered, even though Shannon was certain she'd blown it out. She checked for messages on the answering machine—nothing—then joined Ian in the living room, where he'd slumped on the sofa, staring out the picture window. They did nothing for a while, like two people waiting for a movie to begin. Then he put his head on her lap, and she ran her fingers through his hair, smoothing out the odd tangles. His hair was so soft. She couldn't stop thinking about that man's eyes, struggling against the inner gravity pulling them shut.

"I'm going to call Mercy," she said eventually.

Ian sat up.

"And tell them what?"

"I'm not going to tell them anything. I'm just going to ask them how he is."

"You said he was all right."

"I said he was awake, Ian."

"But what are you going to say?" he asked. "You don't even know his name."

"I'll just ask about the guy on the bicycle."

"Which means they'll know it's the people who did it calling. What if they have caller ID?"

He was speaking so fast that it was hard to keep up with him. She was tempted to tell him to stop being paranoid. But he wasn't being paranoid. This was what was happening to them now.

"We can't just . . . we have to find out how he's doing."

"Shannon, the guy's in the hospital. He's doing the best he can be doing. They're looking after him."

"So aren't you going to tell anybody about this? I mean, is that what you're planning?"

He turned away, his mouth working for a moment.

"Look, Shannon, it was an accident, all right? The car just—I was downshifting, and when I hit the gas, I mean, it just lurched away from me. It was like a rocket taking off. And the next thing I knew this guy appeared out of the middle of nowhere."

"I know it was an accident."

"Then what possible reason would there be for me to get myself arrested? If he was still lying out there or they needed my blood or something . . . he's not going to get any better with us calling the cops. I get busted and that's it for me."

He folded his arms across his chest and bent forward slightly. Shannon put her hand on his back and could feel his body shaking. Headlights appeared on Totten Pike. They watched through the picture window as a car drove by without slowing.

"We'll wait until morning," she said.

He put his head back on her lap. She began to stroke his hair.

"Hey, Ian?" she asked after a while. "How come you drove the Jeep all the way back to Jamie's?"

"I thought it would be easier."

"But what happened on the hill?" she asked softly.

"I don't know. I wasn't even going that fast. It just . . . the car just sort of jumped. It was like the thing was driving itself. I thought . . ."

"What?"

"I don't know what I thought."

He began to cry, a rhythmic stutter of his breathing, his hand gripping her knee. She thought he was shivering at first. She'd never seen him cry before. After a minute of this she felt something hot soak through the fabric on her thigh. Tears. He stopped after that. He was so still that she thought he'd fallen asleep. She slid out from under him, getting one of Ginny's misshapen handmade quilts from the closet to put over his body. But when she came back to the sofa, she saw that his eyes were wide open. There was nothing behind them. They were all pure brilliant surface.

"I thought you were asleep."

"I don't think I'm ever going to sleep again."

She covered him, and then they watched the television with the sound turned off, a Hartford station, evangelists and infomercials, a guy with big rubber gloves cutting up baked chickens. The low ceiling and blocky furniture began closing in on Shannon, a sensation she hadn't experienced since she was a little girl, prone to middle-of-the-night fevers, when she'd lie in bed and it would be as if the air were collapsing around her. Convinced she was about to suffocate, she'd call out in terror, and it would always be her father who came, never her mother. He'd put a cold damp cloth on her head and lie next to her, telling her funny stories and singing to her, until the strangling world eased away.

Finally, just as light was beginning to leak through the trees across the highway, the local morning news broadcast started. They turned on the sound. The story came on a good ten minutes into the program. It was very brief, just the announcer reading from a script, a cheap illustration of a car and a stick figure behind him, some sort of explosive star between them. The newscaster explained that the police were appealing for witnesses in a hit-and-run accident involving a

Totten Crossing man named Robert Jarvis, who was in serious condition at Mercy Hospital. The whole thing took no more than thirty seconds of airtime.

"Serious," Shannon said. "What does that mean?"

"It means he's alive."

She knew it meant more than that but kept quiet. They watched the news on another station, but there was nothing there. Shannon turned off the television.

"So what are we going to do?" she asked.

"Nothing."

"Ian, we can't just do nothing."

He looked out the picture window at the rocky yard. She put her hand on the back of his neck. The muscles were rigid.

"Okay," he said, taking a deep breath. "If he's hurt badly, I mean, you know, really *serious*, then I'll turn myself in. But if he's just, if he's going to get better, then I won't. That's—that's all right, isn't it?"

Shannon nodded, even though she knew it wasn't all right. And then she thought of something else.

"But what if they figure out it was the Wrangler?"

"Okay. That, too. If they start asking about the Wrangler, we'll call them."

They went to his room and lay on top of the covers, keeping their clothes on. They didn't say anything, and Shannon must have drifted off, because the next thing she knew it was very bright in the room, a harsh, headachy light that seemed to be coming from a closer sun. Ian was sitting at his desk, drawing furiously in one of his pads. He hadn't slept. He hadn't been anywhere near sleep.

"What time is it?" she asked.

He closed the pad and looked at her.

"Late morning. Everything's cool."

"I'd better go," she said. "See what's happening."

He nodded unhappily.

"Call me."

"Ian, I'm not going to let you go through anything alone."

"And you won't tell anyone unless we decide together, right?"

"Ian, I promise."

They kissed for a while, and she allowed herself to believe everything was going to be all right. But once she was away from him, the magnitude of what they were doing returned. Keeping the accident a secret had seemed possible when she was lying with him in the quiet house, the world nothing more than passing traffic. But as she drove back into Totten Crossing, moving among all the regular people doing regular things, parents spending money and taking their kids places, she knew this was just an illusion. Someone could have seen them on Orchard; the cyclist would remember the Wrangler's distinctive silhouette. Or Jamie would figure it out on his own. Soon they would have to tell people what they'd done, and the perfect time would be over.

Being in town made everything even more unreal. She couldn't square what was happening with the peace of her neighborhood. The traffic and the squirrels and the coating of light green pollen on everything. The churning growl of Saturday morning lawn mowers. Her street sign that some joker had changed to read RES ENT. She checked the paper once she got it away from her father. There was a small article on the second page, as grimly factual as the television. Robert Jarvis was in serious condition at Mercy Hospital. The police were appealing for witnesses. Serious, Shannon thought. She wished someone would tell her what that meant; she wished someone would tell her the man was going to get better and everyone would forget about this and it could be last night again, before her mobile rang and she'd been stupid enough to answer it.

She wanted to head back to Ian's house, but there was still Jamie to deal with. Although he wasn't answering his phone, she knew this only meant he would still be sleeping it off. She was tempted to take the back way to avoid Orchard, but then Ian would be on his own for that much longer. Besides, something in her wanted to see where it had happened, as if the cold physical sight would yield some guidance about what she should do. She half expected there to be a roadblock. But instead, there was just pavement and trees and a few stubs of the flares they must have lit after she'd left, looking like melting ice-cream cones.

The gates at the Mannings' swung open and her breath seized.

There were at least a dozen vehicles crowded into the forecourt. But there were no police cruisers or news trucks, just the usual collection of sports cars, as small and wicked as bullets. Quint's people. Shannon pulled into the first available slot and started to walk toward the house but stopped when she saw the Wrangler, parked where Ian had left it last night. She checked to make sure no one was around, then went over to look at the front and then at the right side, the part that would have hit the man. The sheets of red metal were pristine, encased in their web of pads and bumpers and black steel. If there was any evidence of what had happened, then she couldn't see it. Men with swabs and gloves and microscopes might be able to find something, but there were none of them around.

She walked to the back of the house, knowing the sliding door would be open. Nobody was playing on the court, but she could hear the sound of clashing male voices coming from the hut. She stepped into the kitchen. Jamie's brothers were watching cartoons in the basement, and Carrie wasn't anywhere in evidence. Shannon went up to Jamie's room, where he still slept soundly, his long body twisted in his blankets.

"Hey. Jamie. Wake up."

Nothing. She began to feel very angry with him. If it weren't for his stupid drinking, none of this would have happened. They would have never left Ginny's house; they would have never been near Robert Jarvis. One of his sponge-light tennis shoes lay at her feet. She tossed it across the room, aiming for his legs but hitting his lower back. His eyes snapped open. He raised his head slightly.

"Why are you throwing things at me?"

"Because you're a jerk."

He stared at her in momentary confusion, then let his head fall back on the pillow.

"You're mad at me about last night," he said.

Shannon felt another pulse of that anger.

"You know what, Jamie? I don't care about last night. Get drunk if you want. Just don't expect me to come fetch you again. I'm not your *girlfriend* anymore."

He sat up, causing the blanket to fall away for a moment, exposing a stretch of naked hip that he quickly covered.

"Shan, why are you so mad?"

"Do you even remember what happened last night?"

"You drove me home." A baffled expression came to his face. "Right?"

She looked into his blue eyes, and suddenly the anger was gone, replaced by the same impulse that had gripped her when she saw her father: to confess everything.

"Yes, Jamie, I drove you home."

"God, for a minute there I thought I was losing it." He closed his eyes, doing momentary battle with his hangover. "Shannon, I'm really sorry about last night. Please don't be pissed at me."

"I'm not *pissed* at you, Jamie. I just don't want to be the one to clean up after you anymore."

"I know." He shook his head. "Look, you were the only person I could count on to keep me from getting in trouble with my father."

"Yeah, well, this is the last time. I mean it."

"I understand," he said meekly.

"All right. I'd better go."

"You want to hang around for a while?"

"Why?"

"I don't know. Just to talk. I was just . . . I thought we could talk about stuff."

She could see in his expression that something was bothering him. Shame, no doubt; shame and embarrassment. He wanted her to do what she'd done so often in the past, put her head on his chest and tell him that it was all right, that it hadn't been as bad as he suspected. She found herself thinking that this might not be such a bad thing to do. Those times last year didn't feel as far away as Shannon would have liked. The idea of crawling into bed with him began to exert a strange attraction. Not to do anything, but just so he could hold her for a while. Jamie wouldn't try to make it be anything more than that. The bed was messy and probably smelled of boy and beer, but it was also the place she'd lost her virginity, and now it felt like the safest spot on the planet. This whole house did. Unlike where she was headed.

"Good-bye, Manning."

"Hey, Shan, hold up, who'd you get to drive the Wrangler home?"

"I gave the keys to your idiot friends," she said as casually as possible.

"Matt and Steve?"

She didn't answer, and he took that as a yes. He fell back on his pillow.

"You're a star."

She left the room before he would force her to tell another lie, moving so fast that she actually, physically bumped into Carrie in the hallway.

"Shannon," she said, taking a step backward. "You scared the—"

They laughed briefly at the notion that anyone should be scared in this house.

"So is he awake?"

"I pelted him with shoes."

"That usually works."

Carrie shook her head in frustration. She looked tired, the skin in the orbits of her eyes doughy soft. For the first time since Shannon had known her, she seemed a little bit old.

"I understand you drove him home last night."

"I got one of his friends to bring the car back," Shannon said, a little too quickly.

"You're a saint."

Shannon had to get out of there before she said something wrong. But Carrie spoke before she could move.

"I don't know what we're going to do with him."

"Send him to Duke."

"Yeah, that's a good place to cut back on the partying," Carrie said, though there was something hollow in her irony now, as if she no longer believed there was that much distance between the wry things she said and her reality. "You want some coffee? It's been a while. I could use a few minutes with a sane person."

"I really gotta . . ."

Carrie tried to hide her disappointment.

"Okay," she said warmly. "But it's good to see you around. We really miss you."

Shannon nodded and briefly held Carrie's eye, struggling not to say what she was thinking: that she missed being here, too. Hanging around in the kitchen, trashing her classmates and their parents with Carrie. Watching movies in the screening room. Knocking his brothers around like a couple of puppies. The feel of Jamie's body in the heated pool at night. Quint hovering quietly on the edge of it all, strong and serene, needing nothing and giving everything.

She hurried back to her car. The automatic gate sprang open as she approached, just as it always did. She considered driving to Mercy to see if she could find out what *serious* meant, though she knew it was too risky. And anyway, there was nothing she could do at the hospital. Ian was right. Nothing depended on them. If the situation changed for the worse, they would know soon enough and they would go to the police. They'd agreed about that. The only thing for her to do now was to get back to Ian and make sure that he was all right.

14 Carrie hadn't slept all night. Just when the wine would lull her into something like unconsciousness, she would be jarred awake by the thought of what she'd let happen. A phrase began to play through her mind, one her mother would utter to mark her abundant childhood transgressions. *Now you've done it.* She could blame it on the pinot blanc, of course, though that would be a lie. In some murky annex of her mind, some peep show booth tucked amid the ganglia and neurons, she'd been planning this for a long time. And the reason was obvious. She'd slept with Jon to hurt her husband. This, evidently, was how she was going to make Quint pay for the Garden and Jamie and everything else. Which was a laugh, since there was absolutely no way that she could ever tell him what had happened. She might just as well have stuck pins in a Quint-shaped voodoo doll. He wouldn't be seized by guilt if he found out. He wouldn't become a changed man. Instead, he would subject her to months of silent, unrelenting anger. And that wasn't even the worst of it. In fact, she could handle the punishment and the disdain. What she couldn't endure was that it would also break his heart.

As dawn approached, she knew she'd have to speak with Jon. She'd put his DVD back in its cunningly designed matte box and drive over to his house and hand it to him, hoping that the gesture was sufficiently eloquent to bring this to an end. If he made her talk, then she would have to be careful not to say it was a mistake; she wouldn't use the language of regret. She could flavor the whole thing with a wistful, if-only tone she didn't for a moment feel. Anything, as long as he got the point: It wasn't going to happen again.

She got out of bed at first light. The entire world was humming. She went to her bathroom to take a couple of Motrin and found the bottle on the counter with its top off, which was strange; she didn't remember taking any last night. She poured a long bath and soaked until it felt as if her muscles were about to dissolve. Downstairs she gave the screening room a more sober check for that condom, then put the damp slipcovers in the dryer. Upstairs, she unloaded the dishwasher and more carefully hid the empty bottles in the recycling can. When everything was clean, she went to check on Jamie, this time using the emergency key to get through his locked door. His room had a yeasty, frat house aroma. His regular breathing made him look like some big Jamie doll in the process of being inflated. It occurred to her that he wasn't young anymore and he would never be young again. Carrie could fuck whoever she wanted, and it wouldn't change that simple fact.

She went back downstairs to call Jon. He answered on the first ring.

"I was hoping you'd call," he said.

Carrie wondered if she shouldn't just do this on the phone, though she knew that would only increase the odds of getting it all wrong. Besides, that would be cruel, and she was not going to be cruel.

"Carrie? Can you talk?"

"Not really," she lied. "Look, can I come over there? About ten-thirty?"

"I'll be here."

The dryer's tone sounded, and she fetched the hot slipcovers. They'd shrunk; wrestling them onto the cushions proved almost impossible. She was tempted to leave it for Sabine, but she knew that she had to do this herself. Her penance, or at least the beginning of it. When she finally finished, she checked for spotting—none, thank God—and then looked around. Everything else about the room looked normal. She went back to the kitchen and drank another cup of coffee. There was an e-mail on the family computer from Quint; he would be back at nine. She underwent a brief spell of panic at the prospect of his arrival, certain that he would be able to read what had happened on her face, that the men accompanying him would be forced to wait while he took her to his office, with its unlisted phone lines and four computer screens and floor safe whose combination was known only to the two of them and Godeep. He would shut the door and force her to confess, watching implacably as she spilled the beans.

But that was wrong. Quint would be too distracted to notice. And even if he did sense that something was different about her, he wouldn't put any sinister construction on it. It just would not occur to him that she had slept with someone, certainly not Jon, who was just another marginal character fluttering around the edges of their life. There was a time when she would have taken pleasure in this refusal to think the worst of her, his absolute faith in their marriage. Now she knew that his mind was elsewhere.

She was actually more worried about Jon. Carrie wasn't sure how to handle this. It had been almost twenty years since she'd broken off with someone. Disentangling herself had been easy during that bad year in New York; none of the half dozen men she'd been with cared too much about exit strategies. Before that, in the third-rate North Carolina drama school she'd attended after Juilliard turned her down, there had only been two major breakups, and she had been on the receiving end of both. First, soon after her arrival there was Marc, the Canadian ballet dancer who'd dumped her cold after a month of revelatory sex, leaving her to hunger like a junkie in withdrawal for the orgasms his long-muscled body provoked in her. And then, two years later, there was Dennis Dunbar, a melancholy director on leave from his wife and three kids in Indiana. Soon after they became lovers, he'd cast Carrie in the lead of his first big production, which just had to be *'Tis Pity She's a Whore*, and was too besotted to give her the direction she needed to master the role. The day after their disastrous opening night he fled back to Indiana, leaving Carrie a long letter explaining in detail why their affair was a mistake. It was just the sort of tough-minded note he hadn't given her during rehearsals. In fact, now that she thought about it, the only actual experience she'd ever had with getting rid of someone was Quint, on that horrible day at the end of her junior year at DWA, when she told him she didn't want to be his girlfriend anymore. Not that this was exactly a useful model, since five years later he came back and claimed her as his own.

Doors were slamming in the driveway. She went to the front window. It was Godeep, bringing back Dillon and Nick from the sleepover. The boys came crashing in, and Carrie let them go without the usual spot-check. She made small talk with Godeep for a few minutes, trying to see in his expression how bad things were with WMV, though of course, he wasn't giving anything away. The gate finally opened to admit Quint's car, followed by a roaring procession of penis substitutes. Carrie, the coward, hurried back inside and watched through the tinted glass as her husband convened the men in the forecourt. She didn't recognize this crew. They wielded tennis rackets like primitive weapons, smacking them into palms as if gauging their ability to inflict damage. She remembered Quint's saying something about their being lawyers, though of course, there was absolutely no way of knowing what they were. Nobody looked like what they were these days. She'd met CFOs who looked as if they played guitar in speed metal bands; she'd met indie film directors who comported themselves like science teachers. Mahabal shepherded the men down to the court along the side path. They were wary and unimpressed, like officers of a conquering army who were billeted in some splendid castle that nonetheless belonged to the enemy.

She met Quint in the front hall. The moment she saw his bloodshot eyes she knew he would not suspect anything had happened. He wasn't thinking about his marriage. His mind was lost in the world of bad fractions.

"So how was everything last night?" he asked vaguely.

Let's see, she thought. Your son came home blind drunk. I screwed another guy.

"Fine. Quiet."

"Did you guys watch your film?"

You guys meaning the entire Garden Film Society board, since she'd neglected to tell him it would just be Jon. She nodded, deciding it was time to change the subject. She'd had enough of this accounting for herself.

"So who is this crew?" she asked. "They look positively Visigothic."

"They represent some of the bigger partners. We're waiting to hear from Barclays about a margin call."

"Do you want me to do anything?" she asked. "Come down and serve canapés? Sing torch songs?"

He smiled grimly as he looked at the floor.

"You can tell me this isn't happening."

His words froze her. There was something in his voice she hadn't heard before, something almost like fear.

"Quint?"

He looked up at her, and there it was. Fear. Pure, unmistakable fear. She put her hand on his shoulder.

"Sweetheart?" she said.

He held her eye a moment longer, then shook his head, dismissing this messy, fragile emotion, knowing that if he brought it to the tennis court, they would tear him limb from limb.

"I'd better get down there and deal with these guys. I don't think they're believing I've only asked them here to play."

She was tempted to grab him as he walked past her, stop him and tell him that whatever was going on didn't have to be happening. If he wanted to wake Jamie and get the boys and fly off to some island, she'd be ready in a half hour. But she knew that he'd only look at her as if she were crazy, a diagnosis she couldn't easily contradict after last night. So she let him go down to his hard-eyed men.

She got some breakfast into Dillon and Nick before sending them out back, where they would be under the proximate supervision of their father. It was time to see Jon. But there was one more delay, Drew Hagel, almost front-ending her in the driveway. He didn't belong with this crew, driving that rusted Saab, his chin covered with crumbs. She remembered Quint saying he was looking to get hurt in the current crisis. She tried to think of something consoling to say, but all she could offer him was a weak smile.

The house Jon rented was a little frame number east of town, not quite old enough to be Victorian. Carrie had dropped him there a few times, though she'd never been inside. She rang the bell, but there was only a dry click within the mechanism itself. So she rapped on the screen door, an empty rattling that couldn't have carried more than a few feet. This was strange; he knew she was coming. She opened the screen and pounded on the door, a sound that would surely penetrate the house. Still, no response. She tried the knob. It spun uselessly in her hand for a few rotations, and then something caught. She stepped into the hallway, which smelled like Other People's Houses. There was a potted tree that was dead and didn't know it yet, a table with a bowl that held mail and coins and Jon's car keys.

She looked into the closest room and found a ratty, comfortable-looking chair directly facing a flat screen television. On either side of the TV were faux-wood DVD holders crammed with films. She thought of Jon sitting in this shabby little room, watching Godard or *In the Realm of the Senses*, dreaming of Carrie Manning. What have you done? she thought.

"Jon?" she called.

"I'm up here," he answered from above.

Carrie waited for the rest of the sentence, the part that explained that he would be down in a minute, that told her to make herself at home, there was coffee. But only silence followed.

"What do you want me to do?" she asked.

"Come on up," he said.

Carrie was starting to worry that some sort of erotic ambush awaited her. Just go, she thought. Leave his movie and drive home. He'll get the picture. But that would be cruel. She owed him an explanation. This was Jon. Gentle, decent, there-for-her Jon. She mounted the steps, piled with junk mail and movie magazines. She paused at the top. A poster in Russian for a Bond film, *From Russia with Love*—she got it—and another terminal plant. There were a couple of long fissures in the ceiling's plaster. Four doors, one of them opening to a small bathroom, the others closed or nearly closed.

"Um, do I get to guess?"

"In here," he said from behind one of the doors.

Not liking this now, convinced there was a surprise and certain she didn't want a surprise, she pushed open the door to what she fully expected to be his bedroom. But it was just a threadbare office. The only significant piece of furniture was a rickety wood table that held a computer and a phone. There were plenty of books and magazines, arranged in piles and overstuffed shelves. Jon wasn't lying for her in some seductive pose; he wasn't perched, grinning and tumescent, on a divan. He simply sat at the table in front of his laptop, fully dressed in khakis and a sweatshirt and his wire-framed glasses. On his computer's screen was the blocky dialogic pattern of a screenplay. Carrie understood. He wanted her to see him at work. He was trying to impress his new girlfriend. On the wall above the computer was a framed poster from an RSC production of *King Lear*, designed by one of those British cartoonists who saw humans as wicked, pointy creatures. The King and his Fool, locked in a tormented embrace.

"Sorry," he said, saving and closing. "Just wanted to finish this sequence."

He stood and moved toward her, just as he had in the forecourt last night. Carrie, working on instinct, took a half step back and raised her hand, unconsciously using the DVD case to block his progress. Jon smiled in confusion when he saw it.

"You didn't have to bring that back."

"I just . . ."

She lowered the case, suddenly unsure what to say. The sight of him at work had weakened her resolve.

"Carrie?" he asked, his voice a little softer. "What's going on?"

"We should talk about last night," she said finally.

He looked puzzled. Any hope she had that this would be accomplished with a few knowing words evaporated.

"All right."

"I think we should try to be realistic about the situation."

"Realistic?"

"What I'm saying is . . . look, this can't happen."

His eyes narrowed. He was getting it now.

"But it already did happen."

"Jon . . ."

"Hold on a second, Carrie. Slow down. Are you . . . you're telling me that's it? You don't want to see me anymore?"

"Things went too far last night."

"Too far?" He shook his head in disbelief. "You can't . . . there's no way you can stand there and tell me that last night wasn't exactly where we've been heading these last few months. I was there the whole time, remember? I was the guy on the other end of all those lingering looks. It was me who listened when you complained about how empty your life was becoming. And then you invite me to your house and there's wine and you sit next to me and I touch you—"

"Jon, stop."

"Stop what? Telling the truth? What is this, Carrie? Are you trying to tell me you were just drunk and angry with your husband? That last night was a little romp?"

"Don't ask me to account for myself. Please."

He looked down at the cheap throw rug between them. Neither spoke for several long seconds.

"And so you're honestly telling me that you don't want to see me. That's why you came over here."

"I'm sorry," was all she could say.

He looked up at her.

"But what am I supposed to do?"

"Do?"

"No, what I'm asking is, what happens to the last five months? Does that just get wiped out? All the time and affection I've devoted to you—does that disappear, just like that?"

Carrie couldn't bring herself to answer him, because the truth was that it *had* vanished, sometime during the long drunken night. Just like that. Their eyes held for a moment, and he finally understood. There was no longer any reason to plead. It was over. He looked away.

"All right. If that's what you want then there's nothing I can—"

He stopped himself abruptly. When he looked back at her, his eyes were narrow and bitter.

"You know what? There's something you should understand about yourself, Carrie. You dabble. I saw this in you from the first, but I thought last night meant you were finally ready to get serious. Clearly I was wrong. You, you make these little reality raids, and then, when it gets messy, you retreat back to your sanctuary up on Orchard. You never think you have to pay for anything. You want to be an actress, but you won't do what's necessary to achieve that. So you marry Quint and have these sons, but being with them isn't enough and so you sleep with me. And then you realize this might cost you something, so you run away from me as well. You just scurry through life and let everybody else pick up the check."

Carrie looked back at that terrible poster, wondering if the man who drew it really saw people that way.

"I'm sorry," she said again as she turned to go. "I really am."

"Carrie . . ."

He was holding out his hand. She thought he was offering her something, an embrace, forgiveness, an invitation to further infidelity. But he only wanted his DVD back. She handed it to him.

Driving home, she tried to imagine some way the last half hour could have come out worse but came up with nothing that didn't involve hidden cameras or a hostage situation. What had made it even more terrible was that everything Jon said was true. She was a dabbler. She didn't live in the world. She didn't pay for things. And now the only thing to do was return to her sanctuary before she did any more damage.

The penis cars were still there. She walked around back, thinking she'd better see if Quint needed anything. At the side of the house two men, locked in sour conversation, strode quickly toward her. They were a couple of truly nasty specimens, clenched and graceless in their arrogance. Their tennis whites looked all wrong, as if they had been cut for a different type of animal. Their conversation froze when they saw her. She flashed them what she considered a winning smile, but they strode right past her with only the vaguest nods. Well, fuck you and the Porsche you rode in on, she was tempted to call after them, though she figured that would hardly help matters. She walked to the edge of the patio and looked down at the tennis hut. There was a short aria of shouting, countered by Mahabal's smooth tenor.

Leave my husband alone, she thought.

Reassuring herself that at least Godeep was there, she went back into the house. It was past noon. Carrie wanted nothing more than to bring the curtain down on this day with a bath and a few glasses of red wine. She'd restart her life tomorrow, Sunday, the customary day for atonement. But she still had one more thing to do. She had to talk to Jamie. As she neared his room, she heard an unexpected voice. It's Shannon, she thought, just as Shannon opened the door and walked right into her. Carrie hadn't noticed her car amid the glut of vehicles in the forecourt. Beyond her, Jamie sat on his bed, shrouded in bed linen, naked as the day he was born.

They spoke briefly, too briefly, Shannon clearly uncomfortable to the point of mortification at being caught in Jamie's room with him still in bed; Shannon, who was usually so relaxed and at home here, now acting as if she had the household silver stuffed up under her baggy sweatshirt. Carrie tried to draw her into conversation, but Shannon made a hasty getaway.

She stepped up to the open door.

"What was Shannon doing here?"

Jamie stared at her.

"Look," she continued, "I think we'd better talk."

"If you let me get out of bed."

His voice was as surly as she'd ever heard it. Carrie was stunned. Jamie never took this tone with her. She immediately cast about for an excuse for him, figuring he must be feeling the effects of last night's bender. She stepped back into the hallway. There was grunting and rustling as Jamie dressed.

"Yeah?" he said, challenge in his voice.

She stepped into the room. Still a dump, but that yeasty stench she'd detected earlier in the morning had been cut by Shannon's altogether sweeter smell. He was seated at his computer, hitting buttons, checking his messages.

"We should talk about last night."

He shrugged in response. Carrie felt herself getting angry. Why was he acting like this? She hadn't done anything to him. She was still his coconspirator.

"Keep looking at that screen instead of me, and we get your father involved. He's down at the court. I can give him a call, and the two of you can go round and round."

Jamie raised an eyebrow.

"He's home?"

"Yes, he is. And he's not in an especially rosy mood."

He hit keys in that superfast manner of the young. Boxes and icons began to retreat in neat precision. He turned to her, that challenge still in his expression.

"You've got to watch this drinking, Jamie," she said, softening her voice. "It's illegal, and it's very stupid."

He looked away in a gesture Carrie would have identified as contemptuous if this had been anyone besides her eldest son.

"Jamie? Are we agreed on that?"

"Whatever."

She gave her head a baffled shake.

"What is it with this attitude? What have I done to you?"

To Carrie's surprise, he was ready with an answer.

"Where were you last night?" he asked with sudden vehemence. "If you're so worried, why didn't *you* come get me?"

Carrie recoiled in the face of this anger.

"I'm sorry if I wasn't totally on call for you last night, James."

"Yeah, well, I don't feel like talking to you about last night, all right?"

"Look at me. *Look at me.*"

He did, though only with the greatest of reluctance.

"Did you drive home drunk last night?"

"No."

"No," she said flatly.

"I told you. Shannon drove me."

"And what about the Wrangler? Did that just trail you home like a loyal dog?"

"Some of the guys brought it back."

"Who? Was it Jazz?"

"No, he wasn't there."

"Then who? Matt and Stephen?"

He nodded.

"Which one?"

"I don't know. Shannon gave them the keys."

Of course, she could check up on this by calling the Dulea or

Petrillo households, but it was hard to see exactly how such a conversation would pan out. Yes, hello, my son came home blotto last night and claims your boys drove his car home, but I think he's lying, so, could you ask them?

"Are we done?" he asked.

There was more Carrie could say, but she knew the only way to prolong the conversation was to let it turn into a fight. And she didn't want that. She'd done all she could. Jamie had been chastened. Jon had been banished, Quint kept in ignorance. The only thing left to do was to take another long bath and hope that there was enough hot water in the tank to wash this wretched day away.

David loved to drive at night. He loved the way the road seemed to be moving, a never-ending black scroll drawing him into the darkness. How the mile markers flashed by like the startled eyes of nocturnal creatures; how the radio stations drifted in from over the western horizon, forecasting weather that wasn't his weather. Tib thought he was crazy to leave this late, but he wanted to get home as soon as possible to talk to Ian. He wanted to let his nephew know that he'd found the perfect place for them to live.

He'd arrived in Beaufort late Thursday afternoon. Things were different at the inlet now. The bait and tackle shops surrounding that big parking lot all were open; the marina's windows were alive with the flashes of welders' torches; the covers had come off the boats. Tib greeted him in the Cove with the news that he would be working that night; the regular bartender had called in sick. David lost himself in the work. He'd forgotten the sheer, engrossing pleasure of tending bar, how you could get a rhythm going, forgetting everything but the task at hand. He and Tib were like an old pitcher-catcher team reunited late in their careers. It took them a few innings to get back into the groove, but before long they were moving effortlessly around each other in the tight space, finishing off orders or taking over conversations the other guy had started.

They met with Gary Jeff Hill the following morning on the deck overlooking the inlet. He was in a new wheelchair, fitted with all the latest equipment, toggles and switches and a powerful motor beneath the seat. His final chair. His Cape Hatteras chair. He had sunk deeper into it, his body curling and shriveling like something subjected to sustained heat. The bright May sun seemed to shine right through to his ice blue veins. But the same intelligence burned in his eyes as he flipped through a daunting stack of papers: gross income and net income, insurance, and how much he still had left on the mortgage.

"So I guess you boys are going to want to know what I'm going to need to let you have this traveling circus."

He showed them a piece of paper bearing a single figure. It was about what David and Tib had anticipated. A little on the high end, but certainly manageable, as long as they had all of Ginny's money.

"And that's it. I don't haggle. Ask Tib here. I ain't got time, and I sure haven't got the inclination."

They agreed, shaking hands, a quiet moment fraught with life and death. There wasn't time to celebrate. They had to prep for lunch. Tib handled the cooking, and David held down the bar, all the while thinking about how it would be when he owned the place. Coming in mornings, when no one else was around except the cleaners. Eating lunch late. Sitting up in that office at night, where he could keep an eye on the crowd. Like Gregg Allman in that drug movie, only without the drugs. There would be headaches—he thought about that pile of paper Hill had shown them—but there were always going to be headaches. The difference was that these would be his own.

"Come on," Tib said when lunch was over. "I want to show you something."

He drove David out through marshland, acres of waist-high grass alive with butterflies and birds and that strange local light he was starting to like. Halfway to Morehead City they turned onto a narrow road that cut through a stand of thick trees and then emerged into another vast marshy meadow. After another minute of driving the journey's object came into view: a small, shingled house at the edge of a coastal pond. Reed fields surrounded it on three sides; on the fourth, the northern side, the house bordered a narrow black water tributary that ran toward a line of balding dunes. Beyond the dunes, David could see the ocean's generous sky. Anvil thunderheads rose from the horizon, though they appeared to be heading out to sea.

"The coast is farther than you'd think," Tib said, tracking his gaze. "But it's there."

"What is this place?"

"Fellow owns it plays music at the Cove. He's a lawyer, but don't hold that against him. He used to rent this one out to a bird artist, but that fellow passed a few months back. This lawyer asked if I knew anybody to rent it and I told him about you and he said that sounds fine to him as long as I can vouch for you. I said, 'Bud, if I can't vouch for David Alan Warfield, my vouching days are over.' He doesn't want seasonal. There's a family in it now, but they're just summer assholes. Come fall it's wide open. And I think he'd be willing to sell eventually."

"Bird artist?"

"Fellow painted birds. Sold his pictures down in Morehead City."

"I could think of worse ways to make a buck."

"Heard that."

Tib had borrowed a key. The house was simple inside: galley kitchen, three small bedrooms, a big den that overlooked the water. Although the tourists had piled their junk everywhere, David could see what it would be like when they were gone. The floors were smooth blond wood; everything was modern and tightly sealed. The builders had cut no corners. There were brand-new storm windows and modern appliances in the kitchen. Bird portraits covered the walls. The guy who used to live here was pretty good if they were his. The best thing, though, was the light, so much of it, pouring through the big window facing the waterway and the Plexiglas skylight in the kitchen. Ginny's house could be so dark, even at this time of year.

"How'd this guy die?" David asked.

"Drowned. Not here, though. He was snorkeling down in the Bahamas."

"Seems like a long way to go to drown."

David noticed a wood table underneath the window, pushed right up to the wall. It was stained and scored. This would have been where the man worked, painting the birds that even now flocked to the elaborate feeders set on poles in the marsh outside the window.

Someone would have to row out to replenish them. David had a vision of Ian sitting here, painting something real instead of those wretched black things he tore out of his mind's cellar.

"This would be perfect for my nephew. He likes to draw."

"I believe you may have mentioned that."

David turned. Tib was smiling. His future partner was smiling.

Gary Jeff Hill didn't come in Friday night; he'd had a steroid injection earlier and wasn't feeling up to getting out of bed. David could see what Tib said about the summer crowd's being very different from the morons back in Daytona. They were steady and respectable. The prospect of trouble was remote; people coming in to be rowdy would have soon left for one of the roadhouses out near Camp Lejeune. Around ten the place got seriously crowded, and for a few minutes David thought he was going to lose his grip on the situation, but Tib gave him a calm down look, and before he knew it, everything was back under control.

After closing Tib offered to let him sleep on his sofa again, but David knew it was time to get back to Connecticut. So he shook his partner's hand in the parking lot and told him he'd be back in two weeks with a bank check for his half of the deposit. By then the lawyer who owned the bird artist's house—David had met him; he played something called a hammered dulcimer—would have drawn up the purchase agreement.

"So this is really happening, right?" David said before getting into the Chevelle.

"It certainly is."

His mind was alive with possibility as he drove home. Now he would be able to present Ian with a concrete plan. First, he'd tell him about that house overlooking the marsh. He'd describe the girls who crowded into the bar, all those tanned limbs and white smiles; the university in Wilmington he could attend if that turned out to be something he wanted to do. Although Ian had hinted a couple times since Monday that he might be thinking about splitting Ginny's money, David was absolutely certain that he could now convince him to commit every penny to the Cove. Just to make sure, he'd bring him along when he went back down in two weeks, parole or no parole, girl or no girl. It was inconceivable that he would be able to turn this down once he saw it all.

He arrived home late Saturday morning. The back door was open, but there was no sign of Shannon's car. The table was a mess, dirty plates and some candles that had burned nearly all the way down. Figuring his nephew was sleeping late, he got the coffee going, making just enough noise to wake him. Ian soon appeared in the kitchen doorway, dressed in a pair of boxers and gray socks. It didn't look as if he'd been sleeping any time recently. His hair was a mess, and there was something strange about his eyes, that caught-in-the-headlights look David hadn't seen in a while. He walked into the room, unsure what to do with himself. He ran the tap, then turned it off for no apparent reason.

"You all right?" David asked.

"Yeah. Sure." His eyes were on the draining water. "You know. Sorta."

Not the answer David was looking for. He wondered if this had something to do with the girl. In fact, it was strange that she wasn't here. Maybe they'd had a fight over their candlelit dinner.

"So what'd you do while I was away?"

Ian yawned shallowly, scratching at his flank as he approached the table.

"What?"

"I was asking what you been up to."

Ian picked off an icicle of wax from one of the candles and crumbled it between his fingers, a half smile forming on his lips, though it soon settled into a frown.

"Just hung out."

"Hung out," David answered skeptically.

Once again Ian didn't show any sign of registering David's words. The coffee machine had reached its last strangulated moments.

"Is this all for you?" he asked, pointing at the steaming glass pot.

"Of course not."

He poured himself a cup but didn't offer David any. Something was definitely wrong. Ian always poured his uncle a cup. One and a half sugars, a splash of milk.

"Ian," David said firmly, "look at me."

Again, that half smile, though he reluctantly obeyed. His eyes looked as if they were plugged directly into the nuclear reactor some fool had built down on the sound.

"What's going on with you?"

Ian didn't answer, though he was beginning to look as if he wanted to speak. David stretched his leg beneath the table and kicked out a chair. Ian sat heavily, his thin shoulders slumping, his chin dropping toward his chest. He shook his head as he laughed bitterly.

"I was just doing the guy a favor."

Whatever exhaustion David had been feeling vanished with a few thundering beats of his heart.

"Okay," he said, knowing that the most important thing now was to go slow. "What guy?"

"Shannon's friend. *Jamie*. Preppy jerk."

"Let's—when are we talking about? Last night?"

Ian shook his head, then nodded.

"And what sort of favor did you do this guy?"

Don't be drugs, David prayed. Do not be drugs.

"He was drunk, so we went to get him from this party they kicked him out of. But he didn't want to leave his car there. So I said, you know, I'll drive it home."

David nodded agreeably, doing everything he could to mask the full-blown dread now gripping him.

"So you drove his—"

"Wrangler. Five-point-oh."

Jesus.

"And where was Shannon?"

"She drove him in her car."

"Okay, and so what happened next?"

"So we're going up this winding hill to the guy's house. You know, on Orchard?"

David knew it well. He must have been up the stretch of road a hundred times, running account clients to the big houses up there. It was just about the last place in the world he'd want his nephew driving a powerful Jeep.

"And there's this guy on a bicycle. I didn't even see him until he was right next to me. I mean, all right, I was definitely punching it up the hill, you know, downshifting like crazy, and maybe I take one of those turns a little too tight. But the Jeep just barely touches him. What's the word? Sideswipes. But not even that. I mean, it's like this."

He brushed the table lightly, knocking some of the crumbled wax to the floor.

"But he went down?"

Ian nodded gently.

"Did you stop?"

"No. I mean, I didn't know he'd gone down at first. Not for sure."

Okay, David thought. Okay. There are no cops at the door. Nobody's in handcuffs. We're still at the beginning of this.

"I did stop at the top of the hill, but Shannon and Jamie just flew right by me. So I followed them there. To the house, I mean. Jamie's. And then I tell Shannon what happened and we go back and the guy was—there were people there and somebody had called the cops already, so I mean, what was the point of saying anything?"

"Ian, is this guy dead?"

"No. Come on! What did I tell you? I barely touched him. He just—I think he had a concussion. But he was awake. You could see him talking to people."

"Okay. So what happened then?"

"Shannon wanted to tell the cops, but I said no way, so we came back here."

"Have you heard anything?" David asked. "On the news, I mean."

"Yeah. They said he was in serious condition at Mercy. But that doesn't necessarily mean anything, right? Serious?"

David gave his head a reassuring shake.

"People are always saying things are serious that aren't. So where's Shannon?"

"Home. She's supposed to be coming right back over."

"And what's she thinking about all this?"

"What do you mean?" Ian asked, growing instantly defensive.

"You said she wanted to call the cops."

"That was last night."

"But what about now?"

"She thinks if the guy's in real bad shape, we'll have to do something. But she wouldn't do it without me agreeing first."

"Are you sure?"

"Yeah, I'm sure."

"Now, this boy whose car it was—what's his deal? Does he know anything?"

"He won't remember. He'd *passed out*."

"But it was his car, Ian. I mean, if there's some kind of damage . . ."

Ian suddenly grew agitated.

"Haven't you been listening? I barely touched the guy."

"Ian, calm yourself, okay? I'm just trying to help here. All right. So the only people who know about this as of right now are you, me, and Shannon?"

"Yeah."

"And she's coming over here?"

"I thought you were her."

"Okay." David slowly pushed his chair back. "Wait here a second, will you?"

"Where you going?" Ian asked, his voice urgent.

"Nowhere. I'm not going anywhere."

David strode as casually as possible to the bathroom. He shut and locked the door, turned on the fan, then knelt before the toilet and proceeded to vomit with great ferocity. His stomach just detonated. It felt as if every one of his 150 pounds was being evacuated. First came the things he'd eaten while driving home, the cinnamon doughnut and potato chips, the sixteen-ounce Coke and medium coffee. Then came the lone bitter beer he'd had last night, followed by the hamburgers and tacos and over-easy eggs that he'd eaten yesterday and the day before and the day before that; he was puking everything he'd ever consumed, all of it streaming out on a cascading river of bile. He was throwing up his entire life. He vomited the bad jobs and stupid whores and lost fights; the drugs and the tequila shots and the nights wasted chasing good times that simply did not exist. Out came the pain of his father's fists and his sister's humiliation. And then there was the quarter ounce of reefer he'd given his nephew the night the cops got him, though it was now sopping and clumped together, incapable of getting anyone high. Finally, out came Ginny's cancer, a half dozen egg-size tumors, green and black and oily, throbbing with death. It came and came, all of it, stinking to high heaven, filling up the bowl, threatening to bubble over. And then, after a few dry heaves to make sure nothing had been forgotten, it was over. He stood, coughing and sneezing and blowing his nose, his stomach muscles throbbing, his throat raw. He flushed away the great putrid mass and walked over to the sink, where he looked at his dog-tired, red-eyed face in the mirror. There was some stuff in his mustache, so he cleaned that away. Now that the attack was over his mind felt bright and empty. For one blessed minute, not a single thought entered his brain, until three unbidden images arrived, one after the other. The first was his nephew sitting in that cell last year, terrified to his core, but refusing to tell the cops about David. The second was the view out of that big window in North Carolina, the birds moving among the reeds. And finally, there was his sister's face, the way it seemed to collapse in on itself after they had moved her into the hospice section.

"All right," David said to his mirror image.

He brushed his teeth and washed his face, then went back to the table, taking a different chair this time, the one right next to his nephew.

"You all right?" Ian asked.

David shook away the question. It didn't matter what he was.

"Ian, listen to me. I want you to understand that you've done the right thing. I know it's been tough on you these past few hours, but I'm home now and I'm going to take care of you on this one. Okay?"

Ian nodded.

"Now, you've got to promise you'll do exactly what I say. Then we'll be able to sort this out. Will you do that for me?"

Ian didn't answer straightaway, and so David reached out and touched his bare shoulder.

"Will you?"

"Yeah," Ian said, smiling weakly. "I'll do that."

Shannon arrived soon after, looking even worse than his nephew.

"I know what happened," David said as she walked through the screen door, keeping it gentle, not wanting to scare her off but also aware that they had no time to waste.

Shannon looked at Ian in alarm.

"And you did the right thing," David added before either of them could speak.

He gestured to a chair. After a brief show of reluctance she took it.

"So how you holding up?"

"Bad," she said.

"But you didn't tell anyone just now?"

She looked at Ian, appealing to him to rescue her from this sudden interrogation, but he remained mute, his leg jostling the table, content to let his uncle handle matters.

"Of course not," she said, trying to sound offended, though it came out as simple fear. "Nobody knows anything. Except us."

"What about this other boy? What's his name?"

"Jamie," Ian said.

She shot Ian a look.

"Shannon?" David asked. "What about Jamie?"

"He doesn't know anything."

"Yeah, but when he sees his car . . ."

"I checked that, too. You can't tell anything from it."

David nodded approvingly, knowing he had to be careful with the girl. She was going to be the key to everything.

"Shannon, you have to understand, I'm on your side here. Totally and completely. I'm going to help you guys keep a lid on this situation. Okay?"

She didn't answer, though he could see that her initial defiance was fading.

"So I guess the next thing we have to do is find out exactly how this man on the bicycle is doing."

"Robert Jarvis. His name is Robert Jarvis." She took a deep breath. "They're saying he's serious."

"*Serious* can mean a lot of things."

She looked down at the table, at the pulverized wax Ian had spread there.

"Look, I think we're going to have to tell the police what happened."

David nodded, as if he were giving this some kind of consideration.

"Well, I understand your position," he said. "But you gotta wonder what good that would do."

"It's the truth."

"Well, yes, it's *a* truth. But there are other truths at work here. Shannon, let me ask you something, you ever been arrested?"

She shook her head. Ian was staring at his uncle. Listening carefully.

"Well, then, you definitely wouldn't know what it's like to be arrested for the *second* time. That's when the fun starts. You see, first time, everybody's trying to figure out if you're wicked or stupid or just plain unlucky. You can negotiate, maybe even make things break your way. Second time, though, they got everything they need. They own you. And that's the *truth*."

"But what if they find out? Won't we get in more trouble than if we—"

"Shannon, I'm sorry to say this, but you already *are* in more trouble. You have been ever since the two of you drove off from the scene."

This was harsh and not really accurate, since the police were always softer on people who made their job easier. They were as lazy as anybody else. But he also knew that the way forward with this girl was to paint a picture of Ian in grave danger. She wouldn't be checking auto bodies and reading the newspaper unless she was desperate to help him get out from under this. That was what David had to work with here. Not threats or anger or lies. But the love.

"So here's what you got to figure," he continued. "You've got to make a little equation in your head to determine if justice is being served. On one side, you call the cops and tell them everything and Ian winds up in jail for my guess is a couple years. Years. As an adult, 'cause seventeen don't mean shit these days. And you may not know this, but the state of Connecticut now prefers to ship its convicts off to such friendly places as Virginia and Texas. And on the other side you have what? Does that man get better? Do we get to rewind the tape to last night and make it all go away?"

Shannon shook her head. She was getting it. As he knew she would.

"So what you have then is an unequal equation. What happens to Ian is a lot worse than anything good that comes of it. You're a smart girl, Shannon, so if you don't like my math, just jump right in here."

Shannon looked back at Ian, whose expression had grown considerably darker at the mention of prison, some of the terror from those days of his mother's dying creeping into his eyes.

"So the question I'm asking you, right here, right now: Do you want to send Ian to jail? Do you want the police to pull up the driveway and put handcuffs on him and take him away for the next couple of years?"

"No," she said. "Of course not."

"Me neither," David said. "Me neither."

He said nothing for a moment, holding her big pretty eyes, making it clear that a deal had just been struck.

"Now here's my idea," he said eventually. "Why don't you two spend some time alone and let me look into this? I'll find out the lay of the land, and if it's hopeless, we'll do what we have to do. But if there's a chance that we can keep Ian out of big trouble, then I think we should give that a try. What do you think?"

"Come on, Shan," Ian said, his first words in a while. "He's right."

She nodded once, so slight a motion it was hard to see unless you were looking for it. Which David most certainly was.

"Well, all right then," he said. "Sounds like we got us a deal."

He shaved and showered and put on a suit, fighting off the exhaustion, trying to stay focused on the task at hand. To help bolster himself, he thought about his passengers in the back of the executive cars, how they reacted when their cell phones rang with bad news. They wouldn't panic. They would take a moment to regain their poise, and then they would *deal with it*. David, soon to be owner of a thriving business, a place subject to hurricanes and fires and biker gang invasions, understood that this was his first real test. If he was ever going to be something more than a cart horse, he would have to handle it, effectively and immediately. The first thing to do was find out about this Robert Jarvis. He had to see what they meant by *serious*. It could mean a coma or it could mean a plaster cast that his friends could sign. Once David had the answer to that question, he would know the best way to save his nephew.

He found the two of them planted on the living room sofa, looking like a couple of little kids who had no intention of going anywhere.

"All right," he said. "I'll be back as soon as possible."

Getting into Mercy wasn't a problem. He knew it well. It was where Ginny had died. It was a busy, wide-open facility; security wouldn't rumble you unless you parked in an ambulance bay or started rifling the drug cabinets. He slotted the Chevelle into an auxiliary lot and walked up to the main entrance, hovering just beyond the laser eye of the automatic doors until the receptionist got busy with an elderly couple. By the time David reached the desk she was on the phone, waiting for someone to pick up at the extension she'd dialed. The oldsters fidgeted impatiently. David sidled in next to them and met the receptionist's eye, smiling at her like an old friend.

"Jarvis," he said, so quietly that he was almost mouthing the words. "His brother."

The receptionist tapped the letters into her computer, then cupped her hand over the phone.

"Critical care," she said, her voice as quiet as David's. "Second floor."

Critical care, he thought. All right. He found the ward easily. There were plenty of signs, the large red one outside the CCU stating that only people having business were allowed inside. He took a deep breath and hit the button that operated the slow doors. There was a liquid, metallic glow in the ward's air; a humming silence. Two nurses were at the main desk, staring down at a screen whose information seemed to be stumping them. They wore austere green scrubs, nothing like the pastel teddy bear blouses they had on the regular wards. Neither looked up. David walked past them with casual purpose. A doctor approached in the opposite direction, swatting a big X-ray envelope against his thigh, giving him one of those bleak doctor nods. As David moved deeper into the unit, he resisted the temptation to stare into the wheezing, beeping rooms that he passed, all of them filled with modern equipment and motionless visitors, big hurt and bad luck. Jarvis's room was near the back of the ward; his name was scrawled on an erasable board by the door. It was surrounded by an indecipherable jumble of letters and numbers. His secret fate. The patient was propped up on an angled mattress. He was a long, skinny man with a jutting Adam's apple and a sharp nose. His skin was sallow; a shock of sweaty hair stuck out from the side of his head. The oxygen tube running into his mouth was held in place by tape; a thinner tube ran into his arm, this one carrying clear liquid. There were wires and monitors. On a small screen above the bed, one group of digits gave way to another. He remembered this from Ginny's last days, how you would start reading the numbers, relying on them, even though you didn't have the slightest idea what they meant.

A woman stepped into view. She wore jeans and a baggy sweater and slip-on shoes; her limp blond hair was held in a ponytail by a black band. She stared down at the man for a while, then used her finger to push a strand of that sweaty hair off his forehead. She was saying things nobody would ever hear. Her eyes were watery and red, but she was done with crying. David knew that this was Robert Jarvis's wife, and he also knew that this man was going to die.

He turned and walked slowly toward the exit. One of the nurses looked up as he passed their station.

"Wrong turn," he explained.

There was an empty waiting area outside the ward, sofas and chairs and a low table covered with old magazines. Concession machines and a pay phone. David dropped into one of the chairs, unable to focus on anything but the woman's drained eyes. All right, he thought. It's still an accident. There's still no reason for Ian to go to jail, no reason for his life to end. There would be no justice in that. Just keep thinking that one thing, David told himself. Just keep focusing on what's right for Ian and the both of you can still wind up in that house in the marshes.

He wasn't sure how much time passed before the slow doors brushed open. Jarvis's wife emerged, holding a cell phone. She walked over to the waiting area and perched on the arm of a chair across from him. She was a little younger than he'd first thought. The way the lines flowed on her face made him think she was somebody who liked to laugh. Her gaze landed on him, registering his sympathetic expression. She showed him the phone.

"They won't let you use it inside," she said numbly. "They say it might interfere with the machines."

He nodded soberly. She summoned a stored number. David picked up a magazine and pretended to read about the ten greatest water holes in North America.

"Tom, it's me." Something caught in her throat. "Well, I just saw the second surgeon . . . No, he was the same. There's nothing they can do. 'Multiple inoperable sites of intracranial hemorrhage.' I've heard that phrase so much today I've memorized it. So it's just waiting now. They're going to move him to a regular room . . . No, they're at home with Ma, who's being great. For once. Teresa's here with me now. What? . . . No, I talked to a nice detective but they're still, you know . . . God, Tom, I want to get mad at him for going out so late, but he'd missed a week with the hamstring and there's Chilliwack coming up . . ." Her voice caught again. "Anyway, so when's your flight? . . . Right. You told me that. You want me to pick you up? . . . Okay. You sure? . . . Okay . . . Yeah. I know."

She hung up, and David allowed himself to look back at her. She put a hand to her forehead in that stiff-fingered way some women had, and then she made a sudden gasping sound, as if she'd just come up for air after spending too long underwater. David wondered what would happen if she lost it now, another human being getting hysterical ten feet away from him and no one else around. He would have to say something to comfort her, and once he started talking he wasn't sure where that would go. But she soon gained control of herself, and then the elevator doors opened and another woman emerged. Teresa. A friend, maybe even a sister. Trying to help and knowing there was no help. She was holding two Styrofoam cups in a cardboard tray. Jarvis's wife put on a brave face when she saw her. As the two women began to speak, David stood and gently placed the magazine back on the low table. It was time to go.

He drove straight back to the house. They met him in the kitchen, Ian even more wired than when he'd left.

"Nobody knows anything," David said. "I checked the hospital and—"

"How is he?" Shannon interrupted.

The truth would be too much for them now. It had been a long day. Maybe tomorrow. Or the day after that. But not now.

"They're moving him out of intensive care," David said.

PART FIVE

16 Carrie knew that at some point she was going to have to get out of the bath. She'd decided on a new regime, and this was as good a time as any to implement it, a late Monday afternoon when nobody seemed to know what to do. Dillon and Nick were in the basement, spellbound by one of their epic video games; Jamie was locked in solitary, grumbling combat with the ball machine down at the court. It was wrong to ignore them when they were so close. If you want to leave this family, then just go. Cash out and start over. Find some third-rate SoHo artist or indie wannabe; move in with Jon and watch the world finish grinding him into dust. Live alone and wind up like your mother, with her muumuus and stashed Gilbey's. Or stick with the man who will never leave you, who will never let you down. Stay with the boys you created. Latch on to all that vibrant imperfection, and let it carry you along.

The bubbles were evaporating, revealing a pale submerged image of a woman. Five more minutes, she bargained with herself. And then she'd be cutting down on the baths. Five minutes, and then she'd find something to do with the boys until her husband came home. The Mannings would have dinner together for the first time in weeks. She'd cornered Quint this morning, making him agree to return at a decent hour.

"Define *decent*," he'd said wearily.

"Seven. And if you're late, I'm going to call the SEC and tell them that you've bought us all one-way plane tickets to Brazil."

He smiled. Physically smiled.

"All right. Seven."

"Promise?" she asked, because if he promised, he would never break it.

"Yes. I promise."

That smile was a breakthrough. It had been a long, bad weekend. On Saturday the angry mob had remained down at the tennis court until midafternoon. It wasn't until a half hour after the last of their irritable little cars vanished through the gate that Quint had dragged himself through the sliding glass door and joined her in the kitchen, where she was making dinner. He sat at the table and began to rub at an invisible smudge, shaking his head slowly. Carrie, vegetable peeler in hand, watched him from the sink.

"Are you hungry?" she asked. "I could get you a sandwich."

He grimaced and nodded toward the forecourt.

"*They're* the hungry ones."

"So what's going on?"

His expression leveled out, his habitual discretion taking over. No, Carrie thought. I won't dwell in the suburbs of his good pleasure. Not anymore.

"Talk to me, Quint."

He looked into the next room and let out the sort of sigh an old man might emit, a lip-flapping evacuation of his lungs. Not a typical Quint sound—not by a long shot.

"The spreads are all wrong," he said, his voice flat and slightly unreal. "They should be converging, and they're not. Which leaves our notional exposure—"

"Quint, English. Please."

"We're starting to have to sell things we don't want to sell to pay back our creditors. We're running out of capital. The fund is going broke."

Carrie laughed nervously.

"Okay, maybe not quite so much English."

"It's . . . the odds of this happening on this specific spectrum of trades are astronomical. This is a million-to-one sequence of events.

And I'm having a hard time figuring out how to get it all back in balance."

"Well, if anybody can."

He nodded in distracted agreement. To an outsider it would have seemed like arrogance, though Carrie knew it was nothing like that. Unless facts could be arrogant.

"It started a couple weeks ago, when the spreads on some Italian government bonds didn't narrow. We could have ridden it out, but then a Swiss bank that'd sold us their risk was defaulted on by a telecom consortium. So now we're saddled with *their* exposure, which we'd hedged with the profits from the Italian bond trade, since the odds of both these things happening were practically zero. But there wasn't any Italian money, and so we had to pay the bank from something else, which threw everything out of kilter. This is just the first chapter, by the way."

"Hey, as long as things get better before chapter eleven . . ."

It was a pretty good joke, although he wasn't laughing.

"We lose money on one trade, and in order to cover those losses, we're bailing out of the next before we should. Which means that we've then lost money on *that* trade, which needs to be hedged with something else. It's like we're sitting at the poker table with a hundred winning hands but we have to fold each one before we can play it." He looked up at her, seeing she was still lagging. "You want to understand what's going on, Carrie? The impossible. Every time it looks like we're out of the woods something else unexpected crops up."

"Volatility," Carrie said, summoning a word she'd often heard.

"The wrong kind of volatility."

"You see, this is what I've never been able to . . . I mean, is there a right kind? Isn't the point of volatility that you *can't* predict if it's going to be right or wrong?"

"But markets aren't supposed to behave as irrationally as this." There was something almost childish in his voice now, an echo of the sophomore who would stay after class to make the experiment turn out correctly. "What's so frustrating is that our models are right. Our theorems are good."

That's comforting, she almost said. Theorems always beat chaos. Just look around.

"All we need is more time. But now the word is getting out. The margin calls from the banks are starting. I just dodged a killer from Barclays."

They sat through a grim silence. Carrie knew there was nothing she could say that he hadn't thought about already. But she still had to speak. She still had to use her voice to make the situation better.

"But these guys all know who you are, right? Can't you get a white knight? Corzine or Bob or the other guys at Goldman Sachs?"

"The guys at Goldman Sachs aren't the guys at Goldman Sachs anymore."

"How about, you know, the feds?"

"After what happened at Long Term? No way. The government doesn't bail out hedge funds anymore, especially this crew. I mean, if we were in Houston, maybe. No, any deal I do now will mean I might lose control of the fund."

She could read the anguish on his face. WMV had been his dream, probably since before he even knew that there was such a thing as a hedge fund. To lose control of it—to have bosses again; people second-guessing him—would be devastating.

"Quint, our voices are very calm here, but you're scaring the shit out of me."

"I'm sorry," he said. "I shouldn't be doing that."

"No, no, wait, if I should be scared, then I want to be scared. I just want to be sure that I *should* be scared before I am. Because I'm not built like you. I can't handle all this uncertainty."

He looked at her, the reserve draining from his eyes.

"Then you should probably go ahead and be scared," he said.

The words shocked even Quint, because he backed off immediately, reassuring her with the usual bromides about cash reserves and market cycles, telling her that the next few weeks would see recovery. They were words that had always worked in the past, though they sounded very hollow now. Sensing he'd said too much, he made his escape to Capital Park. Some people were driving up from the city for

an emergency Saturday night meeting. Carrie knew that once this crisis passed she should make some sort of stand and force him to stop
putting every ounce of himself into WMV. She took a long bath, loading up on the aromatherapeutics and contemplating all the other
things the Manning family could do, alternate lives that would rid
them of the pressure that was obviously driving them all insane. Her
favorite scheme involved Quint's getting his Ph.D. and teaching eco-
nomics somewhere cool, Princeton or Ann Arbor, Cambridge or Stan-
ford. Writing books and being summoned for advice that he would
deliver in his own sweet time, as opposed to whenever the phone happened to ring. They could buy a big rambling professorial house and
the boys could live at home while they went to college, putting off
those particular days of reckoning. Grad students would hang around;
there would be writers and young professors and distinguished visitors, all the usual human benefits of college life. Like Ron Silver's
place in *Reversal of Fortune*, only without any Claus von Bülows
pulling up; there'd been too many of those in the past few years. Or
he could get a job with a foundation, using his skill to raise money for
PBS or the Met. Or he could just retire and be with her. There had to
be something other than this nonstop pressure. As soon as things settled, she would order him to come away with her for a week alone,
and she would get to work on him. Because this had to end. If they
were going to remain a family, this chaos had to end.

It would be a hard sell. He loved this life, the sudden crises and
impenetrable riddles; the complete control. And he hadn't exactly
made secret that this was what he wanted from the first. She'd seen it
as he crossed that street on the day he came back for her, utterly at
home in that surging, filthy, money-soaked city. His timing, as always,
was perfect. Carrie had been back in New York for thirteen wasted
months, living with her mother, drinking too much and dating some
truly awful men. On the day he called she'd cloistered herself in her
room after returning from two beleaguered weeks in L.A. with Dari, a
spoiled Persian sex maniac who wanted to produce Zalman King–type
movies with his father's Savak severance. Carrie had bolted soon after
reading the script he'd written especially for her, or at least reading up

to the point where her character picked up the shirtless hitchhiker. She was neither taking calls nor speaking with Katherine, so when her mother knocked on her bedroom door, she told her to go away.

"Darling, he won't take no for an answer."

"Who *is* it?"

"Some boy from DWA."

He was working for Bear, Stearns for the summer before starting at Wharton. They agreed to meet for lunch the next day. She got to the restaurant early and positioned herself so she could watch him arrive. They hadn't had an actual conversation since the end of junior year, when she broke up with him after caving in to the imagined censure of her classmates and her own restless desire for something more than his steady, unflagging adulation. He'd written her a few unanswered letters during her first year at drama school. After that, there had been nothing.

A cab pulled up on the other side of Fifty-third, and he stepped out, the same boy, only completely different. Taller and broader, his eyes set a little deeper. He crossed the street as if he owned it, holding up his hand to stop an approaching taxi. All that homework and quiet self-confidence had formed something the world would now have to take very seriously. Carrie contemplated bolting through a back exit, worried that whatever image of her he'd been cultivating these past four years would shatter when he saw this frivolous lost creature in front of him. But as he reached the table, his neck blazed with the same autumnal red she'd first seen at his house six years earlier.

They were tongue-tied and smiling. She shrugged off questions about acting school, focusing instead on Princeton. He'd majored in econ instead of his planned chemical engineering and was about to go for his master's at Wharton. Evidently grad school had been a tough call, since a lot of people wanted him to start working for them right away, including his current employers, who'd offered him an astronomical salary to stay put. But he didn't want to be just another trader. He had different plans.

"So," he asked eventually, "are you seeing anybody?"

"You'll have to be a little less specific."

He frowned.

"Don't sell yourself short, Carrie. You've always done that, and I'm not going to let it happen anymore."

He picked her up every night after work, even when they kept him at the office until midnight. They slept together one week after their first date. Or, perhaps more accurately, six years after. Soon after, it became clear that Carrie would be moving to Philadelphia. She knew she couldn't get away without reintroducing him to her mother, who wouldn't remember their two previous meetings at DWA. He took them to dinner, Katherine on her best behavior, toning down the Bozo makeup and the gin. Quint was perfect, barely saying a word to Carrie all night as he charmed the older woman back into some girlish incarnation of herself. He'd left them both with chaste kisses under their building's awning. In the elevator, Katherine grabbed her daughter's arm with such ferocity that Carrie thought she was finally having the stroke she'd been nurturing all these years. But her eyes were lucidity itself.

"Marry that boy or I will kill you in your sleep," she hissed.

As if Carrie needed to be told. A month later she was living with him in Philadelphia; the following May—Carrie secretly pregnant with Jamie—they were married in the small charmless brick church Gloria attended, Katherine happily ceding her parent-of-the-bride duties to the Mannings. The reception was at the farm: a big tent and a decent cover band, plenty of food, and what seemed to Carrie like an awfully large number of strangers from New York, who had made the drive up just to be close to her husband.

After the bath she went downstairs to get going on her family evening. She dismissed Sabine and then started dinner, making a pasta salad to go with the four bloody slabs of prime rib she'd bought at Earth's Bounty. Sweaty and dusted with red grit from the court, Jamie came in while she worked. He ignored her cheery greeting as he gulped down a sports drink, twin fluorescent rivulets running along his chin. It had been like this since Saturday morning: his refusal to talk to her or even meet her eye. The short temper with his brothers. Disappearing without telling anyone where he was going; spending his time at

home locked in his room, coming out only to turn ferocious jets of
sudsy water on his Jeep or murder tennis balls down at the court.
He'd even snapped at his father last night when told to clean up the
balls strewn across the lawn.

"What are you doing now?" Carrie asked in her sweetest, not prying
voice.

"Don't know," he said with undisguised resentment. "Why?"

"Could you at least speculate?"

"Maybe going swimming at Jazz's."

"Oh. Because I was thinking we could do something together."

"Like *what*?"

"Play a game or something."

"A game," he said flatly, fixing her with a look that she could only
define as contemptuous. And then he stalked off upstairs without another word. Carrie was momentarily tempted to clock him with her
Williams-Sonoma tenderizing mallet, though she also understood that
he must still be feeling humiliated about Madison's party. He'd acted
like a fool in front of his classmates, something she'd learned from Diane McNabb when she went to make peace about Friday night's message. Diane had a green thumb for offense, keeping grudges alive
through all sorts of weather. Word would get back to Quint unless she
could be mollified. And so Carrie dragged herself down to Federal at
ten o'clock this morning. As difficult as she now found it to believe,
she had once been friends with Diane McNabb. They first met when
Jamie and Madison were in seventh grade, and for a while Carrie
thought she had found a kindred spirit. They grew close, sharing sardonic comments at school pickup, meeting for lunch at some new
place on Federal and laughing at all the women who were actually
meeting for lunch. Their friendship soon progressed into regular trips
into the city to see movies or shows or whatever else had to be seen,
followed by late visits to the sorts of places where men gathered to
hunt. Although Carrie enjoyed the ensuing intervals of flirtation—
Quint was working fourteen-hour days getting WMV going—there
was no chance she would ever allow herself to cheat on her husband.
They were virtual singles, cruising without consequences, never more
than a seventy-minute drive away from their safe Connecticut homes.

If they stayed out too late, they could always crash at the pied-à-terre Quint kept for his own very different late nights.

But things went too far. Although Diane was still married, she clearly had more in mind than making innocuous eye contact across retro zinc bars. One night they wound up at somebody's place for a party that turned out to be limited to four people; on another occasion Diane had actually invited two horny McKinsey hotshots back to the apartment. Both times it was left to Carrie to cut things off before they got out of hand, making her the stick-in-the-mud, which was exactly what she did *not* want to be. Finally, inevitably, she wound up stranded in her bedroom while Diane cavorted next door with some impossibly young account planner from Saatchi & Saatchi. The ride home early the next morning was terminally strained, Diane nervous and giggly, Carrie smiling tightly. Needless to say, there were no more girls' nights in Manhattan. And now Carrie had to abase herself before the woman.

Diane's shop was called Diane's Shop, which told you just about everything you needed to know about the woman. It wasn't a shop as much as a showroom for the bizarre items she peddled to her friends and, more often, the parents of her children's friends. Most of her stock was remaindered from Manhattan shops and galleries. Carrie doubted she'd be able to get out today without spending any more money.

The proprietor was seated at the sort-of-antique desk she kept at the back of the shop, typing furiously into a laptop, looking for all the world the image of entrepreneurial independence. Bullshit, of course; the monthly rent was paid by her ex-husband's L.A. attorneys. She looked up through black-framed eyeglasses at the sound of the door chime, and her face went through a sequence of attitudes, hostility and hope and resentment, finally settling on cool curiosity.

"Long time no see."

"It's been crazy," Carrie said as she took one of the chairs facing the desk.

She shot a quick look at the computer screen. Instant messenger. Probably chatting with her daughter. Diane tracked her gaze and swiftly closed down the link.

"So how have you been, Diane?"

"You know. Graduation. Rick's flying in. Supposedly."

"Look, Diane, I wanted to apologize for the other night. I didn't get your message until Jamie was already home."

Diane sighed, more in sorrow than anger.

"I have to tell you, Carrie, everybody *loves* Jamie, but he was way out of control. I had to practically fumigate the bathroom. And he broke a gorgeous piece."

Carrie hoped the hot waves of embarrassment coursing through her weren't too obvious.

"I'm really sorry, Diane."

"Oh, don't apologize," she said, though only because accepting an apology would end the conversation. "It's just, some of the kids were a bit upset seeing him that way. He said some pretty out-there things, to Madison in particular. I mean, there was a remark which could be interpreted as racial. You know, he and Madison are real leaders, real *thoroughbreds*, and when the others see him like that, well, you know what I mean."

Carrie shook her head in weary agreement. Taking her medicine.

"I think he's learned his lesson," she said tightly.

"Are you consequencing him?"

"You'd better believe it," Carrie said. "Only, I wonder if you could do me a favor in that regard."

"Anything," Diane said, her eyes wary.

"Could you not mention it if you see Quint? The thing is, I'm going to be the one handling Jamie's punishment. If his father finds out . . ."

"Say no more. Your secret's safe with me."

Carrie began to think that she might now be able to escape.

"But wasn't it Quint who came for the Wrangler?" Diane asked, sensing that the conversation was about to end before she could milk every ounce of humiliation from it.

"No, he was working in the city. Jamie told me it was Stephen and Matt who drove it home."

"I don't think so. They were around until much later."

"You sure?"

"Believe me, Stephen and Matt were *in the house*."

Carrie shrugged. This could go on and on.

"Yes, well, I just wanted to thank you for being a friend," she said. "Now, you have to let me pay for whatever it was my son broke."

"Don't be absurd."

Carrie started to get up.

"But while you're here, there *is* something I'd love to show you . . ."

She wound up buying lawn art, three grazing sheep sculpted out of fencing wire. Twenty-nine hundred dollars, plus a delivery charge, plus taxes, plus whatever it took to dump them somewhere Diane wouldn't find out about. Despite the expense at a time when she should probably start thinking about cutting back, Carrie couldn't help but feel she'd got away from the shop cheap.

So Jamie had disgraced himself. That was why he was acting so badly all weekend. What really hurt Carrie wasn't that her son had been rat-assed drunk but rather that he no longer felt the need to talk to her about his shame. Their secret compact, the unspoken deal that he could always come to her with the foolish things he'd done and she would never betray him to his father, had finally dissolved, it seemed.

This relationship had reached its greatest intensity last year, during the advanced photography fiasco, a crisis of Carrie's own making. It started just before his junior year, when Carrie heard that Warren Tollman was going to be teaching an elective at Country Day. Tollman was a local institution, the owner of In Situ, a Federal Street photography gallery. His work regularly won local competitions, though he was always one step short of gaining acceptance in Manhattan. His main income came from the portraits he did of Totten families, stark, cunning black-and-whites that captured those unguarded moments between poses. Carrie, hoping some last spark might be ignited, ordered Jamie to take the class, even though he'd shown no interest in the Leica or the Hi8 she'd bought him. He protested, wanting to take personal Web site design instead, though he was still young enough to do as she said. Besides, it was just a minor. The understanding at Country Day was that as long as he showed up and demonstrated the slightest promise, he would get an A; if he showed up and was particularly awful, he would get an A-. Major delinquency and nonparticipation would earn a student a B. Anything lower was inconceivable.

But this proved to be an arrangement Tollman, an adjunct who taught only every three or four years, didn't understand. He labored under the delusion that grades bore some relation to their definitions at the bottom of the report card. Although Jamie toiled mightily at the course, his midterm grade came back an unprecedented C. If it held, the effect would be devastating. Grade inflation at the school had reached South American levels. At the end of his sophomore year there had been seventeen students—out of a class of less than eighty—with 4.0 averages. There was even talk of stretching the upper limit to 5.0 to include extra credit. That C would drop Jamie into the middle of the pack, a position from which there would be no recovery. Duke would no longer be a lock. Quint urged him to work harder, but Carrie knew that effort wasn't the issue. Tollman was right. Jamie was at best an average photographer, with a dull eye and no sense of composition. And it was Carrie's fault that he was going to suffer the consequences of his mediocrity.

She chose a quiet afternoon to visit In Situ. After a few persistent rings Tollman appeared. He had sweeping gray hair, tweedy clothes, and a tight smile that indicated he knew this was about Jamie. Carrie, after all, had never once set foot inside the gallery; she'd neglected to have him come up to capture the Mannings gamboling through their orchard.

"I was just in the darkroom," he explained, blocking the door, forcing Carrie to make the first move.

"Are you open? Because I can come back . . ."

"Yes," he said warily, too Totten to be rude. "I'm open."

"Do you mind if I just look around? You must have work to do."

He reluctantly let her in. She wandered the gallery while he finished up in his darkroom. Most of the photos were his. They weren't bad. The portraits had a tendency to pander to the sitter's vanity, which she supposed paid the bills, but the landscapes, if that's what you called them, had an edge to them. Some of them appeared to be commentaries on abundance, like that Russian guy whose stuff she'd liked at the Guggenheim. Yes, Tollman was perfectly fine. Others just happened to be better. He returned after about ten minutes, smelling slightly of chemicals.

"I like this one," she said, indicating a close-up of a dragonfly crushed on oily blacktop.

Carrie noted the sarcastic slant to his head, his way of letting her know that a simple five-hundred-dollar sale wouldn't buy him. But the joke was on Tollman, because she had no intention of buying anything. She knew this guy. His integrity might be more important than mere money, but his ambition kicked the hell out of his integrity.

"Warren, do you know Arlie Kirsch?"

Tollman clearly wasn't expecting the question. A few years ago Kirsch had patented a software suite for digital photo processing that was currently being bundled into half the planet's computers. A failed photographer, he'd used his IPO windfall to buy a couple of galleries in lower Manhattan. He'd also invested with Quint.

"Well, no. I mean, obviously I know who he *is*, but we've never met."

"I was talking to him the other day, and he was saying how there's no good stuff around and would I keep a lookout. Do you mind if I mention your name?"

And that was it. She took a card on the way out. She stopped in to see Kirsch the next time she was in the city. He was surprised to see her but perfectly welcoming. He'd been to the house to play tennis; they'd visited his place in the Hamptons. After small talk she told him about this talented local photographer who was a friend and a neighbor and whose work, in her opinion, had been grossly overlooked. Kirsch held her eye for a moment in which everything that needed to be said wasn't and then told her he'd see what he could do. She left the card.

It all ran according to plan. Kirsch had one of his people look at Tollman's portfolio, and they chose something to hang in the Wooster Street gallery. Luckily, it wasn't scheduled to go up until January, just in case Tollman thought he could double-cross her. Jamie got his A; his 4.0 was intact; the Blue Devils beckoned. The Leica was stowed until she could turn it over to Dillon to ignore.

But then Quint found out. Carrie had believed that a single crummy photograph hung in a small New York gallery would fly beneath the conversational radar of two captains of industry. She was mistaken. People liked to let the self-sufficient Quint know when they had done him a favor. The reckoning came at dinner one night, after Dillon and Nick had bolted down to the basement.

"Arlie Kirsch told me you asked him to hang one of Jamie's teacher's photos," he said to Carrie, his voice calm, the anger inaudible to anyone who hadn't been living with him for the past two decades.

"Come on, I simply told him that Tollman was doing some interesting stuff."

"You went by his office? And Jamie's taking this man's course?"

Carrie didn't say anything. There really was nothing she could say. Quint turned to Jamie.

"Do you understand what's going on?"

"Yeah," he said. "Well, not really."

"Your mother bought your A in advanced photography."

"Oh." He snorted gently. "I was wondering about that."

His expression remained slightly confused as Quint explained that this was not how they did things in this family. Later, without the benefit of an audience, Carrie had it out with her husband, scoring what she considered a rare victory.

"If you want that boy to play fair, then you'd better be willing to have him lose," she'd said after listening to all his arguments.

"What's that supposed to mean?"

"He's not as smart and strong as you, is what it means. And it doesn't matter how much you ride him and micromanage him and let him know how *disappointed* you are in him. You can't put in what nature left out. So I suggest you either adjust your ambitions for him or downgrade your sense of fair play."

"Well, maybe you should adjust your ambitions for him as well, Carrie."

"Don't worry about it, Quint. I already have."

After prepping dinner, she went downstairs to coax Dillon and Nick away from the screen. Carrie recoiled at the sight of them sprawled on the sofa, though the best detergents and machines available had cleansed those slipcovers since Friday night. The boys worked their twin controls in eerie harmony, moving split-screen soldiers deeper into the recesses of some murky labyrinth. The enemy appeared; the enemy was destroyed.

"Hey, guys? I think that's probably enough."

Nothing. She stepped in front of them. They craned their necks to look around her.

"I said I think that's enough."

"But we're on level six!"

"Step off!"

She switched off the television manually. There was a frenzy of last-minute shooting before the screen turned its neutral blue. She expected howls of outrage, but instead they just sat there, weary and sated, as if they were emerging from a deep sleep.

"Is dinner ready?" Dillon asked.

"About an hour."

"An hour," Nick said flatly. "From now."

They watched her. She'd switched off the television and had no immediate food to give them. An explanation was required.

"I was thinking we could, you know, do something."

"What?"

"I don't know. Play a game."

"Dude, we were just playing a game."

"Dude, we were at level six."

"No, I meant a board game."

For a moment she wondered if they even knew what a board game was. But they did. That was the problem. There was a bit more confusion as she tried to find something. Carrie hated Monopoly, so they settled on Trouble, the one with that popping dice shaker in the middle. She led the boys upstairs and arranged them at the kitchen table. She was about to send one of them up for Jamie when he appeared, bouncing noisily down the steps, his wet hair slicked back.

"Jamie?"

He blew right by them.

"I'm outta here."

"Be back by seven."

Her words were swallowed by the slamming door. A moment later the Wrangler's growl filled the forecourt. Carrie turned her attention back to the game. It took a few minutes to set everything up and get the rules straight, but soon they were on their way, racing their plastic markers around the board. The boys particularly enjoyed hammering the dice shaker, vying to see who could make it pop loudest. Dillon started to get a bit too excited, howling triumphantly whenever he sent someone back to the starting post, pounding the table in agony whenever the same happened to him. She let him have his tantrums, intervening only when he suggested he'd made Nick his bitch by capturing him just as he was about to enter the victory chute.

"Excuse me. There are ladies present."

"That's not what I meant."

"Then what did you mean?" she asked.

"You know. I *made him my bitch*. It means something completely different."

"Dillon, you don't know what you're talking about. It's offensive to women, and I won't have it."

She could feel their interest beginning to wane. The game was becoming frustrating. It was clearly developed in an age when instant gratification was not yet the root ingredient of fun. She thought about getting a deck of cards, though she didn't really know any games except war.

She hit the popper.

"Five-oh," Nick said.

She double-checked the dice.

"Nick, it's a six," she said as she picked up her little red marker. "Honestly."

"No. Look."

She tracked his gaze and saw the police cruiser rolling to a stop in the forecourt.

"Wait here," she said. "And don't move any pieces."

Carrie's first thought was that the burglar alarm had gone off, though that would have brought a phone call from the Rapid Whatever crew. It was probably a subpoena for Quint. One would arrive from time to time, especially during his crises. Carrie just signed and turned them over to Godeep. Though she didn't understand why it would be coming here with Capital Park still open.

It was a town policewoman. She was a little shorter than Carrie, with buttery blond hair pulled back in a tight ponytail and black leather gloves on her hands. She had remarkably small ears; they looked like pieces of chilled gnocchi. She looked at the red game piece Carrie clutched before meeting her eye.

"Good afternoon, ma'am. Is Wendell Manning here?"

"No, he's at work. May I help you with something?"

"You are?"

The woman's voice had a hectoring quality that Carrie could see herself disliking in the very near future.

"His wife."

"Are you the owners of a Jeep Wrangler?"

"Well, yes."

"Can you tell me where it is now?"

"My son has it."

"Okay. Was it driven on Friday night?"

Carrie stood perfectly still. The woman began to tug at the bottom of those gloves, pulling them tight, first one hand and then the other.

"Ma'am?"

"Well, yes. I mean, it might have been. Is there a problem?"

"Was it your son who was driving it?"

An image of Jamie swaying in the refrigerator's wan light played through her mind.

"Officer, could you tell me what this is about, please?"

The woman shot her a disapproving look, as if Carrie's question were some grave impertinence; as if she weren't allowed to ask questions at her own front door. Bitch, Carrie thought.

"Ma'am, where is your son now?"

"I'm not entirely sure."

The officer made it clear that she'd had enough.

"I'll need you to ask him to return home *immediately*. I'd also like permission to examine the Jeep."

"All right," Carrie said. "Let me . . ."

She left the woman standing at the front door as she walked back to the kitchen. The boys watched her.

"Did Jamie do something?" Dillon asked.

She shook her head as she picked up the phone. The Mahabals' home number was number four on the speed dial. Quint's cellular was number one.

She pressed one.

17 They were going out for pizza. Shannon had agreed to do this simple thing, driving up to the hippie place near the university, the site of so many perfect evenings together. David wanted them to stay home while he was at work, but she was beginning to get tired of following his orders. Besides, she doubted she could take another evening trapped in the house with Ian, struggling to keep up with his restless pacing and unbridled talking, those quicksilver eyes that were unable to focus on anything for more than a few seconds. Maybe getting him out into the world would help calm him.

She'd hoped he would start settling down on Saturday, when his uncle returned from the hospital to report that Robert Jarvis was going to be all right. But that only transformed his panic into a sort of blind self-confidence that grew stronger as the weekend passed. After David went to get some sleep, he embraced her so strongly that it almost knocked the wind out of her.

"It's going to be all right," he said. "I can't believe it. We're going to be all right."

Shannon had no idea where all his certainty was coming from; a man was in the hospital, and the cops could still come for them at any time. She'd tried to go along with his happiness, though before long she couldn't resist asking him the question that had been bothering her all morning.

"Ian," she said, keeping her voice gentle, "why did you tell your uncle? I thought we'd decided to keep this a secret."

"He was all over me, Shan. He could tell that something was wrong."

"I just would've liked to have a say in the matter before he was nominated our guardian angel."

"Just let him handle it. He knows about stuff like this."

"I'm sure he does," she couldn't resist saying.

"Come on, Shan. Don't be like that."

He put his hand out for her, a peace offering. She took it. There was no reason to torment Ian about something that couldn't be undone. Too afraid to move from this invisible patch of the world, they stayed in the house for the rest of Saturday. David went out only once, returning with several stained bags of Chinese food. His presence seemed to bolster Ian's growing confidence that he would not be caught. The two of them repeated the same phrases over and over. *They can't touch us without a witness. If they knew anything, they'd be here by now.* David's assertions that they were doing the right thing were delivered with the grim authority of the visiting lecturers who came to school during Freedom from Dependency Week, the reformed boozers and crack addicts, with their sticks of gum and patronizing tones. It was the voice of Bad Experience, clueing in the innocent, painting grim pictures of lawyers' fees and prison visits and blasted futures. She couldn't believe that they now depended on this man.

It wasn't until the end of that first long day that she finally got Ian to retreat with her to his bedroom. She hoped spending a few hours alone together would calm him down, but he was too wrapped up in his torrent of ideas to focus on what she was saying. It was as if the words were coming out faster than he could think them. Each time she'd ask him what they were going to do he'd start talking about all those anarchists and rebels he read, Camus and Dostoevsky and the other dead men whose ideas were once so enticing but who now seemed to describe a shadowy world in which everybody was guilty and only fools went to the police. She tried to be patient, knowing this was just a reaction to the pressure he was under. The talking would soon stop; his nerves would settle and his mind slow down.

She left at ten, even though she could have told her father another lie and stayed the night. The truth was that she wanted to be away from Ian for a while. She needed to get some rest so she could start thinking clearly.

"You should try to get some sleep," she said before leaving.

"Maybe later."

"I'll be back in the morning. Call me if anything happens."

"Nothing's going to happen, Shan. Don't you see that? It's like I'm living it now."

"Living what?"

His answer was a long kiss that resurrected enough of their old life to make her believe everything would be all right. She drove around for a long time before going home, trying to think, but all she could come up with were random phrases and fractured thoughts that immediately nullified one another. A man was hurt. They were getting away with it. Justice wasn't being served. There was no such thing as justice. Somebody would have to pay. At one point she found herself on Orchard, slowing instinctively as she passed Jamie's house, thinking how easy it would be just to tell him everything. They could go to his father. Quint would know what to do. He'd call Mr. Mahabal, and they'd be able to take care of this in ten seconds.

But that wasn't possible. She'd promised Ian that she would say nothing unless he agreed.

She snuck into her house undetected. There were no messages from Ian, though there was a sweet e-mail from Jamie, apologizing once again for the other night. Maybe one day when he grew up a little, he said, they could try to make it work again. She started to cry after reading it. Her tears woke her father; she could hear him trying to creep to her door. As he came near, she buried her face so deeply in the pillow that she almost suffocated, and she briefly wondered what that would be like. A stupid thought. A teenaged thought. Eventually she fell into a dreamless black sleep that miraculously lasted until early Sunday morning. She dressed quickly and drove over, expecting to see police cruisers or, worse, to see nothing at all, just the emptiness that signified they'd run away. But his uncle's ridiculous car was in the driveway, and the two of them were slouching in sly communion at the kitchen table, just as they had when she'd arrived the previous morning. The watery look in Ian's eyes told her that he hadn't slept for a second night in a row.

It turned into a long, caged day. David went by the hospital again early that morning and returned to report that they'd moved Jarvis to a private room and taken some of the tubes and monitors off him. And the police still didn't have a clue. As if to prove his confidence, he went out to work in the late afternoon, though he wound up calling in every half hour. Ian was now acting as if the accident were something in the distant past, an almost forgotten event that had no bearing on their present lives. Every time Shannon would bring it up he would smother her with playful kisses or resume the wild monologue he'd begun the day before, riffing on his uncle's belief that the law didn't apply to them. He ordered a movie on cable, some terrible thing with cars and guns, though he could hardly sit still to watch it. Knowing she would go crazy if she spent any more time in that cramped living room, she went to make dinner, spaghetti with pesto, his favorite, though he seemed as little interested in eating as he was in sleeping. After grinding the viscid green mess into oblivion in the food disposal she tried to get him to come to bed with her, but he started pacing and talking again, words feeding new words, a chain reaction of ideas that showed no sign of stopping.

"It's like, you've read Sartre."

Shannon nodded dubiously. At his request she'd once read a play about a group of people trapped in a big hotel room that turned out to be hell. They knew it was hell because there were no mirrors, which struck Shannon as ridiculous, since for a few years mirrors had been one of the very things that made her life hell. And then there was the author photo on the back of the book; the man looked like an evil, pipe-smoking toad.

"It's just like what he says," Ian said. "I can see it now. There are no rules. We really are free to do whatever we want. The cops can't touch me unless I let them."

"Are you sure that's what this guy was talking about?"

"Definitely. Existence precedes essence. You choose your destiny. Well, I'm choosing *not* to go to jail on the back of some rich kid getting drunk."

Shannon almost asked him about his choice to drive the Wrangler up Orchard instead of parking it at the side of Shaker Lane.

"Ian, maybe you should try to stop thinking so much," she said instead. "I mean, these guys you're talking about, they had Nazis and Cossacks and all that European stuff to deal with. We're just a couple of kids in Connecticut."

"So what's your point?"

"I don't even have a point. I just want all this to go away."

"But don't you see, Shannon? It *is* going away. As long as we hold out against the system, it's never going to get close to us." He shook his head. "I mean, why are you resisting this? It's almost like you want me to get busted."

"Ian, I don't want that. I just want to do what's right."

"But there is no right other than what you decide to do. That's the whole point. You can see that, right?"

She didn't even try to respond. He would only come back with another answer, and then another one after that. It used to thrill her, the way his mind would run, even when what he was saying seemed like nonsense. It was like a wicked joke they were playing on the world, something they could laugh about without taking too seriously. But this talk about total freedom was frightening her. Before Friday, all it had meant was they could be together and make love and avoid the timid little lives that adults wanted for them. But now it was starting to mean something very different: that they were free to hide and be scared and let his uncle run things. None of which felt very much like freedom to her.

Finally, just before midnight, exhausted by all the talk and nervous energy, she decided to leave. David was due home, and as hard as this was to imagine, she had school the next day.

"You really should try to get some sleep," she said after they kissed good night by her car.

"I'll get plenty of sleep when I die," he said, smiling.

David's plan, explained so laboriously before he left for work Sunday evening, was that everything would return to normal on Monday.

They would act as if nothing had happened. Shannon would attend school and Ian would go to work and David would work his late shift. Before that, he'd pick up Ian at Earth's Bounty and take him to his appointment with Ronnie, but this time he would bring him home as well. Which meant that Shannon would have to wait until five to see Ian.

The day proved interminable. At school the talk was split between upcoming finals and Jamie's behavior at the party. Shannon had never felt more detached from it all. The idea that she was a senior at a private school in the middle of Connecticut was suddenly as strange as if she'd woken to find herself the beetle in that story Ian loved. She ate lunch at one of the picnic tables outside, her back turned to the cafeteria's glass wall so she wouldn't have to look at her classmates. After a few minutes she heard the leafy shuffle of approaching feet. It was Jamie. She underwent a moment's panic when she saw his bleak expression. He knew. The police were waiting in the head's office. The time had come for her to betray Ian.

"You still pissed at me?" he asked sheepishly as he took the bench opposite her.

They were still safe.

"No," she said, trying to hide her immense relief.

"Yeah, well everybody else is. Supposedly I made some crack at the party about a sympathy vote for Madison because she's adopted."

"Hey, anything bad you say about Madison is okay by me."

They talked for a while about other kids, about graduation and summer. Empty talk, and all the while there seemed to be something else on his mind.

"You sure you're all right?" she asked eventually.

"When your mom, before she left—did you know she was seeing this guy?"

The question was so unexpected that it took Shannon several seconds to understand what she was being asked.

"Well, she didn't exactly keep it a secret that she hated her life. I mean, the woman put a bumper sticker on the car announcing the fact. But no, I guess I didn't know she was having an actual affair."

He nodded, ruminating in that painstaking way he had.

"But after you found out, I mean, did you hate her?"

"Only for about the last seven years."

"How about your dad? Did you hate him?"

"I don't know. Yeah. I guess I did for a while. Mostly I felt sorry for him. Jamie, why are you asking me this? Since when do you care about my parents?"

"I don't know. It's just . . . You want to get together tonight? We could just hang at my house."

"Jamie . . ."

"I really miss you, Shan," he said, a crack in his voice. "I mean, you're the only person around here who knows what it's like to . . ."

He didn't finish the thought.

"Tonight's not so good," she said.

He got up, trying to hide his disappointment.

"Oh. Okay. Well, I'll see you around."

"Hey, Jamie?"

He waited.

"I'll call. Soon. I promise."

She was tempted to head home after lunch, though that would mean dealing with her father, who seemed to have given up going to his office altogether. She endured one more class and then walked over to the lower school, where she did Reading Buddies with her second grader until dismissal. After that she drove around until five o'clock, listening to the university station, conscious that Ian was now in his session with Ronnie. Shannon wondered if she would sense that something was wrong, whether Ian could hold out if she asked him about what was bothering him. Part of her wished he couldn't, that he would tell her everything and this would all be over.

Finally, it was time. The Chevelle was gone when she arrived; the back door was wide open. As she got out of her car, Shannon could almost convince herself that it was going to be the way it was before, the two of them in perfect solitude. But before she could enter the house, she was startled by a sudden noise behind her, a clean crack that echoed through the yard. She turned so fast she almost fell over. There was another sharp sound. It was coming from the side of the garage.

"Ian?" she said, her voice so soft she knew it wouldn't carry more than a few feet.

There was no reply. She went to look. He stood a few feet from the garage's wall, flanked on either side by teetering stacks of split wood. Behind him was a chaotic pile of moldering logs. He was in the process of raising an ax over his head. Strands of hair crossed his sweaty face; wood chips and bits of leaves clung to his naked torso. He drove the ax into an upright log with a ferocity that caused Shannon to take a step backward.

"Fucker."

He tried to dislodge it, though it had been driven in too far. Finally, his thin muscles straining, he slammed the whole conjoined apparatus, ax and log, into the tree trunk next to him. The log shot free, flying directly into the garage with a heavy thud, leaving a hand-size dent in its wall. He didn't pay attention to this; he was already pulling more wood from the pile. Shannon could see now that he'd already sectioned dozens, using them to create those two uneasy towers.

He swung the ax again. The wood splintered. He picked up the three jagged pieces and stacked them on the second tower. It was almost as tall as he was. His lips were moving, forming words she could not hear.

"Ian?"

He ignored her as he reached back toward the chaotic pile. She stepped forward, trying to keep the fear out of her voice as she spoke his name again. He turned and Shannon froze. His eyes were all wrong. The usual arrangement of liquid and muscle had fallen completely apart. They didn't seem capable of focusing. She began to feel afraid, a reaction that was hardly helped by the fact that he was holding an ax.

"Ian, what are you doing?"

He used the ax to gesture toward the pile.

"This shit has been out here for years. My mom let some redneck sell it to her. I thought, you know, get organized. Maybe even burn some of it this winter."

He placed the cylinder of wood on the shattered flagstone he was using as a block and swung at it, a glancing blow that sent the log somersaulting past Shannon, missing her by only a few feet.

"Hey," she said, dancing a few steps backward.

But he didn't notice, reaching instead for a new victim. Shannon looked back at the towers. Something occurred to her.

"Hold on, have you done all this since you got back from Ronnie's?"

"Never went. Didn't go to work, either."

"You didn't go . . ."

"It's cool. David called my boss."

"But Ronnie? You can't just blow that off."

"No, you don't understand, I'm done."

"What do you mean?"

"She called this afternoon. David talked to her. She's stopped working."

Shannon hadn't heard anything about this, though she wasn't exactly plugged into her family of late. A week ago this would have been the best possible news. Now she wasn't sure. She pointed to the stacked wood.

"How about you call it a day? I think that's enough to get you through a few nuclear winters."

He looked unhappy about stopping. But then whatever impulse had sent him out here just vanished. He drove the ax into the trunk of the nearby tree and strode over to her to wrap her in his dirty arms. Shannon recoiled slightly—she hated sweat—though she was glad to have him holding her. And the wildness she'd seen in his eyes a few moments earlier was gone, replaced by sudden desire. He took her hand and led her into the house, moving so rapidly that they were almost sprinting down the narrow hallway. By some miracle of self-control she was able to break free at the last moment to get to the bathroom. She bobbled her diaphragm after opening the case, as if it were a Frisbee someone had tossed her without warning. He was naked when she got to the room, as hard as she'd ever seen him, the sweat and dirt still on his chest and arms, though she didn't care about that, she only wanted to be touching him. He helped her undress, and they kissed for a while and then fell laughing onto the bed.

She was wet and he moved into her right away and she was immediately lost. She held on to him as tightly as she could, afraid that if she let go even a little, he would slip away from her. She followed his headlong momentum, hoping it would take her somewhere far away. He began to move even faster, impossibly fast, but she was keeping up with him now, lifting her hips toward him, understanding that this was how the abandon in his mind must feel, understanding how good it was to let your mind run away from everything hateful and wounding in your life. And then it was just the motion. They came together, their bodies shuddering and frozen, the first time that had ever happened. They said nothing for a long time afterward, Ian breathing deeply, Shannon tracing random designs on his back with her fingers.

"You're going to stay with me, right?" he asked in a muffled voice. "However this goes?"

"Yes, Ian. I am."

He slid off her so they were lying side by side. She plucked a small dry leaf from his hair. For the first time since they'd returned to the house on Friday night the tension had left his body. Maybe this was all he needed, she thought. His eyes shut, but just as she was beginning to think he was finally asleep, they snapped open. He looked confused, like someone awakened by a mysterious dream.

"What is it?" she asked.

"I just . . . I shouldn't sleep."

"Why not?"

"If I sleep, I see him lying there."

He scrambled over her before she could say another word. The house's cheap plumbing rattled as the shower began to run; it sounded as if he'd almost twisted the knob off the wall. She went to the bathroom to join him, but for some reason he'd locked the door. So she went back to the room and pulled the dirty sheet from his bed, using it to clean the grit and leaves from herself. After getting dressed, she went over to his desk and switched on the small lamp to see what he'd been doing last night instead of sleeping. *Swimming Pool World*. He'd filled a dozen pages. But this was nothing like his previous work. The figures were too hastily executed; he wasn't finishing his thoughts. Some of the kids had no faces, while those who did were startled to find themselves underwater. Some even appeared to be drowning, which contradicted the whole point of the story. She closed the pad and pushed it angrily aside, revealing the nude drawing he'd done of her on Friday. It was completely different from what she'd just seen, the work of eyes that were seeing the world clearly.

The shower stopped with a choking clang. He came out of the bathroom a few seconds later, his skin still soaked. He got dressed without toweling himself off; patches of water showed through the back of his shirt. When he was finished dressing, he met her eye.

"Come on," he said. "Let's go out."

"Ian, maybe that's not such a good idea."

"Why not?"

"Your uncle . . ."

"First you don't want to listen to what David says, and now it's like you're letting him run your life."

"I'm not letting him run . . . okay, fine. Let's go."

The pizza place was empty. They ordered what they always had, a veggie supreme. Ian drained his sixteen-ounce Coke in two long gulps, then put his hand out across the table to take hers. His speech was still a bit too breathless for her liking, but at least the topic was something real now, stories about his mother, things Shannon had heard before, though not with this sort of intensity. The way he spoke made her think that Ginny was very close in his mind. But then, right in the middle of a story about her all-cucumber diet, he stopped and looked around.

"Let's go somewhere else," he said. "This place is so *old*."

"Ian . . ."

"No, think about it, Shan. We don't have to slink around anymore. Let's go somewhere on Federal. Have a decent meal instead of this organic slop."

Bad idea, Shannon thought. Simply going out was risky enough; hanging out on Federal felt reckless. But before she could answer, he was on his feet, telling the hippies to cancel the order. There were three of them, two wispy men with wispy beards and a squat woman who always wore the same ratty bandanna in her hair.

"But it's already in the oven," the woman said, more perplexed than angry.

"Well, take it out!" Ian answered, laughing incredulously.

There was a short impasse during which it became clear the hippies weren't eager to discard a sixteen-inch pizza covered with their finest toppings.

"You could have it to go," one of the men suggested.

Ian looked at him as if he were the world's greatest fool, then walked to the counter and lifted the gate. The three of them stepped back in unison, watching warily as Ian headed toward the big steel oven. He paused, then opened the groaning door.

"Hey, that's—"

It was the woman who spoke, and before she could finish her sentence, Ian had reached bare-handed into the oven and pulled out the half-cooked pizza. It flopped like a clock in that Dali painting in the art studio at Country Day. After what felt like a very long time he tossed it away, the last person to understand that he was burning his hand. The pizza landed on the counter's edge. It hesitated for a moment before slithering to the floor.

The owners wanted to apply aloe to his hand, but Shannon knew that it was time to go. Coming here had been a big mistake. She left twenty dollars on the table and led him out to the car. He was smiling quizzically. Once he was sitting down he began peeling something from his hand. She recoiled, thinking it was skin, though when he pulled it off she could see that it was just a patch of mozzarella.

"Let me look."

"It's like it hurts and doesn't hurt," he said. "Pain is overrated."

The burn wasn't as bad as she'd feared, but it was still bad, a bright red patch between his thumb and forefinger. There were small blisters at the top of his palm that confused her until she realized they were from the ax. A few miles down Totten Pike she pulled into a convenience store to buy a bag of ice. She dumped most of it in the parking lot.

"So that was stupid," he said as he plunged his hand into the ice.

There was no more talk about going to a restaurant on Federal. There was no more talk about anything as they drove back to his house. His leg continued to rattle, but his eyes were calmer. Okay, Shannon thought. This isn't right. Robert Jarvis would recover and the police weren't coming and yet Ian's nerves were going more and more haywire. The confidence he'd been showing was just a brave face. She had to do something before he lost control completely.

There was a limo in the driveway when they got back to Ginny's house. Shannon's heart sank as she pulled in beside it. David would be furious with them for going out, especially since Ian had managed to hurt himself. She knew she'd better talk to him before they had to deal with his uncle.

"Ian, wait, what are we going to do?"

"About what?" He looked at her in alarm. "Shannon, you're not still thinking about going to the police, are you?"

"I don't give a damn about the police. I really don't. I'm worried about *you*. This is obviously tearing you up—"

"It's not tearing me up."

She gestured toward his burned hand. He looked at it, driven to silence by the undeniable sight of his own damaged flesh.

"Just go talk to a doctor. Not Ronnie. Anybody. He'll give you something to help you to sleep. And then we'll see what we want to do."

He looked at her for a while, then leaned back against the seat and shook his head. His submerged fingers gently rattled the melting ice.

"I don't know," he said, his voice very soft now.

"Just say you're stressed. Use that exact word. They love to write prescriptions for kids who are stressed."

For an instant it seemed that he was going to agree. But then his eyes traveled past her. Shannon turned. A very unhappy David was coming through the screen door, his small, wiry body tense with anger. He made a rolling motion with his hand before he'd even reached the car.

"What's going on?" he asked as her window came down.

He was talking to Ian, looking right past her.

"We just went out for some dinner."

"There's food in the—Ian, what happened to your hand?"

Ian removed his hand from the ice. The burn had gone a bloodless white.

"Burned it."

"*Burned* it? How?"

Ian didn't answer. David turned to Shannon.

"Look, we just got some pizza," she said.

"Some pizza." He held her eye long enough to register his displeasure, then turned back to Ian. "Come on in. Let's have a look at that."

Before Shannon could say anything, the passenger door had opened. She watched in disbelief as Ian walked around the front of the car. He showed his uncle the burn; David said something she couldn't hear. And then the two of them walked toward the house, the bag of ice now dangling from Ian's good hand, water dripping from the burned one. It was only as they reached the door that Ian remembered Shannon. He started to come back, but David stopped him. They spoke for a while longer, and then it was David who returned to the car.

"I think you should probably go home for a while," he said, his voice chilly.

"Look, I'm sorry about what just happened. It's my fault and I apologize. But I think Ian's . . . I think he's feeling pretty bad."

David looked past her, into the woods behind the house.

"He just needs some sleep."

"I think it's worse than that."

"Shannon, you've got to trust me on this one. I've been living with Ian for a long time. He gets this way when he's under pressure. You've just got to give him time. And I have to tell you, maybe you being around him isn't the best thing just now. I think he's trying to be strong for you, and that's only making things worse."

She didn't have an answer for this.

"Look, just do this for me, will you? Go home. Let me see if I can get him to sleep. You look like you could use some rest yourself." He held her eye. "Please?"

"When can I . . . when can we get together again?"

"Call us tomorrow. And Shannon, don't worry. This is going to work out. You just have to give it time."

As she sped back down the pike, she found herself thinking not about Ian or Robert Jarvis—she'd thought about them so much the last few days—but rather about how it must have felt for her mother to leave. It was a spring night just like this, the same warm, expectant stillness in the air. There had been no big teary scene. Shannon, aware by now that something was very wrong at home, had listened from her room as her parents spoke quietly next door. Their conversation went on for well over an hour. And then there was silence and a few seconds later a knock on her door. Her mother came in and sat on her bed and explained that she was going to be staying with her friend Timothy Purdy while she figured out what to do with her life.

"Am I coming with you?" Shannon asked.

"His place is kind of small," she said. "And we were thinking, your father and I, that for the time being you should stay here."

Although it would be another six months before her mother and Purdy moved to Eugene, Shannon understood that if her mother left without her tonight, they would never live together again.

"Okay," she said.

She'd listened until the front door closed, then gone to her window to watch her mother walk to her car. She must have already packed because she was only carrying a big cloth shoulder bag. Not that she had very far to go. Timothy Purdy lived less than two miles away. She tossed the bag across the driver's seat and then got in the car without so much as a glance at the house. Shannon watched as she drove to the end of Crescent and put on her turn signal. She started to pull out but then stopped abruptly, the taillights flaring, the car rocking. Shannon's breath caught. She'd changed her mind. She was coming back for her. But then a speeding truck raced past on Federal. Her mother's car turned smoothly after it. And then it was gone. She had only been waiting for traffic to clear.

Shannon's phone rang before she'd gone a mile from Ian's house. It was him, calling to apologize, to tell her that he loved her and they would talk about this after he slept, that they would do the right thing. But it wasn't Ian. It was her father.

"Shannon, where are you?"

She remembered what Ian had said about Ronnie's stopping work.

"I'm—why?"

"You should come home."

"I am coming home. Dad, what's going on?"

"Just come home, Shannon. Right away."

18 Drew had just started to read when the doorbell rang. He was tempted not to answer, figuring it was just another kid selling magazine subscriptions, one of those pint-size criminals from Hartford who looked as if they were measuring up the place for larceny. Besides, he was eager to get going on *The Moonstone*. Last night he'd finally reached its "Second Period," in which the narration is taken over by the self-righteous Miss Clack. Only Ronnie's falling asleep had made him stop. It had, after all, been her suggestion a few weeks earlier that he start reading aloud from his father's vast library of Victorian fiction. Although Drew was skeptical at first—he'd never been much of a reader—he was soon hooked. Ronnie believed that the babies took comfort from his voice rumbling through her womb's drum-tight wall, a notion he found too pleasing to subject to much critical examination. It also distracted her from the surging biological process that looked as if it were about to burst her tiny frame. And Drew found the reading soothing as well, his voice's internal resonation loosening all his clenched muscles. He could read to his wife for hours, his feet propped on the bed and the book resting on his lap like a venerable pet, forgetting his own escalating troubles as he lost himself in the story.

The doorbell was doubly annoying since there had already been one delay of tonight's session, Ronnie's dinner. He'd made her promise to eat something before he cracked open the novel. It was black-mail, but Drew wasn't above that when it came to his family's well-being. The only thing she'd had so far today was some miso soup in the early afternoon, bland, substanceless food that could have provided only the most basic nourishment. He insisted she have something more ample before they started. The question was what. She was more terrified than ever of an adverse food reaction, the prime suspect in her miscarriages. Anything with nuts or dairy was out; so was meat; the mozzarella sticks Drew had planned for his own dinner were poison, pure and simple. He finally located a whole grain loaf in the bread drawer, something she'd picked up at Baker's Oven last week. It had the density and heft of a pulpit Bible. After sawing off a few slices he rummaged through the various stores of condiments stashed around the kitchen. A jar of organic honey looked possible until he remembered that was on the proscribed list as well. Evidently it could cause botulism. He didn't blame Ronnie for being cautious. How could he, living with the memory of wiping the blood from the bathroom floor after her second miscarriage; the way it adhered to the tile, refusing to soak into the towel?

It would have to be the Vegspread. Drew hated the gritty gray slop his wife specially ordered from Earth's Bounty at nineteen dollars a tub. The mere sight of it turned his stomach. What vegetables were gray? What pernicious alchemy caused all those vibrant greens and ochers and ambers to merge into a substance the color of old iron? And then there was the question of her breath after eating it. Usually as sweet and welcome as a daiquiri on a hot day, it would become a slightly sour gust of cod liver, multivitamins, herbal tea, and, well, gray vegetables. Drew was tempted to tell her that generations of children, Shannon included, had somehow managed to emerge from the womb fueled only by cheeseburgers and Birds Eye vegetables and mint chocolate chip ice cream. But he knew what Ronnie's response would be, derived from long days spent with the damaged young.

Precisely.

Drew looked away as he unscrewed the top but still couldn't avoid that noxious cloud. He spread it thick, then poured boiled water over the tea bag in Ronnie's big mug. She was propped on her platform of pillows when he came into the room, looking more rested and comfortable than she had in weeks. She unhappily eyed the two iron slabs of bread.

"Once I'm done breast-feeding I want you to take me into New York and buy me the entire right side of the menu at the Bombay Palace."

He reached forward and put his hand on her round, taut stomach. She instinctively covered it with hers.

"They're sleeping," she said.

"You must be eager for this to be over."

"Yes and no. Don't tell anyone this, but it's sort of nice, sitting here with nothing to do but be looked after."

He put his head down on the mattress, an awkward but strangely comforting position. She stroked his hair while eating her toast with her free hand. It was good to have her here, joking and eating. Quitting work had been a smart move. He'd almost physically restrained her from going out the door this morning after he'd seen her bloodless skin, her eyes as slack as a refugee's. She'd resisted him with her usual quiet stubbornness, only to arrive back home at nine-thirty to announce that she was on maternity leave, effective immediately. As if to emphasize the point, she rushed to the nearest bathroom for a prolonged bout of noisy, unproductive retching. Drew half carried her up to their room, where she passed out for the next four hours. He took up a position in the deep chair beside the bed, not at all happy about the violence of those dry heaves. She looked bad, her face moist and her hair haggard, her hands and feet puffy. When she finally woke, she told him she'd decided to throw in the towel moments into her nine o'clock, when she found herself paying more attention to the visceral flutter of her Braxton Hicks contractions than to the borderline bulimic seated across from her. She started closing down her practice from her bed, wrapping up those patients who were nearing the end of their treatments, diverting the rest to fellow therapists. It took only a few hours. By five o'clock her lying-in had begun.

Drew was more than happy to stay home to nurse his wife. Keenly aware that the collections crew at the bank was waiting to pounce, he had no intention of going anywhere near the office now. Although he could buy a few months with the paltry redemption money Quint would be paying him, he also knew that it wouldn't be nearly enough to keep them away. There would be no more hiding behind his friendship with Andy Starke. These new guys would demand to see the records. They would see that there was nothing left to Drew Hagel. And when that happened, they'd call in the loan.

In fact, before Drew dared return to his office, he had one very large order of business to take care of: selling Hagel & Son to the Post Menopausal Girls. There was no other choice after what Quint had done to him. He had to wrap up the company his father had given him and put himself under the power of a loathsome pack of women he'd openly mocked for the past four years. It was his only chance of keeping the house. He would agree to just about any terms they proposed, provided he wound up on their payroll as a junior partner. That was the key. It would put him at the low end of the profit-sharing totem pole, but at least he would be assured enough of an income to service the credit line. Only when he had a new job and Quint's money was in could he finally deal with the bank. It might piss and moan, though a local outfit like Totten Savings was loath to take legal action if the debtor was willing to make some sort of arrangement. A position at Property Management would doubly insulate him; Cheryl Taub O'Malley, its managing partner, was on the bank's board. This would still leave precious little for the babies and Shannon's college; there would be nothing at all for the remodeling. But he'd save 33 Crescent.

He'd called that morning. O'Malley was out of the office for the day, so he wound up dealing with Wanda Crippen, the partner who had handled the purchase of his father's old office. As she listened to his proposal, he was initially under the impression that she was eating, but then he remembered that the Post Menopausal ladies wore telephone headsets that had a tendency to rustle.

"Well, this certainly is intriguing," she said when he'd finished. "Let me get back to you."

"Could you—I'd like to sort this out by week's end. I'm talking to some other people."

There was more of that chewy rustling, and Drew wondered if his bluff was about to be called.

"Okay," Crippen said. "That's good to know."

Ronnie stumbled in the front door just as he hung up, reminding him that he would have to be more careful now to hide what was going on. He'd wanted to confess ever since his disastrous meeting with Quint on Saturday, but the right moment never seemed to present itself. In fact, Drew was beginning to think he might be able to put off the day of reckoning until after the delivery, when she would be too consumed with her children to pay it much mind. By then his recovery would be under way. The business would be sold; he'd be partnered with PMG. There would be no more shortcuts, just hard work and humility. His mistake would be a thing of the past. Ronnie had often spoken of the lethal effect of regret in her patients. Drew would have to hope her belief applied to a transgression this close to home.

"Finished," she said. "Now—Wilkie."

The novel's old paper smell was a relief after the vegetable paste, but the doorbell rang before he could get through the first page. He looked up and shook his head. Whoever was there could go away. But their visitor beckoned again, this time with three raps of the heavy lion's head knocker.

"You'd better get it," Ronnie said.

He was halfway down the steps when he saw the police uniform. He slowed, his first thought this might have something to do with the bank. But the police wouldn't come here. Not like this. Not so soon. The officer was a woman, blond and muscular. Her eyes had a taut, end-of-shift tension.

Shannon, Drew thought. Something's happened to Shannon. He moved quickly to the door and pulled it open so hard it slammed against the stop.

"Hello sir how are you this evening?" she said, conflating the sentence into a few harsh syllables.

"I'm—"

"Is this Shannon Hagel's residence?"

A simple question, though it took him a moment to respond, fear crushing the things in his chest and throat that made words.

"Yes. Is she all right?"

"I'll need to speak with her."

"She's not here."

The woman wore black gloves. She began to tug at the base of one of them.

"Would you be her parent?"

He nodded warily, feeling the beginning of a different kind of fear.

"Would you know where she is?"

The inevitable shaming question. He checked his watch, as if knowing the time would help him answer. It was eight-thirty.

"Not exactly."

"When would you expect her back?"

This line of questioning could go on all night, a deep-sea probe sent to measure the murky trenches of his ignorance about his daughter's life.

"Within the next ninety minutes," he lied.

"Is there some way of contacting her in the meantime?"

"I'm sorry—what's going on here?"

"They need to talk to your daughter down at the police station. Immediately."

Drew remembered the look on her face when he knocked on her bedroom door on Saturday, the sound of her crying later that night.

"What's this about, Officer?"

"You'll have to talk to them."

Drew stood perfectly still. He knew he should phone Shannon but for some reason couldn't bring himself to move just yet.

"It would help if I knew what this was about."

The woman's eyes shifted, as if she were weighing up her options, none of which involved helping him understand anything except that his compliance was required. Immediately.

"All right," Drew said.

He invited her into the front hall, then went to use the phone in the living room. Shannon answered before the second ring. It was his turn to be terse; for some reason he suspected that telling her about the police would be a mistake.

"Look, she might be a while," he lied when he got back to the front hall, wanting this woman out of here before Shannon got back. "I'll bring her straight over."

To his surprise, she accepted this. Although maybe it wasn't so surprising. The police station was five blocks away. And they knew where the Hagels lived.

"Um, who do we ask for down there?" he asked as she turned to go.

"Just tell the desk officer who you are."

Drew walked back upstairs. Now that the initial shock was wearing off, this wasn't necessarily as surprising as it could have been. He'd been aware that something was wrong with his daughter for the past few days. On Sunday she'd left a note saying she would be joining some friends for a day trip to Mystic, but when she got home, she seemed to forget that was where she'd been. He'd been telling himself it was just one of the periodic emotional disruptions in her life. She'd deal with it in her own way. Which, after all, was how they did things now.

"Who was that?" Ronnie asked sleepily when he got back into the room.

"The police."

"The police? Drew, what's going on?"

"They want to talk to Shannon."

"What about?" She was fully awake now.

"I don't know. I'm supposed to take her down there as soon as she gets home."

"Do you want me to come with you?"

"No, you stay here. It's probably nothing."

Ronnie frowned.

"All right. But I want you to call me if anything's wrong."

He collected the tray and kissed her. Downstairs he took up a position in the front window to wait for Shannon. She looked worried as she raced up the steps.

"The police were just here," he said as he met her at the front door. "They want to talk to you."

He could see that she was frightened. Frightened, but not surprised.

"Do you know what this is about?"

"No," she said thinly.

"Shannon, what's—"

"I should probably get down there."

Although she wanted to go to the station on her own, Drew made it clear he was taking her. His daughter's independence could be put on hold for the next few hours. She didn't say a word during the short drive. The new police headquarters was a bland, utterly functional brick building that could have just as easily been a post office or elementary school. He parked in a space marked for visitors. As they got out of the car, he could see Godeep Mahabal's unmistakable white Mercedes slotted a few spaces down.

"Shannon, what's going on?"

She walked on, forcing him to hurry to keep up with her. They entered the lobby through two sets of automatic doors. The officer behind the counter told them to take a seat in chairs near some vending machines. It could have been where you waited while your tires were aligned. The closest wall was covered with an array of photos. Deadbeat dads. The amount each of them owed was printed just below his name. Some owed a little, some a lot. Drew wondered if this really worked. The men pictured looked as if they'd long ago passed beyond shame.

After a few minutes of agonized silence three familiar faces emerged from a door leading back into the station proper. Stephen Dulea and his parents. Stephen's expression darkened when he saw Shannon. He looked as if he were about to say something, but his parents hurried him along toward those automatic doors.

Drew turned to his daughter.

"Shannon, is there something you want to tell me before we go in there?"

She stared at him for a moment, as if deciding whether or not to speak. But then she turned her attention to a short, bulky man in a blue sports coat as he came through the same door as the Duleas. He had bright brown skin and a heavy, prominent brow that compressed his eyes into slits. It was hard to tell where he was from. It could have been Mexico or Fiji or the Philippines. Or Hartford or the Bronx. Drew had seen him around town occasionally, but had never guessed he was a cop. He approached with a shoulder-rolling, bow-legged walk. The buttons on his sports coat were decorated with anchors. His eyes were on Drew's daughter.

"Shannon? I'm Detective Flowers. Thanks for coming in. I'm not keeping you from studying for finals?"

She gave her head a wary shake.

"Good. That's all I've been hearing about tonight. Finals." He turned to Drew. "Are you the father?"

"Drew Hagel."

They shook hands. The man was very strong. Though of course, he would be.

"And you're going to be with your daughter?"

"Well, yes, if that's—"

"Sure, sure."

He had to enter a code into a key pad to get back through the door. It took him several clumsy, muttering tries, and he appeared to be genuinely surprised when it finally worked. Inside was just like anywhere else people did business, track lighting and simulated wood and lazy telephone voices. There was none of the stuff Drew had come to expect from the shows he watched on television, metal cages or racked guns or desperate chained men slumping in heavy chairs. Flowers nodded them into a small, featureless room. There was a table with some moist Dixie cups that he collected and tossed into a garbage can. And, in a corner, a tripod holding a video camera.

Drew and Shannon took the plastic chairs they were offered. Flowers sat across from them and opened a manila folder, shuffled some papers, then stacked and squared them facedown on the table, leaving only a blank yellow pad.

"Okay," he said as he uncapped a pen. "This is just an informal interview, so there's no reason for anyone to be worried or anything."

"Is that thing on?" Shannon asked, pointing to the video camera.

"Oh, shoot, thanks for reminding me."

Flowers got up and pressed a button, once again displaying the exaggerated care of a strong man unhappy around advanced technology. He stepped back, spreading his hands.

"Okay," he said as he sat back down. "There's a red flashing light. They can't ask any more of me."

Drew wondered if he should be challenging any of this, the camera or the interview itself. But he couldn't bring himself to say anything until he knew what this was about.

"Now, your name is Shannon Hagel, right?"

She nodded.

"You have to, I know this seems stupid, but you have to say stuff when I ask you questions. Out loud, I mean."

He gestured back at the camera with his thumb, as if it were some meddlesome, tagalong guest.

"Yes."

"And you're a student?"

"She's a senior at Country Day."

Shannon shot her father a look, as if he'd just given something vital away.

"And she's got to answer," Flowers added pleasantly. "I know it's hard. I've got kids, too. You should see me when my son's at the plate. The league is threatening to make me sit in my car. And you're seventeen?"

"Yes."

"Right. Good. Now, I understand you're friends with James Manning?"

Shannon nodded, then remembered her instructions.

"Yes."

"And how long have you known James?"

"About a year and a half. I mean, we've been friends for that long."

"Did you see James on Friday night?"

"Yeah. Yes."

"And where was that?"

"At the McNabbs' house. Up on Shaker. There was a party. I went for a while. Jamie was there."

"James Manning."

"Everybody calls him Jamie."

"Okay. They didn't tell me that, but what else is new? What time was this? I mean, that you saw Jamie."

"Around midnight. No, earlier."

"So why don't you describe the nature of your contact with him."

"Contact?"

"Did you just see him? Did you speak? Did you hang out?"

Shannon didn't answer right away. Flowers looked up, that heavy brow crinkling, though his expression remained friendly.

"We talked for a while, and then I gave him a ride home."

Drew looked at his daughter, then turned back to Flowers. The detective didn't seem surprised by what she'd just said.

"And this was about midnight, you said?"

"Earlier. I think it was earlier."

"More like, what, eleven?"

"I guess."

"Why did you do that? I mean, give Jamie a ride. Doesn't he have a car? A 2000 flame red Jeep Wrangler five-point-oh?"

"He . . ."

"Go ahead, Shannon. Just tell me what happened. Don't worry about getting people in trouble. We're talking to everybody."

"He'd had a few beers, I guess."

"A few as in a couple or a few as in he was intoxicated."

"I guess he'd had too much."

"So you drove him home in your car?"

"Yes."

"And what is that?"

"A Honda Civic."

"Yeah, my wife used to have one of those," Flowers said, shaking his head with wry affection. "She put ninety-four thousand miles on it, and then somebody stole it. Can you believe that? I kept on hoping I'd catch the guy so I could see the look on his face when he found out he'd stolen a cop's wife's car with almost a hundred thousand miles on it. Anyway. So you drove Jamie home and . . . ?"

"And then I went home."

"And you don't know what time it was when you dropped him off? I mean, exactly. Sorry to be a pain about this, but you didn't, I don't know, look at your watch or anything."

"Like I said . . ."

"Around eleven. Maybe a bit later. Okay." He tapped the table. "Now, what about Jamie's car?"

"Jamie's car?"

"Do you know who drove that home? I mean, to the Manning residence? Was it someone with you? Someone following you?"

Shannon shook her head. Flowers didn't correct her this time.

"So you didn't . . . you weren't in charge of getting someone to bring his car home or anything like that."

"No. I mean, not *in charge*."

"So, you don't know if, for instance"—he peeked at the overturned papers—"Stephen Dulea or Matthew Petrillo might have driven it home?"

"No. They could have, but I don't know. I mean, did someone drive Jamie's car home?"

Flowers didn't acknowledge that he'd been asked a question.

"Okay. So this is the part where we're going to have to get even more specific. You and Jamie leave the party, he's been drinking; do you know what he did with his car keys? I'm talking about before you drive off in your car."

Shannon stared at the detective for several seconds before answering.

"He gave them to me and I left them in the Wrangler and asked this kid to tell Matt or Stephen or somebody to bring it home."

Everything changed in the room. It was almost as if some dense gas had been pumped into the cramped atmosphere. Flowers stared evenly at Shannon for what seemed to Drew like a very long time. With all that flesh crowding down on his eyes, it was impossible to tell what he was thinking. Then he looked back at the yellow pad. Drew noticed he hadn't been writing anything on it, just using the pen to thicken some of the horizontal lines.

"Now what kid was this?" His voice was flat, that jovial undertone gone now.

"I don't know."

"Was he a Country Day student?"

"I don't think so."

"You don't think so? There are like, what, three hundred kids in the upper school over there? Seventy, eighty in your class? We're not talking Florida State here, Shannon."

"No. He wasn't a student at Country Day."

"Then how would he know who Stephen and Matt were?"

Shannon was silent long enough to cause the detective to once again look up from his pad.

"A lot of people know those two."

"Can you describe this individual?"

"He was a bit older. I think he might have been in college. He had short blond hair. Just a normal kind of face. It was dark."

"What was he wearing?"

"Jeans. A shirt. I don't remember."

"And you don't know if he found Matt and Stephen? You don't know if they agreed to do this?"

"No. We left right after I talked to him."

"And the Jeep wasn't there when you got back to the Mannings' place?"

"No. Not that I saw."

"Not that you saw."

"No. It wasn't."

Flowers picked up the papers he'd taken out of the manila folder when they'd first started, shuffling through them a few times.

"Shannon, have you talked to Jamie since Friday night?"

"Um, yeah."

"How many times?"

"Once."

"Not twice?"

She closed her eyes and nodded.

"Yeah. Twice."

"You talk about the Wrangler? How it got home?"

"Yeah."

"And you said?"

"I told him what I told you."

"Exactly?"

"I don't know if it was exact, but yeah."

"You didn't tell him that Stephen or Matt drove the car home?"

"No. I mean, I might have said I *thought* they did. I really can't re-member. It wasn't that big of a deal. His car got home, right?"

Once again Flowers didn't answer.

"Okay." He rapped the table with the base of his pen. "So, to recap. You're at the party. Jamie's had a few. You drive him home, leaving the keys in his car and telling some boy with blond hair and jeans and a shirt to ask Matt or Stephen to bring it home. You drop Jamie, you go home, and that's it."

"Yes," Shannon said softly.

"Okay. One more question because I know I must be driving you nuts." That jovial tone was back in his voice. "Why was it impor-tant that someone bring the Wrangler home on Friday night? Why couldn't Jamie just pick it up the next day?"

She looked down at the table.

"Shannon?"

"He didn't want his father to know he'd been drinking."

"Why's that?"

"He just didn't."

"But you know, most parents, their kid has a few too many, they *want* him to catch a ride home." He turned to Drew. "Am I right?"

Drew nodded dully.

"I guess Jamie, he tends to overdo it sometimes, and his dad's like, if he does it one more time, he's going to lose his car for the summer."

"So you were covering for him?"

"Yeah. I guess that's what I was doing."

"But you're not doing that right now in any way?"

She shook her head slowly, her eyes on the empty table in front of her. Flowers watched her for a moment, then looked back at the notes he hadn't been writing.

"Right. I think . . . yeah, that should do it for the time being."

Shannon pushed back her chair, but Drew stayed where he was.

"What's going on?" he asked. "I still don't understand."

Flowers began to collect his papers.

"There was a hit-and-run on Orchard Avenue late Friday night. You know, where it snakes around up the hill? Some guy was riding a bi-cycle, if you can believe that. He was one of those Iron Man triath-

letes. It might have been a Jeep that did it. We're talking to area owners."

"Jesus. How is the guy?"

Flowers looked at Shannon when he answered.

"Nah, he's not going to make it. Brain damage. They took him off
the ventilator today."

Drew looked at his daughter as well. She continued to stare at the
table. He recognized the expression. If Flowers was waiting for a reaction, he was wasting his time. The detective seemed to understand
this as well because he stood, tapping the edge of the folder on the
table.

"I'd really like to thank you guys for coming in on a school night.
Hey, and Shannon, if you remember anything else about this blond
guy or how that Wrangler might have got home, give us a holler, all
right? It'd be a big help. The more things we can rule out, the quicker
we can figure out what's what."

Drew had trouble keeping up with his daughter as she hurried out
of the building. Mahabal's car was still in the parking lot. They didn't
speak until they were on Federal.

"Shannon, why did you just lie to that man? You didn't come home
on Friday night. You didn't get home until noon."

"I didn't lie. Not about what he wanted to know."

Drew remembered standing outside her bedroom door on Saturday,
listening to the call she was making, her urgent, fearful words.

"Are you protecting Jamie?" he asked as they pulled onto Crescent.
"Is that what this is about?"

Shannon was staring straight ahead.

"Shannon, I want you to talk to me about this," he said after they
pulled into the driveway. "A man is going to—"

But she was already out of the car, sprinting up the steps into the
house. By the time he made it through the front door she was in her
room. He followed her upstairs and, tempted to confront her, paused
outside her locked door. But he knew too well that there was nothing
he could do to compel her to speak with him. Too many times he'd let
her handle things on her own.

He went into his own room. Ronnie was waiting for him.

"Drew? What did they want? What's going on?"

There were sounds in the hallway. His daughter, charging out of her room and hurrying down the steps. Seconds later he could hear the front door slam.

"Drew?"

"I don't know," he said. "I don't know what's going on."

19 David had come home to tell Ian the truth about Robert Jarvis. He'd planned to do it since coming back from his second visit to the hospital on Sunday, though he couldn't bear to shatter the confidence and energy his nephew had shown the last few days. But the truth would come to him soon; he'd see it on the news or Shannon would find out. That would be a mistake. It had to come from David, so he could let his nephew know that Jarvis's impending death wouldn't change anything. They were still going to get through this together.

But he'd arrived home to emptiness. They've taken him, David thought as he tore through the silent house. Ian was once again in jail, and everything he had been planning for them was finished. Lawyers would have to be hired; Ginny's money would soon vanish. Whatever they didn't take would have to go to Jarvis's family; that's how the system did you these days. Punishment was in the air. Make a mistake and you paid. And if you happened to be a workingman, you paid until there was nothing left.

Just go, David thought as he slumped into a chair at the kitchen table. Get the Chevelle from work, fill it with as much stuff as possible, and start driving. If he stayed here, they would want to know why he had been helping Ian hide. There would be court dates and lawsuits and another five years of Traynor. But if he left, there would be none of that. He could sleep in his car tonight and then get his own money from the bank in the morning. And then he'd be free to do whatever he wanted. There was nothing more to be done here. He'd tried to raise Ian and he'd failed. Sitting in his sister's tomb-silent house, he let his mind drift, just to remember what freedom felt like. He thought about the women he would meet, fucking them crazy and not worrying about waking up his nephew in the next room; the parties he could run until any hour; the places he could go, California or Alaska or Mexico.

But David soon found that the only thing his newly liberated imagination could focus on was Disney World. Disney World. A place he hated. A place he'd visited only once. This was three months after Ginny died, when he and Ian had traveled down to Florida to pick up the last few bits of his Daytona gear, stopping by the theme park as a gift to the boy to try to cheer him up. But the long day had been a trial for them both, Ian dragging from one attraction to the next, too listless with grief and road weariness to draw even the smallest amount of joy from the rides and the junk food. By midafternoon David had finally had enough. He made Ian a bed of clothes in the back seat and drove hard through the night, the way he always did, stopping briefly in Georgia to gas up and get some snacks and then again, sometime after midnight, at a rest stop in Virginia, one of the state places that didn't have much more than toilets and a wall map. Ian was asleep for the second stop, and David didn't bother to wake him. When he came out of the bathroom, he glanced at the tangled shadowy lump of clothing in the back and then headed north.

He never did figure out how he came to know that Ian was no longer with him. The back seat was shrouded in darkness; road noise and the radio would have covered the absolute silence. It was probably nothing more than a change in the car's internal atmosphere. Whatever the reason, just a few miles before the Washington Beltway he realized that his nephew was gone. He'd almost crashed as he reached back to rummage frantically through the clothes. He understood right away what had happened. Ian had slipped out of the car while David was in the men's room and had probably wandered off into the woods to pee. Which meant that either he would still be at the rest stop or he would be with the police. Or he would be gone forever, vanishing into that world of lost children. David turned around at the first possible opportunity and powered back down south, figuring it would take him at least an hour to get back. The panic gradually subsided, giving way to a fantasy fueled by his first few terrible weeks as Ian's guardian: the endless crying and the bed-wetting and the long dark silences; the suspicion that he had no notion how to raise this skinny, haunted boy into anything resembling manhood. A daydream in which he just kept on going. Back to Florida or somewhere new. Letting fate take care of the boy.

Not that he could have ever done that. Not after he'd looked into his sister's terrified eyes at Mercy and promised her. Not after he'd stood by so helplessly years earlier, too weak and frightened to do anything on the nights their drunken father came for her, even though he knew where the old man's pistol was hidden, even though it would have taken no strength at all to pull the trigger and send death into that farting, snoring pile of meat. When he got to the rest stop, Ian was sitting patiently on the stone bench beneath the lighted map, having told all the truckers and the travelers who'd asked that his uncle would soon be back.

"I was waiting for you," he said.

He followed David back to the car and crawled into the back seat, where he fell asleep immediately, certain all along of what David had only just accepted: They would never leave each other.

He was just getting ready to go to the police station when Shannon's car pulled up out back. Not only had she ignored his very reasonable request that they stay at home for a few days, but Ian had some sort of wicked burn on his hand. The moment David saw this he knew that he wouldn't be telling his nephew anything. Ian looked even more wired than he'd been when David left, and even though Shannon clearly understood that she'd made a mistake, David wondered what she'd do once she knew the truth about Jarvis. Ian was at the kitchen sink when he came in after getting rid of her, running the cold water at full throttle over his hand.

"You all right?" he asked.

Nothing. Ian was mesmerized by the sight of water coursing over his skin.

"What happened?" David asked in his quietest voice.

"Burned it."

He waited for a further explanation, but none was forthcoming. He fixed an ice pack as a way of getting Ian to turn off the tap. They sat at the kitchen table, Ian's leg going a mile a minute. And then the yawning started, one shallow gulp after the other, like an animal trapped in an airless chamber.

"So how'd you do that to yourself?" David asked, nodding to the wound, as if he were asking an entirely new question.

"At this pizza place."

"Must have been one hot pizza."

Yawn. Nothing.

"So how come you guys went out?"

"We were hungry."

He leaped out of his chair to look in the refrigerator, rattling the door, the racked bottles chiming as he pulled out a can of Coke. David was tempted to suggest that caffeine might not be something he wanted in his bloodstream just now, but that would only change the subject. Ian popped the can and put it on the table without even taking a sip.

"Shannon thinks I should go see a doctor," he said after he collapsed back into his chair. "So I could get some pills. You know, to chill me out."

David watched his nephew closely, thinking about that afternoon's conversation with Traynor. Although her news was good—she was finally quitting—she'd also repeated her request that Ian see this shrink for a "checkup."

"This isn't something you want to do?"

"No," Ian said. "Come on. No way. I feel great."

"Because, you know, you get into a doctor's office, they start asking you questions, that's going to be a difficult situation to control."

"I know."

"The other thing I was going to say, I mean, I think you should probably not be so quick to do everything Shannon recommends."

"What do you mean?"

"Ian, I know you're thinking that you're free and clear on this, but, well, you have to try to keep cool for a little while longer."

"But why?"

Because Robert Jarvis is going to die.

"Just to be on the safe side. All I'm saying is you should stay close to home for the next couple days."

"But what about work?"

"I'll deal with that. I had a talk with your manager. He's cool with it."

This was not necessarily true. When David called this morning to report that his nephew was ill, the moron had actually said that they would have to "see where they stood" if he failed to report for work the following day. But David couldn't worry about that now. He couldn't worry about anything except keeping Ian off the streets until he calmed down a bit.

"Now, if Shannon wants to come over here, obviously that's fine. But, to repeat, I do not want you guys going out. You want a pizza, just let me know. Chinese, Subway. I'll get you anything you want. Movies. Anything."

Ian looked up at him.

"Could you bring me some dope?"

David sat upright in his chair, stunned by the suggestion.

"Say that again?"

"Just a half ounce. Enough to get me, you know, over the hump."

"But what about your random tests?"

"You said I'm done with all that shit."

Another falsehood. He was finished with Traynor, but the parole officer could easily call for a random screening at any moment during the next seven weeks. She'd been slack about that recently, but she might be more vigilant now that Traynor was out of the picture.

"I don't know, Ian."

"Great. I mean, you're real good at telling me what I can't do, but I ask you for this one simple favor and it's like, no way." He shook his head angrily. "You know, sometimes you're so full of shit it isn't even funny."

David couldn't believe what he'd just heard. Ian had never spoken to him like this.

"What did you just say to me?"

"You heard me."

"Ian, you'd better watch yourself. Right now I'm the only friend you have."

"Well, in that case I guess I'm fucked," he muttered as he got up and walked back to his room.

David was tempted to go after him, grab him by his neck, and drag him back to the table to make him apologize. But he knew Ian didn't really mean what he'd said. He was just feeling the strain. His furious music started a few seconds later, louder than ever. David considered Ian's shocking request for dope. It was not necessarily as crazy as it first sounded. He certainly could benefit from the mellowing effects until things quieted down. But of course, it would be insane to supply his nephew again. Backsliding of the worst kind. And then there was the small matter of its illegality. David had been out of that particular life for a long time. It wasn't the way it had been when he was young and getting your hands on a half ounce was no more hazardous than convincing somebody's older brother to buy you a quart of Miller. These days one false step and you could wind up looking at seven years.

He drained Ian's drink and crushed it. And here was something else that was different nowadays. Back when he was Ian's age, crushing an empty can had taken a Herculean effort. Now it was like balling up a piece of paper. Why was everything becoming so much flimsier? Wasn't the world supposed to be getting better and stronger? But it was all headed in the opposite direction. Take inflation, for example. Shouldn't prices be going down now that they had machines and computers and could make everything overseas where people worked for ten cents a day? Fat chance. Ding somebody's car, and it would cost you a thousand dollars. Every time he took his Chevelle into the shop—a common occurrence these days—he was out a week's wages. And look at this piece-of-shit house, its fixtures coming apart after less than twenty years. What was the point of all those people working so hard if things were only going to get more difficult?

One generation after the next, driving themselves to early graves. Ten billion backbreaking hours wasted in lousy, meaningless jobs, and the world was more costly and dangerous than ever. And then there was Ginny. Working hard, paying the bills on time, and what happens? Some evil poison starts growing inside her, depriving her of the solitary joy she'd seized for herself: watching her son grow up. Or Ian himself, turning things around after those bad breaks, and then he does a favor for some rich boy and now he's looking at ruination. Even David's own decision to start living right had brought him nothing but trouble. Could anyone honestly tell him that his life was easier now than it had been when he was dealing dope or getting college kids drunk? That was the thing people didn't understand, all the counselors and cops. Life could be a snap if you just didn't care. The simplest thing in the world. Rent a room somewhere, sign on with the government. Drink and fuck and scam your way through the day. If the world put up obstacles, all you had to do was move around them. David knew plenty of guys who did precisely this and were a hundred times happier than he had been these past few years, if you didn't count that moment three infinitely long days ago when he'd stood in front of that artist's table, looking out at the beautiful marshland through his nephew's eyes. As soon as you wanted something strong and real from this life, that was when your actual troubles started.

So fuck it, he thought. He wouldn't go back to work tonight. And he wouldn't go tomorrow, either. The Egyptians would fire him, but that was just the way it was going to have to be. He'd stay home with Ian until this thing blew over. He'd find something to pay the bills. Sling drinks at a bowling alley or sign on with Labor Ready. Mow fairways at the country club. It didn't matter. They hadn't come up with a job yet that David couldn't do for eight hours at a time.

He doubled-locked Ian in the house and rushed back to Camelot to swap cars, where he told the startled dispatcher he was sick, and no, he didn't have the slightest idea when he was going to feel better. The music still pulsed from Ian's room when he got home. He went to his door and pounded loud enough to make himself heard, then stepped inside. Ian was at his desk, working furiously on one of his big pads, the hooded lamp illuminating his frantic hands as they made their black slashing lines. The way that leg was going reminded David of the paint shakers at a hardware store where he'd once worked. Speaking of lousy jobs. At least he wasn't outside doing any more chores with that ax. David switched off the stereo. Ian kept right on drawing.

"Can I talk to you for a minute?"

David sat on the edge of the bed. Ian turned, tapping his pencil against his thigh. The anger that had fueled his earlier words in the kitchen wasn't even a memory.

"How's your hand?"

"The patient has made a miraculous recovery."

Ian laughed and then seemed to forget why he was laughing.

"What you working on there?"

"Just some stuff. It's great. The absolute best work I've ever done."

David somehow doubted it, but he kept his opinion to himself. And he knew better than to try to look. Ian almost never showed him his work. Another secret he kept from the only person who knew how to protect him.

"Look, Ian, about earlier. I didn't want to come across like I was mad at you. I just really think you should stick close to home for the next few days. You and me both."

"You're not still worried about the accident, are you?"

"Well, matter of fact, I am."

"But, Uncle David, they'll never know it was me. You weren't there. The place, I mean, it could have been on the moon it was so deserted. And if that guy had seen anything, he'd have told the cops by now. They've given up looking."

David nodded, as if he were agreeing with any of this. A well-to-do white man with a family was going to die. The cops would never give up looking.

"But still," he said with a nervous chuckle, "better safe than sorry."

"Well, you can worry if you want, but I'm not going to. They aren't going to touch me."

"It's good you feel that way," David said. "Let's just be cool. For argument's sake."

Ian shrugged, then turned around and resumed his furious draw-

ing. The music came on just after David left the room, louder than
thinking could ever be.

He spent the next few hours pacing the house, Ian's words about
Jarvis making him wonder if the death watch at Mercy was over.
When he'd gone on Sunday morning, he'd discovered that they'd
moved him to a different room, this one in a regular ward. As he came
out of the elevator, he was frozen by the sight of a familiar man standing by the nurse's station. It was Robert Jarvis, that same long body
and beaky nose and shock of brown hair he'd seen through the door
before, though now he was tall and confident and very much awake,
dressed in khaki trousers and a golf shirt. He was speaking softly on
a house phone, jangling change in his pants pocket. David walked
slowly toward him, amazed that after three decades of bad luck he
was being blessed with his second miracle in a week, first the house
in the marsh and now this, the dying victim recovered, all that trouble
vanishing. But then the man turned, and it wasn't Robert Jarvis, just
some near replica of him, his brother, maybe even a twin, uttering the
words *donor people*. David glanced into the room as he passed. Here
was the real Jarvis, stricken and immobile. Tubes and instruments
and people crowded his bed, his wife and that Teresa and an older
woman; more visitors in other parts of the room, though David moved
on before he could see them all, knowing that if he hung around this
time, then someone would make him account for himself. Instead, he
went home and told Ian that everything was going to be all right.

The music had finally stopped. David went to have a look. Ian had
passed out on top of his covers. David wasn't surprised; he couldn't
have slept more than a couple of hours in the last three days. And
even now, while asleep, he looked pumped full of stored energy, his
sheet twisted around his legs like a python, the muscles in his face
and neck trembling. Just waiting for someone to hit the switch. He'd
been like this after Ginny's death, writhing and moaning and sobbing
through long broken nights. It would get better for a while, and then
it would get bad again, only really ending when he began smoking
weed with the crew at Gryphon Games.

Just a half ounce, he'd said. Just enough to get him through this
new bad time.

David went back into the kitchen and poured himself a bowl of cereal. He was chewing listlessly when headlights washed over the garage. He jumped up and turned off the kitchen light. Here we go, he thought. But it was only Shannon. He stepped through the screen door to intercept her.

"I have to see Ian," she said, looking past him to the doorway.

"What is it?"

"Look, can I just talk to him? Please?"

"Talk to me first."

She glanced at Ian's window. She could probably rouse him if she yelled, though David doubted she would do that. This wasn't a girl who shouted or carried on. She looked back at him.

"They know."

Bugs had seen the light. They were clicking against the bulb above his head.

"Who knows?"

"The police. I was just there. They came by my house."

All right, David thought. You knew this might be coming. You're ready for this.

"What exactly do they know?"

"That it was a Jeep. They were asking about the Wrangler. They know it was out at the time of the accident. And they know I was with Jamie."

"What did you tell them?"

"I told them that I drove Jamie home in my car and left the keys in the Wrangler for someone else from the party to take."

Smart girl, David thought. Smart, smart girl.

"Did they believe you?"

"I don't know," she said, her voice cracking. "How would I know what they believe?"

"But you didn't say anything about Ian?"

"No. Of course not."

"Do they know for sure it was Jamie's Wrangler?"

"I think so. If not, they're close to knowing."

"But you told them that you don't know who was driving it."

She nodded her head.

"Did they know you came to the party with another boy?"

"I don't think so. No, I'm sure they don't. Ian wasn't letting people see him. We'd agreed about that."

"So right now all they know is that you and Jamie left the party in your car. Which means that as long as you don't say anything, we're still all right."

She shook her head, resisting his logic.

"Look, I've got to talk to Ian."

She tried to step around him, but David blocked her way. They both eased back, neither wanting to make contact. She met his eye.

"Why didn't you tell us that Jarvis was going to die?"

David looked right back at her.

"Because I don't want to lose Ian."

"But he's going to *die*."

"Do you think that changes anything, Shannon? It doesn't. It only makes it worse for Ian. It means that unless we protect him very carefully, his life is over. Finished. And Robert Jarvis still dies."

She began to tear up.

"Listen to me," David continued. "You've done really well so far. That thing about leaving the keys, that was great. Just keep on saying what you've been saying, and we'll be all right. Buncha rich kids get together drinking, people start piling into cars, anything can happen. I've seen it all the time. The cops might give you a hard time and tell you all sorts of bullshit, but in the end there's nothing they can do to you as long as you don't say Ian's name. You just have to keep that in your mind, Shannon. If you don't say his name, then he will be all right."

She gave a faint nod.

"Now, I'm sorry I didn't tell you about Jarvis, but I think you know why I didn't want Ian to know right away."

"Can I at least see him?"

"He's asleep."

"He's asleep?" she said, lowering her voice. "God, I thought he'd never . . ."

"Shannon, I told you, I've lived with that boy every day for the last four years. I know him. He just gets like this whenever the pressure's on. These nerves—he got them after Ginny died, and it happened again after he was arrested. You just have to give him time. You just have to keep the pressure off him. He'll get better."

"But when can I see him?" she asked. "Can I still call tomorrow?"

"That might not be such a good idea. If the police are asking you questions, maybe you should keep away for the next few days."

"You're telling me I can't see him at all?"

"No. I would never say that to you. All I'm saying is that we have to be really careful now."

She was suddenly looking very young and very afraid.

"So what am I supposed to do?"

"Just keep to yourself. Keep on telling people you drove Jamie home and you don't know what happened to the Wrangler. I'll have Ian call you when things settle down a bit. I promise you."

"When?"

"Maybe on the weekend. Or next week."

"Next week?"

"Shannon, just try to be patient. It's the best thing for Ian. It really is."

She cast another look at Ian's window.

"Will you at least tell him I was here?"

"Of course."

She nodded for a while, accepting what he'd told her, then got in the car and drove off, leaving behind a thin cloud of dust. David didn't know how much longer she'd be able to keep quiet. And even if she did, the police would be talking to the other kids at the party. Someone would remember the boy with Shannon. Sooner or later they would want to talk to Ian. David would have to think of something else before then.

He turned back to look at Ian's window. The light was still burning, but that didn't mean anything. He was sleeping.

PART SIX

20 At first, Carrie couldn't understand the buzzing. It echoed impatiently through the empty house, a harsh industrial noise, the sort of thing she imagined people were subjected to in factories or prisons. She stood perfectly still in the kitchen after it ended, worried that it might be warning of some invisible hazard, carbon monoxide or radon. And then she remembered. The front gate. It was now fully operational, activated this morning by her husband. Visitors were being *screened*, the first time this had happened since they'd moved in. She walked to Quint's office to answer it; he had given her a crash course before leaving for the police station. It was simple, a perfect conjunction of high technology and modern manners. You saw who it was, pressed a button, and told them to fuck off.

She stepped among the Sun Microsystems computers and multi-line phones and neatly shelved binders, all those vehicles for the electrons and fractions upon which the Manning fortune was based. Their visitor's wavering image could be seen on the wall-mounted unit: a tall black woman with an oversize bag dangling from her shoulder. She was excessively dressed, like a character in an amateur play, perched on her toes to look over the iron fence.

"Yes?"

The woman was startled by the unexpected voice emerging from the stone column to her right.

"Ms. Manning?" she said, stooping to speak into the box.

No, I am Oz, the great and powerful.

"Can I help you?" Carrie asked.

The woman's reply was garbled, though Carrie was fairly certain she could hear the name of the local paper.

"I'm sorry," she said. "You'll have to call the office."

The buzzer rang again as she walked back to the kitchen, that abrasive tone reverberating through her already jangled nerves. The new lawyer had warned them that people would be coming now that Jarvis had died. The police liked to use the press to stir things up, especially in vexing cases like this. It was the reason Quint had turned on the system. He'd rerouted all their calls to Capital Park as well. The buzzer sounded for a third time as she took her seat at the kitchen table, a prolonged fit of electronic pique that she hoped would be the last of it. Carrie wondered if this was what the future truly held, locked gates and screened calls and insufferable lawyers sitting at her table. Monday night and then all day Tuesday she had been able to tell herself that a simple explanation was en route, like an express package from some distributor of domestic miracles. They would open the box and pull out a forehead-slapping epiphany, something that would soon have everybody chuckling. Of *course*, that's what it is. How could we have *been* so stupid. She'd fully expected her husband and son to bring her such a package when they returned Monday night. But they arrived empty-handed. Jamie came in first, ignoring Carrie's questions and storming straight up to his room. Quint sat talking with Godeep in the big white Mercedes for a while, and then, after their friend left, he went over to look at the Jeep. When he finally came in, he appeared, in his own way, even worse than Jamie.

"They're going to be coming for the Wrangler."

Not the sort of news she'd been waiting on.

"Who? What?"

"They're bringing a truck from Hartford. Godeep's of the opinion I didn't have to let them have it, but I don't want to start playing those games."

"Them being the police," asked Carrie.

He nodded grimly.

"Quint, what happened?"

"Well, Jamie's sticking to his story."

"What story? Wait a minute, rewind a bit. I'm still at the part where there's a cop in the front hall and you're telling me not to say anything until you get home."

He told her about the injured bicyclist, how a witness saw a red Jeep at the bottom of the hill at around the time of the accident.

"But is he . . . I mean, he's not dead or anything?"

"Not yet."

Carrie felt the jolt move through her. She took a half step away from her husband.

"Not yet? What does that mean?"

"It means they took him off life support this morning."

"Oh, my God. Quint. What is Jamie saying?"

"He's saying that Shannon brought him home and he's not sure who drove his car. He thinks it might be Stephen or Matt, but they both deny having anything to do with it."

"Do you believe him?"

"I don't know, Carrie. It's not a very convincing story. Or a very flattering one, for that matter."

"What about Shannon? Surely she'd know what's going on."

"As far as we can tell, she's backing Jamie up. At least, that's what Godeep thinks, since no one's been arrested."

Arrested.

"Wait, hold on. Who drove the Wrangler home from the party? Surely someone must know *that*. If it wasn't Jamie then . . ."

"That's becoming the big mystery." He shook his head, frustrated as ever to be confronted with the unknown. "I ran into Rob and Andie Dulea in the hallway at the station. They weren't too happy about this, I can tell you that."

"So what happens now?"

"What happens is that the police are going to try to find out what the hell's going on."

"But are they even sure it was the Wrangler that did this?"

"They're a lot more sure now than they were this afternoon." He met her eye. "Look, Carrie, they're going to want to talk to you."

"Quint, I don't want to talk to the police. Can I not do that?"

"We have to cooperate with them. We have to do this the right way."

"But not at the police station. Obviously."

"They're going to want to know what time you saw the Wrangler back here on Friday."

"Well, what should I say?"

"Carrie, you have to tell them the truth."

"The truth might not be so good. It was here right after Jamie got home. Parked in its usual spot. And I didn't see who drove it in, either. Which means I can't say that it wasn't our son."

"Then you're going to have to tell them that." His expression grew even darker. "They're also going to ask about the drinking."

She gave him a helpless look. But he had that merciless cast to his eyes.

"I presume he was?"

"Quint . . ."

"Not that it matters particularly what you say about the drinking. He would have been seen by people at the party."

"Quint, he was drunk, all right? It was like finding Robert Downey junior in your kitchen."

"Why didn't you tell me that, Carrie?"

"Because I didn't want to bother you. I mean, you haven't exactly been in Dad mode of late, have you?"

She knew it was a cheap shot the instant it came out of her mouth, a feeble defense against his justifiable wrath. She waved her hand in apology before he could respond.

"I thought we'd agreed that the next time he drank we'd punish him."

"I know."

"I mean, Carrie, isn't it pretty obvious now why we were going to do that?"

"Yep. It sure is."

He nodded unhappily. He wouldn't belabor the point. Quint never belabored the point.

"I need you to tell me one more thing."

"You want to know if I think Jamie drove the Wrangler. You want to know if I think he's lying about running this poor guy over. Come on, Quint. This is Jamie. He wouldn't do that."

"Drive drunk?"

"No. Hurt somebody and try to hide it."

"What if he didn't know he'd done it?"

"But he'd know *now*. He'd admit if he was behind the wheel. Besides, if Shannon is saying she drove him . . ."

She stopped, remembering the way Shannon hooked her arm through Jamie's after the banquet, remembering her wretched expression coming out of his room on the morning after this accident. And her son's completely out-of-character moodiness and anger these past few days, his refusal to speak with her or even meet her eye, his reckless defiance of Quint.

"Carrie?"

Every instinct told her that Jamie would never do such a thing. The drinking, yes, but not the lying. Not about something this serious. But these were mere instincts. Not exactly her best friends these days.

"I don't know. I really don't."

Quint nodded unhappily.

"So what happens now?" she asked.

"Well, first they're going to talk to everybody at the party. If the truth doesn't emerge from that . . ."

The police arrived for the Wrangler. Carrie presumed it was going to be an ordinary wrecker, but this was a great flatbed beast with pulleys and straps that lifted the Jeep right off the ground with a series of pressurized shrieks and sighs. The men scrambling beneath it looked as if they were from the Islands, their long dreads whipping against their white jumpsuits. They were watched by a short man with a broad, pleasant face. Quint explained that this was Flowers, the detective who'd interviewed Jamie. When the job was done, he came to the door, and the two of them spoke quietly. Carrie fled to her bedroom, not wanting to talk to the police until she'd had time to think.

"Well, we'd better try to get some sleep," Quint said when he came up.

"Oh, yeah, right."

They stood perfectly still, not looking at each other, Carrie perched on the edge of the bed, Quint hovering just inside the door, their son only a few walls away. Carrie was tempted to drag him in here and make him talk to them, letting him know that they were his parents and would insulate him from whatever trouble he faced; they would lie and cheat if that was necessary. But she looked at her husband's unwavering expression and understood that she could offer him no such immunity. If Quint knew that Jamie had done something awful, he would never lie about it. The price would have to be paid.

"Feel free to tell me that this is all some kind of ridiculous mistake," she said after the silence became unbearable. "Just jump right in."

"I can't do that, Carrie. I wish I could, but I can't."

They kept Jamie home the next day. Quint went into work, though he would come straight back if there were any developments. After dropping off the boys at school, Carrie returned home to wait for the call that would tell her that everything was all right. Jamie slept late, or at least he stayed in his room for most of the morning. Carrie couldn't help but wonder if he was online with Shannon. Planning their next move.

"They figure it out yet?" he asked when he finally came down.

She shook her head. Her son suddenly seemed very strange to her. Have you done this thing? she wanted to ask. But she couldn't make the words come out of her mouth. Fearing his contempt if she did, but fearing even more that he would say yes.

"I wish you guys would let me go into school," he said. "I could find out who was driving the car in five minutes."

"I don't think that's a good idea."

He started to walk away.

"Jamie?"

He paused with great reluctance.

"Why was Shannon here on Saturday morning?"

"She just came by."

"Were you talking to her about all this?"

"You know what, Ma? I really don't want to talk to you about Friday night."

He stalked off before she could respond, his fury once again leaving her speechless. They spent the next few hours avoiding each other. Carrie spoke to Quint a few times; he still hadn't heard anything. She almost forgot to ask him how things were going at WMV.

"Not good."

"Meaning?" she asked sharply, resenting the usual ritual of extraction.

"It means I'm putting together a financing deal with a consortium of banks and brokerages. It'll buy us a few months, but unless there's a miracle by the end of September, we're going to lose control of the fund."

"Well, the summer's a long time," she said feebly. "A lot can happen."

At afternoon pickup Carrie thought she could detect a few dark looks and stifled conversations as she made her way along the hedged path to the lower school. When she got home, there were no messages. That express package bearing her reasonable explanation now seemed a lot less inevitable.

She spent the remainder of Tuesday afternoon helping Dillon finish his history project, a model re-creating the gunfight at the OK Corral. Two mind-numbing hours of gluing plastic cowboys in various spots around a toothpick fence. They made placards as well. "Billy Clanton shot here." "Doc Holliday reloads." "Wyatt Earp kills Frank McLaury."

"So, is Jamie in trouble?" Dillon asked as they worked.

It would be foolish to lie. He'd seen too much. The policewoman; his brother's sullen anger; the Wrangler floating above their forecourt late Monday night.

"A little. Your father will sort it out."

"What did he do?"

"He drank too much beer and loaned his car to someone he shouldn't."

"Jerk."

"Come on," she said. "But there's a lesson in this. You know what it is?"

"Yeah. Don't lend people your stuff."

And then Quint arrived home in the early evening, and it all got worse.

"Godeep was at school all day. They talked to the entire graduating class of Totten Country Day, and no one has the slightest idea how Jamie's car made it home."

The entire graduating class.

"So what does that mean?"

"It means that the police are going to start taking a much closer look at our son. Look, Carrie, I'm sorry, but they want to talk to you now. I've arranged for Godeep to be in there with you."

"In where? Quint—"

"Suddenly people aren't so willing to make house calls."

"Now? But who'll look after the boys? Sabine's gone."

Quint shot her a curious look.

"Oh. Right. Of course. Jamie."

Quint went upstairs to tell him that they were going. Carrie could hear raised voices, and then Quint used his absolute tone and there was silence. He came down the steps shaking his head.

"I'll tell you this," he said. "His attitude these last few days doesn't exactly inspire confidence."

Quint drove her down. They said nothing until they reached the spot where it had happened.

"You think he did this, don't you?" she asked.

"It's starting to look that way."

"So do we know anything about Robert Jarvis?"

Godeep had found out about him. He did something with computers, mostly from home, though he went into the city some days, as he had on Friday, which was why he was getting his workout in so late. He was married with two kids at the Catholic school. Evidently he was in training for a big triathlon in British Columbia, one of those races where they go for miles and miles, swimming and pedaling and running, skinny inexorable people with numbers painted on their thighs. The accident had shattered his brain. He'd hit the guardrail at just the right angle; the damage was too deep and pervasive to make operating worthwhile. The family had agreed to pull out the tubes, and now they were just waiting for the end.

They were ready for her at the police station. Flowers was disarmingly polite, but Carrie figured that was just his routine. She'd met too many honey-tongued backstabbers from Quint's work to fall for polite. The interview was very low-key. Godeep was there but said nothing until the very end. There really wasn't that much they wanted to hear from Carrie. She admitted that Jamie had been drinking; his classmates would have said as much, anyway. She said he'd told her that Shannon had driven him home and friends had brought back the Wrangler. She didn't see it arrive but was fairly certain that it was there soon after he got back. No, she didn't know which friends. And she couldn't give an exact time. Flowers asked if Shannon Hagel had been up to their house on Saturday morning, another clumsy trap, since Carrie knew that Jamie had already confessed to speaking with her. So, yes, she'd seen Shannon, though there was no reason to mention Jamie's being naked in bed when she was there. The only tricky moment came at the end of the interview.

"You were home all night, right?" Flowers asked in that flustered, self-deprecating manner she had to remind herself not to like.

"Yes."

"But Diane McNabb tried to call you to come get your son. Just before ten. Didn't you get that message?"

"Not until after Jamie was home," Carrie said. "I wasn't picking up."

She hadn't realized how bad it was going to sound until she'd said it. Though of course, not as bad as the truth. And then Godeep announced that she was done, a fact the detective didn't dispute.

"How did it go?" Quint asked as they walked to the car.

"I'm starting to get a real bad feeling about this."

Godeep joined them just before midnight. They gathered in the kitchen. Jamie was instructed to stay in his room for the time being.

"They're going to want to talk to him again," Godeep said. "I told them not until tomorrow morning. That gives us time to formulate a strategy."

"So where are we?" Quint asked.

Mahabal shrugged unhappily.

"The police had a frustrating day at school, though evidently their interviews did yield one bit of information."

"What?"

"Jamie and Shannon were seen arguing over the keys by the side of the Wrangler."

"By who?" Quint asked after a long silence.

"Jazjit says the rumor mill identifies the witness as Jacob Hsu."

"But he didn't see who drove?" Carrie asked.

"No. But Jacob's saying that Jamie was quite belligerent. He seemed very intent on keeping Shannon from taking away his keys."

Carrie looked at Quint, who bowed his head.

"What about Shannon?" she asked. "What's she say about all this?"

"That's the thing that's giving the police such headaches. They brought her in again this evening, but she must have told them the same story as last night or else . . ."

Or else Jamie would be under arrest. Godeep was too good a friend to say it.

"What time do they want to see Jamie?"

"Eight A.M." He sighed. "That is going to be a tough one, my friends. The gloves are coming off."

"You're going to be there, right?" Carrie asked Mahabal, terrified by the prospect of her son on his own in that bleak little room.

"We'd better talk about this. I think our policy of complete transparency with the authorities may no longer be the most prudent course. We should think about becoming a bit more . . . defensive."

Quint nodded glumly.

"What?" Carrie asked. "What's going on?"

"This isn't my area," Mahabal said. "You're going to need someone. I was thinking Hollis Hardy."

"The guy with the hat?" Carrie asked. "But he's *awful*."

"All right," Quint said. "Should I call him?"

"I took the liberty on the way over. He's available. He says you met last year?"

"Yeah, at that leadership thing in Jackson Hole," Quint said. "There was some talk about him joining the fund, but I had to put him off."

"Well, I get the feeling there might be some of that talk again."

"Isn't he in New York?" Carrie asked.

"Greenwich. So much of his work is up here now that he decided to move office. He said he can meet you for breakfast."

"All right. Tell him to come here at six-thirty, and then we'll go in together."

Mahabal stood.

"Look," Quint said after rubbing his eyes, "you should tell Hardy I'm going to go talk to Jamie now, and you know, he should be ready for anything."

"What about the fund?" Mahabal said. "I only ask because he will."

"Mention that we have a place opening up this week, but don't promise him anything."

Mahabal smiled at Carrie and patted her hand, and she wanted to grab hold of him and not let him go until he told her that it was going to be all right. But she knew he wouldn't because he couldn't be sure that it was true. After he left, she turned to Quint.

"What did you mean, ready for anything?"

"Carrie, if Jamie's done this, he's going to have to confess."

She closed her eyes. Confess. James Warren Manning, seventeen, confesses to hit-and-run while driving drunk and then conspiring with . . .

"The thing I don't understand is Shannon," Quint said. "Why is she lying?"

"Because she's in love with him."

He looked at her in surprise.

"Quint, on Saturday, when I ran into her coming out of Jamie's room. I think they were—"

"What?"

"What. He was in bed with no clothes on."

And then she could see that famous decisiveness in her husband's expression. Coming to the conclusion he'd been skirting for the last twenty-four hours. Their son was lying. Jamie was guilty.

"I'm going to talk to him," he said as he stood.

Carrie watched him go, knowing there was about to be trouble but too weary to stop it. Before long she heard voices across the vast house, and then the voices grew louder. Stop, she thought. Just stop.

But they kept on. And so she went, the stairs feeling very steep. Quint was filling Jamie's doorway, looking larger than he actually was. Dillon and Nick stood at the end of the hallway. Carrie motioned for them to go back to their rooms. They ignored her.

"Tell the truth," Quint was saying.

Carrie took up a position behind him. Jamie stood by the end of his bed. His eyes brimmed with tears, but his mouth was rigid with determination.

"I am *not* lying, Dad. I swear to God."

"Jamie, do you honestly think you can avoid responsibility for this?"

"Look, if I'd hit that guy—I mean, there's no way I'd just leave somebody there."

"*If* you even knew he was there."

"I didn't do it."

"And what about Shannon?" Quint asked. "She's going to get in big trouble when they find out she's lying."

"She's not lying! She drove me home."

"So that's it, then? You're just going to keep on with this ridiculous story?"

"Yes. Because it's true." He sat heavily on his bed, clutching his head. "Jesus, I wish I *had* hit the guy so I could get you off my fucking back for once in my life."

His words silenced everyone for a moment.

"The situation isn't going to stay like this," Quint said. "You know that. Someone is going to come forward who saw you behind the wheel. Or Shannon will understand the mistake she's making. If you tell the truth now, then I can control the situation."

Jamie looked up, smiling incredulously.

"The way you can control the situation, *Dad*, is to believe me."

Quint took a step into the room, and Jamie rose to his feet.

"Quint," Carrie said sharply, "enough."

He turned, his anger directed at her now, though he was able to summon enough self-control to propel him out of the room. He went back down to his office, his sanctuary, where he would work off his fury on some poor fool in London or Zug. Carrie looked at her son.

"I didn't do anything," he said.

"I know."

She wished she believed it. She went to her bedroom, breaking her one-day-old resolve to stay out of the bath. As she soaked, she let her mind empty, preparing herself to accept that her son was guilty. Guilty and lying about it. She had to stop being a fond and foolish mother and start thinking hard truths. Jamie had done this, and then he'd cooked up a stupid scheme with Shannon for keeping him out of trouble. He was guilty and it was Carrie's fault. And Quint's. And every other rotten ambitious cynical adult associated with Country Day and the hundreds of other schools just like it across this rotten, ambitious, cynical republic. Because it was them. The parents. They forced their kids to be perfect students and then told them that the lesson on offer was that you'd better win. If you had to lie and cheat, then you lied and you cheated, but don't worry, Mom and Dad would scramble along after you to clean up the mess. Richard McNabb sends his daughter on some bullshit pilgrimage to Korea and then secretly hires a thrusting young producer to call every shot. And what do you know? Madison's "diary" gets on MTV, and she wins the Carswell. Jonah Fraker-Peerce has an AP history term paper written by an associate at his mother's law firm who is supposedly only *tutoring* the boy. And off he goes to Dartmouth. Some shot-putter over in Darien gets caught with steroids, and it turns out his father has been the one supplying them, willing, it seems, to trade his son's shriveled nuts for a track scholarship. And the funny thing was that people actually thought the kids weren't paying attention, that when it was over, they would somehow turn out to be upright, unblemished citizens.

Jamie knew all of this cold. He might amble and grin through the day, but he knew that his father's famous rectitude served no greater purpose than making obscene amounts of money for people who already had more than enough. He'd watched his mother race down to Manhattan last year to ensure his precious GPA; he saw how his friends were fighting each other tooth and claw for the Ivy League slots and the plum internships. The news was full of kids who were breaking any rule that stood in their way, aided by their folks and the Hollis Hardys of the world. Only in Jamie's case he couldn't even confide in his parents, since he knew his father would turn him in. But the equation was still the same. Get away with it. You'd have to be stupid not to know this. And kids today were anything but stupid. You just had to look at the test scores.

After the bath she lay sleeplessly in bed until 5:00 A.M., when Quint came up to tell her that Robert Jarvis was dead. She cried for a while, and he lay down next to her and held her, neither of them speaking because there was nothing to say. But they were composed and freshly dressed when Hollis Hardy arrived promptly at 6:30, driving a flagrant, self-regarding assemblage of vintage chrome, followed by Mahabal in his Mercedes. Carrie took an immediate dislike to the new lawyer. Although she couldn't remember meeting him in Wyoming—she'd been hitting the wine a bit hard in that thin air— she'd caught his routine on the evening shout fests, the faded Levi's and dusty Australian bush hat that he probably actually had picked up while on walkabout in the Outback, even though any dimwit could order one out of *The New Yorker*. She'd seen so many like him these past few years, men who cultivated surface eccentricities in the hope it would camouflage their lack of imagination for anything except money. She made coffee and cracked open a tin of biscotti, and the five of them sat around the kitchen table. Hardy kept that ridiculous hat on, and Carrie was tempted to ask him if his mother had taught him how to act while in other people's houses. But she knew that they would be needing Hollis Hardy now.

The conversation was strangely listless. Hardy was more interested in loudly crunching cookies with his capped teeth than in Jamie's protestations of innocence. He didn't take notes, and at one point he even stifled a yawn. Carrie could tell the man was convinced Jamie was guilty and that the Mannings were just another family with the means to dodge the blame.

"And that's what you're telling the police?" he asked when her son had finished speaking.

Jamie gave a blatant, put-upon nod. That was what he was going to tell everyone.

"And Shannon Hagel? Can you foresee any situation in which she won't back you up?"

"Only if she lies."

"Will she?"

"No. Not Shannon."

"All right, then." He snapped one last biscotti in half. "Let's go see what they got."

Everybody left together, Quint and Jamie and the lawyers to the police station, Carrie taking the boys to school. Dillon and Nick had wanted to stay home with their brother, but she wasn't sure she could handle their crashing around the house all day, especially since Quint, worried about gossip, had given Sabine the rest of the week off. School turned out to be a nightmare. She would have preferred to drop them at the usual spot, but she had to help Dillon carry his OK Corral replica into school. Near the building the path was sufficiently narrowed by shrubbery that the bulky model would block the way for anyone else. Carrie waited for the oncoming people to pass, then hurried along, expecting that those approaching would wait for her to clear. They did at first, but when she was halfway along the constricted route, a person broke through the lingering crowd and started striding toward her. It was Andie Dulea; her youngest son, Jordan, was in fourth grade. At first she thought the other woman must not have seen her, though as they drew closer, she could tell that she most definitely had. Carrie felt like turning around, but the model's bulk prevented her.

"What the hell's going on, Carrie?"

"Andie, look, I was going to call—"

"We're finishing dinner Monday, and suddenly there's a *cop* at the door saying Stephen has to come down to the police station. And then we hear that Jamie's accusing him of stealing his car and running some guy over?"

"Jamie's not accusing—"

But she wasn't listening. Carrie could feel the pressure of people backing up behind her.

"And if that's not bad enough, we get down there and see your husband and his lawyer standing in the hallway. His *lawyer*. And we're still trying to figure out what the hell's going on."

There was no talking to the woman, no explaining that it was a simple mistake, that Godeep was there as a friend. Carrie looked over her shoulder, but there were too many people for her to reverse track. So she was forced to mutter vague apologies and maneuver around Andie, a move she could accomplish only by dragging the model through the stiff branches, scattering the figures she and Dillon had so laboriously arranged.

"I don't know what you people are trying to pull, but it's not going to happen," the other woman said after Carrie finally got past her. "It is *not going to happen*."

There had been more buzzing after she got home, but Carrie hadn't even bothered to look. Quint and Jamie and Hollis Hardy returned at midmorning, without Mahabal. Carrie understood that he was going to be replaced by Hardy now, one more sad thought to add to the list. Jamie raced up to his room immediately after their arrival, though not before Carrie noticed the black stains on his fingertips.

"Oh, God, they didn't arrest him," she said in a panic. "Quint—"

"No, no," Hardy said quickly. "They say it's a rule-out, but I think they want to be able to say Jamie's fingerprints were the only ones they found in the Wrangler. Not that it matters, since he's driven the car several times since Friday night. He'll have innocently erased the real driver's prints. A point I will be sure to bring up in court."

In court, Carrie thought. They went into the kitchen, once again gathering around the table. Carrie didn't feel inclined to serve refreshments this time. She told them about the woman from the local paper.

"There's a TV van out there now," Quint said, "one of those things with the antenna that comes out of the roof."

"That's the cops, amping up the pressure," Hardy said, continuing to make a big show of his unflappability. "Just keep the gate shut and your heads down. We have people who'll be able to help you with the media should the time come. Hillary Williams? She used to be at News Center Five?"

Take your hat off, Carrie thought.

"So what's going on?" she asked.

"Well, as of this moment no one is actually alleging that your son committed a crime. Jamie says he wasn't driving the Wrangler, and Shannon Hagel concurs."

"But *somebody* ran that poor man over."

"What I'm saying is that for anyone to allege that Jamie is responsible for what happened to that cyclist at this point would be pure speculation. One, you've still got no proof linking the Wrangler to the accident. And even if you did, nobody puts Jamie in the car."

"The police weren't acting like they had nothing," Quint said grimly.

"I'm not going to lie to you here. You could read the room as well as I could. They think Jamie's guilty. The question is what they do about it. As long as Shannon Hagel says she drove him home, it's going to be an uphill battle for them. What's she like, by the way? Is she a flake? Is she going to start changing her story?"

"Shannon is the exact opposite of a flake," Carrie said.

"Well, if she does start flip-flopping now, I can make that play to our advantage. Nothing's better for the defense than a teenage witness with truth issues. No, I'd say, as of now, we still have the upper hand. I'm talking criminal here, by the by. Civil's another story."

They lapsed into a long silence.

"So that's it?" Carrie asked. "Shouldn't we, I don't know, hire someone of our own to help the police find out who was driving?"

"Absolutely not. The best thing for us to do here is just keep playing defense. Jamie's maintaining that he did not drive the car. An eyewitness corroborates this. That's all we need to bring to the table. Don't fix it if it ain't broke, right?"

It took Carrie a moment to understand. Hardy was convinced that the trail of any search for the Wrangler's driver would lead to the upstairs bedroom.

"But doesn't that leave him in a sort of, I don't know, limbo?"

"Legally, no. Legally there is no such thing as limbo, no matter what people say. You're either guilty or not guilty. As of now we're the latter, and I plan to keep it that way."

"I don't mean legally. I mean . . ."

She gestured out the window, at Andie Dulea and Diane McNabb and the Class of 2001 and every single other person they knew.

"Like I say, just keep your head down for a while, Carrie. These things blow over. People have short attention spans." He smiled at her again. "As of right now, I have to say it doesn't look half bad. Just try to keep everything together on the home front, and let me handle the rest."

Quint saw him to the door. Carrie stayed where she was.

"Not half bad," she said when Quint came back to the kitchen. "So here's what I'm wondering: Is this the point in our lives when we get to turn into assholes?"

"I know."

"I mean, is this what we're going to do now? Get away with it? Some guy gets killed and we—"

"I know."

And he did. Any shame she might feel would be infinitely multiplied in Quint. His entire life had been spent in search of solidity and rectitude. And now he was paying Hollis Hardy five hundred dollars an hour.

"I just don't understand Shannon," he said after a while.

"I do," Carrie said. "Shannon's a romantic. She's seventeen and a rebel, and now she gets to spit in the face of the rotten world to save someone she cares about. Which sure beats the hell out of majoring in sociology at Oberlin."

Quint gave a short, dry laugh.

"I'll tell you one thing. I bet this is driving her father crazy. He'd love to stick it to us." He shook his head. "I just don't know what to do with Jamie. Part of me wants to throttle him to get him to tell the truth. The other part wants to protect him."

"Yeah, well, join the club."

"He's going to have to tell the truth, Carrie. It's going to get worse and worse. Something's going to turn up. And even if he gets away with it, Christ, what does that make him then?"

One of your clients, Carrie almost said.

"I'll go talk to him."

She knocked and he didn't answer and she went in anyway. He was lying on his bed, staring at the ceiling. There was a constellation of pale black spots on the wall beside him. It wasn't until Carrie drew

closer that she saw what they were. His fingerprints, arranged in angry clusters of five. Some were smudged; others crystal clear. She took
a breath and sat on the edge of his bed. Snarling, honorable Springsteen, probably as good a judge as the world had to offer for this conversation, looked down at them from the far wall. She'd wait for him
to speak first. It always went better with your kids when you did that.
It became their conversation.

"So *he's* a jerk," he said, staring at his blackened fingers.

"The cop?"

"Hardy."

"Oh. Yeah. But a necessary jerk, I'm afraid."

"What's that supposed to mean?" he asked, finally looking at her.

"Jamie, listen to me. You kids these days, it scares me how much
you know. I'm sure you're perfectly aware how things will play out if
you and Shannon keep saying you weren't driving that car. We hire a
viper like Hollis Hardy, and you just might get off. And we'll still love
you, and you'll still have friends and a future and, you know, the
whole deal. But it's wrong, Jamie. It's a wrong thing. It's just going to
be there and it's never going to go away and it's going to color everything you do." She breathed evenly for a while to keep from crying. "I
know I've put some expectations on you that were unfair, and I've
maybe even been stupid enough sometimes to make you think I was
disappointed with you. But I'm not. I'm anything but. You're a beautiful young man with a beautiful soul, and Jamie, listen to me, people
can lose their souls. They really can."

He raised himself up to an elbow.

"I didn't run anybody over. I swear to God."

"Jamie, Shannon was here on Saturday morning. I saw her face.
The girl looked like she'd been to hell and back. I mean, this is my
point. She loves you, and you're making her—"

"Shannon doesn't love me. I wish she did, but she doesn't."

"Then what was she doing here?"

"She was telling me she didn't want me to call her again."

"Well, sometimes girls will—"

"Ma, please. She dumped me. You think she was playing a game
when she did that? Shannon?"

"But all right, then why have you been so weird since Friday?"

"Come on, the cops are breathing down my—"

"No, I mean before that. Over the weekend. Where was all that anger coming from? You weren't able to say a civil word to anyone, me in particular. And going at it with your father like you have been— Jamie, clearly something's very wrong. Maybe it's because you think that if I hadn't been drinking wine, then I would have come to get you and none of this would have happened, but—"

"Ma, please, just forget it."

"Jamie, I think I deserve an explanation."

He shook his head, although she could see that the truth was there, just below the surface.

"Jamie, I am not kidding around with you. Enough is enough."

"I went to get some aspirin. All right? I went to get some aspirin. Can't we just leave it at that?"

"What on earth are you talking about?"

He lay still for a long time before speaking.

"My head was spinning after I got up to my room. So I decided to take some Motrins. Only I was all out. So I went into your room to get some and then I went to the front window to check if the Wrangler was back and that's when I saw—"

She remembered the inexplicably open canister on her counter on Saturday morning. And then she knew what he would have seen if he'd been looking out the front window at midnight on Friday.

"I mean, you were right there, Mom, kissing that Jon guy in the middle of the fucking driveway. I mean, *kissing* him."

"Jamie, that was just—"

He looked at her, and she knew that she could not lie to him.

"Listen, Jamie, it was—Jesus. I made a mistake. A stupid mistake. It happened, and it's not going to happen again. Twenty years from now you'll understand my reasons, and then they'll *really* seem pa-thetic. But at least they'll make sense. Until then, look, it was a stu-pid, one-time thing. But I'm here now, and I'm not going anywhere, whatever that's worth."

He held her eye for a moment, then fell back onto his bed.

"Jamie—"

"Don't worry, Ma. Your secret is safe with me."

And then Carrie got it. She stood and looked down at him. He'd been upset about Jon over the weekend, not a car accident. That was why he was talking to Shannon, why she was so strange with Carrie.

"Jamie, Jesus—you really didn't drive home, did you?"

He shook his head slowly, and she knew that he was telling the truth.

"All right," she said. "Okay."

She wanted to reach out and stroke his beautiful head, but she didn't dare. Instead, she walked out of the room. Quint was on the phone in his office. He hung up as soon as she stepped through the door.

"Well?"

"Quint, listen, you're going to hate me for saying this, but Jamie didn't do it."

21 The road was all wrong now. Even as Shannon passed the usual landmarks—the abandoned Sunoco station and the house that still had its Christmas lights and the STOP MAKING SENSE sign—she felt as if she were racing into some treacherous, alien landscape. It was so confusing, how familiar things could so rapidly become so terribly unknown. Like saying a common word over and over until it became coarse and obscene, or the way her room would fill with pulsating shadow during those childhood fevers.

She had to see Ian. She had to look into his eyes. If she could only do that, then she would know what to do. Staying away from his house yesterday was the hardest thing she'd ever done. Only David's warning that a visit could get him in trouble kept her away. Convinced the police were watching her, too paranoid to call or e-mail him, she'd spent the day in her room. She'd purged every indication they'd known each other from her life; she'd cleared out her computer's memory and removed his number from her phone. She'd even hidden the drawings he'd given her in the storage room at the back of the garage, beneath some boxes of unwanted things her mother had left behind. Knowing all the while it was futile. There would be records in big computers somewhere, long digital lists that told the whole story of Shannon Hagel and Ian Warfield.

Tuesday would not end. Her father, staying home from work yet again, had come to her bedroom door several times and asked if she was all right. She let her silence answer. Finally, in the late afternoon, he told her that the police had finished talking to the kids from the party and urgently wanted to see her again. She sat glumly in the passenger seat of the rattling Saab, wondering if she could hold out for a second time. Someone had seen her with Ian; the police had a description. Only the image of him locked in some terrible cell had kept her from telling Flowers everything the night before.

He wasn't so nice this time. Those narrow eyes were full of suspicion. Talking to the kids at Country Day had clearly made him revise his opinion of her. There was another man in the small room as well, his long, angular face twisted by a secret irony, as if he were the bearer of incredible news or a bad joke; so young that it was difficult to believe he was anything other than a college student. He told Shannon his name, but she didn't try to remember it. What she did understand was that he was an assistant district attorney. His presence only deepened her belief that everything was about to end.

But they still knew nothing about Ian. They hadn't looked at her phone records or trailed her up to his house the night before. No one had spoken with the hippies at the pizza place; there were no flyers circulating with a grainy fat-faced snapshot of her, asking if the public knew where she had been spending her time. They didn't ask where she'd been before the party or why she had come so late. They didn't care about any of that. It took Shannon a few minutes to understand the reason: Flowers was now convinced that he knew the identity of the Wrangler's driver. It was Jamie. As far as the police were concerned, it had to be him. No one had seen Shannon's key-bearing stranger; everyone who could have possibly driven the Wrangler home was accounted for. Shannon had been seen by plenty of people, inside and out, but in the company of just one person, James Warren Manning, the boy she'd once dated and just might be seeing again. Not long after she led him from the house, one of those junior girls in the living room remembered seeing two cars backing up in rapid tandem, the closest possessing the vertical array of brilliant lights found on customized Jeeps.

"And I guess you forgot about Jacob Hsu," Flowers said.

She really had forgotten.

"Okay, yeah. Jacob. He was there."

"He saw you and Jamie arguing over the keys."

"But that was when Jamie still thought I was going to let him drive."

"Moments before you gave the keys to the mystery boy who no one remembers coming into the party. Though Jacob saw no sign of this boy, even though he had to walk down the driveway to get his car. Did he swing out of the trees, Shannon? Parachute in?"

The assistant district attorney snorted.

"Shannon," Flowers said, "come on."

After that it became very easy. Now that they were convinced Jamie was driving the Wrangler, Shannon was finally free to speak the truth, over and over, no matter how many different ways they asked her. Flowers could try to trick her and threaten her, but he was only wasting his time. Nothing he could say would change the simple fact that she had driven Jamie home.

It was as if they were following a script.

> Flowers: Jamie drove, didn't he?
>
> Shannon: No.
>
> Flowers: He wouldn't give you the keys and so you said [reads from pad], "The hell with this," and you let him drive.
>
> Shannon: No.
>
> Flowers: You didn't say, "The hell with this"? Is Jacob lying?
>
> Shannon: No. I said that. But I didn't let Jamie drive.
>
> Attorney: Do you often say, "The hell with this," before you do something?
>
> Shannon: [sarcastic] Sometimes, apparently.
>
> Drew: Shannon . . .
>
> Flowers: Why are you covering up for him?
>
> Shannon: I'm not.
>
> Flowers: Are you Jamie Manning's girlfriend?
>
> Shannon: I'm his friend.
>
> Flowers: But you guys have quite a long history together.
>
> Shannon: I guess.
>
> Attorney: Are you sexually involved?

Drew: Hey . . .

Flowers: Do you love him? Did you spend the night with him after the party?

Shannon: Look, Mr. Flowers, I'm sorry, but you want me to tell you the truth, right?

Flowers [looks up]: Of course I do.

Shannon: All right, I drove Jamie home.

Around and around they went, the detective refusing to admit he was beaten, the assistant district attorney shaking his head like some sarcastic schoolboy, her father breathing through his nose. At one point the camcorder clicked off, but nobody moved to put it back on. Shannon knew that she was the key. She was everything to them. As long as she kept saying that Jamie was in her car, they couldn't do anything to him. And as long as they didn't think she was protecting someone else, then no one would bother to look for Ian. They couldn't touch either boy. So this is what power feels like, Shannon thought. She could see why Quint liked it so much.

"And what about Robert Jarvis?" the lawyer asked.

Shannon stared down at the table.

"There's nothing I can say that will help him," she said after a moment. "I'm sorry."

"Look, Shannon, are you afraid of getting in trouble if you change your story?" Flowers asked.

Sensing a trap, she didn't answer. Flowers turned to the attorney.

"You aren't going to get in trouble," the attorney said. "You're a minor, you're emotionally involved with Jamie, he's a big strong boy from a rich family; nobody's going to want to get you in trouble for being led astray. But you have to come forward *now*."

"Are you offering her immunity?" Drew asked.

"She puts James Manning in that Wrangler, we're not looking at any problems from Shannon Hagel's point of view."

Flowers's squinting eyes moved between father and daughter.

"You two want some privacy?"

Drew nodded; Shannon did not reply. The only privacy she wanted was with her boyfriend, running her fingers through his soft hair, telling him it was going to be all right. Flowers went to switch off the video camera and realized only then that it had stopped on its own.

"So what do you think?" her father asked when they were alone. "You want to take his offer?"

"His offer to do what? Lie?"

"Why are you so intent on protecting Jamie?"

"I'm not protecting Jamie."

"Listen to me, Shannon. Whatever Quint has promised you, it's a lie. The Mannings aren't what you think they are. They don't care if you get hurt. If you tell me the truth now, I can make a deal here. Otherwise you're risking throwing away your whole future."

"I'm sorry, Dad, but there's no deal to make. I wish you all would understand that."

Shannon could feel the doubt and mistrust coming off him like a fever. He wanted Jamie to be guilty as much as Flowers did.

"Can we go?" she asked. "Can you please get me out of here? I'm not going to say anything different."

They let her go, though not before telling Drew to make her available for further interviews. They drove back home in silence. She went up to her room to switch on her phone, but there were no messages. Nothing on the computer, either. Emboldened by what she'd found out at the police station, she tried calling. There was no answer, just David's sly voice on the machine. She was tempted to drive up there, but her father was hanging around downstairs, keeping an eye on her. Making her available. She kept her cell phone perched on her pillow all night, waiting for it to ring, jolted awake a few times after dreaming it had.

She hoped Ian was getting some sleep.

By Wednesday morning she'd decided that she was going to see him today no matter what. Knowing the police weren't trying to find him would definitely ease his mind. Ronnie was alone in the kitchen when she came down, staring into a cup of herbal tea. She looked up with a pained smile.

"Where's Dad?"

"Asleep. He was up half the night with worry."

Shannon felt brief regret, but then she remembered the way he'd acted at the police station the past two nights, so eager for her to betray someone.

"Well, I'm going to school."

"Shannon, wait a moment." Ronnie's voice was a troubled mixture of warmth and worry and frustration. "I've been wanting to say . . . I know it must be very difficult for you. I just wanted to say, you know, if you need someone to talk to, well, I'm around. And whatever you tell me, it will stay between us two."

Shannon looked into the other woman's pale eyes. She really did want to help. But it was impossible. Even if she meant well, Ronnie was still one of the people who would take Ian away from her.

"Thanks," Shannon said, knowing if she didn't leave, she might give something away. "But I'd better . . ."

She hurried from the room before Ronnie could say anything else.

As she feared, the Chevelle was parked in the driveway. She was tempted to go in, anyway, but that would only provoke David. He'd do something crazy, ban her from seeing Ian or take him away to North Carolina. It would have to wait until five, when he went to work. She would just have to be patient.

Not wanting to deal with Ronnie or her father, she went to Country Day. It was just after first period that she learned that Robert Jarvis had finally died, told by Kensington Smith, the drama queen, who watched Shannon closely for the reaction she would never give. She went out to her car and lay down on the back seat and cried for a long time, telling herself that she knew this was coming, telling herself that it didn't change anything. And then she put on her mask and went back inside to pretend to be this person called Shannon Hagel.

Although Jamie wasn't in school, he was the only thing anyone was talking about. The consensus was that he was guilty—and that he was going to get away with it. Shannon was now the center of attention, the girl who was lying to the police, sacrificing her future to protect a friend, something none of them would have had the guts to do. Eyes that had washed over her with nullifying indifference a few days earlier now locked on her with awe. People she hadn't spoken to in months were trying to get close to her. So this is what popular feels like, Shannon thought, wondering what all the fuss had been about.

Madison McNabb cornered her just before lunch to ask what really happened. Shannon tried to replicate the chilly smile the other girl had leveled at her several hundred times since she had viciously repudiated their friendship.

"I'm not really supposed to talk about this. Sorry."

And so now she had Jamie to worry about as well. People were deciding he was guilty. She'd hardly even thought about him in the last few days. Though Jamie would be all right in the end; he had a rich father to protect him. And he really was innocent. Maybe a scare like this would be good for him. Maybe it would shake him out of his selfishness and his drinking. She wondered what she would do if they arrested him, if she would be able to say anything. She couldn't imagine how that would happen, going to the police and speaking Ian's name. Even if they came for Jamie, she couldn't see how she could do it.

She went back up Totten Pike during lunch break, just in case David had gone out early. But the Chevelle was still there. Shannon slowed down, anyway; she even went as far as putting on her turn signal. But at the last moment she lost her nerve. David was the one person who could take Ian away from her no matter what she did. Not wanting to go back to school, she kept driving north, until the pike turned into another road, and that one into another. Mile after mile, letting the road hypnotize her until she wasn't thinking, only moving. She went as far as Massachusetts, stopping at a diner, where she bought a drink and some fries and watched the people coming and going, all these strangers who had no idea that she was the girl who knew the truth.

She got back to Ginny's house just before five. The Chevelle was finally gone. As she reached the back door, she could hear what sounded like an alarm clock going off. She didn't bother to knock. There was the usual mess in the kitchen, but there was something else, a sulfurous smell, like the charcoal in her father's grill after it had been rained on. The sound, a weak insistent bleat coming from the hallway, wasn't a clock after all. It was the smoke detector.

"Ian?"

There was no answer. She made a quick survey of the kitchen, touching surfaces, opening the oven door. Everything was cool. She walked quickly to the living room. There was still no sign of fire, though now she could see a thin stratum of blue smoke clinging to the ceiling. Her heart began to pound, instinctive fear joining the bad things already in her mind. She raced to his bedroom, passing under the alarm. The charred smell was even greater outside the door. She said his name, afraid to walk straight in. There was no answer. She turned the handle. The room was dark, its curtains pulled as tightly as they had been all those afternoons they'd spent in here, though now there was nothing good in the darkness. Smoke drifted past her, but there was no flame. Ian sat shirtless at his desk, hunched over into the dim glow of a long-necked lamp and the screen-saving twilight of his Dell. She could see the movement of the muscles in his back and his neck. Behind her the alarm continued to sound.

"Ian?"

He didn't turn. She slowly crossed the room. The page he was working on had been subdivided into slanting, irregular panels, nothing like the neat geometric rows he usually made. Most of them were filled with pictures, Michael Sojourner, making his way through a sepulchral labyrinth. The drawing was even worse than it had been on Monday, muddy and childish, lines ending without reason. Michael Sojourner didn't seem to be getting anywhere. The tunnel just went on and on. Terrible creatures loomed from the darkness. Ian was in the process of blackening out the background of one of the lower panels with his pencil's flattened tip.

"Ian, it's me," she said.

He continued to focus on the page, the pencil scratching furiously. His hands were almost black with lead, and there were streaks of it on his face. The bandage covering his burn had also been blackened, its edges frayed and torn, as if some small animal had been trying to get inside it. She could now see the smoke's source. The metal trash can beside his chair was filled with ashes, some of them still rimmed with smoldering orange. Before she could speak again, there was a sudden ripping sound, as harsh and unexpected as the ax had been two days ago. Ian held the thick paper aloft like a doctor examining an X ray, then picked up a cheap Cricket lighter she hadn't noticed. He scraped it on, and Shannon watched, unable to move, as he touched the corner of the paper with the flame. It didn't catch at first, but then the fire was crawling up the paper, a second sheet, this one alive, consuming the first. He held it for as long as he could, then dropped the shriveling paper into the trash can. There was a brief pulse of flame and then only smoke.

He reached for his pencil, but she placed a hand on his wrist. His skin felt so cold.

"Ian, look at me."

His attention remained fixed on the paper. She put her hand on his cheek and gently turned his face toward her. Shannon almost took a step backward in alarm; his eyes were nothing like they'd been over the weekend. The light was gone from them. They were like unpowered television screens, dully reflecting the world, transmitting nothing from within. All she could think to do was kiss his slack lips. After a moment she tasted his breath and almost recoiled from the foul, acidic odor. It was like kissing a wound. This was not Ian. This was not the boy she'd lost herself in kissing. She waited a few seconds before pulling back, not wanting him to sense her disgust.

"Come on," she said. "Let's go."

"Where?" he asked, his voice raspy and mechanical.

"Just out of this room. It's too smoky."

He looked around, as if noticing the smoke for the first time.

"I couldn't get the pictures right."

"You will."

He let himself be led from the room, the quicksilver motion gone from his body. Shannon couldn't believe how drastically he'd changed since she'd been away, all that energy giving way to this lifeless trance. She grabbed a sweatshirt from the pile beside his bed. She had to drag a kitchen chair into the hallway so she could mash the red button in the middle of the smoke alarm, but that didn't stop the sound, so she pried off the casing with her nails and dislodged the battery. Ian was on the sofa in the living room. She made him put on the shirt, and then they sat just as they had six days earlier, watching the occasional traffic.

She remembered the glow from the computer's screen.

"Were you trying to e-mail me?"

"No. I was just looking some stuff up."

"What?"

"Just . . . stuff."

"You want anything?" she asked. "You want a drink?"

"No," he said.

"Where's your uncle? Is he working?"

Ian nodded distantly. It wasn't at all clear he understood her question.

"Ian, are you all right?"

"I just can't . . ."

He left it for her to finish the sentence. Think. Breathe. Exist. Shannon understood how wrong she'd been last night while talking to Flowers. She had no power. There was no way she could let things go on like this. Ian was in trouble. The wild confidence he'd shown in the days after the accident had vanished completely, leaving nothing behind but a darkness so absolute that Shannon was worried it would swallow him completely.

"Ian, we have to get you to a doctor."

"No way," he said, suddenly energized, though it was the energy of a trapped animal. "I'm not going back to jail. No fucking way. Don't try to make me go back there."

"I'm not going to make . . . look, we could drive up to Massachusetts. I'll get money out of my account and pay them cash. We'll make up a name; they'll never know it's you. All you have to tell them is that you're stressed. Just to get you something so you can feel better."

He let his head fall back against the sofa.

"You're going to turn me in. I know it."

There was nothing in his voice. It was completely empty. She put her hand on the back of his neck. Why was his skin so cold?

"I'm not going to turn you in. I just want you to get some help."

"There is no help."

Before she could think of a response, he was on his feet. He shuffled out of the room. After a few seconds she followed, passing under the gutted alarm. Just as she arrived at his door there was an explosion of music. Joy Division, one of his bands from before their life together, when he hung out with the fools at Gryphon Games. Terrible, death-loving music. She opened the door. There was less smoke in the room now. Ian was lying in bed, face to the wall. She switched off the stereo, then lay down beside him.

"If you're turning against me now, I'll . . ."

"I'm not turning against you," she said. "I'm not. Ever."

He started to cry, and she thought that was good, that crying was real and he needed to be doing something real now. She didn't know what to do except stay with him. She couldn't take him to a doctor like this; she feared he would simply give himself up. And then he would be gone. This would have been the time my mother left, Shannon thought. Fleeing when things were no longer good. As soon as some sacrifices were required. She held him close. He shivered for a while, but her warmth soon passed over to him, and he stopped. And then the exhaustion came, and she decided to stop fighting it. Answers would come later. This was good enough for now.

She woke to the knowledge that there was someone else in the room. Hours must have passed; it was very dark outside. She looked up, and for a moment she was reminded of those creatures looming out of the darkness in the drawings Ian had burned. But it was only his uncle, angrily beckoning for her to follow him out of the room. Shannon was tempted to refuse, but there would be trouble and then Ian would be awake.

"I thought I told you to stay away," David said when they were in the kitchen, his voice low and furious.

"Have you seen the condition he's in?"

"I'm dealing with it."

"But what are we going to do? He's . . . it's like he's not even there."

"We've been here before, Shannon. I'm taking care of him."

"Yeah, I can see that. And you're doing a real bang-up job."

She should have known better than to be sarcastic. It was stupid and childish. She could see his fury gather in his eyes.

"Leave, Shannon. Now. This isn't your house."

She wondered if he was capable of hurting her. She'd never thought so, but now she wasn't sure. Not that she cared. He could hurt her if he wanted. But she knew that if they fought, it would be bad for Ian.

"This can't just keep . . ."

She couldn't finish the sentence. She didn't even know what she was trying to say. And words didn't matter. David wasn't going to change his mind. The solution to this wasn't David. It wasn't Ian. It was her.

"You'd better take care of him," she said.

She turned and pushed through the flimsy screen door, careful not to let it slam behind her.

At home, she locked herself in her room. It was all still with her, the harsh smoke and the foul odor coming from inside him; his cold, rigid body and the void in his beautiful eyes. That ugly, mournful music. She had to do something to make this end. For a while she told herself that he would be better if she just called the police. She found the card the detective had given her, with its town crest and the number where he could be reached at any time. But then she remembered the fear in Ian's voice when he spoke about being arrested. And Flowers wouldn't help him. David was right about that much. To the police, he was nothing more than a kid on parole who'd killed a man and run away.

Her mind went around and around until somehow, just before dawn, she slept. The sound of her father coming in the front door woke her. It was still early, a few minutes before eight. It was Thursday, a school day, but there was no question of school. She somehow managed to sit up in bed, even though she felt as if she could sleep for another twelve hours. She e-mailed Ian to tell him she would be with him soon and then went to take a long shower, letting gallon after gallon of hot water run over her, hoping it would wake her up. But when she finally got out, she was more tired than when she had started. She checked her computer; Ian hadn't answered. She pictured him sitting at his desk, drawing furiously, locked in the black caves he was creating. She knew she should go to him, that he would be needing her to comfort him. But all of a sudden, feeling this tired, she wasn't sure she could handle all that misery and fear; she didn't know if she could handle David. She'd be too weak; she'd make a mistake. If only she could get more sleep, maybe then she'd be able to figure out what to do.

She closed down her computer and fell back on her pillow. She'd shut her eyes for just a few more moments before getting dressed and heading over. Five or ten minutes, a half hour at the most. Just enough to give her the strength to get through another terrible day.

22 At first, Drew couldn't understand why he'd set the alarm for such an early hour. It wasn't until his feet were planted on his bedroom's cold wood floor that he remembered his meeting with PMG. Wanda Crippen had called yesterday, summoning him to an early breakfast at L'Oeuf Splendide. Although he wanted nothing more than to stay home to look after Shannon, Drew could not afford to miss this appointment. If he didn't make a deal with Property Management today, he would lose control of his life.

He dressed in the cramped darkness of the walk-in closet, careful not to wake Ronnie. Before leaving the house, he checked on Shannon. She was sleeping deeply. Last night she'd come in late, sneaking into her room without a word. Drew had been tempted to confront her once again about this insane decision to help the Mannings, but there was no reason. She did not trust him. She no longer believed she needed him. As he sat in that interrogation room, it was almost impossible to imagine now that there had been a time when she had no secrets from him. But it was true. Anne's departure had made for a desperate intimacy between them, casting them into a joint exile, where the usual distinctions of age and authority had been leveled by misery. In the few months after they were abandoned Shannon lost all signs of childhood. She became grimly dependable. She would stick close to him when they were in the house and tag along for weekend showings; she was always the first to be fetched from school or par-

ties, waiting anxiously for him by the door no matter how early he arrived. People soon noticed the transformation of the formerly care-
free girl into a frowning, premature little adult. Sympathetic mothers
would offer to have her over for the night, but the phone would inevitably ring after midnight, a politely exasperated, embarrassed voice
asking him to fetch his inconsolable child. Once or twice he was seriously caught out—he was boozing prettily heavily back then—and
was forced to drive across town well over the limit, fooling no one
with his wintergreen mints and breezy chatter. The invitations soon
dried up. Some nights she would sleepwalk to his bed, her boyish
body feverish as she twisted and turned. In the morning she'd be up
first, cooking breakfast and making sure he was out the door in time
to run down his father's business a little bit more. It became a bleak
ongoing game, the way she would fuss over him, ironing his clothes or
bringing him beers as he slouched in front of *World's Scariest Police
Chases*. His requests that she spend more time with people her own
age were met with stony silences. If he pressed too hard, she closed
down. But they never actually fought. There was no reason. Shannon
never did anything wrong.

And then puberty hit, earlier than Drew had imagined it would,
moving through her like a hurricane before the start of the official
season. The somnambulistic visits to his bed ended; she began spending long shrouded hours in her room. There were no more scrambled
eggs or unwrinkled shirts awaiting him in the morning. As she cultivated her unhappiness, Drew learned a hard truth: Nothing could
suck the air out of a room faster than a miserable adolescent girl.
Their desperate intimacy took on the harsh, critical tone of a failing
marriage. She was acutely embarrassed by him in public; she complained bitterly about his slovenly habits at home. Worst of all, she
began to blame him for Anne's flight. Her mother had left because he
was a slob, Shannon claimed; because he was lazy and fat and said
stupid things. Drew never fought back, even though he could have
easily beaten back Shannon's accusations, real and implied. He just
didn't want trouble. Not with the only person he had left.

But she was clearly spoiling for the confrontation that finally came on her thirteenth birthday. She'd refused a party, claiming she had no friends to invite. So he'd taken her into the city for *Rent* and a Chinese meal. Although the rousing musical briefly lifted her spirits, dinner was a disaster. He'd raised his Tsingtao to toast her advent to teendom, and she'd reluctantly picked up her virgin daiquiri, but she wouldn't extend it to touch glasses, forcing him to reach across the table. He'd knocked over the candle jar in the process, forming an instant wax glacier on the tablecloth.

"*Da-ad* . . ." she'd whispered angrily.

"To a better year for everyone," he'd answered, cheerily oblivious.

"Fat chance of that."

He let it go.

"It smells in here," she said after a while. "Boiled cat, I bet."

The appetizers arrived. Barbecued ribs for him, seaweed for her. He looked up after his first few bites to find her pointing at his chest. A strand of gristle clung to his tie.

"Pig," she whispered in that cruel joking manner she'd developed.

She said nothing on the ride home, slumped against the passenger door, her unhappy face lit by opposing traffic. At the house she rushed ahead of him to check the answering machine in the living room. There was nothing, nor would there be until two days later, when a breathless Anne called to say she'd been camping in the Cascades and there was no phone and the roads were still blocked and blah-blah-blah.

Shannon turned on him with a wild fury as he entered the room.

"Thanks a lot for a great birthday," she wailed. "Thanks for taking me to a stinking restaurant so I could watch my father stuff his face."

Drew stood perfectly still, taking it, the heavy bag in some musty basement gym.

"If it wasn't for you, I'd have some friends instead of people thinking I'm a *freak* because my mother left and didn't even want to take me with her. If she was here, we could have had a party and done something fun instead of going to some boring play about a bunch of losers—"

"But you liked the play."

"I don't like *anything*. Exactly how stupid are you, anyway? Are you as big a retard as everyone says? How can I like anything when I have to live with this guy who my mother hates so much that she won't even call the house because she's afraid he'll answer the phone!"

She started to storm past him, and before he knew what he was doing, Drew had blocked the doorway.

"Shannon, that's not true."

She stared at the carpet, waiting for him to move. And so Drew said it.

"She left you, too, Shannon. She didn't want you, either."

A neutral observer might have seen his words as a sober and timely lesson to an out-of-control child. But there were no neutral observers present, just a lonely father and his miserable daughter, trapped in a house that was far too big for two people. Drew knew as soon as he finished speaking that everything had changed. He'd violated their unspoken agreement: that he'd be the scapegoat, taking his daughter's hurt and shame on his shoulders. No matter what vile, neglectful thing Anne did, it would be his fault. Because if it wasn't his fault, then it would have to be Shannon's. Drew knew this, and yet he'd still said it. And now, looking at her stricken face, he knew there was no unsaying it.

He stepped aside. After a few frozen seconds she walked past him. There was no slamming door or tempest of hysterical crying. Things weren't thrown or shredded; music played in her room, some bitter female lament, but at a' reasonable level. The following morning she was ready to go at the usual time. She said little on the way to school, but that wasn't unusual. When she got out of the car, she even wished him a nice day.

Nothing actually changed in the weeks and months that followed. He still took her places and they still talked and she still helped out around the house. But his words had undermined them. He was supposed to be strong, and he'd failed. Shannon made it clear from that moment on that she was going to look after herself. If problems arose, she would deal with them. Her eighth-grade anxiety attacks and then her tempestuous romance with Jamie and now this terrible accident:

Whatever was happening in her life would be for her to manage. As for Drew, she just didn't need him.

He arrived at the restaurant ten minutes early. It was busy. Armed only with his father's battered briefcase, Drew felt exposed, as if he'd wandered in shirtless. Couples passed documents back and forth over demolished bagels and tubs of yogurt; solitary diners spoke into cell phones and scratched the screens of electronic organizers. Even the waitresses had headsets and digital order pads. He got a local paper from the stack by the antique bean grinder and lucked into a table by the window, where he ordered a black coffee; he'd wait to see what his hosts were having before he decided about food. There was an article about Jamie below the fold on the front page. It was written in a cold, slightly awkward style, but there was no mistaking the gathering presumption of guilt. Police had now questioned the Country Day senior twice in the hit-and-run death of a local man after a car with a description matching his was reported near the scene of the accident. Classmates had seen him drinking heavily at a party a short time earlier. Forensic tests were being performed on his Wrangler to determine if it was involved, though an unnamed source said initial reports were positive. The article claimed that the boy's father, who ran a "secretive" investment fund in town, was not returning calls. There was nothing about a girl who was lying to protect the boy, though Drew could take little comfort from this. After all, this was just the first article.

Wanda Crippen arrived a few minutes late, explaining that Cheryl wouldn't be attending. Drew became immediately alarmed, wondering what sort of agreement they could reach without the managing partner in attendance. Wanda Crippen was a short, sarcastic woman with the beady eyes and clawing fingers of an Old World peasant, a look at odds with her burgundy power suit and electronic organizer. She told the hovering waitress that she wanted only coffee. Although his stomach had been grumbling in anticipation of a stuffed croissant, Drew seconded her request.

Crippen noticed the newspaper. She tapped the article about Jamie.

"They've hired Hollis Hardy."

"The guy with the hat?"

"He'll probably get the kid off, too. He takes only cases he can win. Not that the glorious Manning clan are going to fly quite so high when this is over. That little happy family act of theirs is going to be a lot harder to maintain. Quint certainly isn't going to be able to play Mr. Integrity anymore. And that pretentious little wife of his, swanning around like she just stepped out of a Sundance catalog. Time for them to get down here in the trenches with the rest of us." She shook her head. "I know the guy. Jarvis? I sold them their house. The Cape on Montview? Nice people. They really had to stretch for the financing."

Drew said nothing. Although he didn't mind hearing about Quint's humiliation, he was eager for a change in conversation. He didn't want his future partner to know that Shannon was the one keeping Jamie from being arrested.

"So. *Drew.* I spoke with Cheryl about your intriguing proposal. And, while everybody appreciates the legacy of Hagel & Son in this town, there's a feeling that an actual merger doesn't really add much to our mix at this point in time. I mean, we ran your MLS listings, and well, to be honest, a lot of these are properties we decided not to go after when they came on the market. They're more, you know, starters. Fixer-uppers." She chuckled. "Obviously, people have to live in places likes that, but there's no reason we have to *sell* them. So, bottom line, we're going to have to take a pass on Hagel & Son."

The waitress arrived with Crippen's coffee. Drew accepted a refill.

"However," Crippen said after she was gone. "We *would* love to have you come on board. I mean, this is Drew Hagel we're talking about, right? We were thinking as an associate. Most of the people we hire for those positions are just babies. You, on the other hand, would be perfect for us. You'd bring some real substance to the job."

Drew looked down at his coffee. He was stirring it slowly, even though he'd added nothing to it.

"What—could you detail an associate's duties?"

"I suppose your primary function would be to interface with clients at the actual properties? You wouldn't have to worry too much about chasing the listings themselves; we're pretty much old hands at that."

She's offering me a job as a flunky, Drew thought. She's offering me a job as a shower.

"What sort of package would you be offering?" he asked, knowing that if he hesitated for even an instant, then the whole thing would fall apart.

"Well, for the first year you'd be on salary, though a pretty steep bonus scheme would kick in after that. And a man with your experience, obviously this would all be leading toward some sort of a partnership down the road." She frowned. "Though that's off the record. Don't tell Cheryl or she'll *kill* me."

"What's the salary?"

She told him. It was bad, but probably enough to take to the bank along with Quint's redemption. Drew waited a few judicious moments, then made a counteroffer. She didn't even make a show of considering it.

"Let's stick to that original number for the time being, all right? Once the market picks up we'll be in a better position to be flexible."

Drew knew he would have to accept. He had no leverage here.

"When can I start?"

"Can you come in Monday to meet the girls?"

Drew already knew the girls. But he nodded.

"Well, hoo-ray," she said, making parting gestures now. "I can't tell you how exciting it is to have Drew *Hagel* on board. Lucky us! We lose a competitor and gain a valued hand in one fell swoop."

Hand, Drew thought. They split the bill. When they reached the sidewalk, she nodded toward the COMING SOON sign on the Garden's marquee.

"Word is that she's going to have to sell. I guess they don't think people are going to flock to her movies now." She acted as if she had had a sudden idea, a performance so poorly executed that Drew understood he was about to hear the reason she'd bothered to meet with him at all. "Listen, Drew, I was thinking. Since Shannon and Jamie are so close, if you could help bring in the Garden as a listing, I mean, it would definitely go a long way toward putting you on a partnership track. And I'm sure I speak for the whole team on that one, Cheryl included."

And then she was gone, her heels clicking on the pavement. He waited until she was out of sight, then turned back into the restaurant to buy himself some real breakfast.

It wasn't yet eight when he got home. He put his briefcase in its normal spot by the brass hat stand and went into the kitchen. He opened the fridge but then remembered he'd already eaten. He knew he should speak with Ronnie now, tell her what had happened with Quint. It was wrong to keep secrets from his wife. He needed her now if he was going to keep from losing his daughter completely.

He could hear Shannon's feet hitting the floor as he trudged up the steps. Getting ready for another day spent in the service of the Manning family. Drew wondered if she was being so audacious as to go up to Orchard or if they'd established some other means of communication. Kids were clever about that these days, with their cell phones and computers. Though Jamie wouldn't have to worry about being secretive behind his security gate and big opaque windows. Quint and Carrie would be helping him. Mahabal and this new lawyer, counseling and coaching and protecting him. Shannon as well, making sure she didn't speak to anyone, including her father. Not that Drew was surprised that his daughter would choose the Mannings over him. She saw them as her future, just as he once had. But that was a lie. Whatever she'd been promised would mean nothing once the Mannings had what they needed. She would be *dismissed*, just as he had been on Saturday morning.

He had to stop this. He had to make her understand.

He knocked gently on her door. There was no answer. He opened it, anyway, but just then her shower started to run. She hadn't heard him. He began to shut the door, and that was when he saw it. Her laptop, listing slightly on her unmade bed, a thin gray tendril connecting it to the phone jack beneath her window. It was still on. In the bathroom there were slapping sounds as the water sheeted off her.

Drew walked up to the bed and looked down at the computer's screen. An icon flashed in the lower right corner. She was still online. Not only that, but her e-mail program was open, her password entered, six anonymous black circles in the appropriate box. There was a soft thudding noise in the bathroom. He flinched, but she'd only dropped something. He knelt in front of the computer and began to look for the evidence that would prove Jamie Manning had killed Robert Jarvis, just one thing that would allow him to save his daughter. He checked for new mail. There was nothing. He checked the in basket. Nothing for the past few months; she'd been erasing. Of course. They'd be telling her how to do this. The water continued to pound. He checked the computer's recycling bin and the address book. Empty. She'd purged everything. The last thing he opened was the out basket. There was a single message, sent five minutes ago. The surge of excitement Drew felt faded when he saw that it wasn't to Jamie. The address was "ianarchy"; the recipient someone named Ian Warfield. Drew clicked it open.

> Ian my love
> If you're awake write me or call. But I'll be with you soon, I promise. And I'll never turn against you. I'll NEVER tell the police. They think it was Jamie.
> I love you more than anything and will never leave you
> Shannon

The water still ran. After reading the words over again, he closed down the file and left the room. He walked quickly to his study and pulled the phone book from the desk. There was only one entry, a D. Warfield up on Totten Pike. There was no reason to write it down. Drew had a good memory for addresses. He went into his bedroom. Ronnie lay in bed, half asleep.

"How was your meeting?"

"Good. Ronnie, listen, I'm going to pop back out for a while. There's a property I want to look at."

It was a simple little ranch, built cheaply in the seventies, its only exceptional feature a big picture window overlooking a boulder-strewn lawn. The sort of place Drew might have been asked to sell if it came on the market. He drove by it a few times, looking for signs of life. Though it was quiet, there was no way he could risk approaching by that long driveway. So he drove up the pike, looking for a way into those woods around back. The garden statuary center looked like his best bet. He parked and walked through the front gate, telling the smiling woman who emerged from the big shingled shed that he was just browsing. The statues were tastefully arranged over a several-acre lot full of blossoming trees and shrubbery. Buddhas and cherubs and griffins—the whole mythic spread. There was a fence at the back, six feet, easily climbable, unless you were lugging a half ton statue. Or carrying forty extra pounds of flab. After struggling over it, he turned south, trudging through woodland that backed onto the houses on the pike. He'd counted; there would be five of them to pass before he got to the Warfield residence. The going was difficult, hidden ravines and unbreakable vine adding to the threat that somebody would see him out a back window. A chained dog spotted him and went berserk, but no humans responded.

The outline of the sixth house appeared. There was a steep hill just before he reached the property; he almost lost his footing stumbling down it. If the wall of a garage hadn't been there, he would have certainly been propelled right into the backyard. Its wood was soft with rot, almost like damp fabric. He paused by a neatly stacked pile of logs, then looked around the corner of the garage. There were no cars in the driveway, though he could see some sort of compact through the streaked windows of the garage door. It looked as if it hadn't been driven in a while; a patina of dust and pollen covered the back windshield.

Drew watched the house for a while longer, then moved slowly forward. He stopped at a small window to the left of the back door. The curtains were parted a few inches, allowing him to see a boy lying on his back on a messy bed, dressed only in a pair of boxer shorts. He looked to be about Shannon's age, with long hair that clung chaotically to his face and neck. His eyes were closed. He was gone, locked in something beyond sleep. His arm dangled off the side of the bed, twisted so his palm was facing upward in an inadvertent beseeching gesture. If it hadn't been for the slow heave of his chest, Drew might have thought he was dead.

He went to the back door and tried the knob. It was unlocked. He eased it open and stepped into a cramped, filthy kitchen. The table was covered with papers that had been culled from an accordion file. Deeds and certificates and a thick sheaf of documents bearing the familiar heading of Totten Savings and Loan. The name Ian Warfield appeared on most of them. He had a lot of money for someone so young. There was something else on the table, a stack of large drawing pads. Drew picked up the top one and flipped through pages that were covered with pencil drawings. They were no good. The stuff of childish nightmares, stark human figures wandering through a darkness filled with shadowy, demonic apparitions. There were no words to accompany the pictures, nothing to explain what any of this meant. He was about to give up when he came upon a very different image, slotted in after the book's last page. This one was lighter, freer; it showed real skill, picturing a naked woman stretched brazenly on a bed. He held it up to the light, realizing that it was not a woman after all. It was just a girl. It was his daughter.

Drew stuck it back in the pad. He locked the door as he gently pulled it shut, an old realtor's instinct. He drove straight to his office, knowing that if he went home, he would not be able to hide what he'd discovered. He sat behind his father's desk, ignoring the half dozen messages on his phone as he tried to understand. Shannon was telling the truth, or at least some warped version of it. There had been another boy driving the car. Her lover. That skinny, slack figure he'd seen through the window. Drew saw her naked body again, hidden away in that ugly little house. He knew he should call Flowers now. Some sort of deal could still be struck. He should stop this before she ruined herself completely.

There was something on his pants. A burr from the woods. He plucked it off, letting those sharp quills play over his fingers. For some reason he started thinking about one of last summer's tennis Saturdays, when he'd wound up giving one of the players a ride into town to pick up the Aston Martin he'd left for servicing at the European

Car Emporium. He was a short, arrogant man whose name Drew couldn't recall, though he did remember their conversation. They'd talked, inevitably, about Quint. After the usual bland, admiring statements, Drew had asked what made him so special. What gave him the edge.

"He doesn't hesitate," the man said, without hesitation. "He sees an opening, he moves in. Period. He doesn't delay, and then he doesn't second-guess himself. That's why he doesn't have a risk assessment team, or at least one he gives a shit about."

"But isn't everybody in your business decisive?"

"Well, yeah. But you're talking relative. I mean, the average joe on the street might spend a couple weeks deciding what to do with his money. The average trader, a couple hours. The average *good* trader, a couple minutes, seconds on a good day. But Quint, it's like, the decision is made before it's even been made."

"So he's smarter."

"We're all smarter, my friend. He's just *bolder*." He laughed sourly. "Put it this way. We all get eight hundred on our SATs. Quint Manning just turns in his paper first."

Drew understood how he could stop this. How he could save his daughter and his home. How he could wind up with enough. It would be simple. All it required was that he be bold. He placed the burr on his desk and began to flip through his Rolodex. There was an unfamiliar series of tones and clicks and then a woman's voice.

"I was trying to call the Manning residence."

"May I help you?"

"This is Drew Hagel. I'd like to speak with him."

There was a pause.

"May I tell him what this is about?"

"Yes. Tell him I want to make a deal."

23 This was the perfect hiding place. Carrie could stay down here for hours, and no one would ever think to come looking for her. When she left the house, she'd meant to sit on the back patio for just a while, but some stray impulse caused her to step off the flagstones onto the long sloping lawn. She moved down past the clubhouse and the clay court and the bright green balls no one was bothering to pick up, then veered right, behind the leaf-strewn pool and the gazebo. It took her a good sixty seconds to reach the orchard. She hesitated, wondering if Quint and Jamie were watching her, thinking she had finally lost her grip. But no one would be paying her any mind. Quint was trapped in his office, putting the last touches on the financing deal that might lose him his company in the fall. Jamie was in his room, angry and confused and refusing her comfort. Certain she was on her own, she stepped into the woods.

Six years, she thought as she pushed aside the branches. Six years, and this was the first time she had ever entered the orchard. At first, Carrie couldn't understand why Quint had wanted all this land. Their single acre in Upper Montclair had seemed a vast savanna to her after a lifetime of apartment dwelling. When he showed her the plot, he'd told her it was for the boys to roam. Perhaps, but she felt as if she'd hit upon the real reason their first evening in the finished house, when they sat out on the patio and she realized they were completely isolated. They owned everything they could see, except of course the sky, though she was beginning to think her husband had his eye on that as well. This was going to be his place apart, the goal of everything he did. Not adoring press reports or early retirement or great columns of numbers piling up beneath his name in some mainframe. But this suburban oasis, Quint's eight-acre sanctuary for his family.

The orchard proved a thick, hostile tangle. Insects emerged from the trees, mosquitoes mostly. There would be ticks as well, ready to mingle their diseased juices with hers. Come get me, she thought. She'd betrayed her husband and she'd betrayed her son and now her family was in trouble. The infecting snouts of tiny creatures meant nothing to her.

She soon came upon a gap in the trees. A squat circular wall of rocks stood in its center. It was well built, the stones wedged tightly together, the ground inside cleared. She went for a closer look. The niches on the inside of the wall were filled with toy guns and empty sports drink bottles. There was a rusty strongbox as well, poorly hidden beneath a shroud of twigs. She stepped over the wall and tried the latch. It was locked. She wondered what sort of contraband was inside. Dirty magazines and cigarettes and fireworks. There was probably a key stashed nearby, but she doubted finding it would be worth the effort. And anyway, people should be able to keep their secrets.

She brushed off the box and sat on it, then pulled a cracked plastic rifle from a shelf in the wall and pointed it back toward the house. Come get me, copper. All these looming trees began to remind her of Quint's boyhood home, making her wonder whether there had been an element of unacknowledged nostalgia in his choice of this land. Maybe buried somewhere beneath all that cool unhistoric rationality he secretly wanted to re-create the youth he gave every indication of having forgotten. Not that Carrie had ever really understood what was so wrong with it. Yes, his father was a cigar store Indian, but at least he was around, day after day, and there was undeniable pride in his eyes when Quint strode up to give the valedictory address at Deacon Williams. His sweet brother, Warren, may have been dealt some faulty DNA, but he was a lovely soul. And Gloria was a saint. You could laugh at her all you wanted, but then, when you were done laughing, you could only love the woman. She was still on the farm, refusing to move to the places Quint offered to buy her, those blue spruces growing too big for Christmas now that there was no longer any reason to harvest them. Just a flawed loving family living in the middle of nowhere. Where was the crime in a youth like that? Was it nothing more than all that shaggy imperfection that made him run so far from it?

Carrie certainly had spent the best days of her youth at the Mannings' house, the lazy afternoons during junior year when they'd study in his bedroom, listening to Dylan, always Dylan, "Tangled Up in Blue" and "Sad-Eyed Lady of the Lowlands" and "Sara," until she made him put on something else, Joni or Jackson Browne or Carole King. The dinners with his mother chattering away, piling impossible masses of food in front of Carrie, his father hardly saying a word, his bland weather-themed utterances so rare that they took on an oracular weight. On some of her visits Warren would come home from the place in Holyoke. He was completely besotted with Carrie, trailing her around the house so he could run his fingers through her long blond hair. Gloria lived in dread that his bewildered hormones would cause him to pounce, though Carrie assured her that she could handle it. She was from New York. She'd been pawed by pros.

The day they spent selling Christmas trees was the best of them all. It was the Saturday after school had let out for the holidays. Katherine, unwilling to sacrifice a drunken weekend with her coterie of simpering admirers, wouldn't be picking her up until late Sunday. So Carrie had accepted Quint's offer to stay at the Mannings' house for a couple of days, sleeping chastely in the guest room, with its ornamental pillows and framed samplers urging industry and prudence. He knocked on her door very early Saturday morning, and Carrie wondered if she was about to have to make a decision about her virginity. But he only wanted to let her know that it was time to get to work.

"Work? Where?"

"Outside."

It had snowed three inches the night before; her window was latticed with ice.

"Uh, pass."

"No work, no food. House rules."

And so she'd put on most of the clothes she owned and gone to sit by a smoldering fifty-five-gallon drum to watch her future husband sell Christmas trees. Although Wendell IV was out there as well, it was Quint's show. This was serious business, providing a sizable chunk of the family's yearly income. People, most of them regulars, would arrive in their station wagons and pickups, and Quint would greet them with the clipped local accent he'd hidden while at DWA. There would be an interval of terse conversation as he determined what size tree was needed, and then he'd hop on the gear-grinding tractor and vanish into the wilderness. Kids could ride on the aluminum sled; adults were welcome to mount the vehicle's running boards. Carrie went with him the first few times, seated on his lap, actually steering at one point—Carrie Delaney, piloting farm equipment—but she soon discovered that riding a tractor in mid-December Massachusetts was *cold*. After that she was content to stay by the fire, tossing in splintered spruce fronds that would crackle with surprising vehemence, drinking the hot cocoa Gloria brought her, and, most of all, watching Quint sell Christmas trees. He'd never been more beautiful, his cheeks slightly red, his blue eyes alive with purpose. He sold a hundred of them, easily, stopping only when the sun had set. She suspected that every person who walked onto the property that day left with the perfect tree—and that he'd paid a few dollars more than he'd planned when he arrived.

Her reverie was broken by his voice, calling her name from the patio. She'd been wrong. There was no hiding. She would have to talk to her husband. She would have to tell him the truth about her adultery. Last night, after discovering that Jamie was innocent, she'd hoped that the pure energy of her conviction would be enough for Quint. But before she'd even finished speaking, she could see that he didn't believe her.

"Come on, Carrie. We've both seen how strange he's been acting since Friday. He's a totally different kid."

She hesitated before answering, aware that the next logical step in the conversation was to confess what had happened with Jon.

"He was just upset with himself for getting drunk in front of his friends," she said instead.

"But what about Shannon coming over on Saturday morning?"

"That had nothing to do with protecting Jamie."

"Carrie, you're not making sense. You know that he's been acting very strange. I mean, clearly, there was something seriously wrong with him before the police even showed up."

There was only one way to convince him. But she could not bring herself to say it. She was like her mother after the second stroke, struggling to conjure words that just wouldn't come.

"Why can't you just trust me on this?" she asked.

"Trust *what*? Your wish that this wasn't happening? You go upstairs and he cries on your shoulder. Well, fine, that's probably good for him, but it doesn't change reality."

"Jesus, Quint, what is it with you? Where is your faith in him?"

"It's not an issue of faith. It's a question of what I know. It's a question of what I've seen around the house. You might be willing to blind yourself to the facts, but I can't do that. Jamie is getting himself in deep trouble, and he needs at least one of us thinking clearly to help him."

They had said nothing to each other for the rest of the night. She had trouble getting to sleep, and then, just as she drifted off, Nick appeared in the doorway to announce that he'd wet the bed, something he hadn't done in years. For the second time in less than a week Carrie found herself loading the washing machine in the middle of the night. When she came up from the basement, the light in Quint's office was on. He was speaking quietly into his phone. Working. His therapy. What he did instead of crying on anyone's shoulder.

She'd come down at dawn to find him still on the phone, arranging for the private security people to send some muscle down to Capital Park to prevent any incursions by the media. The local paper was spread on the kitchen table. There was an article about the accident on the front page that actually named Jamie. Hollis Hardy had been right. The police must have fed the paper the information. It certainly held nothing back. It even mentioned that the Jeep had been washed and waxed since the accident, as if this weren't something car-proud American boys did whenever the sun emerged from behind a cloud.

Quint joined her just as she finished the article.

"But how can they print his name?" Carrie asked. "He's seventeen."

"Seventeen can be an adult. It's a gray area."

And then Hollis Hardy called with more bad news. He'd got an early look at the lab report. Jamie's fingerprints were the only ones the lab had been able to lift from the stick shift and steering wheel, though Hardy said this was only to be expected, since he'd driven the Jeep several times after Friday night. Infinitely worse, a tiny fleck of metallic blue paint had been found lodged in a crevice of one of the Wrangler's rubberized safety bars. It was the same color and brand as the one on Jarvis's bicycle. The polymers matched. Hardy urged them not to make too much of this; there would be chain of evidence issues, and even if those were resolved, Jamie had yet to be placed behind the wheel of the car. He said the district attorney would probably take the matter to a grand jury now, where he would almost certainly be able to get an indictment. If there was no plea agreement, then it would be followed by a trial that Hardy was still confident they would "not lose."

"Hardy doesn't seem too broken up by the prospect of a long trial," Quint said.

"I'll bet he isn't."

Carrie had fled to the orchard after that, unable to bear the idea of a trial. Jamie dragged into court, day after day, made old before his time. Quint publicly humiliated, cast as just another slick operator. And then there was the image of Jon on the witness stand, explaining why Carrie wasn't picking up on the night of the accident. Although the truth about her infidelity would almost certainly come out before then. The police would interview her again. Jon would see the article and come forward. Jamie's anger at her would boil over, and he'd tell his father what he now knew.

Quint called for her again, his voice growing impatient. She stepped over the little stone wall and used the toy gun to clear the branches from her path. He saw her as she emerged from the trees. She checked her bare arms as she crossed the lawn; there was nothing preying on her.

"What were you doing?" he asked when she reached the patio.

She tossed the gun on a chair.

"Holding down the fort. Is something happening?"

"I was just worried about you."

"You don't have to worry about me, Quint. Save that for our son."

"Drew called a while ago," he said after a moment, his voice charged with dismissive scorn.

"Really? What does he want?"

"He wanted to make some kind of deal. He claims he can get Jamie out of this mess."

"A deal? What kind of deal?"

"We didn't get that far in the conversation."

"So you're not going to talk to him about this at all?"

"Of course not. I'm not getting involved in some sort of conspiracy with Drew Hagel to conceal Jamie's guilt."

"But, Quint, what if it's something else? Shouldn't we see what he has to say?"

"Carrie, the man's a liar," he said impatiently. "I have no interest in anything he says."

His phone began to ring, and he went to answer it, not waiting to be excused this time. Carrie stood on the patio for a while longer, wondering what Drew could possibly know that would make him confident enough to approach them like this. One thing was certain; it wasn't what Quint thought.

He was still in his office when she went back inside. She listened to his voice for a moment, so calm and unyielding, then walked into the kitchen and got the phone book from the desk. She tried the office number first; if she called Crescent, she might have to deal with Shannon or Ronnie. Drew answered on the first ring, not at all surprised that it was Carrie.

She parked in the alley behind the building. He was already there, waiting beneath the rusted awning by the back door, a ragged briefcase in his hand. There was something provisional about him; he didn't seem to know what to do with himself. She could suddenly see him for what he was, a big, awkward man whose sense of purpose was as fragile as the rickety structure currently sheltering him.

"So Quint isn't coming?" he asked as she approached.

"No. It's just you and me."

She unlocked the door and hit the sequence on the alarm. Neither of them spoke as she led him into the auditorium. They stopped on the expanse of moldering carpet between the stage and the seats. The dirty, torn screen rose above them. There was scurrying in one of the dark corners of the ceiling, birds flushed from a nest by this sudden human intrusion. Drew took a deep breath and looked around the theater, his eyes narrowing a little, as if he were trying to understand where they were.

"Shannon's lying about Friday night," he said finally. "I thought she was doing it to protect Jamie, and so I—I looked into it. And I found out your son really is innocent."

"Wait, are you telling me you know who was driving the Wrangler?"

He stared at her without answering.

"Well, who on earth was it? Have you told the police?"

"And so here's the deal," he said, ignoring her questions, his voice slightly breathless, as if he were reciting poorly learned lines. "I want you to give me my money, and then I'll provide the police with the information that will end this thing right now."

"What money?"

"I want you to give me back my investment with WMV, and I want you to give me the profit I should have made. The forty-four percent."

"Drew, I don't know anything about—"

"If you give me that, then your son will be safe."

"Wait a minute," Carrie said. "If there's someone else, you must know that the police will be able to find him eventually."

"The police are convinced it was Jamie. Didn't you see this morning's paper?"

"Then we'll tell our lawyer and he'll—"

"He'll what? Shannon isn't going to say anything, Carrie. You don't know what she's— If you fight me on this, then I'll help her lie, I swear to you I will. And the more you try to prove it wasn't Jamie, the worse you'll look. It'll go on and on. Pay me, and I'll cooperate with the police. I'll tell them what I know, and this thing will be over for you by the end of the day."

"God, Drew, how can you do this to us?"

He laughed bitterly. His face grew strange, its muscles and bones clearly not accustomed to accommodating the things he was feeling.

"What is it you want me to do, Carrie? You want me to save you after what you've done to me? Your husband took everything I had."

"Drew, this is insane. Shannon will have to tell the truth."

"Are you certain of that? Are you willing to take that chance?"

Carrie didn't answer.

"I'm offering you a sure thing," he continued. "No trial. No more newspaper articles. No more investigation. You pay me back, and it ends."

Carrie imagined how good that would be. To have everything just end.

"How much?" she asked quietly.

"Three hundred and sixty thousand dollars."

She held his watery eyes for a moment, then turned away and looked around the shabby cinema. The renovation money was still in the account. There was enough. More than enough. All she had to do was give them some numbers and her clever little password, and they would send the money wherever she wanted. She tried not to think that this was going to be her place. She was going to work here.

"Give me the number of your account," she said. "I'll wire you the money."

After an astonished interval Drew placed his battered briefcase on the arms of one of the front row chairs. Carrie snuck a quick look inside as he opened it. All she could see was a blank legal pad and two packs of shortbread cookies, one of them half consumed, the other unopened. He took out the pad, then pulled a checkbook and a pen from a hidden pocket in the case's lid. The pen was empty; it took him a moment to find another. You lost man, Carrie thought as he copied out the number.

"Carrie," he said after handing her the torn yellow sheet, "you have to understand. I can't afford to lose this money. This isn't about—"

"Don't explain yourself to me, Drew," she interrupted. "Just keep your end of the bargain."

24 Flowers had offered Drew an interview room, but he'd grown to dread those airless little cubicles in the past week. Instead, he took a seat in the small congregation of chairs where he'd waited with Shannon on Monday night. The station was much busier now. There were more police on duty; a steady flow of citizens passed through the automatic doors, ordinary people with ordinary problems. Drew looked up every time he heard the pneumatic wheeze, hoping it would be Ian Warfield in custody. He wanted to get home to Shannon so he could explain what he'd done.

When he first sat down, he unwisely let his gaze wander up to the gallery of deadbeat dads, where it landed on one Gary Randolph Duguay, thirty-four grand in arrears to a woman who must have seen something in those feral brown eyes that the camera missed. The dingy poster forced Drew to contemplate his own unhappy career as a father, all the mistakes he'd watched his daughter make without intervening. The disastrous alliances and impetuous phone calls; that woolly hat that had brought her nothing but ridicule. Allowing her to be self-reliant when she hardly had a self to rely on. He remembered the times Ronnie had quietly urged him to act and he'd done nothing, thinking he was winning his daughter's affection when in fact, he was only pushing her toward that brick house on Totten Pike. But his weakness was over now. Everyone was going to be safe. Ronnie and Shannon and the twins. As soon as Warfield was in custody, he would look her in the eye and let her know that she had a father again. She would be furious with him, but that was all right. He'd avoided her anger long enough. She'd soon come to understand he'd done the right thing.

He'd gone straight to his office after leaving the Garden. Carrie had called a half hour later to tell him it was done. He went to the bank to check; he wasn't worried about Carrie, but if Quint found out, he would probably interfere. There was an ATM in the lobby, although he suspected he would probably have to talk to someone to get evidence of the transfer. The machine seemed to share Drew's misgivings, whirring and clicking for a long time after he entered his PIN number. A receipt finally emerged. The blue ink was faded, but it was still easy to read in the bold fluorescent light. There was just over $361,000 in his account. He looked at the paper for a long time, then put it in his coat pocket and walked to a neutral corner of the lobby, stopping amid an array of life-size cardboard cutouts depicting happy customers. They were all smiling and gesturing with their hands, speech bubbles explaining the services they had so rewardingly used. Drew used his cell phone to call home, careful how he phrased his questions to Ronnie. Shannon was still in her room, asleep, as far as Ronnie could tell. That was good. He didn't want her up on Totten Pike when the police arrived.

It was a short walk to the station. Flowers came right out, listening with that benign scowl as Drew explained about Ian Warfield.

"When did you discover this?" Flowers asked.

"This morning."

"How?"

"She was e-mailing him. Don't worry, it's definitely him."

"You'll go on record with that?"

Drew nodded.

"Where is this kid now? Is he with Shannon?"

"No. He's at his house."

"Does Shannon know what you're doing? Have you talked to her about any of this?"

"Not yet. Look, Detective, what you said the other night about us identifying the driver, how it would get Shannon out of trouble. I presume that still holds."

It took Flowers a moment to answer.

"Let's see what happens with this Warfield kid, all right?"

"Yes, but—"

"Mr. Hagel, I'm really not the person to talk to about this. Though I will say that the best thing for Shannon is that she come down and tell us what really happened on Friday."

"All right. You want me to bring her in now?"

"Hold off on that until we pick this kid up. I don't want her warning him and then I have to chase some teenage joyrider up and down the East Coast. You have his exact address?"

Drew took the legal pad from his briefcase and wrote it down.

"Is this a Country Day kid?" Flowers asked after he took the page. "I don't recognize the name from Tuesday."

Drew shook his head. Flowers looked back at the paper.

"This is a real kicker. I thought for sure it was James Manning."

"Yeah. Me, too."

"I'll tell you one thing. This whole damned job would be a lot easier if I didn't have to deal with teenagers."

The detective went back through the locked door. He came out a few minutes later, that blond policewoman in tow. Neither of them looked at Drew as they hurried from the station. And then they were gone, and there was nothing to do but wait.

The house's phone woke Shannon. She sat up quickly, looking around her room in a panic, her eyes finally settling on her alarm clock. It was almost noon. She'd meant to sleep only a few minutes. She leaped out of bed so fast that she knocked her computer noisily to the floor. She began to get dressed, almost stumbling as she pulled on her pants.

"Shannon?"

Ronnie stood in the doorway, holding herself steady on the frame, her eyes puffy, her hair a little wild. Her big Smith T-shirt was pulled tightly over her stomach.

"Are you all right? I thought I heard a bang."

Shannon nodded.

"Well, I know you don't want to talk to me about what's going on, but I'm going to say what's on my mind, anyway," Ronnie continued, her voice stubborn and tender. "I just think it's outrageous, the way they've been hounding you. Putting a young person under this kind of pressure. Clearly, if you say you drove Jamie, then you drove Jamie. I've half a mind to call Ray Flowers and tell him to back off."

"You know Flowers?"

"Of course, I know Ray. From work. I've told your father that if they're going to continue to harass you, he should hire a lawyer. All right. There. I've said it. I'm sorry to have bothered you."

But before she could leave, something in Shannon broke. She sat back on the bed, her legs giving out beneath her. And then, without wanting to do this, she started to cry, the sobs convulsing her body painfully.

"Sweetheart," Ronnie said.

She made her way across the room's forbidden terrain, lowering herself carefully onto the bed. She reached a small swollen hand out and put it on Shannon's thigh, and this was all it took. Shannon fell forward into her arms, almost tipping her over. It was the first time she'd ever put her arms around Ronnie. Her body was so warm.

"It's not about Jamie," Shannon said. "It's Ian."

"Ian?"

"Ian Warfield."

"What, did he call . . . wait a minute. Ian? You know Ian?"

"I'm in love with him."

Ronnie's shock was evident, though it soon gave way to a gentle smile.

"Really? That's wonderful, Shannon."

Shannon couldn't immediately register her words.

"What did you just say?"

"I'm very fond of Ian. I have great hopes for him. You two, gosh, yes, okay. I can see it. Of course. But how on earth did you meet?"

"Ronnie, no, hold on . . . I met him in your waiting room. A couple months ago. When I came for my keys."

"Months? Have you been seeing Ian all this time?"

Shannon nodded. Here it comes, she thought. But Ronnie continued to smile.

"And you haven't told me because you thought I'd disapprove."

"Don't you?"

"Of course not. I think you're lucky to be with each other. To be honest, having someone as mature as you in his life could help Ian a lot." She looked up. "But wait a minute. Why are you crying? Is Ian all right?"

She shook her head. Ronnie's face took on a sober, professional cast.

"What's wrong with him?"

"He's—he's feeling really bad. His moods have been going all crazy. A few days ago he was pumped full of energy, but now it's like he's not even there. I can't get him to do anything. And he's cold. Really, really cold."

Ronnie nodded, as if this weren't at all surprising to her.

"You know I've recommended he see a doctor?"

"What? What doctor?"

"I've given his uncle the name of a psychiatrist he should see. Has he arranged to do that?"

Shannon shook her head.

"All right. I'm going to call his uncle right now and tell him to get going on this—"

She began to stand, but Shannon grabbed her wrist.

"Ronnie, wait," she said softly. "Ian was the one driving Jamie's Wrangler."

They left right away. Shannon drove. To her surprise, Ronnie didn't want to call the police; she thought having them barge in on Ian might do real damage. She would instead check him into the hospital herself. The police could wait until he'd received proper treatment. Ronnie was certain that once he got some rest and medication he would understand that he had to turn himself in.

"But he still might have to go to jail," Shannon said.

"Shannon, listen to me. It was an *accident*. He didn't deliberately hurt that man. He wasn't drinking or on drugs. For heaven's sake, he was driving some drunk boy's car for him. And I'm sure that his doctors will have something to say about his condition. The court will take all that into consideration. I promise you. And if his uncle's being obstructive . . . I can't guarantee anything, Shannon, but he won't be without friends."

She called the hospital from the car to make sure the attending psychiatrist would be waiting for them at Mercy, ready to help Ian the moment they arrived. There was a somber urgency to Ronnie's voice as she spoke; she used words and phrases Shannon didn't quite understand.

"He's going to be all right, isn't he?" she asked when Ronnie got off the phone.

"As soon as we get there," Ronnie said. "Yes."

Shannon drove a little faster, though her car felt sluggish and weak. Finally, the long rocky yard came into view, and then the house. It took her a moment to understand that there was something wrong. A person was staring in through the big picture window out front. It was a policewoman, her gloved hands held to the side of her face to block out the midday glare.

"Oh, God."

"Shannon, it's all right. We're here now."

There were two cars out back, a cruiser and a sedan. Flowers was walking away from the back door as Shannon skidded to a stop in the pebbled dirt. She could tell by the look on his face that he knew Ian was the driver.

"Where is he?" he asked the moment she got out of her car.

"He's not inside?"

"Nobody's answering."

"But—"

Shannon looked around the backyard and saw that the Chevelle was gone. Which meant that David had taken him. He'd disappeared with Ian sometime in the night and she would never see him again.

The policewoman walked around the side of the house, shaking her head.

"Shannon," Flowers said, "I want you to tell me right now: Where is Ian Warfield?"

She looked back at the quiet house, and a terrible thought started to form in her mind. She ran to the back door, flung open the screen, and peered through the glass. It took her a moment to make out the uneven stack of pads on the kitchen table. All his work, good and bad. He would have never left that behind. She ran over to his window, her chest tightening with fear. His bed was empty, the covers in a twisted pile on the floor. Clothes lay about the place, clothes he would have taken with him.

"Shannon?" Ronnie asked from somewhere behind her. "What is it?"

She banged on the window with her flat hand.

"Ian?" she called. "It's me. Come on."

She turned. They were all looking at her.

"He's in there."

"We've been out here for like ten minutes," the policewoman said. "There's nobody in that—"

"He's in there!" Shannon shouted. "You have to believe me!"

Ronnie turned to Flowers.

"Ray, you'd better go in," she said, her voice thin with fright. "Right now."

But Flowers didn't move. For some reason, he began to talk to Ronnie, and she began to say things back to him. Shannon ran back to the door and grabbed its handle, shaking it as hard as she could. But the door wouldn't open; it wouldn't give. And then very strong hands had taken hold of her, Flowers, pulling her back to make room for the policewoman, who drew the stick from her belt and drove its handle into the panel of glass just above the doorknob. It shattered easily.

David should have left a note. But he'd planned on being gone for only a short while. He hadn't counted on the bank's being so busy, leaving him to pace the carpeted lobby for well over an hour, eating stale candy and trying to avoid the dead-eyed stares of those cardboard cutouts. There was no use calling, since he'd unplugged the phone before leaving the house. It wasn't until just after noon that he had what he'd come for: a banker's draft for nearly twenty-two thousand dollars. His personal savings. His reward for three years of unrelieved, back-clenching work. A fraction of what Ian would be collecting when he turned eighteen, but still enough to get them through the difficult days until then. He waited until he was in the Chevelle to take the check from the unsealed envelope and examine it closely, running his fingertips over the risen numbers like a blind man. He'd never held this much money in his hand.

He raced out of the lot, cutting people off, desperate to get back home. He didn't like the idea of Ian's waking up to an empty house. Besides, the sooner they were on the road, the better David would feel. They were leaving town. Today. No more hesitation; no more debate. He'd made the decision as he kept vigil over his nephew during the night. There was no way Ian could stay around here. He was getting worse by the hour, sliding into an abyss that seemed ready to swallow him whole. It had started before he'd even heard about Jarvis's dying, though that grim bit of news, picked up from the television while David slept yesterday morning, had driven him into an even deeper gloom. Their only chance now was to escape to North Carolina immediately. He had to get Ian out from under all this pressure. It would be risky, since he was by definition violating his probation as soon as he left the state. But David had to gamble that no one would be going to very much trouble about a kid who'd up until now been a model of compliance. At least he was done with Traynor. That was good. There were still two of his monthly probation meetings left, but they could slip back into town for those and also to secure his inheritance from the bank. David would drive back up 95 every night if that's what it took. Anything to rescue Ian from this paralysis.

He'd called Tib first thing in the morning and told him what he was planning, leaving out the part about arriving with a wanted felon. His friend said they could stay with him for the time being, no problem, though he was certain they'd be able to find somewhere else in a matter of days. Come to think of it, that lawyer had mentioned that the family in the marsh house was talking about getting a place closer to the ocean, so maybe something would work out there. Which would mean their new life could begin the moment they pulled into town. Barring breakdown, they'd get to Beaufort before dawn. He'd take the car right up to the beach, so the first thing Ian would see after David woke him was the sun rising over the ocean. A few days in that sea air would jog him out of this gloom; a tour of that house in the marsh would start the process of forgetting.

The biggest obstacle to a swift escape, of course, was Shannon. She loved the boy too much to be careful. And Ian would never accept leaving her for good. David decided to wait until the last minute to tell him that they were going down south for a few weeks, just until things cooled down. Ian wouldn't put up much of a fight, not in his current mood. By the time it became clear that David wasn't going to allow him back Shannon would be on her way to college and Ian would have started over in the bird artist's house and Robert Jarvis would be a forgotten man. He'd even let Ian smoke another bowl before they left, just to avert any trouble that might arise over Shannon. He hated to do it, but now that he'd managed to buy the stuff he might as well put it to good use. What an ordeal that had been, prowling the bars and coffeehouses around the college until he secured a half ounce of seedy, stem-ridden weed. The hippie who dealt it to him had brazenly ripped him off, realizing when he saw David's anxious eyes that he was in a sellers' market.

As if his day weren't bad enough, he returned to find Shannon in the house. He'd come perilously close to losing his temper with her, the sort of mistake that would be harder to avoid if they stayed in town. After getting rid of her, he had to find out about that smoky stench, discovering after nearly tearing the walls apart that Ian had been burning his pictures. Great, David thought. Just wonderful. He sat at the kitchen table after that, drinking beer and hoping his nephew wouldn't wake from his comalike sleep. The crumpled Baggie lay in front of him, a shrink-wrapped patch of poisonous weed that had erupted in the middle of his life, reminding him that he'd come full circle. All the glorious dreams of the past year, and here he was.

And then, because there would never again be peace in this house, the shouting started, a sound so strange and unexpected that it took him several long seconds to understand it came from Ian's room. He raced down the hallway and slammed open the door. Ian sat up in bed, his arms folded tightly over his chest, like someone who'd just emerged from very cold water. His entire body was shaking; his breathing was shallow and fast. His eyes were focused on nothing David could see.

"Jesus, Ian, what is it?"

"I was just . . . there were all these people standing on me. Dozens of them, mashing my face into the bed. They wore these big black shoes. They were pinning down my arms and my neck. I was trying to tell them to *get off* but I couldn't make a sound and they kept getting heavier and heavier until . . ."

He closed his eyes.

"Where's Shannon?"

"She's gone home for the night," David said.

"I thought I was alone. I thought you guys had finally left me."

"Come on."

David draped a blanket over Ian's shoulders and led him back to the kitchen. The moment Ian saw the reefer he went back to his room, hurrying now, and returned a few seconds later with his elbow-joint pipe. David couldn't believe what he was seeing. He thought they'd dispensed with all paraphernalia after the arrest. There was no need to find a match; Ian had also brought the lighter he'd been using to immolate his drawings. Scrape, flame, suck, pop, and then that familiar catch of breath as the smoke was sealed in his lungs. David joined him but only for a couple of shallow hits that he immediately let leak back out into the stale kitchen air. There was none of the cheery, smirking, food-scrounging conviviality normally associated with getting stoned, just the grim ingestion of pungent smoke.

"They couldn't stop the bleeding," Ian said eventually.

David stared at him, expecting more, though Ian had lapsed back into silence.

"What?" he asked eventually.

"Jarvis. There was too much blood in his head. It's amazing how much blood you have inside you. Eight pints. Did you know there was that much?"

"Ian, there's no reason for you to be thinking about any of that."

They remained silent after that, until David finally told him that they'd smoked enough for tonight. Ian shuffled back to his bedroom for what David prayed would be a long spell of dreamless sleep. It was then that he decided they were leaving. He retrieved the accordion folder where they kept essential papers and went over them for a while. Then he packed a couple of suitcases and threw them in the car; he'd borrow Tib's van to pick up the remainder of their possessions when they snuck back for the probation meetings. He confiscated the cord connecting Ian's computer to the phone jack so there would be no careless messages to Shannon. Finally, he locked the dope and the pipe in the glove compartment, wanting to keep the drugs away from his nephew until just before it was time to go.

After that he roamed the house, checking on Ian every few minutes. At one point he took the pads from his desk, bringing them into the kitchen for a forbidden look at what he'd been doing recently. His heart sank even further as he flipped through the pages. He didn't even make it to the end of the top pad. It was like the angry scribbling of a retarded child. He tried not to think about how far away they were from the bird drawings he imagined him doing. But they'd get there. Ian would calm down and get some practice. His hand would mature; he'd start looking out at the world instead of staring back into his mind. They'd get there.

The drive back from the bank took forever. Although David usually bombed up Totten Pike, today he kept it right at the limit. Getting pulled was the last thing he needed, especially with weed in the car. Just before he reached the house, a big refrigerator truck came flying toward him, straddling the center line, its horn Dopplering past. David was so wrapped up in getting around it that he didn't see the police cruiser until he'd begun his turn into the driveway. There was a second car as well, a sedan, slotted next to the cruiser. He straightened the wheel at the last possible instant, sliding his foot back onto the gas pedal and driving on with only the slightest pause. He checked the side mirror; a blond policewoman and a short wide man in a sports coat were walking toward the back door. And then the road curved, and his sister's house was gone.

All right, he thought. It's over. You were a few minutes away from freedom. Closer than most get, but not close enough. Just go. You can be out of the area before people start looking for the Chevelle. You have twenty-two thousand dollars, and your gear is in the trunk. It's a big country, still more wilderness out there than anyone is willing to admit. Ian will be eighteen soon. A man. He'll have Ginny's insurance and the house. There's nothing more you could do for him.

But he hadn't even made it a mile before he pulled to the side of the road. It was no good. Ian wasn't a man. He'd never survive on his own. David thought of him shivering on his bed last night and knew he wasn't going anywhere. He never had been going anywhere. Maybe for the last few weeks, when Carolina looked possible, he'd been on the verge of some sort of new life. But that was over. He switched off the motor and got out of the car. He mounted a small hill at the side of the road and then sat in the thin grass. He looked down at his Chevelle. His muscle car. What a laugh. It was just a piece of shit that got eight miles a gallon and broke down every couple of months. The real muscle cars were the BMWs and Mercedeses and Porsches, the cars people drove in Greenwich and Manhattan and up on Orchard. That boy's Wrangler. Any housewife in a Volvo could blow him away if she felt like it.

He got up and walked back down the hill. He took a few deep breaths, then raised his leg and kicked hard, using his heel. The metal dimpled, a satisfying feeling, a solid sound. There, he thought. That's for Robert Jarvis, riding his bicycle in the middle of the night. He moved a few feet along the car and did it again, this one for rich little Jamie, owning a car no kid should own. Another explosion, another dent, this one for meddling Shannon, all heart and no sense. He circled the car, stopping and kicking every few feet, for the cancer that killed his sister and the troll who hurt his nephew and an especially hard shot for his drunken father. He shattered the headlights and then the taillights. A car passed, an old couple in a sedan, slowing down and then speeding up. David's heart was pounding; his lungs were drawing clean air. The smashing felt so good. Metal and glass yielding beneath his feet. When he'd closed the circle, he dug a sharp heavy rock out of the dirt with his fingernails. It took him a few strikes to get the first window to shatter, but after that there was no stopping him. This wasn't as good as the kicking; the safety glass broke agreeably, without the clean violent sound regular glass would have made. But still. He left the windshield intact. He'd need that.

He chucked the rock into the weeds. The Chevelle looked like a big crushed can speckled with bits of ice, something you'd see at the end of a party. His head felt clear, as if his brain had been wiped clean. All right. It was time to get going. He wanted to get down to the police station before they put his nephew in a cell. He would find the arresting officer, and he would take the blame. He was the guilty one. Always was, always would be. Any justice that needed to be served should be served by him. He would explain that the boy had wanted to turn himself in, but David, his guardian, had forbidden him. He'd threatened force to keep him from calling the police; he'd used drugs to muddy his mind. He'd tell them that he'd done it so he could get his hands on the money. They'd believe that. It was the oldest motive in the book.

He got back in the car, not bothering to wipe the broken glass from the seat. This stuff wouldn't cut him. He started the engine. It turned over first time. The car would still take him where he had to go. He pulled a U-turn, the glass shifting on the floor and on the seat, the few bits remaining in the side window frame falling free.

The police cars were still at Ginny's house. That was lucky; he'd be able to talk to them before they took Ian away. Maybe they'd even let them ride down together, so Ian wouldn't have to go through any of this on his own. And there was another car now, Shannon's Honda. Good. She'd be able to confirm that it had all been David's idea. He pulled in behind her. The kitchen door was half open, one of its glass panels broken. Damn cops probably hadn't even bothered to knock. He would get involved if they were being rough with Ian. It didn't matter what they did to him now.

He heard Shannon the moment he stepped out of his car. At first he couldn't understand what she was saying; all he could hear was the wild fear in her voice. But then the words became clear. They seemed to slice right through the house's thin walls.

"What are they doing? What's happening? What are they doing to him?"

David was running before he'd even decided that was what he was going to do. He had to step over a toppled chair in the kitchen, and then he was in the hallway. Shannon's voice was coming from Ian's bedroom, but the police were in the bathroom, kneeling just inside the splintered door. Ian's bare feet protruded between them. Their backs hid the remainder of his body, though David could see the urgent motion of their arms and shoulders as they struggled to hold him down.

He started moving, yelling at them to stop, telling them to leave his nephew alone. The male cop turned just before he reached the doorway. David froze when he saw the man's narrow eyes. He wasn't hurting Ian. There was no anger there, only fear. David looked past him at his nephew, twisted awkwardly to fit into the tiny space, his skin pale in the light from the frosted window. He wasn't struggling. He wasn't doing anything. The tile floor around him was a shallow pool of red. The Browning knife lay just beyond his head, its evil glistening blade wide open. The woman cop was tying one of Ginny's hand towels around his left forearm; blood streaked the black leather of her gloves. His right arm had already been tied off, just above three long vertical slashes on the wrist. The man pressed the balled floor mat to the side of Ian's neck. It was black with blood. In his free hand there was a radio. He raised it to his mouth as he turned back to the boy, his voice calm and loud as he repeated Ginny's address.

David looked at Ian's eyes. They were open, and for a moment he thought this was good, but then he saw that there was nothing in them, no curiosity or confusion, no recognition or understanding, just fear, ancient and simple, and even that was vanishing now, like mist the moment bright sun hits it.

He began to back down the narrow hall, stopping only when he reached Ian's door. Shannon stood in the middle of the room with Traynor, who held the girl as tightly as she could with her small hands. Shannon looked at David and their eyes locked and she saw what was happening. An understanding passed between them. They had done this. They had let this happen. She broke free and rushed toward the door. David stepped into her path and caught her by the arms. She struggled, but he held on. There was no way he was going to let her see Ian like this. If he could stop anything today, he would stop that.

EPILOGUE

It looked as if Quint was winning, though it was hard to be sure. His game had changed so much recently. He was eager to rush the net now, prepared to let a few winners slip by in search of a weakly hit ball he could volley past his opponents. The man he was paired with was equally aggressive, swiping the tip of his racket through the clay when he'd muff a shot, pumping his fist in the air after winners. He was the newest member of the fund, evidently very big in biotech. He'd made enzymes and proteins do his bidding, and now he was reaping the rewards. Carrie was supposed to meet him today, but just as he arrived, Jamie had put in a rare call from Durham. By the time she was off the phone the game was on, and she didn't think her throbbing head could bear the half hour of small talk that would accompany a visit to the court. Besides, she had to figure out what she was going to do about Jamie's request. So she'd drawn a bath, her second of the day, the first having been an unsuccessful early-morning attempt to avert the hangover now souring her system. As she soaked, she decided she would do what her son wanted. The biowizard could wait until tonight's festivities. Or, if not then, some other day. He'd be back. Once they were locked up, they always came back.

Quint drove one into the net, and everybody gathered courtside to shake hands, as grim as pallbearers. She was wrong; it was a rare loss for the home team. She broke free from the window and wandered back into the bathroom to balm her lips. Her hair was still a little damp, but she could blast it with the car's heater on the way over. She avoided the reflection of her eyes. She knew what they'd be like, watery and swollen, beyond all the available remedies. Her mother's eyes.

There was no one downstairs; she'd seen Dillon and Nick vanish into the orchard a few minutes earlier. Going to that fort, probably; checking their strongbox of secrets. Taking advantage of this Indian summer day. The caterers were due at any minute to set up for tonight's big party. It was ostensibly for WMV's ninth anniversary, though everyone knew Quint was throwing it to celebrate the fund's miraculous recovery. She understood what was expected of her: overseeing the setup, greeting the guests, standing by her husband's side as his genius was toasted. She wondered what would happen if she didn't show; if she just snuck out while the canapés were being served. How long it would take anyone to notice. Or care.

As if summoned by these mutinous thoughts, Quint arrived, stepping through the sliding door at the exact moment she snatched her car keys from the kitchen counter.

"I was beginning to wonder where you were," he said, still a little breathless from the game.

"Right here," she said. "As always."

She endured his cool scrutiny. She'd behaved badly last night. There had been a dinner in the city for those who wouldn't be able to make the journey up to Connecticut. The waiter kept on bringing the wine, and Carrie kept on drinking it, until she was aware of tight smiles and averted eyes and then her husband's hands shepherding her to the car. She couldn't remember much of what she'd said, though it must have been bad, given his flinty demeanor all morning.

"I thought you were coming down to say hello," he said.

"Why? Is there something different about this one?"

He let the remark go. He'd noticed the keys.

"You aren't going out, are you?"

"Just for a few minutes."

"But the caterers are due."

"Quint, don't sweat it. We could serve dog food, and these people would still love you."

He held her gaze for a moment, his eyes filled with the displeasure she'd had to endure ever since he discovered her deal with Drew.

He'd been furious, though his anger was nothing like it would have been had he found out about Jon. He'd threatened to go to the police and have Drew arrested as a blackmailer, but Carrie fought back even more furiously. She told him that she'd paid only to end the pressure on their family, and if he was going to cast them back into the world of police and lawyers, of newspapers and gossip and screened calls, then she would walk out the door and never come back. By the end of their fight she was shaking with anger, a surge of emotion that surprised her even more than her tears before the banquet. Quint understood this was no performance. He agreed to keep it quiet. Money—their money—was quietly paid into the Garden's account, which was then closed down. That would be her punishment, the knowledge that her dream was over. Whatever paperwork was needed to get through the final audit was arranged by Godeep. Not that anyone would be looking very closely. The numbers added up.

"Well, try not to be late," he said.

She didn't answer as he stepped back through the door. It wasn't until he'd pulled it shut behind him that she realized she'd forgotten to tell him that Jamie called.

The usual tangle of cars filled the forecourt. She slowly maneuvered her Lexus through the roadsters, careful not to ding any of that precious metal. Their insurance premiums were high enough as it was. The catering van arrived just as she turned onto Orchard. It braked as it came alongside her, the manager's quizzical smile flashing in the corner of her eye. Carrie drove on, pretending she hadn't noticed.

She'd bumped into Ronnie on Federal a few weeks ago, pushing those adorable creatures, rosy and intertwined in their stroller. Drew was nowhere in sight, thank God. The conversation had been stiff and uncomfortable. Carrie couldn't figure out whether he had told his wife about their deal or it was just the awful weight of everything else that had happened. It wasn't until they were leaning away from each other that she'd summoned the nerve to ask about Shannon. That night she'd called Jamie at college to tell him what she'd learned. He hadn't said anything—Jamie hadn't said much of anything to her since last May—but she could tell that he was curious to know more. He avoided the topic for the next few weeks and finally brought it up again this morning, after they discussed his imminent return for Thanksgiving. It would be his first trip back since leaving, though she'd been down twice, to deliver him in September and then again for Homecoming, with Quint hosting that big dinner at Angus Barn, his first extravagance since WMV had risen so spectacularly from the ashes.

"So have you talked to Shannon?" Jamie asked.

"Was I supposed to?"

Dorm noise intervened.

"Jamie?"

"I don't know. I was thinking I might try to see her when I came home."

"And you want me to check if the coast is clear?"

"I'd appreciate that, Mom," he said, the blame leaving his voice for the first time in months. "I just . . . I've been thinking about her."

"Of course I will."

And so she was doing his bidding, although she probably would have made the trip, anyway. There were things of her own she wanted to say. As she inched along Federal, she wondered if she should have phoned, but Ronnie had given her only the address during their brief meeting. She could have called to get it, of course, but that would have risked a conversation with Drew, something Carrie had resolved never to have again.

The house was in one of the few parts of town that had yet to gentrify. It wasn't even an actual house, just a duplex on a quiet street lined with rusting cars, cheap toys, and a few stunted trees. The exterior had gone a bit to seed, gutters sagging, paint blistering on the window frames. Shannon lived downstairs; upstairs looked empty, the windows lacking any sort of drapery. There was no bell, so Carrie knocked firmly on a slightly warped front door. Footsteps, and then Shannon appeared, a bandanna in her hair. Her eyes were still big and beautiful, but they seemed to have lost some of their mischievous luster. She wore her usual ragged clothes, though Carrie could see that there was a reason for the scruffiness; she was painting, a roller in her hand, fresh bright drops speckling her forearms.

"This is a surprise," she said.

Carrie could tell the moment she heard Shannon's voice that she still didn't know what had happened at the Garden. Drew had said nothing. Her secret was safe.

"I should have called," she said, careful to hide her relief. "I can come back if you're busy."

"No, I meant a good surprise. Come on in. Let me just . . ."

She gestured with the roller for Carrie to step into a short hallway, its walls covered with buckled wallpaper that bore the ghostly, rectangular shadows of someone else's life. As Shannon led her into the front room, Carrie took the opportunity to look her over. She'd lost some weight; that teenage slump had left her body. Her hair was longer and neater, combed evenly and held in a ponytail by a rubber band. They entered a small living room. Music played on a cheap boom box. The Pretenders. Dropcloths covered the floor and the furniture. Lime green walls were in the process of being painted a creamy white.

"Nice choice," Carrie said.

Shannon surveyed her work.

"Yeah, it was looking a bit scruffy. Plus, you know, idle hands make for . . . something. I can never remember."

She put the roller back in its angled tray, then gingerly picked up a wet lid and placed it on an open gallon can, hammering it down with the heel of her hand. Some of the paint splattered, but the cloth caught it.

"So you look like you know what you're doing."

"Well, I'm on a learning curve." She stood and wiped her hands on her trousers, her eyes fixed on the floor between them. "All right. Break time."

She led Carrie into a neat little kitchen at the back of the house. The appliances and surfaces showed their age, but they were sparkling clean and there were lots of plants—ferns and ivy and an herb box in the window. Floral smells filled the room, mixing with brewed coffee and fresh paint. Carrie sat at the tiny, listing table while Shannon washed her hands in the sink.

"You want some coffee? I've developed a taste for it recently."

"I'd love some. Black."

She filled a couple of yard sale mugs from an ancient coffee machine and sat across from Carrie, looking quickly at her face and then away again.

"So," she said, holding up her mug with a nervous, unsmiling laugh, "welcome to my humble abode. With emphasis on the humble."

"It's really good to see you, Shannon."

"Yeah, I've been meaning to call but . . ." She shook her head. "Ronnie told me she saw you."

"God, those babies."

"I know. Why do you immediately want to blow raspberries on their stomachs when you see them?"

"It's one of life's enduring mysteries." She took a sip, searching for something to say. "So are you two getting along now? Because I remember its not being so hot."

"Ronnie's really been great. I mean, if it wasn't for her, well, I don't know where I'd be. I'm trying to return the favor by helping her out with baby-sitting. She wanted me to keep living on Crescent, but I thought it would be better for everyone if I got my own place."

"So how did you find this house? It seems kind of . . . off the beaten track."

"My father bought it over the summer. As an investment, if you can believe that. I think Grandpa used to own it. I'm fixing it up in exchange for rent. He wanted me to have it for free, but I don't want to take anything from him. Ever again." She met Carrie's eye. "You know he's the one who called the police on Ian?"

"No, I hadn't heard that," Carrie said tightly.

"At first, he tried to make it up to me. He'd come up to my room and I'd tell him to go away and he'd come back, anyway. I guess in some part of his soul he means well, but there's nothing he can do. We're just . . . done." She winced. "God, does that sound terrible?"

"No," Carrie answered. "It sounds true."

"Plus, it's not exactly a cozy home environment over there now. Things aren't so hot between him and Ronnie."

"Really?"

"I think she's really disillusioned with him for doing what he did to Ian. With the babies coming there wasn't much of anything she could say at the time, but now it's starting to come out. She's not so patient with all his little habits anymore. She just can't understand why he didn't come to her when he found out instead of calling the cops. I'm not sure they're going to make it, to be honest."

Shannon curled her hands around her mug, and Carrie noticed the fingernails, chewed so low that a thin crescent of whitish pulp was exposed on each of them.

"So how are you, Shannon? You look good."

"I'm fine. You know. Getting better. Keeping busy."

She slid a fingertip into her mouth, chewing at a nonexistent nail, but then jerked her hand away in a sharp-willed motion.

"What about you guys?" she asked, changing the subject. "How's that son of yours?"

"He's deliriously happy. Basketball season starts soon, so he'll be able to paint his face blue and jump up and down twice a week."

"I know how much that must mean to him. But seriously?"

"Seriously? Shannon, I'd be the last to know. Jamie's passed beyond his needing Mom phase." She shrugged. "He's going to be fine. He's going to conquer the world. He's just decided to do it without me. He was asking about you, by the way. I think he wants to see you when he comes home for Thanksgiving."

"Are you sure you want that? I don't seem to have the best effect on boys."

"Shannon . . ."

"Tell him to call. I'd love to see Jamie. We can go to Starbucks. His treat."

"He'd like that."

"And how's Quint? I thought about him after what happened in September. For a couple days I had this terrible feeling that he was in one of those buildings."

"He'd been down in New York the week before, but he was working at home on the day."

"You guys must have known a lot of those poor people."

"We knew some. Well, he did. Nobody too close. Rivals, mostly.

But still. It's just too awful to think about, so, you know what? I don't think about it."

"Did it mess up his business?"

"On the contrary. The fund has been doing incredibly well since then. In fact, we're having a big party tonight to celebrate. Though it *had* been bleak all summer. By the end of August it looked like we were going to lose control of it. But then, after the eleventh, everything changed. All those bad bets suddenly came good. You know, things go down, we go up. In this case quite literally. We're stronger than ever, though we really don't talk about the reasons why." She sighed. "Quint's the same. Well, a little more ruthless. Which is healthy, I guess. Or realistic. Evidently the two things are one and the same. Or so they tell me."

Carrie stopped herself, fearing that she was on the brink of babbling, the last thing she wanted to be doing just now.

"I can't picture him ruthless," Shannon said.

"It ain't pretty."

"And how are *you* doing, Carrie?"

"Oh, you know, the same. Hanging out in the suburbs of his good pleasure."

Shannon gave her a baffled look. Knock it off, Carrie told herself.

"I miss having Jamie around. Unbelievably. It'll be good having everyone home for Thanksgiving."

They were silent for a while. They'd run out of news. They'd done their catching up. It was time to say the things that needed to be said. Shannon was the one who finally spoke.

"You know, I've been meaning to call you."

"Well, I should have . . ."

"No, I mean, I had a specific reason for calling. I wanted to apologize."

"Shannon . . ."

"I just felt so bad, putting you guys through all that. Everybody thinking Jamie was guilty. It must have been awful."

"Shannon, come on. We're all right. We had a few rough days. We got shook up a bit. Other people got hurt a lot worse. A *lot*. Nobody blames you, especially with that crazy uncle character keeping you from telling people."

"But that's the thing. David didn't keep me from doing anything. Okay, he put pressure on us, but in the end it was my decision."

"Whatever happened to him, anyway?" Carrie asked, eager to hear something other than Shannon's apology.

"Nobody knows. He just disappeared. I've driven by the house a couple times, but it was empty." She was silent for a moment. "David wasn't a bad guy. He just wanted what we all want, I guess."

"Shannon . . ."

She shook her head stubbornly, refusing comfort, not just from Carrie but from the whole wide world.

"I just messed everything up so badly," she continued. "Everybody had to pay, didn't they? Robert Jarvis and Ian. You guys. That was the other thing I wanted to say sorry about. All that money you had to give the Jarvises."

"Who told you about that?" Carrie asked, aghast.

"Ronnie heard. Everybody knows. People are always talking about you guys. But I still don't understand why *you* had to pay them."

"Deep pockets," Carrie said with a bitter laugh.

"What?"

"It was our car. Jamie asked for you that night and gave you the keys and . . ." Carrie decided not to tell her about the part of the settlement where it was agreed that Shannon would bear no liability. "Honestly, I can't stand the thought of you worrying about this. It was mostly from the insurance company, and the rest, my God, it's only money."

"How did—?"

She stopped herself from finishing the question.

"What?"

"No, I was just wondering how they came up with that amount. It was so . . . specific."

"They have clever little men sitting in an office somewhere who figured out how much Mr. Jarvis would have made if he hadn't—if not for the accident. His potential. His human capital, I think they call it.

They have computer programs for determining it, would you believe? You feed in raw data, and they give you back the measure of a man." Carrie shook her head; money was the last thing she wanted to talk about today. "Shannon, listen to me. You don't have to apologize for anything. I know you were in love with Ian and the only thing you were thinking about was protecting him, and well, I was about to say I would have done the same in your position, but that would be presumptuous of me. I'd like to *think* I would have done the same, at least when I was your age."

They sat through another silence, the specter of that poor dead boy rising between them. Like everyone else, Carrie had seen his photo in the paper, handsome and gentle and a little bit lost. It had been taken a few years earlier, when he was at the local high school, but there were things in a face that didn't change. She'd read the article's terrible cold words; she'd seen Flowers's stricken expression when he came by that night to explain.

"I went back to sleep," Shannon said eventually, her voice sounding as if this were something that had been through her mind so often that it was now etched there forever. "The morning he died. I told him I would be with him, but I was just so tired and scared that I gave up on him for a while." Her voice caught briefly. "I just hate to think how alone he felt at the end. That the last thing he would have thought was that we'd all abandoned him."

Carrie knew there was nothing she could say that would comfort her. But she still had to try. She still had to speak what was on her mind, what had been on her mind since last May. She tilted her chipped coffee mug a few times, creating some minor ripples that they watched until they'd settled.

"Look, Shannon, there's another reason I came up here besides carrying Jamie's message. I wanted to thank you."

Shannon looked up at her in astonishment.

"Thank me? For what?"

"For helping get Jamie home from the party. It was a decent thing for you and Ian to do. And well, there's not a lot of that going around these days."

Shannon stared at Carrie, her eyes welling. A few tears escaped, and she wiped them away with her forearm, leaving a streak of bright paint on her cheek. Carrie reached across the table and cleaned it away with her finger, glad for an excuse to touch this girl, to provide even this small measure of comfort.

"Well," Shannon said, sniffling in embarrassment, "I'd better get back to work or it's going to dry unevenly. Or so says my *This Old House* manual."

"You want some help?" Carrie asked, the words coming out before she could even think.

Shannon pulled back her head in happy surprise.

"Well, yeah. But I mean, don't you have things to do at home with this party?"

Carrie thought about Quint and the worshipful men at his court; she thought about the caterers and her two hundred impending guests, the speeches and the laughter that would ring through their house tonight. She thought about tomorrow, with its empty hours to fill while someone else cleaned up the mess; she thought about Thanksgiving dinner, everyone counting the minutes until he could be doing something else. And she thought about the wine she wanted to drink, always more wine, chilly and white, stacked so neatly in its own special fridge.

"No," she said. "Not really."

"But do you know how to paint a room?"

"Of course," she said. "You call the decorator."

"Great. Just what I need. A rookie."

"But you said you had a book, right? I mean, how hard can it be?"

"You'd be surprised."

"Shannon, I could use a surprise or two right about now."

Their eyes held for a moment, and for the first time since her arrival Shannon gave Carrie what she now knew she'd really driven down the hill to see, that big, beautiful smile.

"Let's get you a brush, then," Shannon said. "Put the lady to work."